THE BUTCHERS IN:

THE HOUSE OF RA

By Robert Davis

Copyright © 2006 by Robert Davis

ISBN 0-7414-3531-4

Published by:

PUBLISHING.COM

1094 New DeHaven Street, Suite 100
West Conshohocken, PA 19428-2713
Info@buybooksontheweb.com
www.buybooksontheweb.com
Toll-free (877) BUY BOOK
Local Phone (610) 941-9999
Fax (610) 941-9959

Printed in the United States of America

Printed on Recycled Paper

Published October 2006

Chapter 1

Warriors or troops in the field, know that a war is not really over until you make it back home. Ramala and the seven houses agreed to end the war, but they had not met to work out the details. Both sides sent word that their warlords should stop fighting and hold their positions. But holding your position wasn't always that simple. Hostile intentions between combatants don't end so easily.

When the Butchers got the news that the war was over, it had already been three days after the fact. So the Butchers kept pushing the action. The Hayee warlords stopped advancing after the first day. This made it look like the Butchers were trying to put some extra punishment on the Hayee warriors. That didn't sit well with the Hayee warlords. So they moved up from their positions and attacked the Butchers. It was all out war for two weeks after that. Then Ramala's warriors came and gave the Butchers word that they were to return to the House of Ra.

The war had taken its toll on the Butchers. The girls were all but worn out. They were fighting on instinct. They had lost weight and were so tired they could barely think. They would get up every morning and just react to each battle as it came. Dan was just starting to fell the effects of the day in and day out fighting. He had also lost some of his weight, but he was the star player on the team now. Syn let Dan take center stage and fight the one on one battles with the warlords. She fought with the girls and made sure they paced themselves and didn't overwork themselves in battle. And why not. It seemed the Hayee warlords weren't good enough to deal with Dan. He was undefeated in this war. Even though the Butchers left for the house of Ra. This left bad blood between the Butchers and the Hayee. The Hayee warriors and warlords hated the Butchers. They hated Dan more than any of the

Butchers.

On the way back to the House of Ra, every time the Butchers stopped at one of Ramala's strongholds. The Butchers were cheered as heroes. Everyone wanted details of all the battles they had been in. But the Butchers were very tired. All they wanted to do was to get back to the comfort of the House of Ra. They ate and rested just enough to make it to the next checkpoint. They were given elephants so they could ride back in comfort.

When the Butchers finally reached the gates to the House of Ra, the guards erupted into continuous cheers that wouldn't stop. The gates opened up and as the Butchers made their way to Ramala's palace, it seemed like the whole of Ramala's army was there cheering the Butchers on. All of the Butchers stood on the platform on the elephant's back, charged up from the noise of the cheers. The Butchers girls waved at the crowd from time to time. Dan just stood there looking around. He couldn't believe how large the crowd was. Usually when he saw this many warriors, he would have to charge himself up for a serious fight. He had never experienced this many people actually glad to see him. This made him feel uncomfortable and he didn't know why.

Cat and Ma were charged up. They were high from the attention they were getting from the crowds. The Syn, Jara watched it all. She knew the Hayee, Ramala and her cousins had all of these people cheering, whether they wanted to or not. The Syn, Jara looked over at Cat and Ma. She could see it was affecting them a little too much. They both were waving to the crowd and throwing their hands up in victory. Syn said "Alright you two! Calm down! Don't let all of this go to your heads." Dan looked at Syn and said "It's too late for that." Syn looked at Dan for a moment. This was the first time since Syn, Jara found out that it was Dan's father that killed her father that they had looked directly at each other. They both looked away before they had time to think about it. That was enough of an ice breaker for now.

They looked up and could see the unloading docks to the palace. Everyone was there. The Hayee, Ramala was standing out front with her children, the twins Ra, Dan and Ra, Ramala standing by her side. Yaya was right there with them. Ramala wanted to be the first one to welcome Dan and her Butchers back. Everyone else would wait until she greeted them before they walked up. Her two cousins, the Hayee's, Tara and Wana stood right behind Ramala, with the Japha twins, San and Jan. Right behind them were Yin and Backir. Yin and Back were given a heroes welcome two days earlier, but nothing like this. Yin was annoyed that the Hayee, Ramala made him wait behind her and the Japha twins, before he would be able to meet Ma.

When Yin and Backir first made it back to the House of Ra, Ramala saw that Yin and Backir still were in a very aggressive state of mind from the war they were fighting in. They were acting almost like two wild animals and Ramala wasn't going to have her guards intimidated by anyone but her.

The Hayee, Ramala saw this and called a meeting with Backir and Yin, that first evening that they got back. Yin and Backir were escorted into the throne room by Ramala's elite guards. When they got there they saw the three cousins sitting on their chairs in the throne area. Ramala was in the middle of her two cousins. Yin and Backir noticed right off that none of the cousins looked to be in a good mood. Yin took a quick look at Tara, who would not return his glance. Yin looked at Ramala and immediately remembered the last time he saw her and how pissed off she looked then. The look on her face now wasn't much different from that day. But today Yin was a different man. He had defeated seven Japha warlords by himself. Backir had defeated three by himself. Ramala had better recognize who she was dealing with.

Wana waved the guards off and they left the room. Yin and Backir still had not gotten down on their knees out of respect to Ramala. Ramala stared at the both of them. Then Backir got down on one knee. Yin looked over at Backir, then took his time getting down on one knee. Then he stood back up. Ramala stood up and said "Get back on your knees heathen!"

Yin looked at Ramala, then slowly got down on his knees. Ramala said "I give you two a hero's welcome when you get home and you come in here and disrespect me by not getting down on your knees, out of respect for me, in front of my guards!" She paused for a second. Then she said "Then, only after I stare at you, do you remember that you should be doing something besides standing there looking like idiots!"

She paused again staring at both men, daring them to show any sign of aggression. Both men looked at the ground. They knew Ramala was pissed off, and it wasn't going to be good for either of them. With all three Hellcats in the room, Yin and Backir knew they were at a disadvantage if they attacked Ramala. So they impatiently, but quietly listened to their Queen. Ramala continued with "You two come into my kingdom with this attitude! How! Dare! You!" Ramala stood up, and walked slowly off of the throne area, towards Backir and Yin.

These men had faced the toughest Japha warlords, but they refused to move right now, for fear of what Ramala would do to them. They both were a little nervous. Ramala stopped a few feet away from them. She looked down at them, saying nothing for a few seconds. Then she said "Maybe you think just because you have gotten good enough to beat some Japha warlords and have become undefeated, that you don't have to show the proper respect, or do what I say. Well my patience has run out with you two."

Now she was close enough to Yin and Backir, that if they wanted to do her harm they could. Neither of these men were afraid to kill Hellcat Hayee, Ramala, knowing that they themselves would be killed after being frozen by the paralyzing scream of the other two Hellcats, Ramala's cousins Hayee, Tara and Hayee, Wana. The question for both Backir and Yin was that they knew how well Ramala could fight and how quick she was. If they attacked her and she evaded them before they could kill her right away, they knew they would be killed. Neither of them wanted to die not getting the person they intended to kill before they died.

Ramala knew just what she was doing. She said "You two have lost the privilege of looking at me. Your eyes had better never meet mine, unless I order it! Whenever I walk into a room that you are in, you get down on your knees immediately, out of respect. That goes for anytime you see me. From now on, until further notice, you will ask me for permission to speak to me. Never address me without asking permission. I don't care who is around, or if no one is. Always address me as mistress Queen Ramala. Do you understand!?" Yin and Backir both said at the same time "Yes mistress Queen Ramala!" Ramala said "That's more like it! That's what I want to hear every time you speak in my presence. This is the only warning you'll get! Now stand up!"

Both men stood. It was hard to be this close to Ramala without feeling like you needed to defend yourself. She walked over to Yin and stood directly in front of him. She didn't say a word, purposely, to see if Yin would look up at her. He didn't. So she back hand slapped him across the face with a good amount of force. Yin didn't move. He could see that even though Ramala was standing still in front of him, she was on guard for an attack. Ramala had managed to get herself on and off of Yin's list of people to kill when you get a chance. She was number one on the list before she slapped Yin. Now she had just jumped off the list and was dancing in his face. Yin wasn't going to do anything now. But he reserved the right to change his mind at any second.

When Ramala was sure enough that Yin wasn't going to attack her, she said "Yin, you are a great hero in the House of Ra. You will be treated with great respect. There will be a ceremony promoting you to warlord. You will be given territory to control in my name. Besides what I tell you to do, or not to do, you will be able to do what you want. Now look me in my eyes and tell me who has made this possible for you." Yin looked up at Ramala and said in a strong but non-aggressive voice "You have mistress Queen Ramala!"

Ramala searched Yin's eyes. She could see that he had learned his lesson. She lifted her hand, which had a white glove on it. Yin wanted to grab Ramala's neck with both hands and snap it. Instead he took her hand and kissed the glove. If Wana and Tara hadn't seen this with their own eyes, they never would have believed it. After Yin kissed Ramala's gloved hand, he lowered his eyes from hers.

Then she moved over to Backir. Ramala gave Backir the same strong backhand slap that she gave Yin, but she hit Backir again with a returning open hand slap. After seeing Yin get slapped, Backir prepared himself, as much as any man could, to be slapped. It was the return slap that caught him off guard and made his blood boil. He certainly didn't deserve two slaps if Yin only got one! Backir didn't have a list of people he wanted to Kill, like Yin had until this moment. Ramala was the first person on Backir's list now. Oh, he wasn't going to mess up his chance to kill her by flying into a fit of rage. He was going to wait for the perfect opportunity, when he knew he wouldn't fail. That's when he was going to do what needed to be done. Kill Ramala.

Ramala waited a short time to give Backir the chance to do something, or think about doing something. The choice was his. When she was reasonably sure he wasn't going to try to kill her, she said "The same goes for you Backir. The great hero of the House of Ra, who fought side by side with Yin. Look at me and tell me who all of the glory from the battles you fought goes to."

Backir summoned all of the strength he had in his entire body, looked at Ramala and said "It goes to you, mistress Queen Ramala!"

She put her hand up again, and Backir kissed it. Then he lowered his eyes from hers. Then she said "As long as you both live, you had better know that I'm going to be in control of things. So it's in both of your interest to make sure you always do things to impress me and always stay on my good side. Because if you get on my bad side. Well, it won't be for long! Now go and enjoy yourselves. Remember, you're heroes!"

Yin and Backir left the room right away. Right now, neither of them felt like heroes. They didn't say anything until they were far enough away that they knew Ramala couldn't hear. Then Backir said "I can't wait until we get out of here." Yin looked at Backir and said "You had better watch what you say. Besides, you heard her. We're going to be working for her for the rest of our lives. And we had better like it or else!" Backir said "Or else what?" Yin said "You figure it out. You're supposed to be smarter than me, and I already know." Yin paused for a second, then said with total utter disdain "So this is the House of Ra."

After Yin and Backir left the throne room. Ramala turned and smiled at her cousins. Wana said "That was quite a performance you just put on." Ramala said "It was necessary. Now I won't have any problems out of the two of them." Wana said "You think?" Then she laughed. Tara frowned a little and said "You didn't have to be so tough on him." Ramala said "Yes, I did! If I hadn't, Yin would be out of control in less than a week. Lucky for him I did what I did. Otherwise, he would just be a sweet memory for you!"

So that's why Yin didn't move from where he was. Yin knew Ma would make it past the others as soon as possible to get to him. So he waited, impatiently. When Dan saw his twins standing there next to Ramala, that's when he realized how much time had passed since he last saw them. Just before he left, they were just starting to stand on their own. Now they were walking.

As the platform reached the docking area, he could see that they were standing on their own and looking at everything around them, except for the elephant he was riding on. He saw Ramala bend down and point to the elephant, saying "Here comes your Daddy." Dan could see that the young twins were looking at Ramala's finger as she pointed, instead of where she was pointing.

Ramala looked over at Yaya. Before Ramala could say anything, Yaya took off running towards the ramps that the Butchers were now walking down. This infuriated Ramala. She told everyone, including Yaya, that she would be the first to meet Dan and the Butchers when they exited from the elephant. All Ramala saw was that Yaya was deliberately trying to upstage her! Yaya got there just as the Butchers walked off the ramps on to the dock. Yaya ran up to Dan and jumped into his arms, wrapping her legs around his waist. She gave him a hug and a kiss on his cheek. Dan was a little surprised by Yaya's actions. Yaya looked Dan in his eyes, then quickly jumped to the ground and hugged the rest of the Butchers.

By this time, Ramala was on her way with the twins, almost dragging them. Yaya waved at the Butchers. They could see that Yaya was very nervous. They also saw the look on Ramala's face and knew Yaya was in big trouble. Then Yaya yelled at the top of her voice "Butchers! Show your respect to Queen mother of the House of Ra! The Hayee, Ramala!"

Yaya turned towards Ramala and got down on both her knees looking at the ground. The Butchers went down on both knees. Then all of the guards and servants went down on their knees. The place went silent. Ramala saw all of this. She couldn't have scripted this any better than that! Ramala walked past Yaya only giving her a quick look. Yaya flinched nervously, not knowing what would happen later. She only knew that something would.

Now Ramala was focused on Dan. She stared into his eyes and when she got to him she let the twins hands go, and wrapped her arms around Dan. They stood there holding each other for a moment. Yaya had turned on her knees peeking to see what was going on and saw that the young twins were free. Every time someone wasn't holding on to little Ramala and Dan, if Ramala wasn't right there staring at them. They would take off running. Yaya knew this, so she jumped into action as soon as she saw Ramala let there hands go. The young twins were just about to run off when Yaya grabbed their hands and said "Oh, no you don't!"

The young twins could barely get away with anything, when Yaya was around. Ramala took a step back from Dan and said "I've got to put some weight back on you! You haven't been eating well at all!" Dan looked at Ramala and said "Well, I was kind of busy. You know fighting all of your battles while you …." Then Dan remembered who he was talking to. Dan didn't want to argue with Ramala. He was tired and needed rest. The last thing he wanted was to piss off Ramala right away. There would be plenty of time for that. So he finished up with "while you have made yourself more beautiful than I imagined, all of those nights I thought about you."

Ramala had a big smile on her face now. She greeted the rest of the Butchers. Ramala took an extra long look at Ma, then told her to go see Yin. Ma was a little confused by the fact that Yin hadn't run over to see her. Then she figured that Ramala was putting on a show of power for everyone to see who was in charge. She ran over to Yin and jumped into his arms. Yin said "You look unharmed, but stressed. Are you alright?" Ma said "This war has taken its toll on me. I'm alright, but I need rest and relaxation."

Yin peeked over to see where Ramala was, then he said in a voice low enough that only Ma could hear and said "You might get more relaxation fighting Warlords than here at the House of Ra." Ma could tell that something had happened between Yin and Ramala. She just didn't know what. Right now she was too tired to deal with that. So she told Yin "As long as you behave, she won't kill you." Ma was kidding, but Yin didn't smile. He just stared at Ma and whispered to her "I'm not even allowed to look directly at her. I can't wait to get back out there and take my chances with warriors and Warlords."

Now Ma was sure something had happened. That's why Ramala gave her an extra long look. Ma said "Be patient. Things will get better. Besides, I hear you're a hero!" Yin's face lit up a little. It was true! He was a hero. Ma looked past Yin, then greeted everyone else. It was good to see everyone. When Cat got over to everyone, she asked "Where's Chi?" Backir said "He's up in Yee province, with Han. He's become Han's right hand man. At least until Chi gets what he wants."

Now that everyone had greeted each other, Ramala walked over and said "Let's give these great heroes of the House of Ra time to get cleaned up. Then we will all meet and have a feast."

Ramala turned and saw that Dan had picked up the twins. Both the twins just stared at Dan. They didn't try to get away. Ramala could see they were at least comfortable with Dan. Dan walked over with them in his arms. Dan looked around to see how close everyone was to him and Ramala, before he said "Looks like you've done a pretty good job with these two, so far." Ramala said

"I'm glad you approve. Let me show you around." Dan needed to rest, so he said "Show me to somewhere where I can sit down and relax." Ramala said "That would be our sleeping quarters."

Just then, Backir and Yin walked up. They didn't say a word. Dan found it strange that they didn't. Then Backir said "Mistress Queen, may I speak freely?"

Dan was about to say something when Ramala looked at him like don't. Then she said "You have my permission. Both of you, speak freely." Dan couldn't believe this. Then Backir looked at Dan and said "When were you going to come and greet your friends, or are you to big of a hero now!"

Dan looked at Backir, then at Yin. Yin had killed seven Warlords. Dan looked at Yin trying to see something that would tell him, yes, Yin had killed seven Warlords. He didn't see that. He just saw the same old Yin. Yin looked at Dan. Yin knew Dan hadn't killed as many Warlords as he had. It didn't matter to Yin that Dan had not faced as many Warlords, was probably the reason that Dan didn't have as many kills. What mattered to Yin was that, Yin had killed more. Yin's mind told him Dan had better recognize that. They stared at each other for a moment, then Dan said "You and Yin are the big heroes. You took on the Japha and are still here to talk about it. You two are undefeated. That's impressive!"

Yin smiled. Dan had given him the recognition he was looking for. Yin said "You too are undefeated. You didn't do to bad yourself." They both laughed. That broke the tension between these two Butchers. The real question that was running through both of their minds was, who the best was. But they let it go, for now. The servants came up and led the Butchers off to get cleaned up. Ramala turned to Dan and said "Let's go."

Ramala looked around to see where Yaya was. She left with the Butcher girls. Yaya was going to try to wait Ramala out, in hopes that she would forget about what she had done. Yaya and Ramala had that mother daughter type of relationship.

Ramala didn't like anyone carrying her twins for long. So she told Dan "Put them down and let them walk on their own. It's good for them." Dan looked at Ramala and said "I haven't seen them in a while, I'll put them down soon enough." As they walked down the hall, Ramala could see that she was going to have to let Dan know that her young twins were on a strict training schedule, and he wasn't going to mess it up. She wasn't going to make a big deal about it this time, because Dan had just got home, and she knew he probably missed seeing his children.

As they walked, Ramala pointed out some of the different areas in the palace. While they were walking, Dan was finding out that the twins were a handful to keep up with. Little Ramala got herself a handful of Dan's hair and was trying to pull it out of his scalp. She was very strong to be so little. And little Dan kept taking swings at Dan's face every time he thought he could get a punch in. Little Dan was very quick with his hands. Dan was getting a little frustrated, but was trying to deal with his twins. Ramala saw all of this and let Dan suffer for only a few minutes before she stepped in front of him and said "They are just starting to get going. You had better let me take them now, or they will get completely out of control. "

Dan gladly handed them to Ramala, who put them on the ground and stared at the twins, one at a time and said "Follow closely behind mother and don't get far behind!" Dan smiled. He knew these twins were too small to understand what Ramala had said, so he waited to see how soon they would run off, and Ramala would have to chase them.

Ramala stood up, turned and looked at Dan. Then she said "Come on. They'll follow me." Dan and Ramala started walking. Dan kept looking over his shoulders at the twins. They were walking directly behind Ramala. They didn't wonder to the left, or wonder to the right. They just followed her like they were young ducklings. Every once in a while Ramala would say "Keep up with mother. Don't get too far behind!"

Every time the twins heard Ramala's voice, they quickened their pace. Dan was amazed. When they got to the twins sleeping quarters, which was right next to Ramala's, she bent down and told the twins "Me and your father are going to go into our room and talk for a while. I want you two to go into your room and rest for a while."

Ramala pointed to the twin's room. Then she said "Mother is very proud of the way you two have behaved for me." Then she gave them both a big hug and a kiss. Then she said "Give mother a big hug and a kiss!" Both of the twins gave Ramala a hug and a kiss. Then Ramala said "Now give your father a hug." The twins just stood there looking at Ramala. Dan said "It's alright, they just have to get more comfortable around me."

The smile left Ramala's face then she looked down at the

ground. The twins looked at their mother for a few seconds, then they walked slowly over to Dan. Dan bent down, and they gave him a half-hearted hug. Then they turned and looked over at Ramala to see if they had done enough to please her. She smiled at them. Then they ran over to her. Ramala said "That's my good little twins. Mother is very proud of you. Mother loves you!" The twins were smiling from ear to ear, with pride in their little hearts that they had done well for their mother.

Then Ramala said "Now go with the maidens. Mother will see you later." The maidens came over and escorted the twins into their room. Ramala watched until they were inside. Dan was amazed and Ramala could see it. She looked at him and gave him a big smile. They walked into their sleeping quarters. Dan looked around. It was huge. Much bigger than Ramala's quarters at the House of Hayee. It had four large areas. An area for guest to sit at a large table. Another area for Ramala's personal things. A huge private sleeping area. And a personal lounging area next to the sleeping area. Ramala said "It's impressive, isn't it?"

Dan looked at Ramala and said "It's alright, but what was impressive was the way you have our twins trained. That was very impressive! God only knows what you did to them to make them do what you say. I don't want to know." Ramala said "No, you don't." Dan stopped and stared at Ramala. She grabbed his hand and said "I was just joking!"

Dan didn't believe her. Ramala led Dan to a sitting area next to the balcony. They sat down. They stared at each other for a moment not saying anything. Then Ramala said "Are you hungry?" Dan said "Yes, but I can wait until the feast." Ramala said "Nonsense! I'll get the servants to get you something to carry you until we make it to the feast."

Then Ramala clapped her hands, gave orders to the servants that ran in after hearing the claps, then she dismissed them. Ramala stood up. She had on her ruling cape that covered her whole body down to her ankles. She took the cape off, threw it on one of the chairs, and showed off her body to Dan. She walked in front of him, turned slowly around, making sure Dan got a good look at her completely. Dan could see that Ramala was in the best shape he had ever seen her in. She was in better shape than before she had the twins. Her body was perfect. When she was done modeling herself for Dan, she stopped in front of him and waited for his approval.

Dan knew he had plenty of time to wreck that body, but he was curious about something that happened earlier. So he asked about it, before he forgot about it. He said "What's the deal with Backir asking you for permission to speak and calling you Mistress Queen Ramala?" Ramala was dumb founded. What was Dan doing thinking about those heathens, when he had damn near a goddess in front of him. Ramala moved closer to Dan, then she slapped him across the side of his head. Dan grabbed her wrist just as her hand was leaving his head. He twisted her wrist firmly, until he saw her wince in pain. Dan yelled "What's wrong with you?" Ramala yelled out "You're a moron, you shit heathen idiot!" Then she threw a punch that Dan barely avoided. He said "Alright! That's enough!" Ramala grabbed his shirt and wrestled with him until she ripped the shirt down the front of it. That stopped her for the moment, but she still held Dan roughly by his torn shirt.

Dan stared at her just short of anger, waiting on her to give him an explanation of why she was acting like she was. Ramala stared at Dan for a few seconds then said "I try to impress you with all of this perfect body, and all you can think about is those heathen friends of yours. Well if this is the only way I can keep your attention, I don't want it!" Ramala's personal guards peeked in and asked "Is everything alright Mistress Queen?" Then the guards stared at Dan. Ramala said "Go back to your post. If I need you, I'll call you." The guards said "Yes, Mistress Queen!" Then they turned and left quickly.

Ramala stared at Dan, then she said "If you must know. I had to put your friends in their places before they would make me have to kill them, for being disrespectful. Something you seem to do to me a little too much! Since you're so worried about you friends, you can go sleep with them!" She let go of his shirt, stood up and started walking away.

Dan couldn't believe how high strung Ramala was. He stood up and turned towards her. When he started towards her, she turned, and jumped on guard, clinching both of her fists. He stopped. They stared at each other. Dan slowly took his eyes from hers and moved them down her perfectly sculpted body. Making sure that Ramala knew he was paying attention to all of her special places. He smiled at her, then Dan said "You're the only woman I know that could win a war, have children, train them well, and still have time to build a body like that."

Ramala loosened up slightly, just enough to say "You

better recognize you rhino shit heathen." Dan said "You know I like it, when you talk to me like that." Ramala smiled. Dan walked over to her and gave her a hug. He let his hands fall and rest on her firm round behind. Then he moved his lips close to her ear, like he was going to say something, but he didn't. Ramala stood there waiting to hear something. Then just as Ramala was getting ready to pull back and look up at him, Dan said "Why can't you see, how pleased I am with you?" Ramala whispered "I just wanted to hear you say it."

The servants entered with the food and set it out on the table. They sat down and ate. Dan and Ramala always stared at each other when no one else was around. Ramala knew Dan's every move when he was eating. Ramala said "Something I've wondered about and was meaning to ask you." Dan said "What?" Ramala said "Why do heathens eat like they're never going to get another meal, and have to try to eat as much as possible, as fast as possible?" Dan said "Don't worry about that. Just know you're going to get worst treatment than this food, later tonight when I get a hold of you. I'm going to be much more of a heathen, and I'm going to take my time." Ramala said "Don't talk me to death. I'm right here in your face. Now, what are you going to do?" Dan stared at Ramala for a moment. Then he said "I'm going to make you wait." Ramala said "I've had enough of this game! I'm going to rest for a while!"

Then Ramala got up, walked over, and laid down in the sleeping area. It amused Dan when he could affect her like that. Dan walked over a few minutes later and fell asleep next to his Queen, Ramala.

Chapter 2

When Ramala dismissed everyone, the Butcher girls were escorted to one of the many boarding houses for Ramala's special guests. This one was only minutes away from the palace. When the Butchers arrived there, they could see that the building was large, but not one of the largest. They walked in and saw that they were in a large room with several hallways on the far wall, leading to different areas of the building. There were sitting areas on the left and the right side of the room. Backir and Yin walked over and sat down in the seats on the right side of the room. Yin said "Hurry up or we won't be here when you get done!" All three of the Butcher girls stopped, turned and looked at Yin. They were shocked that he thought that he could talk to them like that.

The Syn, Jara said "Come on girls, he won't be anywhere that we can't find him, if that's what we want." Then they turned back around and were led, by the servants, to the bathing area. Yin looked around the room, then he glanced at Backir for a moment. Backir saw Yin. Yin was frustrated and Back knew why. Neither one of them liked the way Ramala was treating them. They both knew, the other, wanted to take Ramala's head, even though both knew they could never say it out loud. It was tough for Back to take what Ramala was dishing out. He didn't know how much more of it he could take. One thing he did know was that Yin was more messed up about it than he was. He knew Yin would explode under Ramala's pressure, way before he would. Then maybe she would ease up on him, even though he knew that wouldn't be good for Yin or Ma. Backir really didn't care. He just wanted some of the pressure off himself.

Yin was getting angrier, as time passed by. He wanted to kill Ramala, but knew he couldn't. So Yin was going to do the next best thing. He had made up his mind. Ramala was now officially on his list of people to kill, when he got a chance. But for now, someone was going to pay dearly, for Ramala's actions. He didn't care who. Backir sat there smiling, struggling to keep himself from laughing. Yin was so easy to read, that even Backir could just about tell what Yin was thinking.

Then Tara walked in. Backir and Yin both stood up. They didn't know how they should be reacting to Tara, since this was the first time they were with Tara since they returned, when Ramala was not there. Tara looked at both men, then said "Relax! La's not here!"

Yin said in a not so friendly voice "How can anyone relax around here!" Tara looked at Backir. She wasn't going to have words with Yin in front of Backir. Tara looked at Yin and said "Come with me. We can talk." Yin looked at Tara for a second without moving. Tara's eyes begged a little. Yin got up and walked over to her. He told Backir "I'll be right back." Backir said "Yeah, okay. I'll hold my breath." Yin turned and looked at Backir. Backir smiled at Yin. Yin turned back towards the door and walked out with Tara. Backir leaned back in his chair, closed his eyes, and waited on the Butcher girls.

Tara and Yin walked for a few moments without saying anything. Then Yin asked "Where are we going?" Tara said "I have a place, not far from here. We can go there, if you want." Yin looked over at Tara and said in a frustrated tone "What did you want to talk about?" Tara said "We haven't had time to spend together, since you've been back. I just thought we could go to my place for a while."

Yin stopped and looked at Tara. He said "You come here like everything is alright! Well it's not! You wouldn't even say one word, in my defense, when that Hayee, Ramala...." Tara cut in with "You had better be careful when you mention La's name. There is no defense when it comes to La. She's in complete control. You gotta know that. And you better know how to act around her from now on. She's gonna test you, just to make sure you know who's in charge. If you're smart, which I know you're not."

Tara smiled at Yin. Then she continued with "You had better show her that you can be a good subordinate. That's the only way to get her to let up on you and Backir. She's in control, so don't fight it." Yin said "Are you done?" Tara said "Yes, now let's go to my place." Yin said "I'm going back to wait on the

Butchers. You can go back and be in control with your cousin."
Tara said "So you're going to let this come between us?"

Yin didn't say a word. He just looked at Tara. Tara said "You're not smart enough to play mind games, so don't try. If you're angry at La, take it out on me at my place. If you do anything else, I can guarantee, you and your sister will end up dead."

Tara had a smirk on her face when she said that to Yin. Now Yin was pissed off. He grabbed Tara by her arm roughly. She snatched her arm away from him. She looked around then looked at Yin and said "Stupid ass! There are guards everywhere. If Wa or La finds out that you think you can man handle me. They'll have your head! Wait until we get to my place. Then you can do what you want to me in private, where no one can see." Yin said "Then, let's go!"

Tara led the way. She could see that Yin was really angry. She didn't know what he was going to do to her. She was afraid and excited. She liked to see Yin's fury, especially when it was directed at her.

When they arrived at Tara's place, they walked inside. Tara put up her hand, stopping Yin from doing anything he planned to do to her. She dismissed all of her personal guards and servants. When they were gone, Tara took a deep breath and turned to Yin and said "Now what?"

Yin smiled at Tara. He put his hand on the top of her head, slowly moving it down her hair. Then he reached around and grabbed Tara's ponytail so fast, that she had no time to react. He swung her around by her hair and threw her across the room onto the floor. Tara had good balance and recovered enough to land on her hands and knees. Just as she was turning around to see where Yin was, he put his knee on Tara's back, and pressed downwards with his weight, while grabbing Tara's ponytail again and yanking her head violently backwards.

Tara let out low painful cry. She feared for her life. The next words that came out of Tara's mouth, she said in a trembling voice. She said "Please don't kill me! And don't leave bruises that anyone can see!"

Yin wasn't smart, but he knew that if Tara couldn't make it to the feast because she couldn't walk, or even worse if she made it there doubled over in pain. His head would be a trophy for Ramala. Even though Yin was a heathen, Tara wasn't going to get his full wrath, at least not right now. But he was going to give her something to think about.

The Butcher girls were lying back, enjoying a hot, soothing bath, when the Japha, Jan and her girls, Nina and Mia walked in. The bath was big enough for six or seven women, so it was more than enough room for the Butcher girls to stretch out. Jan could see that all three girls had lost weight. The stress of battle showed on their faces. Jan said "You girls look good, considering what you've been through. You just need a few good meals and some rest and you'll be good as new."

The three girls were too relaxed to respond, so they just smiled. Jan looked them over again, then said "Really, are you girls alright?" Cat said "It was hell out there."

Cat paused for a moment, while looking up at the ceiling. Jan and her girls sat in chairs that were near the bath. Cat continued with "I love fighting, but this was too much, even for me. I mean, day in and day out, fighting almost from sun up, to sun down. I though it would never end. And just when I thought I couldn't take any more. It was over. On the way back, I wondered what would have happened if we had been out there another week, or a month."

Jan said "Don't wonder about what ifs. That just leads to doubt. Just know that you did what you had to do and you would have done what you had to do to survive had you been there any longer. Thank god it ended, and leave it at that." Cat said "I know, you're right. I'm just tired." Ma said "It was rough out there."

The Syn, Jara was laying back in the bath, listening, but not saying a word. This was down time. She didn't want to think about what had happened on the battlefield. That was over. It was time for something new. They were in the House of Ra, with Ramala in charge. The Syn, Jara knew there would be more fighting. She just didn't know when. She wanted to rest and get back to full strength. Then she would be ready for whatever.

Jan stayed with the girls while they let the warm water wash away some of the soreness their muscles had accumulated over time. The Japha, Jan found herself feeling happy that all three girls made it back in good shape. She was surprised, that when she peaked over at Mia and Nina, she could see that same happiness.

Jan had a lot of family back at the House of Japha. Cousins, aunts, and uncles. Oh, and she still had a few brothers left too.

She smiled to herself. She was going to deal with her brothers as soon as she got home. It was funny to her that, as close as she was to some of her relatives. It wasn't as close as she felt to her girls, the Butcher girls, and Ramala, even though none were blood relatives to her, except for Ramala and her cousins, who were distantly related to her.

Older generations would never team up with members from another House. Teaming up with heathens, was definitely out of the question. They were too afraid that each person from a different House, had to have a different agenda than the ones from the same House. That's why all of the other Houses split from the House of Japha, which was the first and only house in the beginning. Different relatives of the House of Japha wanted more control over the way things were run. These relatives split off and formed the other six Houses. That's why all of the people from the seven Houses are blood related. That's also the reason that people of the seven Houses, only drink the blood of people from the seven Houses. Because it's the same blood. It was taught to everyone, in all of the houses that to drink the blood of heathens, someone not of the seven houses, would turn your own blood in your body, against you, and drive you mad. That's what they believed. Jan snapped back to reality, when the Butchers girls started getting out of the bath.

The, Na Tee had learned a lot about the Japha, Jan, in this time that she spent at the House of Ra. She saw Jan as a laid back Ramala. Tee knew eventually, Jan, just like Ramala, always ended up with what she wanted. So the Na, Tee got smart and started sharing San's free time with Jan. This made Jan easier to get along with. Tee knew her and Jan would never be the best of friends, unless a miracle happened . But Tee knew she wanted to be with San always. So that meant sharing him with his twin sister Jan. The Japha, San had been training like he was preparing for war. He knew eventually he and his sister would be going back to the House of Japha. And although Ramala had made a deal with the House of Japha for the twins to run it, San knew it would be a different story, once they got home. He was sure he would be tested. Some people would need convincing that the twins were in charge, and some people would have to be dealt with.

San liked the Na, Tee because she could keep his attention. They would talk about everything. It didn't matter whether it was about the weather, or the food they were eating, to the houses they came from. They always had something to talk about. Besides that, they had good sexual chemistry. San had a decent sized place, close to the palace. He and Tee were there waiting for the servants to tell them that everyone was on their way to the feast. San was lying down on a bed of pillows. The Na, Tee was laying next to San, half ways on his side, with one of her legs on and across his. Her head was lying on San's chest. Tee asked San "When we get up north, to the House of Japha, how will you tell your family about us?"

San didn't answer right away. That wasn't on the top of his list of things to do when he got back. But now that it was brought up, it was something for him to think about. Tee was a little frustrated that San wouldn't, or couldn't come up with an answer right away. Tee was good about not pushing San on relationship issues. That's one of the reasons he kept her around for this long. But eventually every woman wants to know where she stand in a relationship, and how far is it going to go. Tee enjoyed San's company. She had given herself to San. Now her feelings were getting stronger and she wanted to know if San's were to, or if he was just having fun and toying with her. After a minute of silence, Tee lifted herself up, looked at San, and said "Well, are you going to ignore me?" San said "I'm not ignoring you, so don't get testy with me." Tee quickly said "I'm not. But I would like an answer." San said "When I first get back home, things are going to be tough enough without having to explain you. You being a Na, and me being a Japha. So I think it would be best if you didn't come with me at first. After I see what I'm dealing with, I'll send for you."

Tee lay back down on San's chest. San said "Don't worry about that right now. We have plenty of time before I head home. Let's just enjoy each other until then." Tee didn't respond. That wasn't the answer she was looking for. She had done everything she could to show San that she was perfect for him. She did everything that he asked of her. Her feelings were hurt. She had very strong feelings for San. She knew if she stayed until it was time for the Japha twins to go home. She would be that much more wrapped up in her emotions for San. Tee decided right then and there that she was going to cut her loses. She was going home and suffer with the heart ache she already had, instead of dealing with more of it later.

There was a reason that Wana was head of security. It was

because she was the best at it. Security was so tight at the House of Ra, that none of the rebels knew what Ramala looked like. They couldn't get anywhere near the House of Ra. Not one of the seven Houses could get close enough to make a difference in the war. The only reason the rebels even had a chance up north, near Yee province, was because Wana spent most of her time preparing to defend the House of Ra against war. All of her guards knew what was expected of them. She ran security with an iron grip. Security was tight. Tara told Ramala and Wana about the problems, on the way to, and from, Yee province. As angry as it made Tara, that she had the problem, it wasn't as angry as it made Wana and Ramala. Ramala couldn't believe this type of activity was going on in her territory. Ramala asked Tara if she thought it was Han's, or the Butchers fault, that it wasn't brought under control. Tara told Ramala, Han was busy protecting Yee province from invasion. He didn't have time to chase rebels outside of the province.

Han was the only real warlord Ramala had. He was raised in the House of Hayee, and became one of Ramala's closest protectors. Han understood Ramala. She was a conqueror. Han was too, but he didn't have a name. He was the half Hayee slave. His father didn't want it known he had a son with a slave girl . His father still cared enough about Han, to have him raised in the Hayee military. That's why he was happy to wage war in Ramala's name. He won the battles, while Ramala won the wars. Wana knew Han was more dedicated to Ramala, than her or Tara. Wana was good with that. She didn't need Han to protect her. She could protect herself.

Wana was the oldest, between the three Hellcat cousins. She was also the biggest, and the toughest to fight. Ramala was the fastest of the three. That wasn't always good enough to beat Wana. Tara came in third to both the other girls' skills. Wana had just gotten done checking with her security people, on how she wanted things run for the feast later. She went to her place, which was right next to the palace. She was resting until she heard from Tara or Ramala. She still couldn't believe that both her cousins had sex before she did.

When the three of them first decided to make their move into the south, they agreed that they would pick kings, after they completed their mission. That ended when Ramala met Dan, and Tara met Yin. Now those two had something in common that Wana wasn't in on. Ramala and Tara sometimes made inside jokes about sex that Wana didn't completely understand. She felt like an outsider when it came to sex. That bothered Wana. She was going to find out what this sex thing was all about. She just knew that she wasn't going to let it make her almost a slave to any man. That was going to be the difference between her and her cousins.

Wana was traditional. She wasn't going to be sexually active with anyone that wasn't from the House of Hayee. So that meant she would have to get more of her relatives to the House of Ra, from the House of Hayee. She knew that wasn't going to be a problem. The Hayee Hellcats had just won a war. They were on top. Everyone loves a winner. Everyone wants to be on the side of the winners. Wana knew that. She knew if she sent for Tara's brothers, Tito and Tim, that they would bring some of her other cousins. She would have more than enough Hayee to choose from. For now, she would be patient. Pretty soon, she would be in on all of the sex jokes.

Yaya didn't get to miss her workouts, just because the Butchers were back home. Still, this was better than anything she could have imagined, when she was back in Yee province. She had an hour practice. After that, she would go and check on the twins and get instructions from Ramala. Ramala treated Yaya like her own child, after the Butcher girls went into battle. It made Yaya very happy that Ramala had accepted her, after first acting like she wouldn't. Yaya always worked extra hard to make Ramala proud of her.

Yaya would sometimes do things that neither she, nor Ramala could figure out why. Ramala knew what was up with the way Yaya acted around Dan. You would have to be a fool not to recognize that this young girl liked Dan a lot. That didn't bother Ramala as much as the other lapses in judgment that Yaya would have. It tested Ramala's patience, and gave her insight on how to deal with little Ramala, when she got to be Yaya's age. All of the servants and guards in the palace were used to Yaya running down the hallways of the palace. When she wasn't running, she would dance to where ever she was going. The only time she walked was when someone made her. She was always full of energy. You could see it in her eyes. Her eyes were always eager to learn or do something. Before Ramala went to her sleeping quarters with Dan, she gave instructions to Yaya's trainers to push Yaya hard, for an extra hour. This was Ramala's way of punishing Yaya lightly, for what she had done earlier, when the Butchers arrived.

Yaya was weighted down in a fifty pound vest. Her teacher had a wooden pole of four feet. Yaya had to avoid getting hit with the pole. She wasn't allowed to fight back. This was purely for defensive skills. Usually after an hour of this. Yaya would take a short nap. Today, she was being push to her limits. She didn't complain when the teacher told her that Ramala wanted her to practice for an extra hour.

She just pushed herself until she could no longer get out of the way of the swinging pole. The teacher didn't take it easy on her either. The teacher punished her enough to let Yaya know that next time she had to be better. When the teacher was done, Yaya thanked him, just as Ramala had taught her to do. Then she went to get washed up. Yaya was beat up and tired, but after she got cleaned up, she went and checked on the young twins, Dan and Ramala, because she knew they would be waiting on her.

The twins Dan and Ramala were a lot to deal with. Ramala had five maidens who took care of the twins needs on a regular basis, when Ramala was busy or didn't want to. The five maidens had a small army of servants to get whatever they needed, so they wouldn't have to leave the twins or drag them all over the palace to get whatever they needed. The maidens and the servants to the maids were watched closely by Ramala's elite guards and Ramala. It was suppose to be a great privilege to be able to serve the twins. There were a lot of good people waiting in line to take these maidens places, so they had to do their most impressive job to make sure that Ramala wouldn't have them replaced by someone better. Yaya also kept a close eye on the twins for Ramala.

Young Ra, Dan was strong like his father and he was gifted with Ramala's quickness. When he learned how to control his hands, he found that he liked hitting people with them. He was very quick and usually caught you with his first swing. If you were quick enough to avoid the first swing, he would keep swinging with increasing speed, until he hit you, or you put him down. Ramala and little La, were the only ones he wouldn't try to take a swing at, unless he was extremely tired or hungry. Then he was more than willing to take whatever punishment he had coming. When young Dan wasn't hungry or tired, he was no trouble at all, unless little La got him worked up.

Little La was the new version of Ramala. She was quick both in mind and body just like Ramala. Only now, she had Dan's strength. The Ra, Ramala, little La, or Lala was who she was called by everyone, loved to test her strength every chance she got. If you picked her up, she would grab your hair, or your clothes and pull as hard as she could one way, then another. She would quickly get carried away and would be out of control wrestling you.

But just like young Dan, she knew not to try that with Ramala. Ramala was very loving with her twin. But if they did something she didn't like, she was very rough and stern with them. Little La didn't like being roughed up, so she tried to do what she thought Ramala wanted her to do. When Ramala wasn't around, or looking at her, Little La tried to do whatever she thought she wanted to do at the time. That included trying to rip young Dan apart every chance she got, or sometimes, if she just felt like it. Little La gave young Dan his first lessons on how to defend himself. Even though Dan had some of Ramala's quickness, his mind wasn't as quick as little La's. So she was a continuous exercise in defending himself. At this young age, he just couldn't compete with his sister, although that never stopped him from trying.

Yaya arrived at the twin's room shortly after she got cleaned up. She had two drummers come with her. Even though she used a lot of her energy practicing, she always had enough left to put on a dance show for the twins.

When Yaya first walked into the room the twins were calmly sitting. They had recently wakened from sleep. When they saw Yaya, they jumped to attention, their eyes lit up, and they started getting up. They ran and met Yaya in the middle of the floor, where she threw them both to the ground and started tickling them. Both of the twins roared in laughter. Every once in a while, little La would let out a scream. It wasn't developed enough to freeze anyone yet, but it could disorientate you for a second or two.

The maidens knew when Yaya came around it was time to put cotton in their ears to protect them from the screams. Yaya didn't use cotton. She thought it was fun to be off balance for a few seconds.

Yaya pointed to the drums and looked an order to the drummers to start up. Yaya got off the floor and started dancing. She was a master at moving to the beat of the drums. The twins got up and started watching Yaya. Then they started dancing.

Doing the best they could, they would stumble and sometimes fall, trying to imitate the moves they saw Yaya doing. They were going on for about ten minutes.

Both the twins were revved up to a fevered pitch. Then little La stood still, put her arms to her sides. She leaned her shoulders back slightly, clenched her fist, and let out a scream. Yaya immediately covered her ears and stumbled backwards. Young Dan stumbled too, but he didn't know enough to cover his ears. He looked at his sister curiously and wondered how, and why she did that.

This was the most powerful scream La had put out and it was enough that the maidens covered their ears and nervously got low to the ground. La looked at everyone in the room. It puzzled her that she could make everyone react this way by screaming. So she did it again. This time a little louder. Yaya fell to one knee still covering her ears and trying to recover. Young Dan fell over sideways landing on the ground. Then they heard "Ramala! That's enough! Be quiet!" Little La jumped to attention, after hearing her mother's voice. It was very loud and stern. That was enough to shut La up. She stared at Yaya. Then she ran over to Yaya, looking nervous. Yaya said "See what you did. You have annoyed Queen mother." Young Dan got off the ground and walked over to Yaya. He looked at his sister. He didn't like being yelled at.

Ramala was sleep in her quarters, next to Dan when she heard the drums beating. She knew it was Yaya. She knew Yaya loved to dance to the beat of the drums. Ramala figured she was entertaining the twins. Ramala rolled over, peeked at Dan, and then closed her eyes.

What seemed like a few minutes later, Ramala and Dan where startled out of their sleep by a scream. Dan drowsily asked "What was that?" Ramala smiled and said "That was your daughter. You had better get used to that. You're going to be hearing a lot more of it." Then there was a second scream. Without realizing how close she was to Dan, Ramala yelled so loud it shook the room. She yelled "Ramala! That's enough! Be quiet!" Dan quickly covered his ears. Ramala's yell was deafening. Dan looked at her and said "Did you have to yell so loud with me being right here!"

Ramala, realizing Dan was yelling at her, looked at him, removed the smile from her face, saying "I wanted to make sure she heard me." She paused for a second, then said in a serious tone

"Anyway it's time to get up. We have to get ready for the feast. And another thing. Don't yell at me." Dan said "I wasn't yelling at you." Ramala said "Well don't use that tone of voice with me. It's going to do nothing but cause problems."

They stared at each other for a moment. Then Dan said "Since I've been back, I've noticed you have been short tempered with me. What's up with that?" Ramala got up and said "It's been hard on me with you not being here. You know, training the twins, dealing with a war, and getting back into shape. All at the same time. Not to mention, trying not to worry about whether you were alright." Her face tightened a little. Then she said "Then when you get here, you don't release me from my frustrations. You think it a game to make me wait for what I need from you. I'll wait because it's you. Don't think I like it! And don't think things will be pleasant for you if I don't get what I want!" Ramala turned and started walking towards the exit, before Dan could respond. Dan was looking at Ramala as she walked through the doorway with her perfect body. She was his drama queen. He knew that was just the way she was. He wondered if he would get to a point where he couldn't put up with her attitude. Dan watched as her perfect body disappeared into the hallway. Well, one thing was for sure, he knew as long as she kept that body, he would be dealing with her drama for a while.

When Ramala walked into the young twins room, first she looked around the room and then at the maidens. They had their heads lowered, looking at the twins. The twins were in the middle of the floor with Yaya. Yaya turned the twins towards their mother. Yaya stayed down on her knees. Ramala looked at Yaya and said "I see you all have been enjoying yourselves." The twins had already taken off towards Ramala the second they saw her. Yaya didn't move or say a word. She didn't want to give Ramala another reason to punish her. The twins ran into Ramala's legs, trying to climb up into her arms. She bent down and held both of them. They wrestled each other, as well as Ramala, to get the most attention from her. Ramala pushed both of them back a little and said "Alright, that's enough pushing." Then she looked at little La and said "I see you discovered a new skill today. Mommy heard you scream." Ramala put both of her hands to her mouth, gesturing a scream, so that little La would understand what she meant. Then Ramala said "Mommy's going to teach you how to control that voice and make it stronger!"

Chapter 3

The feast that the Hayee Hellcats had that night wasn't for the guards, warriors, or the warlords that did the fighting. The feast was a celebration of the Hellcats victory. Not everyone was invited to the feast. Only elite guards and the top warlords that Wana thought could be spared, without compromising security, were invited.

That's the reason Han, Chi, and the Death Squad were not present. Wana couldn't take the chance that something wouldn't go wrong while they were gone. There would be plenty of time to let Chi and Han come and give praise to the Hellcats. That's what this feast was really about. The Hellcats wanted to see who would give them the most praise out of their top warlords, and which warlords would try to take some of the glory for themselves. Wana wanted to see if she was going to have to replace people now that the war was over. You couldn't have ambitious warlords serving you, when they thought they were the reason for your victories.

The Hellcats knew they were the ones that put all of the warlords in good situations to be successful. Otherwise, the warlords could have taken over themselves. But they couldn't. So in their minds, all of the praise for winning the war should go to the Hayee Hellcats Tara, Wana and Ramala.

The reason the Hellcats were a great ruling team was the fact that each of them respected each other's strengths, and they each knew their place. Ramala was the conqueror. She was smart and always came up with the best plans. Wana was a mastermind at security. No one could lock down a place and secure it like she could. Tara was a great negotiator, and the voice of reason to the other two girls. As long as Tara kept her sometimes, uncontrollable anger, in check, she could out think anyone.

They all knew each others strengths and didn't invade the

others specialty. Wana and Tara didn't want to rule, and Ramala didn't interfere with security issues. Ramala also never wanted to negotiate for anything. With her it was always, what she wanted, when she wanted it. So she would always listen to her cousins, and if what they said made since, or they pushed her hard enough, she would take their advice. But make no mistake, Ramala was running the show. Her cousins were alright with that.

The feast was held in the guest building, which was huge, and could house a couple hundred people. Almost no one was allowed in Ramala's main palace. That was sacred ground. A person could lose their head for trying to enter her palace.

The Hellcats were seated on a stage that had three ruling chairs, and a round table with chairs on both sides. The tables were for the Butchers, the Japha twins, and any other very special guest. All of the top guards from the House of Ra took turns giving praise to the three Hellcats.

Then everyone enjoyed a big feast. It was very formal. After it was over, Ramala invited The Butchers and the Japha twins to a private party with her cousins. It was in a building very close to the palace. When they got there, they could see that food and drink was already set up for them. There were drummers and dancers off to the side, preparing for a show. Everyone came in and sat at a huge table that had more than enough room for everyone to get comfortable. Yaya, who had been to the feast, and had been bored to death, started to liven up a bit. She knew this was going to be the real party.

The drummers started up, and the dancers went out on the floor. The dancers stretched a little, then got right down to it. They put on a show that got everyone's attention. Ramala watched Dan closely. This was Ramala's first time seeing Dan's reaction to dancers. She could see that he was enjoying it very much.

After about twenty minutes, Yaya couldn't hold back any longer. She joined the dancers out on the floor. Yaya was a very good dancer. She was putting on a good show, almost out dancing the more experienced women. But at nine years of age, there was no way she could compete with the moves of grown women. The dancers took a break and everyone clapped in appreciation for the show they had just put on. Yaya was just getting warmed up. She went over to Cat and Ma and begged them to dance until they finally gave in. Yaya waved at the drummers to start up again. The drummers knew that Yaya liked a heart pumping fast beat, so that's what they played. Yaya, Cat and Ma started dancing. The Syn, Jara and Tara joined in. Then Jan, her girls, and the Na, Tee got up and went to the floor with the other girls. Wana turned to Ramala and said "Let's show them how it's done."

Wana and Ramala headed towards the floor. This caught Dan's immediate attention. When Ramala got to the dance floor she started dancing with her back to Dan. She knew he was watching her. She could feel it. All of the girls were shaking it up pretty good now. Then Ramala turned so Dan could get a side view of her. She watched as Dan was almost drooling over her moves. They locked eyes, and that's when Ramala really put on a show for Dan.

Her performance wasn't lost on the rest of the Butchers either. Yin and Back were getting a good look, while trying not to get caught looking by Ramala, for fear of her thinking that they were being disrespectful. Even San couldn't help but notice Ramala, although most of his attention was taken by Tee's dancing. But Ramala was focused on Dan and shaking her body for all it was worth.

Ramala had not told Dan that she had learned how to dance. She wanted to surprise him. She knew if she had told him, he would have been somewhat prepared for what she did, and would try and play it cool. Like he wasn't affected. Looking at Dan, she could see that he was caught off guard and staring to the point that she had all of his attention. Just like she planned. All three Butcher men were now standing in front of the table watching.

The drummers stopped and took a break after a half hour. The girls headed back to the table. All of the men were affected by the dancing. Ramala could see how pleased Dan was with her. As she walked past him, neither of them could take the smile off of their faces. Ramala knew this would be a good night. San was just as pleased with Tee. Even though San had seen Tee dance before, it seemed that the added competition between the girls forced Tee to shake it up more that she ever had. Yin couldn't take his eyes off of Tara. She saw that and walked right over to him. When he sat down, she sat on his lap. That got the immediate attention of the two other Hellcat cousins. Before they could say something, Tara said "Relax you two! It's a party and I'm having some fun!"

Still that wasn't good enough for Tara's cousins. They stared at her and she quickly stood up and sat in the chair next to

Yin. Yin didn't want to be involved, so he acted like nothing happened. Everyone enjoyed each others company a little while longer, then Ramala ended the party. She had waited long enough to get what she needed from Dan. Soon after her and Dan got back to her palace, Ramala got what she was waiting on, and she got it good.

The next day, Dan and Ramala ate twice in bed before either of them had enough strength to get up. They put on just enough clothes so that they could lounge around, without being naked. They stayed in their quarters so long, that Yaya asked if she could, and then brought the twins to Ramala's quarters. The twins played and climbed all over the bed. They knew Ramala was giving them more freedom than usual, and they were taking advantage of it. Yaya sat quietly at the edge of the bed watching Ramala, Dan, and the twins.

Ramala looked over at Dan and said "Do you know why I couldn't take my eyes off of you the first time we met on the road?" Dan looked over at Ramala and said "No, I don't." Ramala said "Of course you don't. But I'll tell you. I saw you in my dreams many times before we met. My dreams told me that you would be my King. I didn't know if it really was true until I saw you that day out on the road. That's why I stared at you for so long. I also know that I will be Queen for a very long time." Dan said "Have your dreams ever been wrong?" She said "It's not a matter of them being wrong, it's a matter of me understanding them." Dan asked "What else have your dreams told you about me?" Ramala said "Nothing. My dreams only tell me about things that affect me. They don't tell me about other people's future. Or at least they haven't yet."

Ramala moved closer to Dan, looked up in his face and asked him "Of all the weapons you faced in battle, what would you say was the best." Dan didn't hesitate. He said "The Hammer-Axe is the best. I started out with machetes. Once I got a taste of the Hammer-Axe that was it for the machetes. I'll never go back, unless I can't get to my axes." Ramala said "That settles it then. I'm going to turn our children into Hammer-Axe champions! You're going to be very proud of them!"

Dan was listening to Ramala, but he had his hands full, wrestling little La. She, it seemed to Dan, had an unlimited reserve of energy. Dan kept tossing her around and she kept coming back for more. Little Dan wanted to join in, but he was more comfortable fighting with Ramala, who was lazily keeping him at bay with her light kicks and skillful foot work. Dan said "But still, you should also train them to be machete masters also, especially the girl. You should know that a machete is a girl's best friend." Ramala said "That's right! I'll teach them both all of the weapons, but they will become machete and Hammer-Axe masters." She paused for a second, then said "What's the weakness of the Hammer-Axe?"

Dan was puzzled. He questioned "Weakness?" Ramala said "Yes, weakness. Every weapon has a weakness that can be taken advantage of. If I know what it is, I can make sure our children won't fall prey to it."

She looked at Dan for a response. Dan thought for a moment and then he said "There is one slight weakness. When the Axe blade is sharp it slices through skin and bone effortlessly. But after so much use, the blade gets dull and you use much more energy hacking through bones instead of slicing. So you become that much slower, once your Axe blade becomes dull. Also, the Hammer-Axe is heavy. The longer you fight, the heavier they get. If you're not in great condition, you'll get worn down. I don't know if anything can be done about that." Dan looked at Ramala to see if that was any help to her. He could see that it was. Ramala said "Something can always be done, if you know what the problem is. It's just figuring out how to solve the problem, or get around it."

When the Japha, San woke up that morning, the first thing he thought was that Tee really got her money's worth out of him last night. He rolled over and didn't see her. He thought she must be having breakfast, or practicing. He wondered how she could practice so early, after a night like last night. San dragged himself out of bed and got cleaned up. He was going to find her so they could meet every one else for breakfast.

When the Na, Tee woke up, she rolled over slowly, as quietly as she could. She looked at San. He was sleeping soundly. Tee smiled. She surprised even herself last night with San. She rolled back over slowly, and got out of bed. Tee got her clothes and watched San as she put them on as quickly and quietly as she could. She backed up to the doorway, looking at San. Then she walked out of the room.

The Na, Tee walked outside, and went straight to the Japha, Jan's place, which was two buildings down. When she got there, the servants announced to Jan, that she was there. Then the servants escorted Tee to Jan's sleeping quarters. The Na, Tee walked in and was surprised to see, not only was Jan and her girls up, but it looked like the Butcher girls had camped out there for the night. All of the girls were very surprised to see the Na, Tee, knowing that Tee and Jan weren't the best of friends. Tee greeted every one, and all of the girls could hear in Tee's voice that something was wrong. The Japha, Jan walked over to the Na, Tee. Nina and Mia walked over right behind her. Then they moved on both sides of Jan, as she stopped right in front of Tee.

Tee tried to talk in a normal voice, but her words come out low, with a slight sadness to them. Tee looked at Jan and said "I'm leaving now. I didn't want to wake San. You can tell …." Jan was shocked at the fact that Tee was leaving and didn't tell San. So she interrupted Tee with "Why are you leaving?"

Tee looked down, then back up into Jan's eyes and said "I guess you were right." Then tears started welling up in her eyes. Tee said "I just thought he really liked me." Then she looked down and wiped the tears from her eyes. While still looking at the ground, Tee said "I don't want to be hurt anymore than I already am. Right now, San would talk me out of leaving. But I know eventually he's going to get tired of me. That's why I have to leave now. Please tell him that I'm going to miss him."

All of the Butcher girls had been listening. They got up and walked over to Tee. Tee looked at them, and said "No sappy good-byes." That's when all of the girls gave Tee a hug. That forced Jan to give Tee a hug too. A few tears from Tee weren't going to make Jan change the way she felt about Tee. Jan didn't want to do, or say anything that might make Tee change her mind. So Jan said "Do you need guards?" Tee said "I already made those arrangements with Wana. She's waiting on me now." Jan said "Don't worry, I'll tell San for you. Be strong. Do what you need to do to make yourself right. Things have a way of working themselves out." Tee said "Thank you sister." And quickly turned and left, before Jan could respond. Jan was happy, but tried not to let it show. She didn't know what happened between San and Tee, and she didn't care. All Jan knew was that Tee was leaving, and she would have her brother back.

Because Yin had Tara, and neither Chi, nor the Death Squad was around, Backir had his pick of the dancers from the party. On his way back to his place, which was a pretty good sized house, Backir gave orders to the guards that were responsible to him, that he not be disturbed in the morning. Backir smiled, now he was giving orders. That was a long way from being the strong arm protector for restaurants and inns.

Although, Ramala was a tough task master, the benefits were great. He figured, as long as he didn't let her get to him, thing would keep getting better. Backir didn't have to like her. He just had to make sure she stayed in power. Eventually, when he got his own territory, he would hardly see her at all. She was right about one thing. She had made all of this happen. Backir didn't want Ramala dead anymore. He just wanted to be as far away from her as possible. He laughed to himself, and thought, ' Long live Mistress Queen Ramala! '.

Wana came and got Tara, shortly after she saw Tee off. Wana had already told Tara and Ramala about Tee leaving. Tara was just getting dressed when Wana got there. Tara was an early riser. It didn't matter how late, or what had happened the night before. She was always up and out early in the morning. Yin was passed out cold. If a group of assassins walked in right now, he would be easy pickings. Well, maybe not. Yin knew he was in the House of Ra. Even though he knew there was no danger, his guard wasn't all the way down. He knew Tara was the only one in the room. When she left, he would be sensitive to any noise. No one would dare disturb him, unless it was on the orders of the Hellcats.

Yin was in a deep sleep. He was dreaming that he was in a very intense battle. He was holding his own, but he was under a lot of heat. After a few more minutes, the three men that Yin was fighting, started to get the advantage. Yin was on the defensive and taking a beating. He was taking severe punishment just when he was turning and saw the blade of a Hammer-axe arriving at his throat.

Yin jumped up out of his sleep swinging and trying to block the axe from taking off his head. His eyes looked wildly around the room. Yin was sweating profusely, and breathing heavy. He realized he had been dreaming. He wondered why he had such a dream. Yin had never dreamed of himself being killed. In his dreams and in real life, he did all the killing. Yin quickly labeled this dream a nightmare. He was glad that Tara hadn't seen him jumping up like a scared little girl, and he was glad the dream wasn't real.

By the time the Japha, San had gotten dressed, the Na, Tee

was gone. Jan caught up with San, as he was looking for Tee at their sparring gym. She asked her girls to wait outside, while she talked to San. Jan didn't waste time, she said "You won't find her, she left before you got up." San turned, and started for the exit, saying "Left? When did she leave? How long has it been since she left?" Jan put her hand up to stop San and said "You're not going to go running after her, are you?"

San stopped. He looked at Jan, wondering if Tee and Jan got into it. Then he wondered if Jan decided to make Tee disappear. San asked in a stern voice "What happened between you two that she would leave without telling me?"

Jan watched her brother. She could see that he was very affected by Tee not being here. She could see that he was near panic, thinking that she might have killed Tee. Jan said "It wasn't me. This time brother it was all you're doing. And I didn't make her disappear either, if that's what you're thinking. No dear brother, she told me that you were leading her on and her feelings are involved. She told me that sooner or later, you would tire of her. She decided to cut her loses and leave right away." San searched Jan's eyes to see if he could detect the slightest deception. He couldn't. Jan saw that he was more disappointed that she wasn't lying to him. San said "It's just a misunderstanding. If I can catch her and talk to her then ...."

Jan said "Then what? Begging! I would definitely have to kill her then! No Japha, let alone, my brother, should be chasing after a woman who left him of her own will. A word of advice from your sister, never chase after a woman who runs from you, because if she's running, she usually has a good reason why." San was confused. He asked "Why do you think she's running?" Jan said "I couldn't know for sure. But I suspect that something you said or did made her realize that she had no future with you."

Then San thought about the conversation they had. He sighed. San wanted to go after Tee and let her know that she misunderstood him. Jan just stood there and watched San. She wanted to see if he would come to his senses. San realized Jan was right. Then he thought that as much time that he and Tee spent together, she would miss him more than he would miss her. Besides, she came back once, she would come back again! Jan could see San coming back to his senses. She said "Let it go for now. These things have a way of working themselves out. Let's go have breakfast. I'm hungry!" San smiled at Jan and they went and got something to eat.

Ramala gave the Butchers a whole week to recuperate, then she called a meeting. She had a plan, and wanted to go over it with everyone. She told her cousins and Dan the day before, what her plan was. None of them cared much for her plan, but they were willing to go along anyway.

The meeting was after a big lunch that was held in the strategy room of Wana's security building. As soon as the servants cleared all of the dishes, Ramala started talking. She said "Butchers, now that you are my warlords. It's time to teach you protocol. There is a way to act in formal meetings like this. The Hellcats, my King, and the Japha twins are the only names recognized, and that can speak freely in this setting. Everyone else must ask permission to speak."

Ramala looked around the room at all of the Butchers. Her eyes then looked right past the Butchers at the wall behind them, then she said "There are consequences for not following protocol. Isn't that right, Yin and Backir." They both said "Yes Mistress Queen Ramala!"

Ramala continued with "It's very important to remember who's in control here. It's me!! I make the plans. And yes, I do need all of you to help me with my plans. But make no mistake, my plans are good enough that they will work, with, or without any of you. This is an opportunity for all of you. I am in position to give each of you whatever it is you want. Help me, and you will be able to have, and do whatever it is you want, after my orders. Impress me with what you will do for me, and I will impress you with what I can do for you."

Tara, who was sitting next to Ramala, could see that the Butcher girls felt that they were being bullied by Ramala. Tara stood up and said "What my cousin means is she has a special place in her heart for all of you, that you are even here to be a part of this meeting. Her plan is bold, and is going to take all of our best effort to make it work."

The Butcher girls looked at Ramala. They knew Ramala meant exactly what she said. Ramala smiled at the Butcher girls, then said "Now that I am Queen. I think it is important for the people in my territory to know where I stand on things. So I'm going to travel throughout the whole of my territory and meet all of the families in it."

She looked around the room and said "Oh, I know what you all are thinking. Don't do it Queen Ramala, it's too dangerous. Well, who told you to think! That's what I'm here for! I heard tales of my own cousin being attacked in my own territory. These heathens are rebelling against me. I can't have that! This is going to be taken care of right away! Let there be one attack on my caravan, and I will lay down a massacre that will never be forgotten! Make no mistake about that. If I have to kill everyone in my territory to make sure there are no rebels, I will. That's the plan. Wana will work out a security plan, and you Butchers will be expected to execute it. We leave in ninety days."

Ramala paused for a second, looked at the Japha twins and said "We have to figure out how to get you two safely into control of the House of Japha. Do you have a plan yet?"

Jan said "As you already know, when we get back, the House of Japha will only be willing to give me and San control in name. They are going to run the House of Japha as they see fit. Of all of the bodyguards we had, there are only two left. That's not a show of force. Maybe not even enough to keep us alive, if someone brought foul play."

Ramala said "We can supply you with all of the guards you need." Jan quickly said "Not one of your guards can step foot in the House of Japha, without starting a war. They won't care if they're there to protect me. The guards would never make it past the first checkpoint. We have to think of another way to take real control."

Ramala smiled at Jan and said "Whatever plan you come up with, we will back you. If it leads to war, then so be it. One thing's for sure. One way or another, you two will rule the north."

Jan smiled. Now everything was on the table. Jan could see that Ramala wanted to control the north, through the Japha twins. If the House of Japha didn't comply, Ramala would try to destroy them through warfare. If that happened, Jan knew her and San would have no one to depend on except Ramala, and the House of Ra. She knew some of her cousins would back her up in her bid to rule the Japha House. She would be able to control her cousins and most other family members.

Jan liked Ramala a lot. But she wasn't going to bet her and San's life that Ramala wouldn't turn them into her puppets. Jan was going to take the chance that she could convince her father and the other elders at the House of Japha that she could rule the House of Japha, without interfering with traditions that they were used to. She knew the only way to do that was for her and San to return to the House of Japha alone.

Jan said "I have decided that we want to be escorted to the House of Japha and only be delivered to my father. Then me and my brother will enter the House of Japha alone, with my two girls." Ramala's face had genuine concern for the twin's lives. Ramala said "That sounds very dangerous. Are you sure you want to do that?"

Jan said "Thanks for your concern, but that's the only way the Japha might be willing to deal with me. Me and San will meet with Han and Chi once every moon. I will make sure that we are there. If we don't show up, that means we're dead. If that happens my sister, I want you to take revenge for me and my brother's deaths. Leave not one Japha alive. Not even my father. Because if he can't protect me, then to hell with all of them."

Ramala walked over to Jan. Jan stood up. Ramala said "No harm will come to you as long as I can stop it. If it does, I won't stop until I kill everyone who didn't stop it from happening. You have my word on that." The two girls stared into each others eyes, then hugged each other. Then Ramala walked back over to her place and said "We have a lot of work to do before we leave. So let's get started!"

The meeting left the Butcher girls with mixed feelings about Ramala. On the one hand, they definitely didn't like the way she talked to them. On the other hand, they had become close to her and genuinely liked her. Ramala was aware of the affect she had on the girls and met with them later, along with her cousins. They all ate, drank, and danced together. That put the Butcher girls at ease, for now.

The next three months were filled with heavy training for all of the Butchers. Ramala didn't want to have to treat the Butcher girls like she had to treat Yin and Backir in order for them to have complete respect for her.

But still, Ramala wanted the Butcher girls to know that she was in complete control, and not just a figure head. She was their leader, and they had to know that. So Ramala set up a practice with the Butcher girls. She didn't tell them, but she was going to fight each of them, one on one.

Ramala had been practicing very hard with Dan before he went to war. After she had the twins, she worked even harder to get back where she was before. Now she needed to test herself. She didn't tell her cousins about her plans. She thought that the Butcher girls might hold back if the other Hellcats were there.

Ramala showed up at the courtyard where the Butcher girls were practicing. Everyone greeted each other, then Ramala said "I'm glad we have the chance to practice together today. I need to know the skill level of my new female warlords. Today I'm going to test the skills of each of you. All of you will fight me one at a time. I want to see your best. Don't hold back. And if you happen to best me, don't kill me."

Ramala smiled sarcastically after her last sentence. All three of the Butcher girls weren't to sure about this. If they put a beating on Ramala, where would that leave them? Would the other Hellcats come for revenge? Syn, Jara said "Can't you test our skills against some of your elite guards. That way you can get a better look at our skills."

Ramala said "This is the best way for me to really know what you can do. My mind is made up." Then she paused for a second, as she looked over the three girls. Then she said "Ma, you're first." Ramala walked into the middle of the courtyard and motioned for Ma to join her. Ma hesitated. Ramala said "If you need to warm up a little, I can wait." Ma took a quick peek at Cat, and Syn, then said "I'm ready."

Ma walked out into the center of the courtyard. She looked at Ramala. If Ramala thought she wasn't good enough, she was going to find out she was wrong. Both girls slowly circled each other, while closing the distance between them. Then Ramala attacked. She was lightning fast and Ma was forced to go on defense right away. It didn't take Ramala long to work her way through Ma's defense and delivered a three blow combination, all to Ma's body. Ramala said "Come on, I know you can do better than that."

Ma charged herself, then attacked. Ramala dodged everything that Ma threw at her then stepped back and said "That's enough." Ma wasn't ready to quit yet, even though she knew Ramala was much better than her. Ma decided that it wasn't a good idea to push things. She backed up. Ramala looked at Cat and said "Alright Cat, your turn."

Cat had watched the first match and was aware of Ramala's speed. She walked out, fully on guard. Cat didn't wait on Ramala, she attacked and didn't hold back. But it was very hard to catch up with Ramala. She didn't run from you, but she managed to stay just out of harms way. And she was a great counter attacker. She would force the action to such a fast pace that sooner or later one or more of her counter blows would hit its mark.

It took longer with Cat, but the results were the same. Ramala got four straight counter blows to Cat's body. She put something on them, and they backed Cat up a little. Cat attacked again. If Ramala thought it was going to be that easy, she had another thing coming. Cat fought hard, but got caught with a four piece combination that had her off balance.

Ramala could have turned it into a seven or eight piece combination that would have finished Cat off, but she didn't. She backed up from Cat and said "That's enough. You're tough to take those blows!" Cat said "You're really fast, and very hard to catch up with! I have to practice much harder. Thank you for the lesson."

Ramala smiled at Cat, then looked at the Syn, Jara. Syn walked into the middle of the courtyard. Ma and Cat watched very closely. They didn't want to miss any of this. They were confident that Syn was going to win, but they could see that Ramala was much better than the time Syn put her on her butt, when they first met her.

Syn relaxed herself. She knew that after the first match with Ma that Ramala really wanted to test herself against her. Ramala just didn't want to single out Syn for a challenge, so she made up this practice thing. Syn wasn't fooled! When Syn looked into Ramala's eyes, she knew she was right.

Ramala didn't waste time, she attacked. Syn wasn't going to let her use her speed as an advantage like she did when she first met Ramala. Back then, Ramala's speed caught up with Syn, and she got hit. This time, Syn counter attacked immediately. Then both girls were giving it every thing they had. Ramala was doing well enough not to get hit by Syn, but she couldn't catch up with Syn either.

They went on for twenty five minutes, then Ramala backed up from Syn. She knew she was dangerously close to getting hit by Syn. Ramala said "You're still the best! I'm just glad I didn't get hit this time! I'm impressed!" Syn smiled at Ramala, then walked over to Cat and Ma. Ramala walked up to all three Butcher girls, hugged them one at a time, and said "Take what you want from this, but know that we all have to improve our skills." Ramala walked off.

Ma looked at Syn and said "Even though it didn't look like it, you had to be holding back, right?"

The Syn, Jara knew that Ramala had vastly improved her skills. Even though Syn was better, Ramala seemed to have closed the gap in their skill level. Syn gave both of the girls a serious look and said "If I was holding back, it wasn't much. She definitely proved that you two are no match for her. If I were you two, I'd be working as hard as possible to improve your skills."

None of the girls ever mentioned what happened that day, but they did work harder to improve their skills. Just as Ramala knew they would.

Chapter 4

Ramala was carrying another child, after the second month that Dan had returned from war. Tara became with child in the third month. Both girls decided not to tell anyone until it was absolutely necessary. Tara, who was subject to fly into fits of fury, became calmer. Ramala, was pleasant most of the time because she was trying to hide the fact that she was with child. But every once in a while she would fly off the deep end and surprised every one.

By the middle of the third month, Ramala's thirst for blood had returned. That was a signal to Tara and Wana that something was going on. When they questioned her she admitted it. Tara thought that this would be a good a time as any to let them know about her. So she did.

The ninety days before they left, felt like the longest ninety days that San had ever faced. At first he told himself that he didn't miss the Na, Tee. After three weeks he couldn't even lie to himself. He missed Tee. He knew he was strong enough to put her out of his mind, as long as he kept busy. It was the times when he didn't have anything to do those thoughts of her creped into his mind.

The Japha, Jan knew that San was having trouble keeping Tee off of his mind, so she spent as much time with San as possible. Jan also made sure that San had concubines to keep him from getting lonely at night. All of that did help, but San found himself fighting, not to miss Tee. And it seemed the more he fought it, the more he missed her.

By the middle of the third month, Yin had had the same dream about having his head close to being chopped off several more times. When he jumped up out of his sleep, he would tell Tara that he was dreaming about battles that he had fought. Yin wasn't scared of dying. He just didn't want to dream about it over and over again.

The dream was starting to annoy him. He wanted to tell someone, but he didn't want to be looked upon as being weak. He definitely didn't want Ma to find out about it. She would start to worry about him. He didn't want that. So he practiced hard to defend himself from what he could remember in the dream. Was the axe coming from one of the three men in the dream, or was there a forth man that he didn't see? Yin couldn't see the faces of the men. In practice he would always go up against four or more of the guards. After Yin ended up killing several of the guards on different occasions, during practice, he was warned to tone down his practices by Wana. Yin told Wana "If I don't practice as hard as I can, how can I be sure that I will be good enough to protect Queen Ramala?"

Wana said "Practice as hard as you want. Just don't kill my guards!" Every one knew something was bothering Yin, especially Ma. It bothered her that he wouldn't tell her what it was. She decided not to push him about it. Ma figured he would tell her when he was ready. Tara wasn't pushing Yin on it either. But after seeing Yin jump up out of his sleep several times, she figured he was on edge because of his dreams.

One night after a vigorous session with Tara, Yin was relaxed and comfortable enough that he told Tara about his dream. He made Tara promise not to tell anyone about his dream. He didn't want Ma to find out about it. Yin never once made eye contact with Tara while he told her the story. After he was done, he looked at Tara to make some kind of since out of it. Yin said "It sounds like I'm losing my mind, doesn't it?"

Tara said "There's no doubt you're crazy, but I don't think you're losing your mind. It's just a dream. Don't let it get to you. When It's your time to go, there's nothing you can do about it. Enjoy this life while you have it. Besides, you're going to be a father soon."

Tara turned and looked to see Yin's reaction. Yin stared at Tara, letting what she just said sink in. Then Yin said "I'm going to be a father?" Tara smiled and said "Yes. We are going to be parents. Can you imagine us raising a child?" Yin smiled a little. He wondered what kind of father he would be. Yin dismissed that thought and looked at Tara.

This was the first time he had opened up to anyone besides Ma. It still didn't get him the answers that he needed. He thought that he probably wouldn't be sharing anything else, anytime soon. Now he had to think about Tara and their child. He definitely wasn't ready to think about that, but he did wonder. How long do I have to live? Will I live to see my child? Then he put it out of his mind. He was a Butcher. If his dream was real, that's what he was going to do, until he died.

The young twins became very comfortable with Dan during the ninety days before they left. Now the twins were old enough that Ramala would let Dan rough them up a little. They couldn't get enough of being tossed around by Dan. Ramala made sure that the family ate at least two meals together every day. Most of the time it was breakfast and dinner.

The twins were sitting in restraining chairs that were the equivalent to high chairs. They were making a mess of their food, while eating it, as they usually did. Maidens and servants were there to take care of the mess the twins made, so Ramala could enjoy her meal, while she supervised her twins.

Dan noticed that Ramala was drinking blood with her meals again. Ramala noticed Dan staring at her, while she drank her blood. She ignored him until she finished drinking. Then she looked at him. They stared at each other for a moment. Dan knew this could lead to trouble, but that rarely stopped him before. Dan said "The way you're drinking that blood, It's almost like you're with child again." Ramala didn't break eye contact when she said "I am with child again." Dan said, while still staring at her "Are you sure about that?" Ramala said "Yes, I was going to tell you today."

Dan didn't believe that for one minute, but he let it go. It seemed to him, that he stumbled upon that information. He said "Are you going to postpone this trip of yours." Ramala asked "Why?" Dan said "It's obvious, isn't it? You have two children to take care of, and another one on the way. I know you take pride in knowing what you are doing, but you haven't even discussed with me who will be watching our children while we are gone." Ramala said "This trip is going to take four to five months. I know you didn't think I was going to leave our children with anyone for that long, did you? They're going with me."

Dan looked away from Ramala, then he looked back at her. His face tightened a little. He didn't like the sound of this. He said "I don't think that's a good idea. I think you should wait."

Ramala smiled at Dan. She was in a playful mood and said "Who told you to think?"

Ramala was joking, but Dan didn't find what she said funny "He said "What!?" Ramala, still playing around, mocked Dan, saying "What?" Dan said "You think you can just say anything to me!" Dan calmed himself, then said "If you weren't with child, you would have gotten slapped across your behind, to teach you some respect."

The smile immediately left Ramala's face. She looked around the room at the maidens and servants. She looked back at Dan and said in a slow angry voice "You shit heathen!" Little La was starting to repeat words now. She found one she liked and started saying it over and over again, right after Ramala said it. Little La said "Shit! Shit! Shit!" Ramala said "La, don't say that!" Dan said "You shouldn't talk like that around her. She doesn't know any better. So don't yell at her."

Ramala was fed up with Dan. She said "You can go to hell!" Dan had a chalice, full of water. He threw the water out of the chalice, straight at Ramala. She instinctively put her hand up in front of her face to block the water. The water splashed on, and around her hand, into her face, and all over her.

The servants ran over with cloths, and tried to wipe the water from Ramala. She snatched one of the cloths from a servant and waived the others away from her. She ordered the maiden, saying calmly. "Take the children to their room. I'll be there shortly to check on them. The rest of you, get out of here." Dan sat there, waiting. He knew Ramala was upset. He knew there was going to be a big fight. He didn't care. One way or another, she was going learn some respect.

Ramala finished wiping the water from her face and hair, just as everyone was leaving the room. She put the cloth down, and stood up. Dan also stood up. Whatever was going to happen next, he didn't want to be sitting down.

Dan and Ramala had managed to not fight the entire time since Dan returned. Now it seemed that things were coming to a head. Ramala looked at Dan and said "You just had to humiliate me in front of my servants! What did you think would come of that!?"

Dan was fed up with Ramala's attitude and said "You know Ramala, I really don't care. I've had enough of your attitude. Go ahead, do whatever it is you're going to do. Scream and freeze me if you want. If you don't kill me, afterwards, I'm out of here anyway. I'm tired of all of your shit!" Then they heard, from down the hall, little La saying "Shit! Shit! Shit!" Ramala and Dan were trying to be serious, but La sounded so funny that they both erupted into laughter. They laughed for a few minutes, and when they stopped they realized that they weren't as angry as they were before.

Ramala said "I wonder why she picked that word." Dan said "She probably got it from you. You know, Rhino shit heathen." Ramala said "Oh yeah, I have to be more careful what I call you around her from now on." They stared at each other for a moment. They still had unfinished business. Ramala said "Don't say things like that to me. It's gonna cause trouble." Dan said "I told you, I'm out of here." Ramala said "Where are you going?" Dan said "Away from you!"

Dan could see confusion in Ramala's eyes. She was unsure of what to do next. Dan still wasn't sure whether he would be blasted or not. The last time when he thought for sure she wouldn't, she did. He braced himself as he started towards the door. Ramala followed him. She didn't want to say anything that might push Dan further away.

When Dan got into the hallway, he turned and said "Where are you going?" Ramala said "Where ever you're going." Dan said "Well I'm leaving the House of Ra." Ramala said "Then so am I. If you can leave our children, then I will to. I'll follow you until we die."

They stared at each other for a moment. Dan said "I wouldn't have to leave if you could tone it down a bit. Can you show me the respect I deserve?" Ramala whispered "Yes." Dan said "Then I'll stay for now." Just then, Wana, Tara, and Butcher girls came running into the hallway where Dan and Ramala were.

The servants had alerted them that something was about to happen between the two. Wana looked at Ramala, and then at Dan and said "Mala, you alright?" Ramala put her arm around Dan and said "If you're going to come running every time you think me and Dan are fighting. You're going to be doing a lot of running." Wana said "That's alright. I'll do a lot of running, but if you're not alright just one time, it won't be a second." Ramala scolded "Wa!" Wana said "I'm just saying!"

During the week before the meeting, Wana got down to the business of getting her relatives to the House of Ra. She sent a messenger telling her two cousins, Tito and Tim to bring young relatives, both male and female, to the House of Ra as her guest. She knew Tim and Tito would bring as many Hayees that wanted to come. Wana was good with that. There was more than enough guest and guard housing to accommodate them when they got there. If there wasn't, she would have more built.

It was a month before the Hayee, Tim and Tito arrived with one hundred of the Hellcats cousins. When they arrived, the Hellcats partied with them. They partied for two days uninterrupted. They were happy to see blood relatives, and cousins that they hadn't seen for a long time.

After the two days, Wana got her relatives into the daily routines of the House of Ra. She found out what each person was good at, if anything at all, and put them to work at that. The ones without skill were given minimal task, until they could learn real skills that were helpful to the House of Ra. The Hayee, Tito and Tim found it hard to deal with Ramala as a ruler. Back at the House of Hayee, she was one of the favored daughters of their uncle and grandmother. Her and Wana trained with, and helped in security matters. They knew Ramala was strong willed and very difficult to deal with, if you didn't agree with her.

Now their younger cousin, Ramala was Queen of her own territory and acting harsher than normal . Tito and Tim weren't even allowed in Ramala's palace. The palace was Ramala's sacred ground. She told them they could go most places except the palace. What kind of person would treat her own cousins like that? Wana and Tara made excuses for the way Ramala treated her Hayee cousins. Ramala was happy to see her relatives, because now she could drink Hayee blood exclusively.

Every Hayee that came to the House of Ra, had to give blood, at some time or another. That was the price every Hayee paid to stay at the House of Ra. The Hellcats also made it clear to all of the Hayee that if they challenged, or even offended Ramala, there would be severe consequences that neither Wana nor Tara would be able to get them out of. All of the Hayee children had a strong dislike for Ma, and they hated Dan. All of the warlords that Dan killed from the House of Hayee, were related to them in one way or another. The only reason they weren't trying to kill Ma and Dan was because of threats from the three Hellcats. Both Dan and Ma could feel the dislike from the Hayee. So could Cat and Syn. They never let Ma go anywhere, without one or both of them by her side. Usually it was both.

Wana was very close to her cousins, Tito and Tim. Both were older than her. Tito was six years older than Wana. Tim was two years older than her. She was closer to Tim than any man besides her father. Tim would do anything for Wana, and she knew that. If there had been any sexual energy between these two, they would have already been together sexually. But there wasn't, so nothing happened.

One evening a bunch of Hayee were over at Wana's place. When they were leaving, Wana stopped Tim and told him she wanted to talk. They walked back into the lounging area where Tim sat down. Wana came over and sat next to him. Tim asked "So what's so important that we had to talk right now?" Wana said "How's Meka doing?" Meka was Tim's wife, and a distant cousin to Wana. Tim said "She's doing fine. The baby isn't due for another five months." Wana asked "Does she let you have concubines to help relieve your stress?" Tim said "Yes, she does, but you know I do what I want anyway. Why?"

Wana said "I need a very big favor from you." Then she paused for a moment. She continued with "Ramala and Tara have experienced sex. It seems to have made them dependant on the men they chose. I don't want to be dominated by a man. I did look at all of the men to choose from at the House of Hayee before I left. I didn't want any of them. Now I'm out here at the House of Ra with a bunch of heathens, and a few Hayees. I thought about this for a while and decided that I want to do this my own way. I trust you, so I want you to take me and teach me sex."

Tim turned and looked Wana in the eyes. He said "You're joking right?" Wana shook her head no without breaking eye contact. Tim said "One day you're going to find a man that you like. He's going to want you to be unused by another man. You're going to want that too. Don't be in a rush to find out about sex. It's going to happen when It's time."

Wana said "It's time now! I get these urges, but there is no one to take care of them. So I suppress them." Tim said "Then you're doing a good job. You're supposed to suppress those feelings until you find someone that you want to live your life with." Wana said "That's easy for you to say. How long have you been having sex?" Tim said "About five years."

Wana said "Were you good at it right away?" Tim said "It took some time, but now I know what I'm doing." Wana said

"Was it always with the person you plan to spend the rest of your life with?" Tim hesitated for a moment then said "No, but it's different because I'm a man."

Wana stood up and turned her back to Tim. She started undoing her shirt. He couldn't see what she was doing. She said "I want to have control over sex, like a man. You know what you're doing, so teach me. That way I won't be a slave to a man." Wana turned towards Tim and let her top fall to the ground. A better pair of round firm, pointing to the sky breast, you couldn't find on the planet.

Tim stared for more than a few seconds. Not only were her breast beautiful, but her stomach muscles were tight and flat all of the way down to her pants. Tim stood up and said "I don't think we should do this. Get some rest. We'll talk about it tomorrow. "

Tim started to leave, but Wana blocked his way, pushing her firm breast up against his chest. Tim thought holy mother of mammary glands! If she keeps this up, something is definitely going to happen! Then he grabbed both her arms and said "Stop!" Wana stopped struggling and said "Alright! I won't force you." Wana dropped her head and looked at the floor. Tim let go of Wana's arms.

Wana, with disappointment in her voice, said "Just send in the first guard you pass. I'm sure he'll do what needs to be done. I'll live through it." Tim stared at Wana for a moment. There was no way he was going to make her have to disgrace herself like that. If she was that determined to do this, he would help her. He took his hand, and lifted her chin up. She looked at Tim. Tim said "Are you sure this is what you want?"

Wana said "Yes, I'm sure." Tim took his time with Wana and in the next two months, he taught her everything he knew about sex. Wana's experience was much different than her cousins. She felt more in control of her urges, and she didn't need it as much as her cousins, at first. Wana waited until just before they left the House of Ra before she told Ramala and Tara that she was having sex. She didn't know that they already knew. It wasn't much going on in the House of Ra, which all three Hellcats didn't know about.

From the time that Wana put a severe beating on Ma, back at the House of Hayee, Ramala was firm in her orders that these two not practice together. If things got personal between these two, which it already was, at least from Ma's point of view, and one of them was killed in a fight, the alliance between the Butchers and the Hellcats would be destroyed. Ma was much better now, than she was then. She was practicing hard to get better, but she was also practicing to beat Wana. Ma knew that eventually they would fight. No matter how much both sides tried to keep them apart, it was going to happen. The reason she knew it was going to happen was because , when she was ready, she was going to make it happen.Ma and the other Butcher girls had been training very hard and learning security details. All three of the girls took advantage of their week off, relaxing and eating. After that week, they trained extremely hard. They polished their skills with the hooked blade, and the baby axes. It had been a month and a half, and the Butcher girls were confident in their fighting skills with all their weapons, and without them.

This day, the Butcher girls were at afternoon practice. It was hot, dry and a little dusty outside. The sun was beating down, but they were used to that. Practice was held in harsh conditions like this for endurance.

The Butcher girls were surprised when the three Hellcats showed up. The Hellcats had on their ruling capes as usual. All of the girls greeted each other. Wana told her cousins to come with her so they could see the progress the girls were making. The girls had just finished warming up.

Wana said "You girls have made a lot of progress since we first met." Wana purposely looked at Ma. Then she said "I need to know how good you have gotten. That way I know how to use you in securing that we have a safe trip. Everyone step back except for Ma. I want to see what you got."

Wana pulled the string holding her cape around her shoulders. The cape dropped to the ground, just as Ramala turned to Wana and said "Hold on. This ..." Wana interrupted with "This is a security issue. I'll handle this." Wana looked down at the ground towards Ramala, then she looked back at Ma.

Wana was the security expert, but Ramala definitely didn't like the fact Wana didn't tell her and Tara what she was planning. Ramala stepped back, letting Wana know to proceed. Tara looked at Ramala, then stepped back. Cat and the Syn, Jara looked at each other. Syn could see Cat was worried about where this was going. Syn gave Cat a reassuring smile, then they both stepped back. Wana turned her attention back to Ma. Ma looked in the direction of Wana, but not directly at her. Wana said "Back at the House of Hayee, I beat you easily. You weren't much of a challenge. If you think you've gotten better, let me see what you got."

Both girls looked at each other. Ma couldn't believe what she just heard. Ma took a quick look at Tara and Ramala. She had just been challenged by the girl that put a beating on her. It didn't matter to Ma that Ramala and Tara were there. Ma was determined to make Wana pay for what she did to her back at the House of Hayee, and for what she just said.

Wana said "We're not going to use weapons, so my cousins will only stop it if my life is in danger. And then, they will only break it up. You can start whenever you want." Ma didn't hesitate. She stepped up and attacked Wana. Ma's attack was strong. Wana played on defense, before mixing in some offence. Then both girls found themselves in a fierce battle that had them both punching, blocking, kicking and avoiding each other's attacks.

They put heat on each other for twenty minutes straight before both backed up to see the affect they had on each other. Both of the girl's breathing was normal, not hurried at all. Neither one had managed to get a blow in yet. As they stared at each other, they knew this was going to be a test of endurance. Ma walked over to Wana and attacked again. The girls went through a chess game of fighting strategies. Neither one was willing to be hit first by the other. That meant that they had to be the one that got the first blow in.

After another twenty minutes, they both backed up again, but not as far apart as before. Tara said "Haven't you seen enough yet?" Wana said "We've been fighting for less than an hour. A practice is two hours long. An attack from enemy forces could last longer than that."

Everyone there knew what that meant. These two girls weren't finished fighting yet. Ma attacked again. Now the girls were fighting so hard that they were starting to grunt and make other guttural sounds. Ramala was concerned about if she should stop this fight now. Cat and Syn kept looking at Ramala like it's been enough, stop it. Ramala let the action go on for now, but she wasn't going to let it go on for much longer.

Another ten minutes passed. Wana and Ma were right on

top of each other raining blows towards each other. Then finally Wana's speed caught up with Ma. Ma knew she was going to be hit. She braced herself, then swung as fast and as hard as she could at Wana's mid section. Wana's blow landed solidly, just above the stomach, in between the two rib plates. Ma's blow landed a split second after Wana's did. It landed in the middle of Wana's left rib.

Even though Ma was starting to move backwards from the force of Wana's blow, Her punch had enough steam that it stopped Wana from getting a second blow in on Ma. Ma stepped back to a safe distance, while she took back control of her breathing. The blow Ma took was solid and powerful. It shocked her body. Ramala could see that Cat was near panic. Syn was watching both Cat and the fight. Syn was on edge, ready to do something. Ramala and Tara both were seeing all of this and the fight. Wana could see that Ma was getting herself ready to attack again. Wana put her hand up and said "Hold it."

Then she looked at Ma until Ma made eye contact with her. Wana said "Just to hit me, you refused to move back and took the full force of that blow when you didn't have to, if only you had started moving back. If I were your enemy and we kept going. I would be beat up from your willingness to exchange blows, but you would be dead. You are quicker and you are stronger than you were before. But you are not a better fighter. Fighting with anger can only take you so far. Fighting with a grudge will get you killed. You hold on to something that means nothing. So you took a good beating from me long ago. What has that got to do with anything now? We are past that point. Think of it as practice. Everyone takes a beating in practice. That was like practice back then. This is practice. I hope it never becomes real." Ma was getting ready to say something when Wana said "Go get cleaned up. That's enough practice for now."

Then Wana quickly turned her back to Ma. She knew Ma wouldn't attack her from behind with her cousin's right there. Wana walked over and picked up her ruling cape. As she bent down to pick it up, she felt a twinge where Ma hit her. As Wana stood up, she turned, smiled at Ma and said "That was a pretty good blow." Ma stared and said "Yours wasn't bad, either." Ramala said "Girls we'll see you later." The Butcher girls barely waved. Then the Hellcats left.

When the Hellcats got far enough away from the Butcher girls, Ramala, who was slightly annoyed that Wana hadn't told her what she was planning, said "We're suppose to be a team. What was that all about?" Wana said "I have to know where I stand with Ma. It's going to be very difficult protecting both of you as it is, without having to think about whether Ma is going to try to take revenge. I need to know that she has our back in whatever situation we get in."

Tara said "So, have you figured it out Yet?" Wana said "You don't get someone like Ma to change her mind about killing you this quickly, if at all. But don't try to help me on this one. And another thing, if she does manage to take revenge one day. You two had better make sure she doesn't live long after that." Tara bumped into Wana while they were walking, then said "Come on! Did you think you had to tell us that?" Wana said "No, but I'm just saying."

The Butcher girls thought they were in heaven the first month after the meeting. To them, they were being treated like queens. They had servants that got them anything they wanted. All they were required to do was practice and meet with Wana for security strategies. The rest of the time was theirs to do whatever they wanted to.

Then the Hayee children arrived. Since all of them disliked Ma, she got dirty looks from most of them. That kept the Butcher girls on guard. They did everything together. None of them were ever alone without the others. They always bathed together.

After Ma's fight with Wana, the Butcher girls went to their private bathhouse to get cleaned up. They had a large bath, big enough for ten people that they would sit in and soak the stress away. They were laying back in the bath, trying not to bring up what had happened earlier when Ma and Wana had their so called practice session. Then Syn, Jara looked at Ma and said "Maybe you should let go of the past. Things are different now." Ma and Cat both looked at Syn.

Syn said "We're a team now. Wana is part of our team. It's best if things don't get personal between you two." Just then they heard someone in the hall. Wana walked in with a bathrobe on. The Butcher girls watched, as Wana came over to the bath, dropped her robe and got in the bath with them.

Wana said "I came here so we could get to know each other better." Then she looked at Ma and continued with "When my cousin Shaia died and I found out her killer was in our home, the House of Hayee. I told myself that that person wouldn't leave there alive. I'll never apologize for doing what I did. Tell me Ma, what would you have done if you were me?"

Ma didn't answer. Wana said "Now things are different. As much as I loved my cousin. Maybe Shaia's death couldn't be avoided. So I no longer feel the way I felt then. What about you Ma? Can you let go of the past?" Ma quickly looked at Syn and Cat. Then she looked at Wana, and said "Even if I could, I know the other Hayee won't."

Wana said "That's not completely true. Ramala and Tara don't want any harm to come to you and neither do I. The rest of the Hayee here know they can't deal with you Butchers. If they test, do what you have to. A girl has to defend herself if she is attacked. I came here because we need to know we can trust each other. We will practice once a day and then we will take a nice relaxing bath together afterwards."

Wana leaned back and said "I like spending time with my sisters. Who would have ever thought I would be bathing with heathens!" Then Wana realized what she said might have been offensive to the Butcher girls, so she looked at all of them and said "I didn't mean it like it sounded. I just never thought this would happen." Cat said "Neither did we."

All of the girls thought that was funny, but wasn't going to laugh. Ma looked at Wana for another second, then relaxed, and leaned back in the bath. She knew everything that Wana said made since. Wana wasn't trying to win Ma over with kindness. Wana was appealing to Ma's intellect. What bothered Ma more was the fact that she didn't dislike the fact that Wana was there with them. She actually felt comfortable around Wana. Ma really didn't like that.

After Wana's and Ma's first practice or second fight. They went at it almost every day for the next two months. Ma rarely paid any attention to Dan now. He could barely get a dirty look from Ma, let alone a fight. Dan wondered if he didn't miss those fights with Ma. Ma just didn't have time to fool around with Dan. Her day was filled with the Butcher girls, Yin, and Wana. Besides, at the House of Ra, you don't fight with Ramala's King.

Cat had managed to gain all of her weight back and she added a few more pounds. All of it solid. Just like Ma, Cat trained hard, knowing that Ramala would put them in hell's belly and expect for them to come out. Cat was good with that. She was getting tired of all of the practice. Cat was ready for some real action. She had watched Wana and Ma closely when they fought. Cat was sure that neither of them could beat her in a one on one fight.

The person that Cat wanted to beat was the Syn, Jara. Even though the two of them were sisters. Cat felt like the younger sister, even though she was older than Syn. Cat didn't have anything personal against Syn. But to best the Syn, Jara, that was the ultimate test. Cat knew if she worked hard enough, one day she would beat Syn.

The Syn Jara trained hard with the Hellcats, the Butcher girls, Jan and her girls, and Ramala's elite guards. She loved the House of Ra. Where else could she get treated so well, and not have to watch her back. Syn didn't care about all of the petty differences or even the fights that happened between them all. She knew things would work themselves out one way or another. The Hellcats were very careful to keep their Hayee cousins from bothering Syn. The Hellcats knew Syn would put down any challenge to her. Because all of Jara's family was dead, the Butchers, the Hellcats, and the Japha twins and their girls were her family now. Syn loved all of her sisters and brothers. She even found herself missing Chi from time to time. That's the only thing that kept her here. This was her family now.

Chapter 5

On the day the Hellcats tried to wipe out Whirlwind Wa's family, twenty-five of the Wa made it into the forest. There were eleven girls, and fourteen young men. They ran for twenty minutes before they stopped to see how many of them had escaped. All of them were under thirteen, except for five. And those five were all under twenty years of age.

The oldest male was Mobo. He was nineteen. Mira was the oldest girl. She was sixteen. Nicko was seventeen. Then there was Massiko, he was sixteen. Hilando was fourteen, China was twelve, and Yawu was eleven. The other twenty were between five and ten.

All of the children were afraid and were crying hysterically. Mobo and Mira took control. Mira calmed everyone down as much as possible. They told them that they would have to be very quiet so that they wouldn't get caught. Mobo was very angry, but he knew all of the others were looking to him for guidance. He didn't know exactly what to do. All he knew was that if they got caught, they all would be killed. To give them a better chance of surviving, Mobo said "If we all are caught together we will be killed. We have to split up."

Panic ran through the young Wa. Mobo said "Stay calm! I know you're scared. I am too. But we have to survive so we can take revenge for our family. That means being strong and doing what's best." Mobo looked at Mira and said "Mi, you take all of the girls and head to the Mid-Range mountains. There is a convent of nuns there who are protected by the House of He. I want all of the girls to train there until they are experts in fighting. That will take many years, but that's the only way we can be sure that we will get our revenge. Massiko you will take the boys to the Spiritual fighter's temple and beg them to take you in for training." Mira asked "What about you?"

Mobo said "Me and Nicko will try to find out if any more of our family escaped. Then we will help them take revenge. But first I will take you girls to the mountains safely." Mira was concerned and said "You should just go to the temple with the rest of the boys. "Mobo said "Don't worry about us. If we find more Wa, we will send the girls to the mountains, and we will send the boys to the Spiritual temple. If we get our revenge, we will send for everyone. If we don't come for you, just keep training until you are good enough to fight. Then meet up with each other and take revenge for our family. Another thing, don't let anyone know that you are Wa. We don't know who's trying to finish us off."

Mobo turned to Massiko and said "You take good care of the youngsters and keep them up in the trees as much as possible until you reach the temple." Mobo wanted Massiko and Hilando to keep the younger ones in the trees as much as possible because he knew the trees would keep the younger ones safe from wild animals.

Mobo, Nicko, Massiko, and Hilando all were men. That meant they had passed the test of manhood, which was killing a lion, or a tiger with their weapon of choice, by the time they reached thirteen. None of them were grown men yet. Massiko and Hilando were capable of killing a lion or a tiger. But if they ran into a pride of female lions hunting. Well, they would need the young Wa to be in the trees to have a fighting chance. Hyenas were the worst. If they were caught on the ground by a pack of hyenas, there would be no escaping.

Mobo told everyone that it was time to split up. All of the older Wa looked at each other. They didn't know whether this would be the last time they would see each other. Then Mobo took the girls and crept off into the jungle heading towards the mountains. The young men watched until Mobo and the girls were out of sight.

Then Nicko turned to his cousins and said "Stay close to me. When I say get in the trees, I mean do it right now. Don't be playing around. This is serious. If you don't listen, it might get you killed and it'll be your fault, not mine. Come on, let's go."

Then they crept into the jungle going in the opposite direction as Mobo, towards the Spiritual temple. It took them three weeks to get there. They ran into other tribes or families that had been almost wiped out, or were now under the rule of the House of

Ra. These families felt sympathy for the young men and gave them shelter, food, and direction to the temple. When they got to the temple, Nicko told the head priest the story of what had happened to his family. The priest decided to take them in. The priest looked at all of the young men. He shook his head. He knew it would be at least seven to ten years before they would be able to deal with Butchers. But still, that didn't include dealing with someone like the Syn, Jara.

Mobo and the girls weren't so lucky. To get to the mountains they had to make it through Ramala's guards. The mountains were north and east of Tan province. Three of the seven Houses were located in the mountains. The House of He was located at the base of the mountain. They had a monastery that trained young orphan girls to be nuns. The House of Tere was a little further up the mountain. Even higher up the mountain was the House of Tat. We'll get to those three Houses later.

Right now, Mobo and the girls were moving mostly in the evening, just before dark. That's when most of the patrol guards headed back to camp to avoid being ambushed. That strategy worked pretty good, until they got near Yee province.

Ramala had Yee province heavily guarded. That was her supply route and the most northern territory that she had. Mobo and the girls tried to go around Yee province when they saw an army there. They had managed to make it completely around Yee province. It was close to dark, so they were trying to cover as much ground as possible.

Guards were just leaving the area that they were passing through, when Mobo and the girls were spotted. The guards were moving to surround them when Mobo saw them. As soon as the guards started pulling out their machetes, Mobo yelled "RUN!" All of the girls tried to take off running, but the guards managed to trap Mira and four other girls.

China took off with the other five girls. Mobo attacked the guards that started to go after China and the other girls. That gave China enough distance that the guards didn't chase after them. It was to close to dark and the guards didn't want to be caught in an ambush. So they turned their focus on Mobo and the other girls. Mira knew they only had one chance of surviving, so she grabbed the girls and went to the ground, hoping for mercy from the guards.

Mobo was surrounded now. Most of the guards had put

away their machetes and were giving Mobo a fierce beating. It was getting late and the guards had to get back to camp, so one guard split Mobo open from his chest down threw his stomach. As his guts spilled out of him, he stopped for only a second. That's when the second guard took his head clean off. His body dropped to the ground like a sack of potatoes. Mira and all of the girls saw it. Mira screamed and the only thing that kept her from passing out was the four girls that clinging to her in shock. She tried to gather all of the girls into her arms.

One of the guards yelled out "Who are You!?" Mira was in shock and afraid. She didn't answer quick enough for the guard. He lifted his foot and sent it crashing into Mira's back, sending all of the girls on the ground. The guard grabbed Mira by the hair and dragged her away from the other girls. He pulled out his machete and said "What's your name and the name of the ones that got away? I won't ask you again!"

Mira was shaking and could barely get her words together. She said "Please don't kill us! We are just wondering orphans! Our name is Seko!" The guard asked "Where were you going?" Mira was still terrified but now she was a little more composed, and she was lying for her life and the lives of the other girls. She said "There is war everywhere. We were just trying to run as far as possible from the fighting." The guard stared at her. He asked "Who were the ones that ran?"

Mira said "I don't know them. They joined us while we were traveling." The guard didn't believe her. He looked over at the young girls, then he looked back at Mira. He said "All of you belong to the House of Ra now. We will do with you whatever we want. Give us any trouble and all of you will be killed." The guard let go of Mira's hair. Mira said "Yes sir! Thank you for sparing our lives!" Another guard walked up and threw some rope to Mira and said "Tie those girls together." Mira did as she was told. Mira whispered to the girls "Do what they tell you to do and don't make any trouble. The main thing is that some of you survive. Don't talk, just watch and listen. Be brave." Then one of the guards yelled "Hurry up and finish! And no talking!"

Mira finished tying the girls up. The guards had her move them next to one of the guard huts. Mira looked at the girls. They could see sadness and hopelessness in Mira's eyes. Then Mira heard the guard say "Come here you heathen shit!" He was looking right at Mira and she knew he was talking to her.

All of the girls were under ten, except for Mira. Mira was sixteen, and she saw the way these men were looking at her. She knew what was going to happen to her. She looked down at the ground. She started walking forward. She couldn't stop herself from trembling.

When she got to the guard, he grabbed her arm and threw her in the middle of the rest of the guards. When he let her arm go, Mira realized that she was surrounded. She stood there looking down at the ground, trembling and confused. She begged "Spare me, please!"

One of the guards move in and ripped Mira's top off. All of the other guards erupted into laughter at the sight of Mira's bare breast. Mira covered her breast with her arms. She was so scared that her already unstable legs gave way underneath her. She fell to her knees.

Then one by one, all of the guards had their way with Mira, while the other guards held her down. Mira was still a virgin. This night, she took punishment that an experienced concubine would not have been able to take. Mira was in so much pain, that she screamed and yelled until she separated her spirit from her body. The last thing she thought was ' God please protect my sisters from the hell that I'm going through.'

The four little girls, who were tied up on the side of the guard hut heard everything. They went through the hell of hearing Mira screaming for her life. All of the girls were so terrified they were shaking. They all were trying to be quiet, because they didn't know if they were next. Mira's screams went on for so long that Hania broke down and just kept saying in a low defeated sobbing voice "Mi , Mi , Mi ."

Najay started to get nervous, thinking the guards would hear Hania and come for her. Najay whispered "Please! Be quiet!" Then she took Hania's hand in support. Then all of the girls grabbed each others hands for strength, until they finally fell asleep.

The next morning the girls were awakened by the guards moving around and talking loudly. One of the guards came over and grabbed the rope that attached the girls to each other. The guard dragged the girls until they got to the other side of the camp. Then he stopped and pointed. Mira's naked body was laid out, in the dirt, badly beaten and bloodied. Her throat had been slit open. The girls were so shocked that they just stood there and stared, trembling. They had never seen anything so horrible. The guard said "If you don't listen and do what you are told, the same thing is going to happen to you." All four of the girls knew that Mira hadn't done anything to deserve that.

The guards took the girls back to Yee province. Once there, they were interrogated. None of the girls let it be known that they were Wa. Because all of them were so young, the guards figured that they might not know their tribes name.

The girls were sold to one of the restaurant combination inn owners. He put two of them to work in the inn cleaning the rooms before and after guest were there. Those two were Najay and Mayho. The other two girls were put in the restaurant to clean tables and carry supplies.

After the girls were done working, they would see each other in the slave quarters at night. The girls would be very tired and their spirits would be low at the end of the day. But one of the girls would always dance for everyone. She studied the female dancers every chance she got. Then she would put on a show for the servants. That lifted the spirits of all of the other slaves as they watched her dance without the beat of drums. One of the girls that worked in the restaurant was Hania. The other girl, who danced for everyone, was named Yaya.

The four girls knew that the chances of them learning to fight in order to get revenge was very slim. They decided that they would learn whatever they were taught and somehow use it to help the others when the time came. Life was hard on these girls, but when you're young, it's easier to adapt to tough situations. So that's what they did. They really had no other options at the time.

China only looked at Mobo for a split second when he yelled "RUN!" Then she took off with the other girls. They ran and ran for what seemed like forever. Then they stopped. At first China didn't even know who all was running with her. When they stopped to catch their breath is when she saw that only five other girls had escaped with her.

All of the girls were panting heavily. China said "We have to keep going!" The girls took off again. This time they ran at a steady pace, instead of the all out sprint that they had been running at. They didn't see any more guards, but they were to afraid to stop.

Once it got dark, China had all of the girls get up in the trees like Mobo had made them do when he was with them. China thought about her cousins. She wondered if they were still alive. She was very sad but didn't shed a tear until she was sure the other girls were asleep. Then the tears ran down her face, but she didn't make a sound.

China made a promise to herself that some how she would get these girls to the monastery. She had to. Even if she had to give her own life just to make sure they got there. She also promised that she would never forget what was done to her family and that if she couldn't take revenge herself, that some of these girls would stay alive to take that revenge.

When China woke up the next morning, she got down from the tree, checked and made sure the girls were all there and safe. The second and third youngest girls Uma and Jami started complaining about being hungry. China was already stressed out because she really didn't know where she was going. She could see the mountains. They weren't that far off now, but how to get there safely and as quickly as possible. She just didn't have the answer to that. She told the girls "You have to eat some grass for now. When we get to the mountains we will be safe." The grass was bitter, but the girls got enough down to get rid of the hunger.

The Wa girls started out for the mountains again. China was being as careful as a twelve year old could. They were moving cautiously through tall grass when several men jumped out at them. The girls tried to run but were quickly caught. China was desperate. She begged "Please let the others go and keep me! They are to young to be of any use! I'll work hard! I'll do anything! Please let them go!" One of the men walked up and said "I already have all of you. Why would I let any of you go?"

Then the men dragged the girls back to their camp. When they got to the camp, the girls could see that it was a tribe and not an army. Still they tied all of the girls together by the waist and put them in the care of the older women in the tribe. Then the men left. China was defeated. The tears roll down her face as she looked around. She knew she had failed her family. She wasn't good enough to get one of the girls to the mountains. She was to ashamed to even look at any of the other girls. So she held her head down and cried.

The other girls were scared, but they were also worried about China. She just wouldn't stop crying. The other girls had no clue of what to do. China's crying just made them more nervous and scared. One of the old ladies of the tribe brought over some food. All of the girls were suspicious and looked to China for what to do. The old lady tasted the food, then said "See, it's alright."

Still the girls wouldn't take the food. They just stared at China for guidance. China looked at the old lady, then she looked at the girls. She took some of the food and said "It's alright. Go ahead and eat. They won't kill us, at least until they get some work out of us."

Then China stared angrily at the old lady. That didn't bother the old woman. She had been stared at by more fiercer people than a young girl. The girls started eating. The old lady said "What are you young girls doing out in the wilderness by yourselves?" China didn't answer. Then Gia, who was the youngest, said in a desperate voice "Every body is dead! We needa get to the mountains!"

All of the other girls immediately stared at Gia. Gia knew they meant for her to shut her mouth. Then Gia looked begging at the old lady and said "We just needa get to the mountains." The old lady said "Don't worry about the mountains. You're safe here. Eat your food. You're going to need your strength." Then the old lady walked away. The other girls didn't scold Gia. They all were just as desperate as she was.

The girls were given small jobs carrying things around the camp, while still being tied to each other. China could see that all of the women did work inside the camp. She saw that men were everywhere on the outer perimeters of the camp. It looked impossible to even get to the outskirts of the camp from where they were.

Later that night, after the girls had eaten, several women came. The women looked the girls over for a few minutes, then one of the ladies asked "Why are you trying to get to the mountains?" China said "Our family was murdered. We are the only ones that survived. I didn't want us to become slaves. That's why we are trying to get to the monastery in the mountains. Please help us get there!" The lady cautioned "Be quiet! If the men hear you, you will be beaten, or killed."

The lady paused for a moment. She looked at the young girls. She could see how frightened they were. She said "You've already been through enough. You don't deserve this." Then the lady cut the ropes. She told the girls "My son will take you out of the camp and a ways past that. Then you will be on your own. I hope you make it."

A young man about sixteen came up. The young girls got nervous. The lady said "This is my son. His name is Koto. Follow him and do exactly what he says." China looked at Koto for a quick moment, then gathered the girls, and they followed Koto out of the camp. Even though it was very dangerous to travel at night, because that's when most predators were out, they had no choice. They rested for a while and traveled most of the next day.

China would sometimes catch Koto staring at her. She tried to ignore it, and hoped it didn't mean anything. Koto caught himself looking at China. She was a beautiful young girl, and her breast were just starting to come in.

Koto was at the age where his mind was sensitive to the sight of the female body. All that day, between scouting for danger and looking for food, Koto found himself staring at China's body. He had never been given this much responsibility before. All kind of thoughts ran through his mind. Koto had never been with a female before. Out here, he could do whatever he wanted and his mother would never find out. He put it out of his mind for the moment. He had to make sure they didn't get caught in the daylight.

That evening, Koto found a suitable place that he thought the girls would be safe for the night. He got the girls something to eat, and sat there with them. He was very careful not to let the other girls see that he was looking at China. But China was very aware that something was not quite right. She didn't know why Koto was watching her so much. It wasn't like she was trying to escape. She was doing everything that he asked of her, just like the lady told her to. She also tried to smile in appreciation for the help Koto was giving them every time she saw Koto staring. She put it out of her mind as her just being nervous from all that she had been through.

Now it was dark, and the only light was that the full moon provided. Koto told the girls to hide in a small area that was safe, and that he and China would keep guard. He said that they should get a good nights sleep, because it would be a long day of traveling come tomorrow.

The young girls had no reason to doubt Koto. He was their protector. They were grateful that they had someone looking out for them. Then Gia came over and gave Koto a hug. Then, one by one all of the girls gave Koto. When China gave Koto a hug, he felt her breast pushing up against his chest. It shocked Koto that these girls showed him affection and they weren't his family. But still, Koto had a plan.

After the girls were settled in, Koto led China away from them. China thought they were a little to far from the girls, but she trusted that Koto had a good plan for their protection. Then Koto stopped and turned facing China. China instinctively looked around to see if Koto had seen or heard something. She quickly looked at Koto for a sign that there was danger. Koto's face was calm so she didn't think there was any danger. China looked around again. This didn't look like a good place to watch for danger.

Koto had never touched a woman's breast before. He had seen many of them. All different shapes and sizes. Now was his chance to see what they felt like. He put his hand on China's breast and started feeling them up. That startled China and she took a step back. Koto grabbed her wrist with his other hand, while continuing to rub her breast.

China's body stiffened and her eyes got as wide open as they could. She knew Koto had a machete on his waist, but she was never more aware of it than she was right now. Now she figured that since he had gotten her away from the other girls that he would surely kill her when he was done. Her mind was racing crazily, wondering what was going to happen. She feared for the other girl's lives. She looked at Koto and begged, whispering "Please! You don't have to kill the others. I won't make a sound." Koto pulled China closer to him. Koto could feel China trembling as he rubbed her breast again. He stepped back and looked at China.

China saw Koto reach for and pull out a small knife he had concealed on his thigh. China closed her eyes and waited. Koto said "Here, take this." China opened her eyes to see Koto handing her the small blade. He said "Take this and hide it. Always keep it with you." He paused for a second, then continued with "Someone could really take advantage of you out here. They might even kill you when they're done. Keep this with you all the time, everywhere you go. Be careful who you trust. It could get you killed."

China took the blade. Koto said "Hide it under your clothes." China did as she was told. When she was done, she looked back up at Koto. Koto couldn't believe that China thought he was going to kill them. All he wanted to do was touch some breast. He told China "Go right over there and get up that tree and get some rest. Don't make a sound. If you hear anything, I'll be right over here." China climbed the tree, and laid on a large branch, with her arms and legs hanging down on both sides of it. China was glad that Koto had taught her a lesson and gave her the blade. China felt a little funny because she didn't trust Koto any more. That's exactly how Koto wanted China to feel, and he got to feel some breast. He climbed up the tree next to the one China was in and fell asleep.

The next day, Koto got the girls up early. They traveled until they got to the monastery for nuns at the base of the mountains. When they got to the main gate, they were met by nuns. One of the nuns told Koto "You know that no men are allowed here. What do you want?"

Koto stared at the nuns. They seemed to be a bit mean for not knowing him. China said "He escorted us here. We want to be nuns. Our whole family was wiped out and we have no place to go. Please take us in! please!" All of the girls looked at the nuns with begging eyes. The nuns could see in their eyes that these girls had been through a lot. One of the nuns said "It's not going to be easy here. There's a lot of hard work that's going to be expected of you."

China said "We'll work as hard as we have to. We'll do whatever it takes to make you proud that you accepted us." The nun said "We'll see. Come girls." The nun motioned with her hand for the girls to come and join them. All of the girls looked up at Koto. He said "Go ahead, you've been accepted!" Then the girls, one by one hugged Koto and joined the nuns, China was last. She gave Koto a big hug, in which she made sure she pressed her breast firmly up against his chest. When they let go of each other, China said "Thank you for everything. I won't forget it." Koto gave her a smile then he turned a walked away. China walked over to the nun. The nun said "Now you will learn to be a nun. Soon you will have no need for men, and you will forget all about that boy." China nodded in agreement with the nun, but she knew she would never forget Koto.

Chapter 6

In the months before Ramala's Planned trip, she had her clothes makers make even heavier weighted clothes for her twins. They created a clothe tunic, or poncho, that had large, sturdy pockets for weights. Ramala would increase or decrease the weights in the tunic according to what she wanted the twins to do. If she wanted them to walk around, she only put enough weight in to make them work, while walking.

Now that the twins were repeating words, she wanted them to get a lesson on language. When she had low level meetings with the Butchers, or her cousins, she would load the tunic full of weights, until the twins could not walk, but not to heavy that they couldn't stand. Then Ramala would make them stand still weighted down, and listen to the conversation.

From time to time Ramala would address the twins to make sure they knew she was watching them. That kept them at attention. Little La had always watched her mother's every move from the time she could focus her eyes. Ramala fascinated La with the tone of her voice and all of the movements she made. La would often try to imitate the moves she saw her mother making. Ramala was aware of this and made all of her movements precise and deliberate, with obvious purpose when La was around her. She ordered, and directed La's movements. Ramala also corrected La's diction whenever it was not perfect.

La knew her mother was the boss and expected perfection. Ramala made sure of that. La was three and was getting use to the routine that Ramala had set for her. It was almost the same every day. That made it easy for La to figure out the times when she had to be perfect for her mother, and the times she could do what she wanted until someone caught, or stopped her.

Young Dan was easier for Ramala than little La. He was a

little more obvious than La. Ramala could look at Young Dan and see everything that he was planning on doing before he did it. She would be right on top of him, and get physical with him if it wasn't what she wanted him to be doing. Dan couldn't figure out how his mother knew everything he was thinking about doing. That, and her getting physically stern with him kept him in line around Ramala most of the time. Ramala would get more physical with young Dan, than she would with La. It also helped keep La in line seeing Dan get roughed up.

La didn't like being roughed up by her mother. She like roughing up Young Dan and being roughed up by her father. With her mother it was different. Mother didn't play nice! If you didn't do what mother wanted, mother didn't play at all! Both La and Dan knew that. They both found that if you did what mother wanted, she showered you with love, later. They both loved when Ramala was showing them the love that only a mother can show her children.

Young Dan had to be very careful around his sister when his mother wasn't around. That's when La would unwind and get a little out of control until someone calmed her down. And since Young Dan was always there, closest to her. La would, most of the time, start with getting physical with him.

This evening, after a long day with Ramala, the twins were with Yaya and their maidens. Yaya was dancing and doing her fighting moves that she had learned in practice, to keep the twins attention. La and Dan were watching intensely.

Dan looked around and spotted a small piece of bread on the floor. He looked around to see if anyone was watching, only to see La staring at him. Dan looked back at the bread, then looked back at La. La looked down at the piece of bread. She peeked around the room to see if anyone saw what they saw. When she was satisfied that they hadn't, she started moving side to side, getting closer to the bread, while still pretending to pay attention to Yaya. When La was close enough, she reached down to get the bread, but was beat to it by one of the maids. The maiden cautioned "Miss La, you don't eat things off of the floor. It's almost time for dinner. You'll eat soon enough." The maiden walked away with the bread. La didn't like being caught. That was her bread that the maiden took. Then she saw the maiden get rid of the bread. The maiden didn't even want it! She just didn't want La to have it. That was La's interpretation of the situation. One day she would be smart enough that the maidens wouldn't catch her. But for now, she would protest in the only way she knew how. First she charged at Young Dan and wrestled him, then threw him to the ground.

That was for him showing her the bread that she could not get. Then, as the maiden came closer to see if Dan was alright, La let her have it with a scream as loud as she could. The maiden was stunned and disoriented to the point that she lost her balance and fell. Everyone else in the room, including Yaya, covered their ears a second to late. Now La was really upset. Everyone was going to pay. Yaya knew La, and knew she was getting ready to start blasting screams until Ramala came and stopped her. Yaya ran over and got to La just as she was taking in as much air as she could. Yaya moved behind La and put her hand over La's mouth and held it for a moment. La had to exhale. Yaya moved her hand and La let out the air she was holding without screaming. Yaya grabbed La, turned her around, and said "Mother's going to come if you keep that up." La stared at Yaya. Then Yaya let go of La before La thought that she was being handled, and said "You know she's going to be angry. Then we won't be able to do this." Yaya took both of La's hands and started doing a stupid dance with her. After a few seconds, this tickled La and she started laughing. They danced in the middle of the floor and La forgot all about being angry. Dan came over and joined in, once he saw that La was under control.

La was quick witted, but she was very young. Yaya had a few years on La and was smart enough to manipulate La. Yaya always managed to control the twins without the twins thinking they were being forced to do anything. Yaya was their older sister. They loved Yaya dearly. The maidens also loved Yaya because she could control the twins almost as well as Ramala. The twins would tolerate the maidens guiding them to do things. But that's all. When the twins felt like it, and Ramala or Yaya wasn't around, the twins would give the maidens pure hell. The maidens weren't allowed to get rough with the twins. Ramala would have their heads if she thought that they were abusing or even intimidating her royal offspring. The maidens would have to put up with the twins until they were rescued by one of the two. They also couldn't complain about the twins. It was suppose to be a privilege to help raise them. One wrong word about the twins could also cost a maiden her head. That gave Yaya some control over the maidens. If they managed to piss Yaya off, by not doing or doing something Yaya didn't like. Yaya would be purposely late to see the twins. That made the twins unruly when Yaya didn't show up on time. The maidens learned real fast who was in control of their fate after Ramala. For the maidens, it was tough dealing with the twins. But that was their life in the House of Ra.

Today was the day before it was time to start the trip Ramala had planned. Her and Dan were eating breakfast with the twins, and Yaya. Ramala would allow Yaya to have breakfast with them. Dan still wasn't completely convinced that they should be taking this trip now. He knew he wasn't going to change Ramala's mind, only a day away from leaving, especially after all of the planning her and her cousins had done.

It seemed to Dan that Ramala had thought of everything. Her and Wana had reinforced platforms built for the elephants, to guard against spears. The platforms all had thicker wood for walls. The larger platforms were so heavy that they had to be carried by four phants. They also had large openings or windows on all sides so you could get a good look in all directions. There were many different sized platforms, according to what they were needed for. Platforms for the attack elephants. Platforms that the personal servants stayed in. There was even an open topped platform, with borders, for the twins and Yaya to play on.

Dan enjoyed his breakfast, while he watched Ramala tell her twins and Yaya about the trip the next day. If she wasn't talking to the twins, she was talking to him, her cousins, the Japha twins, the Butchers, or somebody. He wondered if she talked to herself when no one was around. Ramala saw Dan looking at her. She could tell his thoughts were about her. To Ramala, Dan was almost transparent. She could just about see what he was thinking, because she had studied him for so long. She pretended not to notice him staring.

After sitting there for a while, Ramala ordered every one out, including her personal servants. She had the maidens take the twins to get cleaned up. Yaya knew after breakfast was training, so she got up and slowly walked out the door. When everyone was gone, Ramala got up and walked over to Dan who was still sitting in his chair at the table. He watched her as she moved slowly and deliberately towards him. When she got there, she sat on his lap, put her arms around him, put her lips right on his ear and said "Don't worry, I've planned everything perfect. You'll see, this is going to be a great trip!" She pulled back a little to look at Dan's reaction. She could see that even though he wasn't in one hundred percent agreement with her, she knew he was going to back her all the way.

The next day, everyone headed to their assigned platform. There were eighty platforms in all. The eight center platforms, which were also the largest, housed Ramala, Dan, Yaya, and the twins. They also housed the Japha twins and their girls, the Butchers, and the Hellcats Tara and Wana. Behind those platforms were the ten that housed the servants and maidens. Another ten platforms carried food, water, and supplies. There were two military platforms, one in front of the royal caravan and one behind the supplies. The military platforms had twelve foot towers on them. The towers were used for surveying the areas ahead and behind the caravan. Then surrounding the whole of the caravan were fifty attack elephants with four of Ramala's elite guards on each one. There was an advanced guard of two hundred troops that would scout the areas ahead and would clear a path for the caravan if needed. There were one hundred forty elephants carrying those eighty platforms.

You probably wonder how they kept all of those elephants under control. Well, certain elephants were trained for specific modes of travel. The elephants that carried the royal family, their guest, the servants, and the supplies were all trained to march to the beat of drums. That kept the caravan moving at the same speed. Each one of those plat formed elephants had a captain, much like a ship or airplane, to make sure the elephants were moving at the pace set by the drummers. Those captains also controlled the direction, left, right, or straight, that the elephants traveled.

Now the military and attack elephants could move to the beat of drums, but were under the strict direction of the captain of each. The captains of the military and attack elephants had long reigns that they controlled the phants with when they wanted them to do individual maneuvers. This was an extremely well organized military caravan. It took an hour and a half just to get everyone on the proper platforms. The Butchers had never seen anything like this before. They figured Ramala and the other Hellcats were making sure that they would be able to deal with whatever they came across. Even though they had all went over the plans with Wana, they still couldn't believe how large the caravan really was.

As they started out, they looked back at the city of Ra and Ramala's main palace. The city was still functional. There were a large number of Hayee still in the city. The main palace was closed and guarded by a large number of the Hellcats elite guard. No one was allowed in the palace no matter who they were. The elite guards knew that if the Hellcats came back and found one thing out of place, they would lose their heads. They also guarded Tara's and Wana's palaces the same way. As if their lives depended on it. And it did!

This was the first time that the young twins had ever left the city of Ra. They were curious and very excited. Ramala gave them a little more latitude than normal to look around and investigate. She gave Yaya one job on this trip. It was to never leave the twins side, no matter what. Yaya was armed to the teeth with two machetes hanging off of her waist, two large gutting knives just above those, and a smaller blade on the inside of her thighs. Yaya wasn't the only protection for the twins. Ramala made sure that each and every one of her guards knew that they should protect her twin even over her. This was just training for Yaya as one of the twin's personal protectors. Yaya liked having responsibility and wanted to impress her Queen Mother with how good of a job she was doing. Ramala would, every once in a while, give Yaya a look of approval of the job that she was doing.

Dan and the other Butchers were able to relax. There was so much security that they would be alerted if any danger was near. The Japha, Jan knew that her Hayee sisters were smart, but at first she didn't think it was a good idea for the Hellcats to be traveling so soon after a war. Now that she saw the scope of the caravan, she was impressed. The Hellcats weren't gambling that they could make it through the whole of their territory. They were going to let everyone in it know who was in charge. Ramala was going to prove that it was what she wanted, when she wanted it. The Japha, Jan knew that nothing could help whoever showed opposition to the Hellcats.

The first stop on the trip was the area that the Hellcats grand-aunt's tribe occupied. They visited with their aunt who's name was Mishay. Mishay was very impressed with the young twins. They seemed to accept her hugs because they could see that Ramala was very comfortable around Mishay and had explained to the twins that she was family. Mishay questioned why and where the cousins were heading with their army. Ramala didn't like being questioned, but she needed something from her aunt. So she said "I'm going to let all of the tribes in my territory see their Queen. I have to make sure that no harm will come to me or my family. That's why my guards are with me. To protect their Queen."

She paused for a moment, then said "I need four of your best singer to travel with me. I admire the singing skills of your tribe." Tara who was right there with Wana and Ramala, knew this was a demand from her cousin. She wanted to take the edge off of it. So Tara said "You know our guards have strict orders from us not to bother your tribe and to protect you from any harm. As long as we are in control you will never have to worry about your lifestyle being changed by outside forces. Please do us this one favor and we will be most grateful."

Mishay looked at all three girls. She could see that Tara was begging with her eyes for Mishay to agree. Mishay also saw that Ramala had been as polite as she was going to be before she took what she wanted. Wana just stood there waiting to see what would happen next, so she could decide if she needed to get involved. Mishay knew she had no choice, so she agreed. Not even her sister Mashaya was as ruthless as Ramala. With her cousins with her, she just might succeed in whatever she was planning. One thing that Mishay knew for sure was that these girls had something planned. She just didn't know what it was, and she really didn't want to know.

The Hellcats only stayed one day with their grand-aunt before moving on. They had an uneventful night, then got moving the next day. The guards on the towers, that were on the military phants, reported that tribes were on the move, trying to avoid the caravan. Wana ordered the ground troops to push ahead and try to surround the fleeing tribes. They did as they were told and managed to trap three good sized tribes with about fifty to sixty people each. Once the caravan caught up with the trapped tribes, the attack phants took over guarding the tribes. The ground troops moved ahead again to try to trap more fleeing tribes.

The three tribes were separated and searched for weapons before being sent to meet with their Queen. The first tribe had about sixty members. They aged from in their eighties down to a few newborns. Ramala, and her cousins were carried forward on portable thrones. The Butchers walked right beside the thrones. The Japha twins and their girls walked behind, watching the show that the Hellcats were putting on. When the guards sat down the thrones, the Butchers took defensive positions right next to the Hellcats. Everyone in the first tribe was brought up close enough for the Hellcats to get a good look at them. The other two tribes were brought close right behind them. Then Ramala stood up. She had on her black ruling cape that was outlined in blood red. The same capes that her cousins wore. The colors of the House of Ra. When she stood up, one of the lead guards said "Get down and show your respect to your Mistress, Queen Ramala!" Everyone got down out of fear of what would happen if they didn't. When Ramala stood up, was the first time any of this tribe had ever saw her. They got a good look before they were ordered to get to the ground. Ramala said "This is a great day, that you get to see your Queen. Consider yourself blessed. I know most all of you are thinking of what you can do to show your appreciation for this honor that your Queen has bestowed on you? But before you try to shower me with gifts, tell me, what the names of your tribes is?"

The lead guard pointed to the first tribe, and one of the older men stood up with his head lowered and said "We are the Seezu." The lead guard looked at Ramala. She looked in the direction of the tribe to the right. The guard ordered "You! Give your name!" A man from that tribe stood up and said "We are Tazi." Then Ramala looked to the tribe on the far left and the guard pointed to them and said "Your name!" Again a man stood up, and he said "Our name is Hakma."

Right after the man said his name, he looked into Ramala's eyes for a split second. Ramala yelled "What's this!" The guards headed straight towards the man with bad intentions, until Ramala pointed at the guards and said "Hold It!" The guards stopped in their tracks. Then she ordered the guards "Get him and bring him closer!"

Two guards went over and each grabbed the old man roughly by one arm each and started dragging him towards Ramala. One of the Hakma teenagers stood up and Yelled out "Grandpa!" A second Hakma teenager stood up and looked at his grandfather with concern in his eyes. Ramala squinted her eye, shot a sharp stare at the lead guard, and said in a stern deliberate voice "Rebels!"

All of the guards drew the weapons. Again Ramala stopped the guards from killing the Young men, by waving no with her hand. Both young men were nervous and surrounded by guards with weapons. All they had were their hunting knives. Almost the size of machetes. They hadn't reached for them, or they would already be dead. She ordered "You two! Stand there and don't move or my guards will butcher you before you breathe again!"

They didn't move. Then she turned to the old man that dared look at her. She looked at him and said "When I first came up, I allowed all of you to look at me because you had never seen your Queen before. You heathen! Even though you knew you could get your head taken off for looking me in my eyes, you got greedy, and did it anyway. Then I see you have rebels with you." The man looked confused and said "They are not ..." and that's all he got out before one guard plowed his fist into the old man's gut. As the old man bent over in pain, the other guard came down on his neck with a powerful blow that sent the old man on the ground into the dirt. The old man shook on the ground, trying to catch his breath. Ramala said "My guards are completely offended that any heathen think that they could address me without permission. I'll give you a chance to talk. Tell me what your family does that might impress me?"

The man stayed low to the ground and would not look up when he said "We are just simple people, we live off the land." Ramala said "You have no special skills?" The man said "I'm sorry, we have none." Ramala motioned for the guards to pick the man up off the ground, then she said "Young people can be trained to do. So heathen, listen well to what I have to say. You have to be strong if your tribe is to survive. Because of your disrespect, I won't kill you. I want you to live so you can raise the young members of your tribe to never disrespect their Queen." She then told the old man "Show the proper respect and the younger ones live. If you don't, you get to watch them all die. Then I'll have no use for you. "

Then Ramala turned to her guards and ordered "Guards! Kill everyone that looks over eleven! Now!"

Everyone was surprised when Yin jumped into action and started killing the Hakma's along with the guards. The old man watched as the two young men who were standing were sliced up first. Then the guards gathered everyone that the thought were younger than eleven, and quickly moved them out of Yin's path of destruction. The women screamed until Yin got to them and silenced them for good. The old man stood there silently horrified at the sight of his family being slaughtered. He saw what Yin had done. He didn't want to do anything that would get the others killed. The guards barely got to kill anyone because of Yin's rampage.

Ramala told the old man "That man there is the Butcher Yin. He'll kill the instant I say. You did the right thing to save the rest of your family. If you would have so much as looked wrong or made a sound. The rest of your family would be dead. Now I want you to know that whatever I want to happen, is going to happen. You and your young will be trained to do services for your Queen. If you resist, you will exist no more."

She paused, then said "You can turn your young ones into rebels if you want. You'll never get them good enough to change anything. I had better never find out that you are rebels. All I know is that when you are given a task from me, it had better get done!" She waved her hand and the guards took the man and who was left of his tribe away. Then she turned to the other man who was still standing, and looking at the ground. She said "Now you Tazi. Tell me what special skills you have that would impress your Queen." The man did not speak. He didn't want his tribe to meet the same fate as the last one. He said in a very shaky voice "Mistress Queen, May I have permission to speak?" Ramala turned to Tara and said "I told you heathens can learn proper respect if you give them the right motivation." Then she said "Speak Tazi."

Then the man proceeded to go down a long list of what the members of his tribe did from cooking to hunting and everything in between. He didn't leave out anything, hoping that Ramala would hear something that she liked. She said in an unimpressed voice "Well that's more than the last ones could do. I would not be a good Queen if I didn't let you prove how eager you are to serve me. Go, talk with my guards. They will tell you what is expected of you. Know that you are blessed to be able to serve me." Then she looked at the man. He nervously said "Thank you Mistress Queen." Then the guards led that tribe away. Ramala looked at the last man standing and said "Seezu, what do you have to say for yourself?" After asking for permission to speak, and given permission to do so, this man proceeded with a list that was longer than the last tribes list of skills.

Yin had made his way back over to the throne area. Ramala didn't look at Yin but was aware of him moving back in place. Ma had watched Yin, and now that she saw him coming back, she knew there was something bothering him. She had left it alone up until this point, to see if he would tell her. Now she knew since he wasn't going to tell her, she would have to push him to find out. That way she could advise him. Ma didn't understand why Yin wouldn't come to her. He always had, if he had something he couldn't figure out himself. Which was anything that didn't have anything to do with killing.

Ma hoped that it wasn't Tara twisting Yin's mind into circles, confusing him. Because if she was, to hell with her. If it was one thing that got Ma in a Yin state of mind, it was some one she thought was doing harm to her brother. Right now she didn't know if it was Tara. Cat caught Ma staring into space, almost in a trance. Cat moved closer to Ma and whispered in her ear "Snap out of it. You have to stay sharp. Whatever is going on with Yin, we'll figure out later." Ma turned to Cat to protest, but Cat stopped her with "I said, don't let it bother you. We'll figure it out." They stared at each other for a moment, then Cat smiled. Ma didn't smile back. She would listen to her sister, for now.

Dan was on guard with the rest of the Butchers by the thrones. He watched closely as Yin put in some work. Ramala wanted him sitting on the throne next to her, but Dan didn't think he would be able to react quick enough if serious trouble came up. He wasn't taking any chances seeing that his children were out here. This was the most focused Ramala had ever seen Dan. She knew if any of those tribe's people had put up any resistance, Dan would have been the second one over there, slaughtering them. Everyone moved back to their platforms, and the caravan was on it's way again.

The Caravan made a few more stops to let tribes on the way offer contributions of labor to their new Queen. If they didn't have any skills, the Hellcats would except, at least two of their young, depending on how large the tribe was, to be trained by the House of Ra. They would serve their Queen for a number of years, then they would be allowed to return to their tribe. Plus they would have a new skill. In Ramala's eyes, who could ask for more than that?

Now that they were back on the platform, Dan looked at Ramala and realized what this trip was all about. It was about more than these people seeing their new Queen. It was about making sure that every tribe was accountable to their new Queen in some way. Whether it be by working the land, using the skills you already had, or being trained to do what she wanted. You were going to be accountable for doing something for your Queen. Through this plan, the Hellcats would be able to replace all of the guards they lost in the war. They also would have an endless supply of servants and free laborers. Most of the tribes called this slavery, because that's what it was.

Dan knew that Ramala would be able to bully all of the tribes, but what about when they got to the seven Northern Houses. Would she be this demanding of them? He somehow knew she would. How would the Houses respond? Even though they were in a military caravan, it wasn't like she was running a war from the safety of the House of Ra. If the seven Northern Houses attacked them out here, they would be in for the fight of their lives. Ramala caught Dan looking at her. She smiled at him and said "What?" Dan already knew what. He figured if the seven Houses didn't start something, he knew she would. Dan deflected by saying "Are the children alright?" Ramala said "They couldn't be better. They're having the time of their lives. They won't be a problem." Dan pointed his finger at Ramala, and said "You're very smart." She moved closer to Dan and said "Thank you. Isn't this great traveling through our territory? It has so much to offer!"

Wana told her cousins that the next stop on their trip would be to the Spiritual Temple. Wana sent guards telling the Temple that their Queen, Ramala would be visiting. The Temple was asked to show their respects to their Queen, by setting up a tour of the grounds for her. The guards told the priest that their Queen wanted them to know that she would not be staying long, depending on the level of respect that was shown to her. If she didn't like the level of respect, she would stay until it was to her liking, or until she dealt with it in her own way.

Normally, the Temple would never set up a tour for a female. But since it was their Queen Ramala, they would make an exception. Mainly because word had gotten back of what happened to the tribe that didn't show the proper respect. The top priest were well aware that this was the same Queen Ramala that had taken on the House of Japha, and the House of Hayee. Not only did she still have her head. She beat them in the eyes of everyone. That is, except for the Japha, and the Hayee. They knew it was in their best interest to show the proper respect. They were going to keep the young refugees, that they had taken in, out of sight, while the Queen took her tour. The priest that Ramala would see, knew to show the proper respect.

The caravan arrived around mid day. Wana had all of the caravan stay about a mile from the temple. She had the guards on high alert, protecting the caravan while the royal court was gone. The royal court consisted of the Hellcats, the Japha twins and their girls, and the Butchers. That's who visited the Temple. They took no guards. They rode in on four elephants. When they got to the gate of the temple, young priest opened the gate. When the gate opened, the Royal Court was met by the head priest of the temple. There were six of them. All of them were at least sixty, but their bodies were in the condition of men half their age. Ven was one of the priest. He had seen Tara and the Butchers before. He recognized the Syn, Jara right away. This was the first time he had seen the other two Hellcats, and the Japha twins. He looked them all over carefully, as did the other priest. The Hellcats looked the old men over before Tara said "We are the Hellcats. Rulers of the House of Ra, who's territory your temple resides in. I'm the Hayee, Tara." Then Tara pointed to her cousins and said "This is the Hayee, Wana." She paused for a second, then said "Now get down out of respect for your Queen of the House of Ra. Mistress Queen, the Hayee, Ramala."

The priest got down, then stood back up. Ramala looked around, then said "This is a very nice Temple you have here. I'm sure you are doing very good work here. Introduce yourselves and tell me your position here." The priest all introduced themselves and told their positions. Then Ramala said "I'm not going to take up much of your time if I don't have to. Show me around and afterwards we will have a meeting. After that, I will be on my way."

The priest showed the Royal Court around the grounds of the temple. The priest paraded a good number of priest past the Hellcats. When the tour was done, and the priest were ready to meet with the court. Ramala stopped the priest and said "I have seen most of the grounds, and you have done a fair job of letting me see the priest. I know you take in refugees and help them. That's a good thing. Molding young boys into men. I want you to show me all of these young men." The priest knew this could be a bad situation. If they showed the Hellcats the young refugees, they might recognize some of them as rebels from the tribes they conquered. On the other hand, if they didn't show them the refugees, there would surely be big trouble for the Temple.

The top priest ordered the junior priest to go and bring out the refugees. He had studied the Hellcats carefully. He could see that these young girls were very professional, and meant business. Even though they were women, he was impressed with them. Although, he didn't like seeing women with this much control. He would play along until the timing was right. He decided whatever the Hellcats did to these young men would be better than the Temple being destroyed. The junior priest marched out about thirty young men from about the age of five up to about seventeen or eighteen. They stopped in front of the court and got down to the ground, out of respect. The young men stood up, and all of the court took a good long look at these young men. Then Ramala said "You have a good group of young men here. I trust that you will train them well. I won't keep them from their duties any longer. We can meet, and then I will be on my way." The priest all were relieved that the royal court didn't recognize any of the young men as rebels.

The priest escorted the Hellcats and the Court to a large meeting room. After everyone was seated, and offered food and drink, the meeting started. Ramala took the lead as usual. She said "First order of business we need to address is when my cousin was visiting north and some of the priest from this Temple attacked her caravan, trying to kill one of our most trusted guards, the Syn, Jara. That was a serious show of disrespect. Disrespect won't be tolerated anywhere in the House of Ra. I'm going to assume that those priest did that on their own, and didn't have the blessing of this Temple. That way we can try to get past it. But if I'm wrong in assuming that, please tell me right now." Ramala waited on a reply. The head priest said "Those priest should have never attacked the Royal Court. I apologize for that disrespect. We will keep a better eye on all of the priest." Ramala looked at all of the priest there, then said "Does the priest of this temple have a problem with my Warlord Syn, Jara?" The Priest all said they didn't. Ramala continued with "You priest are doing a good job here helping the youth. Training their minds and bodies. Your training produced the Syn, Jara. Her fighting skills are superb. I'm going to leave some of my guards under your care, to be trained by you in your fighting techniques. These guards will report back to me and show me the skills that they have learned. I need to be impressed by them, so that I know that leaving this Temple untouched is a good decision. Right now, that has yet to be proven. Make no mistake. If I'm force to, I'll destroy this whole Temple."

There was an uncomfortable silence after Ramala's last sentence. Tara quickly said "What my cousin means is that the House of Ra respects the good work that the Spiritual Temple does. She want you to show your respect by training her guards to the best of your abilities, so that they can protect your Queen." The priest had no choice but to agree. So they did. And with that, the Hellcats ended the meeting and were on there way back to the caravan. As they were going back, Wana questioned Ramala "Most of those young men are rebels. Are we going to deal with them right away?" Ramala said "No, not yet we won't. We have a chance to learn some fighting techniques of this temple. That will keep our guards strong. If we go in and demand to take the heads of those young men, we might have to destroy the Temple. Then we wouldn't get any use out of them. Those rebels are young. They won't give us any trouble for at least ten years. That's how long it's going to take to train them at a level that might make them a nuisance to us. Anyway, we know where they are. It's always good to know where your enemies are, and what they are doing. Just remember, all we have to do is kill all of the rebels before they get good enough to cause a problem."

After Nicko and Massiko got the other young men to the Temple, they made sure all of them worked hard. All of them were given very strenuous duties that made them very tired by the end of the day. In the evenings, after dinner, was when they had a little time to meet. Nicko would always stress how important it was for them to do their best. He and Massiko would make them train extra, for a short time before bed. Nicko didn't know if the girls made it to the mountains. He hoped that they had, but since Mobo hadn't come to the Temple to at least check on them, he didn't know if they were still alive. All he knew was that the young men with him were the only ones that survived. They had to be good enough to one day take their revenge for their family. He was making sure that none of his cousins were taking that responsibility lightly. Nicko pushed himself and the others hard. When he needed a break Massiko reminded Nicko what was at stake and pushed him and the others just as hard as Nicko would. It was a hard life, but they accepted that it was their fate.

Chapter 7

On the day that the Royal Court was to visit the Temple, all of the orphans that the Temple had taken in, including the Wa, were taken to the far end of the Temple and hidden in one of the storage buildings. The young men were told to stay there and not make any noise. They were told that they would be sent for later in the day.

Sometime after noon, a few of the junior priest came and got all of the orphans. One of the priest instructed the young men not to say a word. They all followed the priest to a large courtyard where they saw a group of people that the Head priest were treating like they were very important. The orphans were lined up and told to get down out of respect for their Queen Ramala. All of the young men did as they were told. When they were allowed to stand, they memorized the faces of everyone in the Royal Court. They weren't one hundred percent sure that these were the people responsible for their family's death. But they felt that they were. After the Royal Court was gone, the priest confirmed that they were the one that were responsible for wiping out the Wa and most of the other tribes that the orphans belonged to. Now Nicko and the other young men had faces to channel their hatred to.

At the Mid Range Mountain monastery, China and the girls had it just as rough with the nuns as the young men had with the priest. It seemed to China that the older the nun, the more stern and bitter she was. For Nicko and the other orphans, they found things just the opposite. The younger the priest, the meaner they were. The older priest seemed to be calmer, although they could be very stern when they had to. When China and the girls first arrived at the monastery, they were led to a bathing hall. When they undressed to wash themselves, the nuns saw that China had a medium sized blade that she had hidden on her upper thigh. The nun held out her hand and said "Give that to me. You're safe here. You won't be needing that." China shook her head no. The nun reached to take it from China and China pulled out the blade and went on guard. One of the other nuns immediately called for one of the head nuns. China said "Please! I have to keep this with me at all times! It's very important to me! It's all I have to remind me of my family!" The head nun had just arrived to hear what China had said. The nun looked at China. China saw the head nun when she came in the bath room. China pleaded "Please! I have to keep this with me! I won't be a problem! Please!" The nun could see that the other young girls were starting to get nervous. The nun thought that one of this girls dead relatives must have given this blade to her. The head nun said "Calm down child! I will allow you to keep your blade, but I don't want to see it at all, unless it's next to you while you are bathing." China said "Yes Mistress, I will keep it out of sight always."

After the blade incident, the nuns were very hard on China. They wanted to see if she was a trouble maker and would become rebellious if they pushed her hard. China took everything they threw at her and didn't make a fuss. She knew if she got kicked out of the monastery, the other girls would soon follow. She had to make sure that her cousins trained hard so they could take their revenge one day. Almost every day she would force herself to remember when she heard Mobo yell "RUN!" She remembered the look of desperation on his face. China wondered if Mobo, Mira, and the rest of the girls were still alive. She was going to take whatever these nuns dished out because someone was going to pay for what happened to her family!

After the run in with the Syn, Jara Delun decided that he needed better fighters and a lot more of them. He started recruiting the best fighters that he could. He gave important information to Han and Chi about rebel attacks. That kept them from bothering him and his operations just south of Yee province. He had his men training to the best of their abilities. During the war, Delun managed to build a small army. Han and Chi knew Delun was getting larger, but since he never threatened them once, they let him go on with whatever illegal operations he was doing. Besides dealing in extortion of good from the tribes in the area, Delun also captured and sold people as slaves. Another one of his illegal schemes included stealing an elephant or two.

The scouts from the Royal caravan spotted Delun's well

guarded village. Wana had her guards surround the village with a very wide perimeter. She didn't want to get close enough for Delun to know he was surrounded. Eventually Delun's scouts told him that he was being surrounded. By that time it was to late to do anything about it. He would bring his toughest guards close around him and the others would also be as close as possible. By now, everyone knew Ramala was marching north with her military caravan. They knew what she had done so far. Delun wasn't sure what she would do when she got there. But if she had a problem with him, he wasn't going to make it easy for her to take his head.

Now that the village was surrounded, Wana could see that most of the fighters were concentrated in the center of the village, and outwards from that point. Wana told her cousins that whoever was in that village was taking up a defensive position. Readying themselves for a battle. Ramala said "If it's a battle that they want, it's a massacre that they'll get."

The Hellcats called a meeting with the Butchers. The Syn, Jara told them that the man who ran that town was Delun. She called him a two bit bandit. He harassed, and bullied everyone that passed through. Ramala told Wana that she wanted most of those guards dead, quickly. She wanted the leader unharmed, so she could address him. Wana knew just how she wanted this handled. Wana had the Syn, Jara, Cat, and Ma get to the attack elephant and head to the backside of the village. Once there, they were to massacre all of the guards protecting the village. When they got to the main buildings in the village, they were to contain the fighters, but not advance on Delun.

After the girls were gone, Wana had the Butchers Dan, Yin, and Backir advance on the village from the front. They were to slaughter every fighter in their path, until they got to where Delun was. The Hellcats would be right behind the Butchers, so they could meet with Delun. The Japha twins decided to back the Hellcats up, just in case of an ambush. The three Butcher girls all decided to use their baby axes. They had plenty of time to practice with them. Now even Ma felt comfortable enough to use hers. The girls were by themselves, with no guards, when they got to the first of Delun's guards. They kept advancing on the guards. One of the guards asked "What do you girls want?"

He didn't get an answer, he got attacked immediately by Cat. Syn and Ma attacked also. There no time for conversation. The Butcher girls had their orders. None of the orders included answering questions. As they were chopping and slicing these guards, more appeared and joined the battle. These guards were more skilled, but it didn't matter. Cat and Ma had become killing machines. And the Syn, Jara, well she had gotten better than the Butcher she was before. All three of the girls were competing for the most kills.

When Cat attacked the guards who asked the question, he managed to block the first swing of her axe. He wasn't fast enough to block the second swing, which sliced open the left side of his chest. That was enough to weaken his left arm to the point that he could not get his weapon up high enough, fast enough, and Cat took his head clean off, swinging her axe across the left side of his body and through his neck. Before his head hit the ground she was on to the next guard. That's when Ma and Syn knew they would never catch up to the head count that Cat was about to have, if they didn't get started right away. So Ma jumped between two guards and attacked them both. She was very quick with her baby axes. She swung and hacked off the first guard's right arm. Then she immediately followed that with a lightning fast swing that sliced downwards through that same guards neck, with her blade coming out down through the front of his chest. She ducked just out of the way of the second guard's machete. While still low, she swung her axe lightning fast again, and spit the guard's stomach wide open. As his guts started to spill out, Ma came up with both of her axes, with so much force, she took off both the man's arms. Before his body could fall, she came across with her axe again and took his head.

Not to be outdone, the Syn, Jara ran full speed at the guards. Two of them had their machetes aimed at Syn from both sides of her. When they swung, she jumped up in the air in a tight ball spinning, extended her arms in that revolution and took both men's heads clean off. She hit the ground and with lightning speed she repeated the same move taking off another two heads, then another two.

By this time the guards that she was quickly approaching, saw her coming. They protected their necks, and swung their machetes at her, while she was spinning in the air. Instead of swinging at their necks, which would have left her open for the killing, she turned the flat side of her axe towards the swinging machetes and blocked them from both sides. When she hit the ground, both men swung their machetes again. Syn blocked with the flat side of her axes again, but this time she twisted the handles, which caused the blade of her axes to push down on the machetes. Then she twisted the handles in the opposite direction, pointing the blade of the axes at the guard's throat. She plowed the blade of the axes into the throat of the guards, just as they were about to swing and take her head. She was just that quick.

The Syn, Jara had managed to kill eight men, just as Cat was finishing off her forth, and Ma was finishing off her third. Still she wasn't done yet. She had managed to get ahead of the other girls when she was spinning taking heads,and found herself surrounded. The guards were already somewhat disoriented, after seeing what Syn had already done. That made what she was going to do a lot easier. She spun into the guards with blinding speed, and all you saw was a hand flying here, an arm flying there, followed by heads twirling and flipping into the air. None of the wounded guards that Syn had not killed had a chance to retreat, because Cat and Ma were right on top of them.

The Butcher girls reached just outside of the back door to Delun's headquarters, when About twenty men jumped from the roof top and attacked them. Syn, Jara charged and sliced up one of the men before he hit the ground. Cat and Ma tore into the men until there were no more. As soon as all three girls had finished off the last of the men, they turned quickly around, looking with a sharp eye for any movement that they would surely consider hostile, and deal with right away. When they didn't see any guards alive. Cat Started swinging her axes very fast around her body for a few moments, then she stopped them on a dime, pointed at the back door of Delun's headquarters. As soon as the blades stopped, Cat screamed "AAAAHHH! BUTCHER GIRLS KILL!" Ma was so hyped up that she screamed next, then said "That's Right!"

Syn looked at both of them. Those screams were nothing like the Hellcats screams. But still, she had never seen or heard her sisters scream like that before. Then Cat walked to the back door and kicked it in. The Syn, Jara warned "We are supposed to wait back here until they finish up front." Cat was pumped up and wasn't ready to stop killing yet. Cat said "We can't wait here and do nothing! We have them on the run! Let's force them out front to the others. "Ma said "Yeah, that's a great idea!" The Syn, Jara wasn't going to argue. They were in the middle of warfare. The Hellcats would stop them if they went too far.

Out in front, the Butchers Dan, Yin, and Backir had gotten

a head start on the girls. These three Butchers made short work of Delun's guards in the front of his headquarters. Backir and Yin had seen each other in battle, and weren't surprised at how much better they had gotten since recuperating from the war. What surprised them was how good Dan had gotten. Dan was also impressed with the other two Butchers. It seemed to Dan, that they were just about unbeatable. This wasn't even a workout. It was a massacre. The three Hellcats watched their Butchers and knew they had something special. This was a fighting team that couldn't be beat. They were going to take full advantage of them. Then everyone in front heard a scream, followed by Cat yelling "Butcher Girls Kill!"

Then they heard Ma scream, and add in her two cents. Wana yelled to the Butcher men "The girls should be at the back door. Go in and bring me whoever is in charge." The Butchers were about to follow those orders when they saw Delun and about twenty of his guards come out of the front door. The Butcher girls saw all of Delun's guards surrounding him and following him out of the front door. They followed them out, but did not attack. The girls could see Wana and the other Butchers from where they were. They were just waiting on a signal from Wana to finish off Delun and his men. Delun and his men stopped outside of his headquarters. All of his men were dead, except for the ones surrounding him now. He saw the Butchers on guard in front of him. They weren't attacking. He looked around and saw the three girls behind him. Immediately, he recognized Syn, Jara as the girl he tried to recruit. His eyes only paused on her for a quick moment. There were more pressing issues he had to deal with right now. When Delun turned back around, he saw Three very well dressed women walking up. He knew they were the Hellcats he had heard about.

Delun was above begging for his life. He had faced death many times in his life from starting out as a two bit bandit, to taking or extorting whatever he wanted from the tribes in his area. He knew since he wasn't dead yet, they must want to talk. That meant there was a chance he could talk his way out of this situation. Ramala walked up with her cousins on both sides of her. The Butchers moved out of the way, but stayed on guard, focused on Delun and his men. Tara said "Down on your knees! Show respect to your Queen Ramala!"

Delun got down on his knees. When his men saw him go

down, they went down too. Ramala saw it a sign of disrespect that Delun's guards only got down on their knees after they saw Delun go down. Ramala's face tightened. She looked at Delun and said "Who is the leader here?" Delun said "I am." Ramala ordered him "Stand up!" He did as he was told. Ramala pointed to Delun's guards and said "You two! Stand up!" Two men looked up and saw that she was pointing at them. They stood up. She asked "Who is the leader here?" The two guards looked at Delun and at the same time said "Delun." Ramala looked down at the ground, with her head still held high. Wana looked at Yin and Backir and made a motion. They attacked and took the heads of the two guards. Then they stepped back and looked to Ramala for further instructions. Ramala raised her eyes and looked at Delun. Then she said "Tell me, how is it possible that you could be in charge when I'm in charge of everything?" Delun knew he had to be careful if he wanted to keep his head. Before he could answer, Ramala turned and pointed to two more guards and said "You two! Stand up!"

When they had done so, she asked "Who is in charge here?" The men knew they had to do better than the last two. They both said "You are." Ramala gave the men a look that said she still was not pleased. She looked down again, and this time Wana didn't have to look at Yin and Backir. They knew what to do. They gave these two guards the same treatment the last two got. Ramala threw both her hands in the air and said "I try to be kind to my subjects. I try to be a good Queen, but still they don't show me the Proper respect. Am I not your Queen?" Then she pointed again and said "I'll try to be nice only once more. All of you! Stand up!" The guards got to their feet. Ramala said "Who is the leader here!?" The guards didn't hesitate. They said "Queen Ramala!" Ramala looked right at them, then said "That's right! You better know that when I give an order it had better be carried out right away!"

Then she turned and looked at Delun. She pointed to his guards and said "Take the one you call Delun and bring him to me!" Delun's guards grabbed him by both his arms and took him over, right in front of Ramala. Then she ordered "Hold him tightly!" Then she pointed to another one of the guards and said "Pull out your machete." The guard did as he was told. Delun's guards were now following orders from Ramala, as if Wana had trained them. Then Ramala looked at Delun and said "When I asked who was in charge, You said you were. Tell me, how can that be?"

Delun looked as high as Ramala's chest, but would not look her in the eyes. He said "I meant that I am the leader of these men, after you. I'll make sure they do whatever you order." Ramala quickly said "I don't need you for that! They'll do what I want whether you are here or not. There can only be one master. In this case it's your Mistress Queen Ramala. You run around here taking from my loyal subject. They have a hard enough time doing what I want them to do! They can't be doing extra for you! What kind of ruler would I be if I let outlaws harass my subjects. And on top of that, you sell slaves that you steal from families in my territory. You even steal my phants and sell them. I have not seen one offering of goods or slaves. That's very disrespectful. Disrespect won't be tolerated. Give me your best reason why I should let you keep your head and serve me."

Delun knew his life depended on his answer. He had never been under this kind of pressure, to suck up to someone before now. And it was a woman. He couldn't believe how nervous this young lady made him.

Delun was an outlaw who bullied tribes and took what he wanted. He had no real marketable skills, except taking from the meek, or people that couldn't defend themselves against his thugs. Now those same thugs that worked for him were ready to kill him if this young girl told them to. Delun thought about all of that in only a couple of seconds. He knew this Queen wasn't going to wait long on an answer. So he said "I'll do whatever you order me to do without hesitation." Ramala yelled "I already know that! Tell me what skills that I might think important enough to let you live." Delun said "I am a good organizer of men. I'm very smart." Ramala said "You said you can follow orders without hesitation?" Delun replied assertively "Yes, I can." Ramala said "Then hold your head as far from your body as possible, so this guard can get a clean swing at your neck with his machete." Delun was a little confused by this request, and hesitated. Ramala stared at him and said "I knew you couldn't follow orders, without hesitation. You're to smart for that. Being smart isn't always a good thing. Following my orders without hesitation is always the right thing. You failed that test. You're no good to me. Guard! Take his head."

After the lesson that Queen Ramala gave on following orders without hesitation. This guard decided that he was not going to fail this test. He walked over to Delun and took his head off with one swing of his machete. Blood squirted from Delun's neck into the air. The guards holding Delun threw his body to the ground, then stood there waiting, with their heads lowered, to see if they had done a good enough job for their Queen to keep their heads. Ramala smiled. Seeing that out of the corner of their eyes, a great relief came over the guards standing there waiting on their fate.

Ramala said "That was good. Your lives will be spared, and you will serve me as long as you remember, don't think about what I say. Just do it! Make sure I'm impressed with whatever orders I give you. Impressing me should be number one on your list. That's how you keep your head around here! Now, here are your orders. I'm going to have my guards take you and beat you, and then cut you with their machetes. Some of you will get sliced up pretty good. Be strong and take it like the good servants you are. Then my guards will let you go. I want you to tell everyone that you run across, that you barely escaped my guards and your leader Delun was killed. Make everyone believe that you want revenge at all cost. Your orders are to find and join rebellious opposition to me. Wait until you know their chain of command and top leaders. Ways will be made for you to contact my warlords and get me important information that will crush that rebellion."

Then she dismissed them. Wana and Tara watched their cousin closely. Tara watched to make sure that Ramala didn't get to outrageous with her demands. Wana watched to see how far her cousin would go and if she would have to back her up with military force. Wana really didn't care if Ramala wanted every tribe slaughtered. That's what Wana and her army were here to do, if she had to.

When the Butchers were on their way back to the caravan, Yin, who was walking next to Ma, asked her "What was all the screaming about." Ma said "Cat got a little hyped up back there. She couldn't help herself." Cat looked over at Ma and said "I wasn't the only one." They smiled at each other. Dan looked over at his sisters. They had blood splattered all over their clothes. As much as the male Butchers had on them. Dan wondered what happened back there to get the girls so hyped up. Whatever it was, he wished he could have seen it.

Chapter 8

After setting up a small regiment of troops to run Delun's headquarters, the caravan was on it's way again. Yaya and the twins were brought to the large platform that Ramala stayed in. The twins were demanding more of Ramala's time. They were a little uncomfortable with their surroundings changing everyday. They missed home. The only thing to them that was familiar from home was Yaya, the maidens, the Butchers, the Japha twins, Wana, Tara, and their parents. They needed to see all of these people every day out here in the field. They also needed to see Ramala before she went on her missions, and right after she got back from the missions. Otherwise the twins got out of control, and not even Yaya could calm them down.

When Ramala got back, the twin were already acting out. Ramala walked in and called them both by their names. When they saw her, they raced over to her. Ramala looked at Yaya's face and saw that the twins had been difficult to deal with today. She smiled at Yaya. Yaya lowered her head, to show respect to her mother. Ramala said "I know they were tough on you today. You're doing a great job. Take a break. You can come back later." Yaya's eyes lit up. She turned and took off running. Ramala thought 'That girl's always running! ' and was about to yell for her to stop running, but didn't. She let it go this time because it had taken them so long to get back. Besides now the twins were on her legs clawing at her, trying to climb up her. Little La was whimpering and they both were crying "Ma, Maa , Maa." Ramala bent down and grabbed them both in her arms. She kept looking at both of them, while saying to them in a reassuring voice "Don't worry. You know mommy's never going to leave you for too long. I always come back, don't I? You two have to be brave while I'm gone, and not give big sister Yaya too much trouble." The twins listened, but weren't to concerned with what Ramala was saying. They were just glad she was back and giving them the love that they needed so much from her right now. Then she turned to young Dan, and said in a tougher voice "I expect you to be brave while I'm gone." Then she turned to La and said "I expect that from you, too." Then she stood up and took the twins over to the sitting area. She let them climb over her while they calmed themselves that she was not going anywhere for a while. Then La looked at her mother and said in a stern voice "Where's my Daddy!?" Little La had a tone to her voice like her mother, that sometimes could be mistaken as disrespect. Ramala locked eyes with La for a moment, letting her know that she didn't approve of that tone of voice. Then she said "Don't yell at mother like that. Your father is getting cleaned up. He'll be here as soon as he's done." La looked at her mother for only a few more seconds. Ramala stared her down. La looked away and started pulling on her mother's arm and then went back to playing. She knew not to challenge mother to much, because that could lead to trouble. But she was going to go as close to the boundaries as she could without getting herself roughed up. She watched her mother closely, and was learning how far go. After all, she was learning from one of the best.

La was also a daddy's girl. When Dan came in from getting cleaned up, La jumped up and ran over to meet him. She jumped into his arms and wrapped her hands around his neck and squeezed as tight as she could. Dan held his daughter tight while making his way over to young Dan.

Young Dan was a mama's boy in the sense that he wouldn't go running to Dan like La would. He knew his Dad would come over to rough him up. La knew this too, and when Dan started walking over to get his son, La quickly looked around and when she saw where they were headed, she started squirming to get more attention from her father. But it was to late. Dan grabbed his son by his shirt and threw him up in the air. Ramala's eyes got big with fear in them every time Dan was recklessly rough with young Dan. Dan caught his son out of the air, with the one arm that he threw him up with, and said "How's my little man doing today?" Ramala warned "Be careful! Don't drop him!" Dan looked at Ramala, then he looked back at his son and shook him roughly in his arm. Young Dan started laughing. Then Dan said "Your mother babies you to much. She doesn't understand that you like the rough stuff."

Ramala didn't like it when Dan talked against her to their children. If he made one more statement like that, there was going to be trouble. Then Dan saw Ramala staring at him. He knew not to push it any further.

La had had enough of this too. She had run to meet her father, to show him love and get attention. But he goes over and picks up Dan and gives him the attention that she thought she deserved. Young Dan was wrapped up in happiness from playing with his Dad. La saw this as an opportunity and threw her fist at Young Dan, hitting him across the side of his head. He looked at her, and she launched another swing, but this time Dan moved his son out of the way of that blow and said "Alright La. That's enough. You don't try to hurt your brother."

Then she swung again. Dan put them both down, then he grabbed La and gave her a kiss and said "Go play nice. I'm going to relax for a while." La watched as her father walked over and gave her mother a hug and a kiss. Then Dan sat next to Ramala. La wasn't going to be pawned off that easily. She ran over and forced herself between her mother and father. This was the only time La would be willing to have a confrontation with Ramala. It was over the attention of her father.

La got between them and started squirming and using her body to push Ramala away from Dan while trying to get closer to him. Ramala couldn't be outsmarted by a grown woman, let alone a three year old. It was time to get rough with La. She grabbed La by her arm and lifted her off the ground and said "That's enough! Now go play or mother will find something for you to do!"

La winced in pain and a tear rolled down her face. Her feeling were more hurt than her arm. Dan reached over, wiped the tear from her face and said "Go and play. Daddy will be right her watching you." La looked at her father. She noticed that when she cried, he was affected by it. She knew that meant something. She would experiment with that later. Right now, mother was two seconds from busting her butt, so she walked over and started playing with Dan, while watching her parents closely, as she usually did.

Little La was right about one thing. Dan didn't like seeing his daughter roughed up by anyone, not even her mother. Just about as much as Ramala always thought that Dan was getting to rough with their son to soon. Dan said to Ramala "You didn't have to be so rough on her." Ramala said "You haven't seen me get rough with her yet. I was just teaching her a lesson." Ramala was two second from getting angry, but was giving a half effort not to. Dan said "We would have been back a lot sooner if you didn't have to give a speech to someone who you were going to kill anyway."

Now Ramala was offended. She said "I wouldn't expect a moron shit heathen like yourself to understand what I was doing out there. It's best if you don't let your ignorance show."

Dan couldn't believe some of the statements that came out of Ramala's mouth sometimes. He stared at her, shocked at what she was saying, while she continued with "Let me explain what I was doing. I had to make sure that everyone there knew that I expect their best when I give orders. I need to be impressed by their actions. That includes you too. I keep hoping that your ignorance will fade away, but I see it hasn't yet."

Now she was sure that she had offended Dan as much as he had offended her. And she had. Dan hadn't found a name to call Ramala that would be as offensive as her calling him names like moron shit heathen, or shit heathen idiot. Which she had gotten used to calling him when she was angry with him. Shit heathen didn't bother him, but add something else to it, and that was the best way to start a fight.

Ramala stared at Dan waiting on a response. She knew he wasn't quick witted enough to beat her with words, so she watched him closely for a sign that he was going to grab her and hold her down. She hated being man handled, unless she was having sex. Dan knew that and would do it just to get back at her. Dan said "We are to far away from home to start fighting. I'm going to let it go this time. Calm down and try to relax. Go drink some blood or, whatever it is you do when you're not talking shit."

Ramala's family tradition was always a low blow that Dan knew he could get in whenever he wanted. For some reason it offended her when he would make light of her drinking blood. She instantly took a swing at him. He caught her arm and wrestled himself on top of her. Even though she was red hot at Dan she said in a whisper "Not in front of the children! Let me up!"

Dan looked at her. He knew she was hot, and would say anything to get him off of her. He also knew that if he didn't let her up, she wouldn't care if the children were there or not. She was going to do something stupid. He got up off of her. She stood up, so he got up too. Dan quickly grabbed Ramala and pulled her close to him. He said "If you weren't so smart and beautiful, I wouldn't put up with you. You know I love you." Then he kissed her. Even though she was still a little angry, she always liked when Dan would tell her how much he loved her. For some reason, that always made her feel special. Even if she wanted to be mad at Dan right now, she couldn't. So she let it go, for now.

Cat couldn't believe that after all of the practicing she had done, she still wasn't in the same league as the Syn, Jara. It seemed that Syn had gotten good enough to keep the other girls behind her in their killing skills. When the Butchers got back to the caravan, Ma and Cat gave the Hellcats, and the other Butchers a blow by blow account of Syn's last battle. Both girls said although they thought they did a good job with their level of killing, they were disappointed that they couldn't keep up with Syn. The Syn, Jara told Ma and Cat "You'll never get more kills than me if you're spending time watching me." Cat said "That's easy for you to say. If you were seeing what we were seeing, You'd be looking too." Both Cat and Ma agreed that they shouldn't be watching so much, but for them it was hard not watching the greatest fighting show that they had ever seen.

The caravan made it to the heavily guarded Yee Province. Han's guards met the caravan at the edge of Yee Province. They cheered their new Queen and showed her the respect that she expected. Then after a very short meeting with Wana, the Yee guards escorted the Royal caravan to the main town.

When the caravan reached the main town, there was a steady, continuous roar of cheers for the Queen. The Butchers thought the reception that they got, coming back from the war, was loud. But this was even louder. Ramala and her cousins stood and waved to the crowd of warriors and guards that lined both sides of the road. The caravan was led to a building set up for The Royal family. Han was there waiting with his personal guards. The Death Squad was with him.

Ramps were set on the platforms, and then the Hellcats and their entourage exited the elephants. When Ramala's feet touched the ground, Han yelled out, "Loyal subjects get down and show your respect for your beloved Queen Ramala!" Han and everyone there got down on their knees. The whole place went silent. It was so quiet that all you could hear was a hawk crying out off in the distance.

Ramala was impressed! She walked up to Han, with her cousins by her side, the Japha, and Butchers behind her. She said "Rise Han!" Then she took a look around and said "You have done a great job here. I am impressed!" Then she held out her hand. Han quickly grabbed it and kissed it. He said "Thank you my Queen for giving me the opportunity to show you that you made the right choice in putting me in charge of protecting Yee Province in your name." Han pointed to the building that he set up for Ramala to stay in while she visited. Then he said "I hope you are impressed with the accommodations I have made for your visit." Ramala motioned for Han to lead them in.

Dan always found it quite the show when Ramala was playing the part of ruler. He had spent time with Han here in Yee Province and had never heard him talk submissive like that before. Han knew just how to talk to Ramala with the proper respect. He seemed to have a special love for his Queen that made him genuinely subservient, without looking like he was sucking up and being fake for the sake of it. When they walked in they saw servants lined up along the wall. The place was immaculately clean. There was a large table with fruits, vegetables and nuts in large bowls. Han said "I didn't know if you wanted to have some food, so I had a light snack prepared. If you desire anything else, just let me know."

All three of the Hellcats smiled at Han. He had always done the best for them. Wana said "Join us. We will have a light snack while you update us on what's going on here in Yee." Tara looked around and then questioned "Where's Chi?" Han was about to answer, when Chi came in with bodyguards surrounding him. The guards parted and Chi walked up. He got down on his knees and said "Mistress Queen Ramala, your humble servant, Chi, pays his respect."

Ramala stood up. She stared at Chi for a moment, then said "I bless you with my presence and you have something better to do that makes you late! That's what you call respect!?" Ramala's personal guards pulled out their machetes when they saw that she was offended. She put up her hand to freeze them in their position. Then she said "Tell me heathen, what was more important than being here to meet your Queen?" Chi said "I was making sure that security was tight. I took one last check and it took me longer than I expected. Please forgive me."

Ramala didn't trust or believe Chi. She ordered "Stand up

Chi!" Chi did as he was told. She then ordered him "Put your hands behind your back." He did so. Then she turned to Han and said "Han, pull out your machete and put it to the throat of the heathen Chi." Han didn't hesitate. Once Han did what she had ordered, Ramala said "Han you are my most trusted Warlord. If this heathen has not been truthful with your Queen, take his head off now." Han lowered his head a little, still keeping the blade of his machete at Chi's throat, he said "My Queen, Chi is late because I sent him to do another check of security. If you still wish for me to take his head, I will." Ramala said "Is rebel activity such a problem?" Han said "No. Not since the war ended. I have been able to spend more time securing the area. Still, I would not be doing my job if I didn't take extra precaution to make sure that my Queen's stay was not interrupted by rebellious heathens." Ramala paused for a second, then said "Alright Chi, you get to keep your head."

Then she extended her arm and held out her hand. Chi hustled over and kissed it. Then Tara said "Join us Chi." They sat down and Han went through the formalities of explaining to the Hellcats what he and Chi were doing. Now Chi remembered why he never wanted to see Ramala ever again. Wana could see that her cousins were getting tired. She ordered everyone out, and posted Ramala's elite guards outside of the building. The young twins, Yaya, and the maidens were brought in. After everyone was settled in, the Royal family took a mid day nap.

Now that the Hellcats were out in the field, Tara wouldn't make time to spend with Yin. Tara was different than Ramala when it came to her man. Tara would focus all of her attention on security and military issues, when she was out in the field. She didn't need Yin to fall back on and keep her grounded like Ramala did with Dan. She was the opposite. She ignored Yin and treated him like hired help. Tara didn't have time to think about what Yin needed. He was a big boy. He could handle whatever he had to, until they got back. Besides, she knew she couldn't let Yin do what she wanted him to do to her out here. She could possibly lose focus. More than anything, Tara didn't want to get side tracked and miss something that might get her cousins or her niece and nephew hurt or killed. That's how she kept her focus.

Wana was on top of everything. She watched everything from her guards, the position of all of the attack elephants, the servants, The Japha twins, The Butchers, her cousins, and everything else. She was good at spotting when something was out of place. She even double checked her own strategies. She was so good that she would reward herself special treats. Wana was different from both of her cousins. She only needed a man to serve her. If he wasn't taking orders from her, the only other thing he could do for her was pleasure her. She used her guards as if they were her personal whores. Wana found that after good sex she was more focused, and energized for making up her military strategies. When they were back home, she would test herself, to see how much sex her body could take.

Out here in the field she couldn't do that. Wana wasn't going to let that keep her from what she wanted. So she perfected the quickie. Wana had learned what it took to satisfy her body. Knowing her body like that, made it quicker to get where she needed to be. The quickie was getting just enough sex as quickly as she could, to get her to that point of satisfaction, until she could get some more at another time.

After a quickie, she would be energized, and right back on top of things. This wasn't about the guards getting one bit of pleasure. It was about them following orders. Just like with all of her other orders, they did exactly what they were told to do. They were expected to perform like the elite guards they were. When they didn't, they were killed, or just punished severely if Wana thought they had the potential to do better. Wana's cousins knew what she was doing and tried to warn her. But just like them, she would listen to what they had to say, then she would do what she wanted. Ramala and Tara didn't make a big deal out of Wana's sex life, because Wana hadn't slipped one inch in her security duties. But one thing was clear to the other two Hellcats. Wana was going to get some sex one way, or another. She had to have it.

The Royal caravan only stayed in Yee Province for a little over a week. They used that time to restock supplies. It also was the last down time they would have for a while. The Royal court visited the restaurant- combination Inn and had dinner there. Everyone was there, except for the young twins. They were left in the care of the maidens. All of the regular customers were cleared out so that service to the Royal court could be the best possible. Yaya was allowed to come with the Royal court. She sat opposite of the Hellcats. She was happily looking around, squirming in her seat, with her usual bright, wide eyed enthusiastic look, that she always wore on her face. The Hellcats didn't miss much, so they noticed that Yaya and one of the young servers at the restaurant recognized each other. The girls would stare at each other when they thought no one was looking.

Yaya could see that Hania had grown since the last time she saw her. She was taller, and still slim, but not to the point of looking like she wasn't eating good. Yaya remembered that working in the kitchen always provided opportunities to get extra bites of food here and there. Her and Hania always managed to get extra to eat and not get caught.

Hania was the only worker from the kitchen that the Hellcats noticed Yaya's attention was on. To provide the best service possible, Najay and Mayho were brought over from the inn to help out. Again the Hellcats realized that Yaya knew these two girls also. Yaya's face had a look of concern when she saw her other cousins. Najay and Mayho's faces both showed signs of stress. They both had gotten taller since Yaya had last seen them.

Najay was heavier than Mayho, even though Mayho wasn't thin as Hania. The Hellcats communicated what they had seen to each other in a glance, without saying a word. That's how close in thought to each other, the Hellcats were. Wana wanted to see what kind of reaction she could get out of Yaya, so when Hania walked past, Wana said "You server, what are you doing?"

This immediately caught the attention of the guards and the restaurant owner. Hania was confused. She didn't know of anything that she had done that might have been out of line. Yaya was near panic now. She knew what could happen to a server if they offended a guest. Wana saw Yaya out of the corner of her eye, and it confirmed in her mind that this girl was someone that was close to Yaya. The owner was on his way to Hania with bad intentions written all over his face. Just as he got to Hania, and before he could do anything, Ramala said "We are impressed with her level of service."

The owner's whole attitude changed towards Hania instantly. Now he looked at her like he was a proud father. Ramala continued with "She should be treated well and promoted because of her level of service." The owner said "She's one of our best." Ramala turned to the owner and said "I've already told you that! Just make sure that my orders concerning her are followed." The owner replied "Yes, my Queen." Then Wana said "As you were."

Then Hania continued with her duties and the owner moved back out of the way. The Hellcats could see the look of relief on Yaya's face. Wana wanted to take things a little farther, but Ramala had seen enough, and wasn't going to let Wana play with her adopted daughter's emotions. Wana was good with that. She knew that her and her cousins would have conversations later on this matter.

When Hania came out of the kitchen with a tray of fruit, she saw the Royal court. The owner had warned her to be very careful and to keep her head down. She was not to look in the eyes of these important people. That would lead to her losing her head.

Hania carefully walked up to the table and placed the tray on it. Just before she turned to walk away from the table, she recognized her cousin Yaya. Yaya was as well dressed as the other important people. She had never seen Yaya look like this. Yaya was taller and very healthy. She looked like a fighter to Hania. Hania and Yaya locked eyes in recognition of each other. Hania realized that she had been staring for a moment. She quickly walked away.

That's what the Hellcats and the rest of the girls at the table saw. The same thing happened when Najay and Mayho recognized Yaya. When Hania came out the second time and when Wana questioned her, she froze in fear that this woman might realize that she knew Yaya. Then she thought there was no way she could know they were cousins. Hania was confused and didn't answer. That's when the restaurant owner came up and deflected the attention to himself. Hania knew that she had to be more careful around grown-ups. She knew if anyone found out that they were Whirlwind Wa's family, all of them would lose their heads.

Later that night, the Royal court got a show at the spot in the back of the restaurant. Ramala was so impressed that she told her cousins that she wanted a spot like this built in the city of Ra, when they got back home. The Hellcats met for a short time privately at the spot. They had their own private booth. As they watched Yaya dance out on the floor with the professional dancers, Wana said "Ya has a special connection to three of the servants here. Do you think they are her relatives? I should have them interrogated." Tara asked Ramala "Have you questioned Ya about her past before getting here?" Ramala answered "No I haven't." Tara said "Well there is a definite connection. They could be orphans from one of the families we wiped out." Wana said "It wouldn't be a problem to eliminate all four of them." Ramala Shot daggers at Wana with her eyes, then said "You'll do no such thing!" Wana said "Don't look at me like that. I'm just saying."

Then Wana looked at Ramala like this had to be at least investigated. Tara looked at Ramala for a second, then at Wana and said "Wa there are ways to keep things under control without going to the extreme. All of them are still young. Have them watched, and if we find out that they are doing anything against the House of Ra, then we will eliminate them."

Then Tara looked at Ramala for a reaction. Ramala knew Tara was right, so she didn't object. Wana had been watching closely. Tara turned back to Wana and looked at her. Wana knew that it meant that she could investigate, but to proceed with caution. They knew that Ramala had become fond of Yaya and would not let them harm her unless they had concrete proof that she was a threat. The next day Wana had a meeting with Chi. He was to have the three servants watched closely at all times, but not to change things for them. He was to leave them to their destiny and give Wana updates through her messengers. Chi found that to be a strange request, but knew he couldn't question Wana. So he did what he was told.

Once the Royal caravan was full of supplies, they were on there way again. The Japha, Jan was enjoying this trip. The next stop on the way was the House of Na. Jan knew they would get great treatment there. After all, that was the Na,Tee's home. She looked over at her brother Japha, San. She knew he missed the Na, Tee even though he tried not to let her see it. Japha, Jan tried to fill the void left by Tee. San would spend his spare time mostly with Jan. Jan loved spending time with her brother. When she was not practicing, or spending time with either the Butchers, or Hellcats, she spent her time talking and relaxing with her brother. These two were very close, and it was nothing to see Jan huddled very close to San when they were relaxing. San was Jan's personal pillow, or get comfortable spot when they were lounging around. Up to this point, Japha, Jan hadn't been interested in men.

Jan was laying, relaxing very close to San. Jan was talking about seeing their father when all of a sudden she found that her body was having a strange reaction. She was instantly aware of every inch of her body that was touching San's. Her heart rate increased almost instantly. She didn't know what to make of it. She was a little uncomfortable with this, so she moved slightly to get more comfortable. When she did that, a flash of heat ran through her body. She was instantly hot for her brother. She wanted to move away, but the sensation of his body up against hers was keeping her right there. Then she felt her body involuntarily press and squirm closer on San. Japha, Jan willed and then forced herself to get up.

San hadn't noticed a thing. Jan was always using him as a pillow, so he thought all of the squirming was her getting more comfortable. When she abruptly jumped up, San looked around and asked "What's wrong." Jan was embarrassed, but could see that San had no clue as to what just happened. Jan Said "My leg just got stiff on me." San said "Lay back down and I'll rub it out." Jan didn't know how her body would react to San's touch and she wasn't about to find out. She said "I'm going to go see my girls. I'll just walk it off. I'll catch you later."

Jan walked out on the balcony of the platform. She took a few deep breaths and tried to compose herself. Then she thought about what the Na, Tee said to her a while back at the House of Ra. Na, Tee said "He's gonna be a man, and men have needs. I know you can't take care of that, can you? "Jan knew her body wanted to take care of that.

Japha, Jan knew she was thinking crazy. She had to calm herself down. She thought all she had to do was avoid San for a while, then this feeling would go away. Nina and Mia were watching to see when Jan would come out of San's quarters. When they saw Jan, they made their way to the elephant she was on . The girls knew their mistress so well that when they got to her, they could see something was not right. They could see water welling up in Jan's eyes. Nina said "What's wrong mistress?"

Jan said "I really miss my father. It just got the best of me. I must be tired." Mia said "Maybe a good nap will make you feel better." Jan nodded in agreement, but her body told her what would really make her feel better. She ignored it.

Yin was relaxing with Ma. Every since they had been out in the field, Tara had been ignoring Yin. He tried to act like it didn't bother him, but it did. That's why Yin would never let anyone get close to him except his sister. He was worse than Dan when it came to dealing with his own feelings. It didn't make it any better that he kept on having the same nightmare. Yin wasn't smart, but he had to figure this thing out before it ate him up inside. He tried to eliminate some of the possibilities. He knew it couldn't be a conscious, he didn't have one of those. He wasn't afraid of dying. He always thought when you're dead, it's over. You don't have to worry about much after that. That's about as much as he could figure. Anything after that, he needed help with.

Yin looked over at Ma. She said "What?" Yin hesitated. Ma knew something had been bothering Yin that he wouldn't tell her about. She knew if she was patient, and he didn't figure it out himself, that he would come to her, his ace in the hole, when it came time to understand something. Ma said "The sooner you tell me, the sooner we can figure it out, together."

Ma always knew what to say to Yin to get him to talk. The only problem was Yin didn't want Ma to see his dream as a premonition and start worrying about him. Yin said "It's that Ramala. It just gets under my skin the way she treats me. "Ma said "Don't lie to me. You're not good at it."

Ma moved closer to Yin. She said "We never use to keep secrets from each other. That's probably why whatever you're thinking about is still bothering you. Come on, tell me what it is." Yin looked at Ma for another moment. She was putting on her most reassuring face. He still wasn't sure if he should tell him Ma. So Yin tried a truth, instead of a lie. Yin said "I think this thing with Tara is starting to make me think about her a little to much."

Ma could spot a lie coming out of Yin's mouth before he finished it. She was relieved that it was only Tara that Yin was worried about. She told Yin "Tara is a good girl. You be patient with her. When she gets back home, she'll make it worth your wait." Then Ma smiled at Yin. Ma knew that Tara was so busy with her cousins that she wasn't spending time with Yin. So Ma had no problem believing that's what was bothering Yin, because it really was.

This was the most comfortable that Cat and Syn, Jara had felt out in the field. Things were going so smoothly that these two took naps most of the day, between eating. They were laying stretched out on a platform, out cold.They had learned a lot from being out in the field during the war. Now they knew the value of conserving your energy. They only used as much energy as they needed to. They were almost like two female lions without cubs. Since these two weren't going into heat, they rested, until it was time to hunt and kill.

Chapter 9

The Royal caravan sent messengers to the House of Na, Telling them what Ramala expected when she got there. The Na had been a neutral during the war. That was to their advantage. The Hellcats knew they had to respect each of the Houses, and couldn't bully them the way they did all of the tribes in the area south of the seven Houses. But since the Hellcats had the largest House, or the most territory of any of the Houses. The Hellcats felt that they were the strongest House now. That's how they were going to be treated as far as they were concerned. On top of that, the Japha twins were the heads of the seven Houses. The Hellcats wanted to see how the seven Houses would treat their new Queen and King.

Now that the Hellcats were in the north, they would let the Japha twins take the lead. They and the Butchers would become the twins protectors, much like the role the twins played back in the House of Ra. The Japha, Jan had been trained by her father to be a general. That was a lot different that being a ruler. The Hayee, Ramala taught Japha, Jan as much as she could about being a ruler. Jan was a Jett, so she learned quickly. Now it was time to see what kind of ruler Jan would be.

The only demands that the Japha twins made on the House of Na before they got there was that the Hellcats and the Butchers be able to keep their weapons with them upon entering the House of Na. Ordinarily, no outsider would be allowed to enter any of the Houses with their weapons. The second request was for the Japha twins to be introduced as the King and Queen of the Seven Houses. This was to test the Na and see if they would respect the wishes of their new Queen. Matt, Nott, and Bor were the leaders as well as the elders at the House of Na. They knew they had a good relationship with the Japha twins. They also knew the

Butchers would be respectful. What gave them slight concern was the Hellcats. Even though the Na were assured that the Hellcats were only Jan's escorts while in the north, they knew these girls were very smart.

The three elders had met the girls a very long time ago when they were very young. That was the only time they had ever saw them. Now they were curious to see the girls that waged war and carved out their own territory. These girls were so bold and reckless that they would travel through the north and all of the seven Houses, thinking that they wouldn't encounter resistance. That alone made the elders want to meet these girls.

When the Royal caravan reached the gates of the House of Na Only the Japha twin, the Hellcats, Ramala's twins, their maidens, and the Butchers entered the House of Na. The rest of the Royal caravan waited outside of the main gate.

Once inside, they were greeted by the three elder and all of the important heads of family in the House of Na. Matt announced "All the Na welcome the new King and Queen of the northern Houses. King Japha, San and Queen Japha, Jania Jett!" The House of Na erupted in cheers. Japha, Jan was almost over come by this. Even though she tried to prepare herself, she found that it still came as a shock when she was announced as the Queen. Her and San gave a quick wave to the crowd, then the Na got down out of respect to their new rulers. After a few seconds, Jan motioned for them to get up.

Then the Na were given a chance to walk past and see their new rulers. After this ceremony was over, the Japha twins requested a meeting with the elders. They met for most of the day. The twins assured the Na that they were one of the Japha twin's closest allies. They were also a close ally to the House of Ra. The Hellcats pledged that as long as the Na fully supported the Japha twins, the House of Ra would be a strong ally to the House of Na.

The three elder watched the Japha twins and the Hellcats very closely. They could see that the unity between these girls was very strong and would be very hard to break. This was a strong team that seemed to have a plan. The elders would support their new rulers. That would help keep the Hellcats in the south. None of the seven Houses, including the Hayee, wanted the Hellcats in the north. The last request the Japha twins had was for blood. They wanted the Na to give them an offering of blood to solidify the unity with the Na, the Ra, and the new King and Queen of the north. This was the ultimate request of a House. All of the Houses reserved their blood for their own family. To share your family blood was a show of complete trust. The elders agreed. This was the best move for the House of Na. The Na gave blood and drank it with the Japha Twins and the Hellcats. The House of Na was already in good with the other Houses. Now they were in good with the new rulers of the north, and the largest House of them all, the House of Ra. There would be nothing that the Na wouldn't be able to get through trade.

In the few days that the Royal caravan was at the House of Na, the Japha, San knew the Na, Tee would come to him. He saw her when they first arrived. She was with the greeting party. Na, Tee showed the proper respect to the new Rulers, but she didn't make a effort to see Japha, San.

When the greeting party disbanded, Tee went with them. Japha, San knew he couldn't go running after Na, Tee, so he sent a messenger requesting that Tee meet with him. Tee came to meet with San in one of the many gardens in the House of Na. When she got there, she tried to put on a formal act. Tee didn't walk up to San, she kept a respectable distance. When San saw this he said "What no hug?" Na, Tee said "If that's what you request of me, I'll do it."

San stared at Tee for a moment then said "If you're not going to give it to me of your own free will, then I don't want it." Na, Tee just stood there. San said "Oh, so it's like this now?" Tee said "You know I'm glad to see you. It's just. It's just I'm already confused and I need time to sort things out." San said "Sort what out?" Tee said "My life. I need to find out where it's going."

San smiled at Tee and started towards her. Tee took a step back. San stopped and looked at her. He knew if he pressed the issue, she would let him take advantage of her. He would do that with other girls, if he felt like it. But not with Tee. He wanted to ask her why she acting like this, but after she backed away from him, he took offense. He said "Alright then, go sort out your life." Tee stood there looking at San with a hurt look in her eyes. San said "What do you want from me?" Tee immediately replied "What do you want from me!?"

San thought for a moment, and before he could say any-thing, Tee said "That's what I thought." Then she turned her back and walked away. San wasn't going to run after her, or even say anything to her once she turned her back on him. He watched her as she walked and disappeared into one of the buildings, not looking back. Japha, San told himself he wasn't going to let Na, Tee Spin his head around, thinking about her. But still, he didn't like what had just happened.

Japha, Jan knew that San and Tee would be meeting. She had her girls watching them at a safe distance. They were to let Jan know when the two got finished meeting. She knew Tee had been avoiding San. She also knew that San had to at least meet with Tee once before he left. After Tee walked off, the girls alerted Japha, Jan. Jan came to see San.

San noticed that Jan had been acting strange the last few days. He didn't know it was because of the incident of their bodies touching that Jan had with him. Jan came up to San and gave him half a hug. Not like the ones he usually got where they were very close on each other. Before Jan completely pulled away, San grabbed her in his arms and said "What's wrong? You've been acting strange lately."

Jan gently moved San's hands from around her and said "I'm trying not to make a mistake in my ruling protocol. It's making me think to much." San said "Just try to relax. You're doing just fine. If Hayee, Ramala can be as good as she is at it, I know you can do just as well." Jan smiled and said "Thank you." She paused for a second, then said "What about you and Tee? Was she happy to see you?" San's face looked angry and confused. He said "Who knows. What do I care." Jan could see that San cared. She knew that was his pride talking. He did care. Jan didn't push it any further. She just spent time with her brother, while trying to figure out how to get San and Tee to spend time together. Jan was starting to think that her and San were to close. That's how she explained her feelings for San to herself. If Tee could occupy San's time, that would give Jan more time to think her way through her feelings.

On the day before the Royal caravan was to leave, Jan asked the elders to have a feast prepared to seal the alliance that was made between them. Jan went directly to Tee, and asked her to sit at the same table as her. Tee looked at Jan. She didn't know what Jan was up to, but she wasn't about to be a part of it, unless she was forced to. Jan could see that the history between them made Tee hesitant. Jan looked at Tee and said "I know we haven't seen eye to eye in the past. Over time, I have come to realize that my brother has real feelings for you. I was wrong thinking that you were a play toy to him."

Na, Tee looked away from Jan, then said "Why doesn't he act like he cares." Jan said "He's never felt this way about someone. It's confusing him. He refuses to be weak."

Tee looked back at Jan and searched her face when she said that San never felt this way about anyone. Tee's eyes had a glimmer of hope in them. Japha, Jan knew that she almost had Tee. She just had to be careful. Jan kept the same look of needing help on her face when she said "Talking to him won't help. That's why I want you to come and sit with me at our table. Don't say a word to him. Let him sort out his thoughts on his own, while seeing how beautiful you are to him, and how much you really mean to him. That's how you get San."

Tee didn't know what to think. She asked with a suspiciously confused look on her face. "Why help me?" Jan looked away and said "My brother has become distant to me since you left. I think he somehow blames me for your leaving. I need my brother, but I can't give him what you can. When I help you, I help me. We both can get what we want, if we work together." Then Jan turned to Tee and came just short of begging her with her eyes. Now this made since to Tee. She knew Japha, Jan had to have a reason for wanting her to sit with her. Tee did want San. She said "Alright, I will try your way." Jan said "Thank you."

That evening, Na,Tee came to the feast. When San first saw her, he put up his defenses. He wasn't going to show any signs of weakness, if that's what she thought. He went about his business, paying no attention to Tee. Jan pretended not to notice anything. Tee did just as Jan told her to. She made sure she was looking her best. Then she pretended not to notice San.

After San became more comfortable that Tee wasn't watching him, he found himself looking over at her more and more, from time to time. She had always been beautiful to him. Tee felt San watching her. Jan told her not to look at San. It took everything in her not to. But halfway through the feast, Tee couldn't help herself. Nervous energy was building in her.When she knew San wasn't looking at her, she had to look at him. Then finally they locked eyes for a moment. Tee looked down, then away from San. Jan saw all of this and inwardly smiled. She had managed to do what neither one of them was willing to do. She made them realize how much they really missed each other.

After the feast, Jan was talking to Tee. Jan saw San and

called him over. Just as San got there, Jan said "Excuse me for a second San. I need to see Mali for a quick moment. I'll be right back." Before San could say something, Jan was gone. San looked Tee over. Tee looked up at San and said "So you're leaving in the next day." San said "Yes we are." Then he looked Tee over again. San said "You're looking beautiful as usual." Tee said "Thank you. The garden is beautiful also. Can we take a walk?" San nodded in agreement and they walked off together. They talked for a while in the garden. As much as they wanted to, both of them knew that they wouldn't be able to enjoy each other like they really wanted in the House of Tee's ancestors. They both also knew that they would find a way to see each other. Sooner or later.

The next stop was the House of Hayee. When they got close, all of the Butchers went on guard. None of the Butchers ever had good dealings with the Hayee. Ma had her thing with the Hayee, because of killing the Hayee, Shaia. Dan, Cat, and Syn, Jara had killed more than a few Hayee during the war. Backir was a Butcher, so he figured he would have trouble just because of that. This was enough to make the Butchers concerned about what would happen when they got there. The Hellcats assured the Butchers that things would be different because they had won the war. The Butchers didn't believe one word of that bullshit! They knew the Hayee were hotheads. That's probably what they would have to deal with. If not, they didn't mind being wrong about it.

The Hayee were part of a large group of family members that broke off from the House of Japha and the House of Hoo. This group then split up, going in their own directions. One group went to the base of the mid-range mountains and formed the House of He. From the House of He, came the House of Tere. The Tere lived in the lower mountains. The House of Tat was formed from the Tere and was even further up the mountain in the colder air regions that the other six Houses didn't want to deal with. The other groups that left the Japha and the Hoo moved south of the mountains. They formed the House of Hayee and to the south of Hayee was the House of Na. Everything south of that, the seven Houses considered to be inhabited by savages and heathens. That way, they could feel justified, to themselves, when they went into that area and took, or did whatever they wanted to.

When the House of Hayee was newly formed, they had to fight for survival. The House of Na to the south had more family members and was much stronger at the time. The Three Houses at the mountain were also putting pressure on the House of Hayee to join them. The Hayee had to fight and resort to aggressive tactics to keep their family together. After the Hayee multiplied in numbers, they became strong enough that the other Houses had to respect them. Even though the other Houses embraced the Hayee, the Hayee kept their aggressive nature.

The Hayee built up an army only second to the Japha. They had guards and spies everywhere. So they spotted the Royal caravan from the House of Ra before it got close. Messengers were sent back and forth. The Hayee would greet the Japha twins as King and Queen of the northern Houses, and they would accept the Hellcats as guest. But they would not guarantee the safety of the Butchers. The Butchers could enter the House of Hayee at their own risk. There were more than a few Hayee with scores to settle with the Butchers. The Hellcats knew this and when the Royal caravan got to the main gate of the House of Hayee, the Hellcats said that the Butchers would not leave their weapons unless the Hayee could assure them that they would be safe.

The guards escorted the Hellcats to meet with the elders of the Hayee. Mashaya and Roe were there, along with some of the Hellcats older cousins. After everyone greeted each other, Mashaya asked "Where are my babies?" Ramala got right down to business. She said "You'll see them after you guarantee that all of the Butchers will be safe once they enter the House of Hayee." Mashaya said "Now how can I guarantee that?" Ramala stared at her grandmother and said "I'll destroy this whole place if my children's father runs into foul play!" Mashaya said "You come here to the home of your ancestors and threaten to destroy our home! Just who do you think you are!?" Mashaya looked at Tara and Wana, then said "I know you two don't agree with that, do you?"

Tara didn't say a word. Wana said "Mala didn't mean it like that. We just want to visit and enjoy our time here with you. Can't you see that?" Wana paused, while begging her grandmother with her eyes. Then Wana said "But I wouldn't put it past those two, both of them being with child. You never know what they might do."

Roe's face lit up. He smiled at Ramala. She saw his happiness and smiled back at him. Mashaya looked at Tara. Tara didn't smile at her grandma, she looked away from her. The look on Tara's face told Mashaya that Tara had probably taken up with a heathen too. Mashaya said "The last time you said that, it took more than a year before you had those children. That was the longest I've heard anyone carrying a child. Are you really with child this time? Are you trying to raise a hoard of half heathen degenerates?"

A Degenerate was what they called children made from heathens and royalty. Royalty was considered to be any of the direct descendants of one of the seven Houses. Degenerate was the equivalent to a racial slur. The same as the word heathen was offensive to the people that were called it.

Ramala was offended. The smile came off of her face. Tara and Wana knew that if anyone but grandma had said that, they would be dead. Because if Ramala hadn't killed them, one of them would have.

Roe stared at Ramala to be careful what she said to his mother. Ramala had a lot of respect for her grandma, and would not look at her with her eyes as angry as her's were. She looked at her grandma's feet and said "I come here happy to see you. All you have is bitterness for me and my King. On top of that you insult me and my children. Well I can tell you one thing, you don't have to worry about seeing my children or me again! I'm leaving!" Mashaya Yelled "Hold it! Don't you talk to me in that tone of voice!"

Mashaya knew that Ramala would stand there and listen to whatever she had to say, out of respect. But when she was done, she knew her stubborn daughter wouldn't be past doing what she said she would do. Mashaya softened her tone just a little, and said "If you had brought them with you, instead of using them as a bargaining chip, I never would have said what I did. You bring me my babies and I promise that if there is a challenge to your King, it will be fair. He will not be ambushed in the House of Hayee."

Ramala looked up at her grandma. She knew this was as close to an apology as she was going to get. Ramala said "I'll bring them to you, but don't call my children degenerates." Mashaya said "Don't tell your mother what to do! I'll be respectful!"

Roe didn't like it when these two went at it. It always made him nervous. It seemed to him that since Ramala had become a teenager, she would, a little bit at a time, start talking back to his mother. She had never done that before then. Now it had escalated into them having heated conversations. Roe didn't want to get between these two women if he didn't have to. He knew his daughter was going to speak her mind, no matter what. He also knew that his mother and his daughter loved each other very much, and would argue like this one minute and be loving to each other the next minute . It was too much drama for Roe. He wished he didn't have to be around them when they were together. Most of the time he made sure he wasn't.

Once Ramala and her cousins were on their way back to the Royal caravan to get everyone, Mashaya stared at Roe, and said in a scolding voice "I don't know why she acts like that!" Roe looked at his mother and thought ' She acts like that because you raised her. She grew up watching you!' But he said "You know how she is. She's very stubborn." Then he walked off.

Wana told the Butchers that they would not have any problems at the House of Hayee. They just had to leave their weapons upon entering. The Butchers all looked at the three Hellcats trying to figure out if they were lying. The Hellcats put on their most reassuring faces. The whole of the Royal caravan was allowed to enter the House of Hayee because mostly all of the Hellcats guards were family members. The ones that weren't, were not enough to be considered a threat. Besides they had been with the Hellcats longer than any of the Butchers.

Everyone greeted the Japha twins as King and Queen of the northern Houses. Even though the greeting was not as enthusiastic as when they were in the House of Na, it was sufficient. Mashaya had gone back to her palace. She wasn't going to be a part of the ceremony. She knew Ramala would bring the children to her later. Roe was there. He saw the Young twins walking very close to their mother, while looking at the new surroundings. He saw Dan, but would not look at him. He didn't even look at Dan when Dan got down on one knee, out of respect. Dan had killed some of his younger cousins during the war. Roe didn't like Dan to start with. Now things were worse than that. Roe focused on the young twins. Ramala took them right to him. Yaya was there, but she stayed with the rest of the Butchers.

The twins didn't like strangers. That's the way Ramala raised them. Roe saw this and didn't try to pick them up. He smiled at them. Ramala told her twins "This is my father. Like Dan is your father. "She pointed and made gestures to help the twins understand what she was saying. Still they were focused on Roe, making sure he didn't get close enough to make them uncomfortable. Roe got down on one Knee, and said to the twins "I'm your grandpa! You two look great!"

The twins just stared at Roe. Then they took a look at each other. They both agreed that this was a stranger. Roe looked up at Ramala. He stood up and hugged her. He said "They look good! The girl looks just like you, when you were her age." The twins relaxed a little once Roe stood up. He knew they would. He waited a second, then he snatched La up before she knew what happened. Once in Roe's arms, she looked at his face and realized that this was to close for her liking. She pushed him back with her hands and let out a piercing scream that made Roe put her down immediately.

Roe was used to screaming. His mother was a screamer, his daughter and nieces were screamers too. So La's scream didn't bother him. Young Dan backed up between his mother's legs so he wouldn't get snatched up like La.

When La's feet hit the ground, she ran to her mother in a panic, grabbed her leg, and then turned around looking at Roe, to make sure he didn't try that again. Ramala rubbed her hand over La's head and down her back. Then she said "It's alright. He's your grandfather. He won't hurt you." Then Ramala walk over to Roe, hugged him, and turned to the twins with a big smile on her face and said "This is my daddy!"

Both La and Dan knew what the word daddy meant. To them daddy meant Dan. La looked at Ramala and said "That's not your daddy, mommy!" Then La pointed to Dan and said defiantly "That's your daddy mommy!" Ramala smiled at La, pointed to Dan, and said "That's your daddy." Then Ramala pointed to Roe and said "This is my daddy!" La grabbed Dan's leg, looking at Ramala and thought ' That's not how she acts at home! Now that she has her daddy, I'll see if she tries to get my daddy later!'

Roe erupted into laughter. He said "She's just like you! You're going to have a lot of trouble when she gets older." Ramala said "No I won't. I have her under control." Roe started laughing again. He said "Alright, we'll see about that." Young Dan stood there and watched the old man. He didn't know why, but he wanted to laugh every time he heard this old man laugh. He wasn't going to. He didn't want the old man to think it was alright to pick him up. Young Dan did smile. Mostly because he could see that his mother was happy.

After Ramala let her other relatives get a look at her twins, she took the twins to see her grandmother. Dan stayed with the Japha twins and the Butchers. He knew how the Hayee, Mashaya felt about him. After seeing the way he was ignored by Roe, he didn't want to deal with Mashaya's reaction to seeing him.

Mashaya's guards let her know that she had visitors. Ramala walked in and saw her grandma sitting on her throne. When the twins got close enough to get a good look at Mashaya, they had a different reaction than they had with Roe. Ramala looked a lot like Mashaya. So much that she could be mistaken for her daughter. The young twins noticed this right off. They stared at Mashaya and then back at Ramala. Ramala saw this and told the twins "That's my mommy!"

Ramala got down on one knee, then got up and hugged her grandma. Mashaya was as focused on the twins as they were on her. She barely acknowledged Ramala. After Ramala let her go from hugging her, Mashaya smiled at the twins. She said in a very soft and reassuring voice "How are my babies doing?" The twins got another shock. This old lady also sounded like their mother! She had the same soothing tone to her voice. Mashaya bent down, not moving towards the twins, and said "Come to grandma!" La smiled and looked up at her mother for instruction. Ramala said "It's alright. Go to grandma." As she motioned for both twins to go over to Mashaya. La hesitated, then slowly walked over first. She studied Mashaya's face. When she got to Mashaya, La touched her face, then turned and looked at Ramala's face. She did look like mommy!

Mashaya was patient with La. She didn't want to scare her back into the arms of her mother. She waited until La finished investigating, then she slowly and deliberately reached for La and hugged her. La allowed it to happen. La didn't feel uncomfortable. Dan watched all of this. Once he saw that La was relaxed with Mashaya, he walked over slowly, looking for some attention. Mashaya watched him.

When he got there she hugged him too. Ramala watched as her twins seemed to be at ease with Mashaya. They were so comfortable that La started trying to get more of Mashaya's attention from her brother. Ramala had to call La's name to let her know not to get out of control. Mashaya was lost in the moment with her great grandchildren. Ramala watched and couldn't remember when she saw her grandmother so loving to someone. It was also amazing to Ramala that only after a few moments of ever seeing Mashaya, her twins were totally comfortable with her. They almost didn't notice their mother. Ramala sat down and watched as Mashaya played with and had the twins laughing.

Mashaya looked up at Ramala with approval in her eyes. She said "They are beautiful and very strong. I wouldn't have done it this way, but you've done well with these two." Mashaya sat down with the twins laying in her arms. They looked up in her face from time to time.

Mashaya was never prouder of Ramala than she was right now. She asked Ramala "So are you really with child right now?" Ramala answered "Yes I am." Mashaya then asked "What about Tara? Who's the father of her child?" Ramala didn't answer right away. Mashaya stared and waited on an answer. Ramala finally said "It's the warlord Yin. "Ramala wanted to make Yin seem more significant than the heathen he was. Mashaya couldn't believe this. She blurted out "Another Heathen!" She was interrupted by La saying "Heathen!" Mashaya continue with "I've seen this Yin. He's an accident waiting to happen. What could she possibly see in that heathen!?" Ramala said "That I couldn't tell you. You know Ta has a mind of her own." Then Dan said "Heathen!" Then he looked at Mashaya. Mashaya looked down at Dan and said "You got that right! It seems there're everywhere these days!"

Wana knew there could be trouble for Ma. She made it clear that no Hayee was to try to do harm to Ma. Wana didn't know if that was enough for the Hayee children. They were very resourceful when they wanted to get something done. They wanted Ma dead. Wana wasn't worried about them doing something while she was around. But if they caught Ma without one of the Hellcats around, there would be trouble. So to avoid trouble Wana spent almost every moment with Ma. Wana dared the Hayee children to disrespect her by trying something against Ma. Since Cat and Syn, Jara also never left Ma's side. Wana became closer to the Butcher girls than she ever had. That didn't bother her at all.

At first, Ma didn't know whether Wana was looking for an opportunity to set her up. After seeing the precautions Wana was taking, Ma figured that Wana was on the up and up about keeping the Hayee from starting something. After seeing that Wana couldn't stay away from men. Because Wana wasn't shy about what she was doing. The Butcher girls got to see, first hand, what Wana was up to. Ma didn't have urges for men yet, but she found that she didn't mind watching. Cat and Syn always found somewhere else to be when Wana did her thing. Knowing that Ma was watching made Wana put on a good show for Ma, every time. What bothered Ma more than anything was the fact that she was starting to like being around Wana. How do you kill someone that you really don't want to? Ma wondered if she needed revenge for the beating she took. Could she let it go as just practice? Even though she liked Wana, she wasn't ready to go that far yet.

After spending time and talking to her grandma, Ramala told Tara to keep away from Yin while they were in the House of Hayee. She also told Wana to make sure to keep Yin out of Mashaya's sight. That was probably the only way to keep her from killing Yin. Tara didn't have any problem staying away from Yin. A couple of months after she became with child, she didn't have much use for Yin. When Yin was doing whatever he was doing to her sexually, she would put up with him. Now she didn't have those urges, so she basically ignored Yin. That was something else that didn't sit well with Yin. He thought it was because he told her about his nightmare, and now maybe she thought it made him look weak. That was all he could come up with. So that's what he went with. He knew he couldn't prove to her that he was the same man, right now. He would have to wait until she had their child. Yin's nightmare, Tara and their child and the House of Hayee all had Yin on the edge of insanity. Sooner or later he would have to release that pressure the only way he knew how.

In the next few days the Hellcats drank as much blood as they were allowed to. Now that two of the Hellcats were with child, there would be no stopping Wana from joining in the blood drinking feast. While that was happening, Mashaya was spoiling the young twins rotten. She would take them early, keep them most of the day, and feed them whatever they wanted. She took them to all parts of the Hayee House and show them off. Ramala didn't mind that Mashaya wanted to spend as much time with her twins as she could. What bothered Ramala was the fact that the twins never acted out while they were with Mashaya, and they didn't seem to miss her when she came to get them.

To the young twins, Mashaya was the best thing that ever happened to them. When they were with grandma, they could do whatever they wanted and grandma would let them. Not like their mother. And the treats they were getting! Mother never just let them eat until they were about to burst. But grandma would! Dan even got so full one time that he vomited everything that he ate. When he was done, he started eating again. And grandma let him! They didn't have to look around to see if mother or the Maidens were watching. Yes, this was great, and they loved this treatment!

They had spent a whole week at the House of Hayee. Dan could feel the tension from the Hayee building against him. He and Ramala were having breakfast, when Dan said "We've been here a week already, When are we leaving?" Ramala said "It's not that often that I will be able to spend time with my family. I'm enjoying this time. What's the hurry?" They stared at each other for a moment. Dan couldn't believe Ramala couldn't or wouldn't see that things for him weren't that good here. For the most part, he had to hide in Ramala's quarters to avoid confrontations with the Hayee. Well, he wasn't hiding, but that's what it felt like to him. Dan said "The longer we stay here, the greater the chance of a serious fight breaking out with me and your family." Ramala said "Nonsense! They know better than to test me like that. You have nothing to worry about. Relax, we'll be leaving in a few days." Knowing that they would be leaving relieved Dan for the moment. He couldn't wait to get out of there.

Chapter 10

Later, after noon, a challenge was issue from the Hayee to Dan. Ramala tried to stop it by appealing first to her father, then to the elders of Hayee. As a last resort, she even tried to get her grandmother's help. You can guess how much Mashaya helped. None! The most they were willing to concede was not using weapons. They told Ramala that it wouldn't be a death duel. The fight would go on until one person conceded. Ramala knew that meant someone would be near death or dying. She knew Dan was good enough to beat most any Hayee in a one on one battle. What she wasn't sure of was what was going to happen after he won that fight. She had Wana get all the guards ready for a hasty departure. The Hellcats knew that their guards would only half heartedly fight their own relatives, so leaving quickly was the only option. Even though Dan would have to fight. When the fight was over, the Hellcats would be out of there.

The contest was being held in the largest courtyard the Hayee had. There was enough seating for anyone who wanted to be there. The seating encircled the area where the fight was to take place. Just before the contest was to take place, another challenge was made to Ma. Wana told the Hayee elders that she would fight in Ma's place. That anyone that attacked Ma would have to deal with Wana. That kept any Hayee from taking that challenge. All of the Hayee girls knew that Wana was almost unbeatable, and the Hayee young men weren't willing to fight Wana, just to have a chance at Ma. So Ma didn't have to fight the Hayee, this time.

All of the Hayee were anxious to see Dan defeated by one of their own. He was the one that killed several of their uncles and cousins. The courtyard filled up quickly. Mashaya had a ringside seat for this one. Mashaya was sure that she would be rid of Dan after this competition. He would be dead, and she wouldn't be blamed by Ramala for causing it to happen. Things couldn't have worked out better, as far as she was concerned. Ramala and her cousins, along with the Japha twins, their girls, and the Butchers sat together. Yaya, and the twins, were sent back to the caravan. The Royal Guards were on high alert. The Hellcats decided if things got out of hand, they would blast a scream to freeze their relatives, so they could get out of there. Things got very tense when Dan came out into the center of the courtyard. He looked past the grandmother and around at the crowd. Dan was calm. He wasn't overconfident, but he was ready. He didn't start this. He had no choice in the matter. Right now, all he knew was that who ever the Hayee that came out into the courtyard had to be dealt with. That was the fact of the matter. Whatever happened after that would be dealt with then. Dan took a quick look at the Butchers. Last time they had to deal with the Hayee, they were all captured. Dan was sure that they were going to do better than that this time. He looked over the Hayee in the crowd without staring at individuals. As Dan waited for his opponent, he thought ' A lot of Hayee won't like what's going to happen her today '.

Ramala didn't tell Dan, but she already knew who Dan's first opponent was. She had a lot of cousins here. It couldn't happen that one of the Hellcats wouldn't find out who Dan would be fighting. Ramala was nervous, and anxious to for this to be over.

Once it seemed that every Hayee there was seated, one of the Hayee announced "We, the House of Hayee issue a challenge to the Heathen Dan. The fight will be one on one. If you manage to beat the first fighter, you will face two more of our top fighters. If you defeat all three, the contest is over." Ramala protested right away. She said "He was only to be challenged by one fighter! Now you say he has to face three! How is this fair!?" The announcer said "Whether you think it's fair or not, this is the way it's going to happen." Ramala stared at the announcer. He refused to look at her. If she was still living in the House of Hayee, no one would dare talk to her like that, except for Mashaya and Roe! Even though she knew he was following orders, she would deal with that announcer later. Ramala looked at Roe and Mashaya. They weren't going to help her. Tara stood up and put her hand on Ramala's shoulder, and gently pressed for her to sit down. Now Ramala was pissed off! The slightest sign of trouble and she was going to blast a scream that all of the Hayee would never forget.

Tara and Wana looked over at their cousin. Then they looked at each other. They thought that even if Dan won all three matches, Ramala might blast a scream just out of spite. They turned their attention to the crowd, then the exits, before looking at Dan, waiting to see him face his first opponent . The Butcher girls sat between the Hellcats and the Japha twins, with Ma between Cat and Syn, Jara. They tried to stay as relaxed as possible, while still on alert. Yin, Back, And Chi sat right in front of them. They knew there was going to be trouble. They knew it would be right after Dan finished off the last fighter, if he got that far.So, as Butchers, they were going to wait, then do what had to be done. After all, that's what they were here for.

Dan stood out there for about three minutes before his first opponent came out. Then his opponent walked on to the courtyard. Dan could see the family resemblance. He looked in the man's eyes. They both had immediate dislike for each other. The man was in excellent condition. Dan judged that he was in as good condition as Yin, and Yin was in excellent condition. Dan could see that this was going to be a good test for him, if this man had any skills at all.

The Hayee that Dan was facing, was the Hayee that was picked to be Ramala's mate. His name was the Hayee, Surick. Ramala had always liked Surick, but not as a mate. He was humiliated when Ramala chose a heathen over him. Now he was face to face with this heathen. He was going to give this heathen a real beating before he killed him. Ramala would see that no heathen could ever be as good as he. Surick walked towards Dan. No one had to tell these two when to get started. As soon as Surick got into striking distance of Dan, that's when the fight started. Surick threw the first blow that Dan moved out of the way of. Then a steady Rain of blows came from Surick. Dan could see that speed was a skill that the Hayee mastered. He blocked and moved out of the way of all of them. Then the moment Dan saw the chance to switch to offense, he did. He gave Surick a variety package of punches and kicks. Dan didn't connect with any of them. He could see that Surick had good defensive skills. The two men kept going at it without a pause in the action, until they both met with forearm blow intended to knock the other back. It was a test of strength to see if you could over power your opponent.

As both men took a couple of steps backwards to regroup from the contact. They knew they were evenly matched in strength. They both looked at each other for a second, letting the other know that it was going to take more than that to win this fight. Then they went at it again. They both knew what the next test would be. Who could take a good solid blow.

Of course neither of them wanted to take a solid blow, just to see if they could take it. The other would have to earn it. But Dan was a good chess player when it came to fighting. He let Surick earn the first blow earlier than he actually had. Just so he could see what he was dealing with. Also it allowed Dan to choose the blow he was going to take.

Surick's technique was tight. So when he did connect, it was a very solid shot. It shocked Dan's body. Surick had a lot of power. After seeing Dan's reaction to that blow. Surick knew if he could keep up the pressure, Dan wouldn't be able to take many more of those. But Surick hoped that Dan would at least be able to take enough of those blows, so he could get a slow punishing beating in on Dan. Surick never believed in giving up anything for free. He figured that if it takes longer to hit him, his opponent had to work harder before he himself took a blow. To him that meant that he wouldn't take his opponents best shot, while his opponent was his strongest. He would take the blow from an opponent later, if at all, after the opponent had wasted some energy fighting through his defense. By then, he might have gotten in a few more blow of his own.

Dan knew it wouldn't be that long before he got a good one in on Surick. Surick did manage to get the next blow in before Dan. But Dan followed with a two piece, that was followed by Surick's two piece, that ended up in an exchange of blows that totaled eight for both men. Now they both had taken some punishment from each other. Neither of them liked what had just happened to them. After they made eye contact for a split second, they attacked each other again. The action was fast and furious for another twenty minute, with both men taking some more punishment. They stopped for a second. Now it was a test of endurance. Who's technique could stay the tightest under fire.

They went at it again. This time it was almost a half hour. They both needed to regroup for defensive purposes. Dan didn't let it happen. He forced the action, which resulted in both men taking more blows. Dan was done with taking breaks and checking for damage. He wasn't going to stop until he was sure that this fight was over. He forced the action to where there was continuous heat on both fighters. Dan was going to see what Surick was really made of. They went on for another twenty-five minutes without a break.

The crowd was on the edge of their seats, knowing that something would give sooner, rather than later. Dan started with a three piece that turned into nine straight solid blows that sent Surick to the ground, unconscious. It was clear that this fight was over whether Dan walked over and finished Surick off or not. Dan didn't advance. He waited for the announcer to say the fight was over, or for Surick to wake up and get to his feet. He knew Surick couldn't recover for those blows. If Surick got up, he would take some serious punishment.

After the shots that Dan took from Surick earlier in the fight, it didn't matter to Dan if he got up, or not. But if he did, Dan was going to really punish him this time. Surick rolled over on his side trying to get up. He looked unsure of where he was. Men came out and helped him out of the courtyard. Dan stepped back and watched closely. He turned to see Ramala walking out on to the courtyard. Dan didn't need her out here at this time. But with her family surrounding him, he wasn't going to tell her that right now. She walked up to Dan, checking him for damage. Even though Dan had taken some good shots, he wasn't hurt. Ramala peeked at the crowd, then said "You gave him too much of a chance. Don't play around. Put the next ones down as quickly as possible. I'm ready to leave, and I know you are too. The sooner you get done, the sooner we leave."

Dan couldn't believe Ramala. Did she really think he was out here playing around? Maybe this was her way of motivating him. Dan said "Go sit down. I'll finish this as soon as possible." Ramala smiled and said "I know, but don't kill them unless you have to." Ramala was trying to give Dan as much rest time as possible. Then she rubbed her hand across his face gently. After her hand left his face, she quickly returned it with a backhand slap. Dan caught her wrist, just as her hand left his face. Then he remembered where he was. He let her go. She smiled and said "I'm still quicker than you." She turned and went back to her seat. Ramala knew the one thing that would get Dan's blood boiling was slapping him across the face. She was right. Dan still felt the sting of that slap as Ramala was returning to her seat. He was going to make her pay for that later. Right now, whoever was next was going to pay. He took a deep breath and calmed himself.

heat on him sobered him up. Now Dan could see that even though Opert was putting heat on him, Opert was trying to set Dan up for another powerful blow. It seemed that Opert was willing to take Dan's shots, patiently waiting to get another thunder blow in that he was sure would take it's toll on Dan. Dan had fought brutes before, but none this quick and none with this much endurance. This fight was into it's second hour. Dan was tiring a little, but not enough to affect his fighting. He was taking more chances, trying to put more on his shots so that they would start taking a toll on Opert. Dan had not used his feet on Opert because if O caught his leg that would be it for Dan.

In the middle of a stiff four piece combination, Dan got caught by another blow from Opert that he blocked but was still sent to the ground from the force of it. O was right on Dan again. This time when Dan tried to roll to get some distance O closed the gap and was right on Dan just as Dan was getting to his Knees trying to get up. Dan fought while on his knees but couldn't maneuver from that position to get out of the way of another one of O's blows that connected solidly. Dan went rolling in the dirt. This time he quickly got to his feet. Opert was right on top of him. This time Dan put a powerful five piece on O. It stopped O for about a second. That was the only opening that Dan had this whole fight, so he put his foot into O's mid section. O took one step back, then Dan put a powerful six piece on O that sent him to one Knee. Opert was open for the kill for a few seconds.

Dan had spent so much energy that he went down on one knee, taking in as much air as he could. Opert got up. So did Dan. They both were spent. They started up again. This time O wasn't as quick. Dan wasn't either, but he was quicker than Opert. He got more than a few good shot on Opert. It was hard for Opert to get out of the way of Dan's blows. Dan could see that O was done for, but refused to quit. Dan backed up from Opert. Then he went down on one knee, while keeping an eye on Big O. Dan said "We have pushed each other to our limits. This has been the greatest one on one battle I've ever been in. I admire your skills. I don't wish to continue fighting. Much respect to you and Your family." Opert stared at Dan. He knew he had been beaten by Dan, yet this man was on his knees giving him and his family praise. Opert looked over to his brothers and sisters. They knew he couldn't continue and win. They nodded that it was alright for him to end it. Opert looked at Dan again, then he walked out of the courtyard,

His second opponent came out. He was a brute like Back. He was almost twice the size of Dan. His father was one of the Warlords that Dan killed in the war. His name was the Hayee, Opertshepsky. They called him Opert, or Big O for short. He was about a year or two older than Dan. When he came out, he had fire in his eyes. Ramala was also familiar with Big O. She had practiced with him on many occasions. She was a little nervous because he was a very good fighter. Dan could see that although Opert was a huge brute, he looked to be in very good shape. His muscle were just as defined as Dan's. Dan knew he had to come up with an excellent strategy, or he was going to take a severe beating.

Just as the last fighter, Opert didn't waste time. He attacked Dan immediately. Dan was put on defense right away. Opert was dishing out some very powerful blows that had pretty good speed on them. Dan knew if he got caught with just one of those, he could be disoriented enough to be finished off. He wasn't use to dodging and running, but that's what this fight called for. So that's what he did. Sooner or later he would find an opening and punish Opert.

Finally Dan found that opening, and was able to get two solid blows in before he had to move out of the way of another one of Opert's powerful swings. Big O was unaffected by the shots. He kept up the heat on Dan. O knew that smaller fighters figured if they stayed out of his way, that he would tire. Opert worked hard on his endurance and could fight like this for hours. Dan had already fought for over an Hour with the Hayee, Surick. Now he was just past an hour with the Hayee, Opert. Dan was use to practicing for six to eight hours a day. Usually he would only go for two hours at a time. He could see that Big O wasn't tiring. Dan was getting two to three blows in here and there and still hadn't been hit by Opert.

Then right after a three piece, that Dan put everything that he had into, Dan got caught with a body shot that lifted him off of his feet, sending him backwards landing hard on to the ground. That shot shook his whole body. Dan didn't have time to regroup because Opert was in the air on his way to Dan. Dan rolled on the ground, just out of the way of a powerful forearm smash from Opert that sent dust flying from the ground.

After rolling, Dan quickly got to his feet. Even though he was roughed up by that shot, the intensity in which Opert kept the escorted by his family.

Dan stayed down on his knees. He didn't know how he was going to deal with another fighter. He took in as much air as possible, trying to regroup. Then to make matters worse, Ramala came running out to see if he was alright. This embarrassed Dan. When she got to him, Dan while trying to take in as much air into his lungs as possible, said "Please, don't slap me. That's not what I need. I'm having a rough enough time as it is." Ramala forced a smile onto her face for Dan. The she put a serious look on her face as she turned to the crowd and said "He's had enough for one day! Let him rest and he'll fight anyone tomorrow." She looked around the crowd. Then she saw Roe come out of the crowd. She smiled because Roe was coming to help her. Roe said "I'm his next opponent."

That shocked both Ramala and Dan. Dan stood up. He didn't want to fight Roe, the father of his Queen. Especially in the condition he was in. Ramala knew Dan didn't want her to beg for his life. She walked up to her father, looked him in his eyes, and said in a low voice that Dan couldn't hear "After you kill him, you're going to watch me end my life. Then decide if it was worth it to you."

Then she walked back to her seat. Roe looked at Ramala as she walked away. Then he turned slowly and stared at Dan. He knew he could kill Dan. Dan wasn't at full strength. Even if Dan went for a while, he wouldn't be able to go as long and as hard as Roe could. Dan readied himself.

Then Yin stood up and said "Let me fight in his place." That shocked everyone. Dan looked over at Yin. Dan said "This is not your fight. I'm not done yet."

Yin stood there for a moment, giving Dan another chance to let him fight in his place. When Yin saw that Dan wasn't moving, he sat down. Dan turned back to Roe and got down on one knee, then stood back up. Roe was staring at Dan, but he was wondering if Ramala was bluffing. Would she actually kill herself?

Roe looked at Ramala, then back at Dan. He knew he didn't want to see that happen, and have to live, remembering it. The question to him was did he hate Dan more than he loved his Daughter. Roe had been staring at Dan for a few minutes. Dan didn't know what Ramala said, but it seemed to be weighing heavily on Roes mind. Dan hoped she hadn't begged for his life.

He definitely wasn't going to do anything that would make this fight happen. He was going to wait until Roe attacked. Roe said "You are not welcome in the House of Hayee. Leave right away." Roe didn't have to tell Dan twice. Dan got down on one knee again and said "Thank you Father." Roe immediately said "I'm not your father, so don't call me that!"

Dan said "Right now, you're the only father I have living." That pissed Roe off. He turned and walked away. As he was walking out of the courtyard he looked at Ramala for a moment. He hated that she put him in such a position. Roe refused to look at Mashaya because he could feel the heat coming from her stare. She fully expected Roe to finish Dan off. He knew he would have to deal with her later.

The Royal court didn't waste any time getting out of the House of Hayee. They were back on the road a couple of hours after Roe told Dan to leave. Ramala went to see Roe right after he left the courtyard. She hugged her father and thanked him profusely. She promised him that she would be back to visit him, with his grand children. He didn't say it, but he hoped Dan wouldn't come with her.

Ramala also wanted to take two of her cousins with her. Mashaya gave her permission to take them. The first cousin's name was the Hayee, Tagowa. Tagowa liked to melt different metals and alloys together to see what he would get. He was a weapons maker. The elders at the House of Hayee didn't like him burning and melting metals. They just wanted him to make weapons the way they had been made always. Ramala liked that he was always trying to come up with something new. She figured that one day he might.

The second cousin's name was Hayee, Chuseechan. Chu is what they called him, or Chusee. He had two huge front teeth that pointed out towards you, and when he talked, saliva would spray out at you. His special skill was that he could repeat whatever he was told to the letter. So that made him a valuable messenger. The only thing was, no one wanted to receive any messages from him, for fear of being sprayed with saliva. The Hayee didn't have much use for him, so Mashaya didn't care if he went with the Hellcats.

When Chan and Tagowa got to the Royal Caravan they were introduced to the Butchers. Each of the Butchers found themselves jumping out of the way of a saliva spray, except for

Yin. Yin looked a dare to Chusee that if one drop of saliva got on him, Chusee would loose his head. Chu wasn't crazy. He kept his spray well away from Yin. He knew what kind of effect he had on people. Chu liked to have fun with it.

Yaya watched from behind Cat. She instantly decided that she didn't like Chusee. She wasn't going to take a chance on getting sprayed if she could help it. When the young twins saw those choppers that Chusee had, they didn't want any parts of him. Chusee looked at the twins and said "Hi! How are you two doing?" The twins watched in horror as a spray went shooting to the left of them. La looked up at her mother and said "Something's wrong with his mouth!"

Chu extended his hand to La. La didn't like being scared, so she let out a scream that made Ramala call her name to stop her. Dan just stood there by his mother. It took a lot to scare Dan. A tear rolled down his face. All he knew was that he didn't want to hit by whatever that was coming out of that man's mouth. He moved behind Ramala's leg and put on his best mean look. Ramala had enough of Chusee for now. She said "Don't try to scare my children again." Chusee said "You know I was just having fun." Ramala said "I know. Find your fun somewhere else. Don't have any more fun at the expense of my children. That I won't tolerate." She stared at Chusee and he got the message.

Ramala always liked Chu every since they were young children. She even had to keep her other cousins from beating him when he accidentally sprayed one of them with his saliva. He didn't go with Tito, Tim, and the other Hayee to the House of Ra earlier because he knew he would be harassed severely.

Now that the caravan was on it's way again, the Butchers could relax. They could see the mountains off in the distance. That's where the Houses of He, Tere, and Tat were. They would get to the female monastery before they got to the House of He. Dan was recovering from the bumps and bruises he took at the House of Hayee. They were nothing serious. Just a reminder that he would never be welcome there.

Today Dan was on the platform with Ramala, Yaya, and his children. Yaya was keeping the twins busy, while he and Ramala relaxed and watched them play. Yaya was getting good with her fighting skills, and was showing them off to the twins. The twins were trying to imitate the moves they saw Yaya doing. Yaya would try to correct the twins. That always tickled Ramala and Dan. La was having a good time jumping around.

La stopped and looked around. Then she looked at Ramala and said "Where's grandma?" Ramala said "She's at her home." La said "When's she coming?" Ramala said "She's not coming." La questioned "Why?" Ramala said "We have places to go that grandma doesn't want to. She's happy staying home." La's face lit up with enthusiasm, because she had just thought of a great idea. She said "Let's go see grandma!" Ramala said "I told you, we have places to go. We'll go see grandma another time." La said "Why?" Ramala said "Because I said so."

La didn't understand why they couldn't go now. She wanted her mother to know how much she really wanted to see grandma. La stared at Ramala, stomped one foot then the other, and said in a serious tone. "I wanna go see grandma now!"

Dan was sitting next to Ramala. It tickled him when La got defiant with Ramala. He knew Ramala wasn't going to put up with that. Yaya had only slightly been paying attention to what La was talking about. When she heard the tone in La's voice, she turned to see what was going to happen next. Yaya knew she could never get defiant with her Queen mother. She knew nobody could get away with defying her Queen mother. Not even Little La. Yaya watched and waited to see what would happen next.

Every since La started putting sentences together, Ramala found that half of them she didn't care for. This was one of them. She gave La a serious stare. It instantly shocked La. La knew she was in trouble, but didn't know why. Ramala ordered her "Come here!"

La put on her best, let's forget about what I did and let's just be happy smile for her mother. Ramala said "NOW!" La jumped, and her feet started moving towards her mother before she thought about it. She looked at her father. Dan had been watching her. He knew Ramala was angry. He said jokingly "Take it easy on her."

That annoyed Ramala even more. She kept her stare on La. Just as La reached her, she bent down, not breaking her stare, and said "He can't help you when it comes to me." She grabbed La by her ponytail and lifted her by her hair, until La was on the tips of her toes. Then Ramala let go of the ponytail, and grabbed La by both of her shoulders and tightened her grip to where it was very uncomfortable for La. Ramala continued with "Don't ever stomp your feet at me again. And never look at me with angry eyes. Next time I won't be so nice. When I say we have to something to do, that's what we are going to do. Once I tell you, don't question me. And you don't say I wanna. You say I want to. Always remember, Mother knows what's best. Now you stand right here for a moment and don't move, so that I know you understand me. Mommy will let you know when you can move." Dan said "She understands now. Let the girl go play."

La looked over at Dan with a glimmer of hope in her eyes. Then Ramala told La "Don't move!" La stood there at attention. She put on her I'm going to do what you say, but I'm frustrated face. Ramala stared at her, then she straightened up her face. Ramala only made her stand there for a minute or two, at the most, then she let her go back to playing. To La it seemed like an eternity. She didn't understand why her mother had to get so stern. She just wanted to go see her grandma.

Yin rode on a platform with Backir, and Ma. He needed something to think about, other than his nightmare. He focused on Dan's battles. Back at the House of Hayee was the first time he got to see how good Dan really was. Now Yin knew why Ma always picked fights with Dan. He could see that Dan was good enough to deal with Ma without killing her. Yin couldn't help what went through his mind next. He wondered who was the better killer between him and Dan. He was sure he could beat Dan, if it came down to it. Yin knew the only way to find that out. Only a fight to the death could tell who the better killer really was. Ma rolled over close to Yin and said "What are you thinking about?"

That snapped Yin back into reality. Yin said "What's the next House we're going to?" Ma said "I think It's the House of He." Backir said "Yeah, that's it. The House of He. I wonder what He's like?" Yin said "I guess we'll find out." Ma said "At least we don't have any enemies there." Backir said "None that we know of."

Now that the Royal Caravan had passed two of the seven Houses, the other five Houses were aware that the Hellcats were away from the safety of their palace. There wouldn't be a better time to ambush the Hellcats and put things back in order. The Tere and the Tat wanted nothing to do with this plan. The He wanted to wait and see what the House of Japha would do.

Once the so called Royal Caravan dropped off the Japha twins, they were going to be dealt with by the Japha from the north, and the Hoo and He to their south. The plan was kept secret between the three Houses. The Houses of He and Hoo were to treat the Royal Caravan with respect. That was the only way to keep the Hellcats from realizing something was up, and sending for help from Han back in Yee province. If they could catch the Hellcats right after they left the House of Japha, there would be no way the Hellcats could get word to Han. Even if they did, they would be dead before help could arrive.

Ma and Cat had many memories from the all female Monastery run by the elder females from the House of He. It was a very strict and disciplined life being a nun. Cat had spent more than half of her life there. She was sent there by her mother, who thought Cat needed more structure in her life. Ma spent eight years there after her parents died. That's where Ma and Cat met. They liked each other right off, and became very close.

Yin lived outside the Monastery with a uncle that wasn't related by blood. That's where he learned fighting skills to add to the ones his mother taught him. Ma would go see Yin every chance she got and teach him what she learned. Ma made sure that Yin kept up his practices by putting a severe beating on him if she could. That kept Yin at least good enough to not get beat up by his sister.

When a messenger came and gave Cat word about Chi's parents, the elder nuns wouldn't give Cat permission to leave. So Cat, along with her best friend Ma, and Ma's twin brother Yin, decided to go anyway. That was the last time the two girls saw the Monastery. They told this story to Syn, Jara as the Royal Caravan approached the Monastery.

Since the Monastery was very strict about not letting men enter, the Japha, Jan and the Hayee, Ramala decided that they would respect the nuns, and make this a very short visit. One compromise they wouldn't make was on weapons. They weren't going in there unarmed. It was the Hellcats, the Butcher girls, Yaya, Japha, Jan and her girls. They were met by ten elder nuns, who gave them a tour of the grounds.

All of the nuns and the nuns in training were brought out to pay their respects. Yaya saw her cousins. Again she had to act like she didn't know them. China and all of her cousins were there. China and her cousins were a little older, and now had three years of training under their belts. They were working hard, but they had a ways to go. This was the first time they got to see the people who killed their family.

China looked at her cousins, letting them know to memorize these faces. These were the faces that they were going to take their revenge on. Then China took a look at Yaya. Yaya was dressed in fine clothes. China could see that the people she was with accepted her as one of their own. China knew Yaya wouldn't forget where she came from, and when the time was right, she knew her cousin would help in any way she could.

It didn't go unnoticed to the Hellcats that, just as in Yee province, that some of the young girls at the Monastery looked a lot like Yaya. Tara and Wana again told Ramala that something had to be done about Yaya, before she got old enough to create trouble within the House of Ra.

Wana reminded Ramala that Yaya already knew most of the layout of the House of Ra. She could easily help an enemy find all of the important security areas. Wana wanted to have Yaya eliminated right away. Ramala said "Right now we know where the rebel children are. Wana you have your spies keep an eye on them. Let me deal with Ya. I'll let you know when it's time to eliminate her. Until then, we'll be careful to limit her access to a minimum. Our advantage is that they don't know we know about them. If they join up with other rebels, Wa's spies will know who they are."

Wana said "She has already become close to your twins. How much longer are you going to let that go on?" Ramala said "Until I'm ready to stop it." Wana said "I'm just saying."

Tara didn't say anything. Both her and Wana thought that Ramala had become attached to this heathen girl. They looked at each other for a quick second, and they both thought that maybe they could find a way for this young girl to have an accident, or an on purpose, without Ramala finding out.

The Royal caravan moved closer to the base of the mountains where the House of He was. Now the mountains were towering over the skyline. They could see that the House of He was very large. The Royal caravan was met by messengers. Terms of entry were worked out, just as they had been at the other Houses. The Japha twins insisted that their personal body guards, the Butchers, and the Hellcats be allowed to carry their weapons in order to protect their Queen and King of the Northern Houses. The other guards would stay with the Royal caravan. The elders of He begrudgingly agreed.

The He were gracious host. They treated their new King

and Queen very well. Even the Butchers were treated well. They didn't get the dirty, or suspicious locks they got at the House of Hayee. The He were very careful not to give the Hellcats any reason to be suspicious.

The stay at the House of He was short. The Japha, Jan asked the He elders to give them guides to lead them to the House of Tere, which was a little ways up the mountain. As the Royal caravan started up the mountain, they found that the elephants were having a tough time adjusting to the rocky terrain. Also the further they got up the mountain, the colder it got.

Even though they all put on extra clothes, they found it hard to adjust to the change in temperature. When they finally reached the House of Tere, they could see that it was mostly on a flat plain on the side of the mountain. When they entered the House of Tere, they saw many big fires going. The heat from the fires warmed the air. They also found that fires inside of the buildings kept them somewhat warm.

The Hellcats, the Japha twins, and the Butchers didn't like this place at all. They couldn't figure out why someone would want to live in such adverse conditions. Not much vegetation grew here. The Tere had to get most of their goods through trade. That's why they didn't want the war to go on for long. The only advantage of living here was that your enemies could only come from one direction.

The Tere were also known for their intelligence. They were very scholarly. They studied nature and natural science. The Tere elders studied the new King and Queen very closely. When they weren't studying the Japha twins, they watched the Hellcats and the Butchers very closely. This made the Hellcats a little nervous. Wana and Tara made mental pictures of the buildings that they visited. If they were going to be studied, they were going to make sure they studied their surroundings as well. After the first night at the House of Tere, the Japha twins and the Hellcats had a private meeting amongst themselves.

The Japha, Jan looked at her brother, then at Ramala. Jan had concern on her face when she said "I can't take much more of this cold weather." She paused, then continued with aggravation in her voice "We still haven't been to the House of Tat, which is even further up the mountain. It has to be even colder there. I don't know about the rest of you, but I'm sick tired of this cold weather already!"

Japha, San looked at his sister. He could see that she really didn't want to go any further up the mountain. He said "We should send for the elders of Tat to meet us here. Surely they would respect the request of their King and Queen." Japha, Jan's face lit up. She liked San's idea. She said "I agree!"

Then Jan looked at Hayee, Ramala and said "What do you think? Should we go up the mountain just to make a formal visit?" Ramala Looked at Tara, then at Wana. All three of them were in agreement. They didn't see why they should suffer going any further up the mountain. Ramala said "I'm with you all the way. I don't want to go any further than we have to. It would be a sign of respect to their King and Queen if they honored your request." Jan smiled at Ramala and said "That settles it then!" San said "I'll go talk to the Tere elders and make the request that they send a messenger with our wishes." Jan nodded in approval, then San left. Jan looked at Ramala, then said "I'm not built for cold weather. Once we leave, I don't care to ever come back here again!"

Messengers came back with news that the elders of the House of Tat would send representatives to meet with the new rulers. They arrived a day after the messenger returned. There were six of them, accompanied by their servants. Dan, Backir, and Yin were the first to see the Tat elders. Although they didn't care for the cold that much, the three Butcher men weren't as bad as the women from the Royal Court. In fact, they were more than a little fascinated seeing snow for the first time.

Snow was falling for the first time that they had been on the mountain. The three Butchers were outside staring in amazement, like children, at the snow. Neither of them said a word to each other. They just watched. They were outside when the Tat elders arrived. They turned their attention to the Tat.

All of the Tat elders had long white hair. It was almost as white as the snow, but not as bright. The Butchers also noticed that even though these men had on heavy clothes, and they looked in decent shape, they didn't seem to have the build of fighters. As the Tat walked up and were introduced to the Butchers, the Butchers could see that the cold didn't seem to affect these men. The Butchers tried to look like they weren't affected by the cold either.

All of a sudden, all three Butcher girls came running outside. Ma was beside herself with excitement. She yelled to Yin "Yin look! Fluffy petal are floating, and falling from the sky! It looks so beautiful!" All of the Butchers were letting the snow hit their hands and faces. They watched in amazement when the snow flakes melted into water after hitting their hands.

Cat tasted the liquid on her hand. She said "Its water! So this is what rain turns to when it gets cold. Fluffy petals!" Cat and Syn, Jara were standing there trying to look at the snow, and the Tat at the same time. One of the elder Tats said "Fluffy petals. That's the first time I've heard it called that. It is special seeing the snow for the first time. Its frozen rain, but we call it snow. Sometimes it still amazes me."

All of the Butchers found themselves absorbed in what this man was saying. They lost focus on their surroundings while he was talking. Syn noticed something wasn't quite right. She always kept focus on her surroundings. But now it seemed that her mind was telling her to focus only on the man, and what he was saying. She knew she would never tell herself that, in any situation, let alone with someone she just met.

Syn looked at the rest of the Butchers. She could see that they were as focused on the old man as she was, before her internal warning system told her that this was not her thought, even though it was in her head. She looked at the other elders that weren't talking. Syn knew that one of them somehow put thoughts in her head. Syn, Jara didn't know how to deal with that, so she said in a firm voice "Cat, Ma, Dan, Yin, and Backir! Don't be rude. Come with me, so that we may tell The Royal Court of the arrival of the House of Tat. Let us go now!"

The Butcher men heard Syn, but stayed focused on the man. Cat and Ma both looked at Syn. They realized that what she had said was code for time to go, now. Ma called to Yin "Yin! Time to go!" That got Yin and the other male Butcher's attention. They looked at Syn, Cat, and then Ma. They knew it was time to go. They all got down on one knee and then left. As the Butchers followed Syn, Cat asked "What's wrong?" Syn looked around and at some of the Tere guards that they passed and said "I'll explain later."

When Syn got to Jan's room, she saw that the Hellcats were already there. Syn didn't waste time explaining how she was affected and what she observed of the Butchers when they were affected. She said that she was sure that the men were putting thoughts in their heads. Syn said "I couldn't tell the difference from my minds voice and the voice making suggestions to me."

Yin blurted out "That's impossible! I would know if someone besides me was in my head. They might have got you, but they sure didn't get me." Syn said "What did I say before Ma called your name?" Yin started to say something, but couldn't remember. Syn said "You can't remember what I said, can you? I bet you can remember what the Tat said."

Everyone looked at Yin for a response. Yin wasn't going to say it but he could remember what the Tat had said. Even though Yin didn't think so, everyone in the room could see on his face that he did remember. Dan thought for a moment about what had happened, then he said "Syn might be right." Ma and Cat thought about it and said at the same time "She is right!"

Tara said "Then we have to think of a way that we can know that our thoughts are our own." Wana said "Until we figure that out, we have to make a plan of what we are going to say to the Tat. We stick to that plan, that way, everyone will know if something is out of place. Even if they trick all of us, we will realize that the plan has changed. That will alert us that something is wrong. At that point, we leave and discuss what happened in private."

San said "That was pretty good! How'd you think of that?" The Hayee, Wana smiled at San and said "I think of the best solutions to problems. That's what I do!" Tara said "Wana, don't get overconfident! "Wana said "I'm not. I'm just saying!"

The Tat elders noticed that the girl called Syn, Jara released herself from their mental grip. They could have turned their mental focus up a notch to see what it would take to control her, but they didn't. They didn't want anything to do with their new King and Queen, or the House of Ra, more than just a formal visit. The Tat elders used a form of suggestive thought. They could put thoughts into your mind and suggest things. As long as the suggestions weren't so much out of the normal way of thinking, most people considered the thoughts to be their own. If the Tat elders would have known that something would have triggered that girl's defense, they never would have tested the Butchers like that.

The Tat elders were taken to a meeting hall where the King and Queen of the Northern Houses waited on them. Everyone greeted each other, and was introduced. The elders studied Ramala just and much as they studied the Japha twins. They could feel a strong presence from this girl. They entered her mind to see what they could find out about this girl who had carved out her own territory and made an alliance with the Japha children.

Ramala was watching the meeting closely. At all of the Houses, except the House of Hayee, Ramala would sit back and let the Japha twins take the lead. She would pay close attention, then give Japha, Jan any insights she had, when they met later in private. This time was no different, but she found herself thinking of things about herself. She thought about her upbringing, her children, Dan and how they met.

Ramala was very disciplined in her thoughts. She could focus on the task at hand. Thinking about other things, while in an important meeting, let her know that someone was running through her memories. She used all of her focusing powers to concentrate, but found herself thinking about her past. She looked at the elders of Tat, one at a time. Ramala started to get up out of her seat. Then she heard a voice in her head that said "Don't make trouble. We mean you no harm."

Ramala spoke in thought to the voice in her head. She said "Get out of my head right now or there's going to more trouble than you can handle!" The voice said "We respect you, but you are not in a good position to give us trouble. We have tested your top guards. We know we can get the Yin and Backir, as well as the Catismalianne and Mamiaa to do whatever we will them to do. If we decided to make them fight you right now, all you would be able to do is kill them. And that would only be after an intense battle in which one of your beloved cousins might end up dead. Like we said before, we mean you no harm. Your destiny is in the open plains, not in the mountains."

Ramala thought "If you can read my mind, you know I hate this cold weather and have no intentions of ever coming back here." The voice in her head said "Right now you have no intentions of coming back here, but this conversation we are having now will convince you that it's not in your best interest to send armies here later. Right now we are having a similar conversation with Japha San and Jania."

Ramala, Jan, and San all quickly looked at each other. The voice inside Hayee, Ramala's head continued with "Entering your minds is just one of our skills. Just like your soul splitting scream, we have mind skills that are just as dangerous. If we used them on you, you would be dead before you could scream." Before Ramala could stop her thoughts, she thought "Then why don't you stop us now, while you have us here?"

The voice said "If we killed you now, things would get much worse than they will get. Someone would take your place that would do more harm than you can imagine. You are necessary. Now go and remember that this mountain is off limits to your armies. And know that if you do send them, they won't succeed, and we will be force to come and deal with all of you personally."

The elders of Tat smiled at Ramala. They could see and feel that she was very offended by what had just happened. They also knew that she was too smart to risk trying something. They also knew that Ramala thought that she would one day come and impose her will up in the mountains. But the elders knew what Ramala didn't know, and couldn't tell her. That she didn't have as much destiny as she thought she had, and she would never make it back to the mountains.

After the meeting the Royal Court left as quickly as possible, and made their way down the mountain. They didn't do much talking, and tried not to think until they were off the mountain. Once they got off the mountain, they discussed the mind controlling very little. Everyone was thankful that they didn't have to deal with the cold anymore.

One thing the Japha twins and the Hellcats did decide was, they wanted to know if any of the Tat came down off the mountain. They would keep spies in the area to let them know if that happened. The Tat were not a threat, as long as they stayed up on the mountain. The moment they came down from the mountain, the Hellcats would deal with them, from a safe distance.

Both times that the Syn, Jara fought the Hayee, Ramala she wasn't fighting to kill her. Syn was fighting to beat her. The first time was relatively easy, once Syn got serious. The second time Syn, Jara had to do her best, without trying to kill Ramala. She knew, just like Ramala knew, if they had kept going Syn would have caught Ramala with something.

Syn laid back on the open platform, enjoying the warmth of the sun that she had missed so much, while on the mountain. It was hard to believe that Hayee, Ramala could get that much better in just four years. She spent time off from practicing while having the twins. Yet she was still able to raise her skill level to almost match Syn.

Syn could see that Ramala was using her to get the best fight possible from someone better than her, without being killed, just like Ma was doing with Dan, when she got the chance. It didn't bother Syn that Ramala was getting better. What bothered Syn was that Ramala had shortened the gap between their skill levels. Syn knew she was still much better than Ramala. She just knew she had to practice harder because Ramala was going to get better. Ramala had already proven that she could beat the other Butcher girls easily. She was going to keep trying Syn until she could beat her. Syn laid there thinking that there is no way Ramala is going to beat me! If that means taking her down, so be it. Nobody beats the Syn, Jara!

Chapter 11

The Royal Caravan traveled two days before the guards on the towers of the military elephants saw the House of Hoo. They alerted Wana, who sent messengers telling the Hoo that the Royal caravan would be arriving. The Hoo sent a messenger back telling the Royal Caravan that the Butchers and the House of Ra was not welcome. That the Japha twins should head north to the House of Japha and not get involved in anymore of the nonsense that the House of Ra had forced on them.

This reaction from the Hoo was a surprise to the Japha twins, but not to the Hellcats. The Hellcats knew that they had only defeated armies from the Houses of Hayee and Japha. The Hellcats expected that if there was any opposition to the Japha twins and the House of Ra. It would be from the Houses that hadn't fought them yet. Still the Hellcats didn't know if the House of Japha was going to be involved in what now was starting to look like an ambush of the Royal Caravan.

Wana immediately started formulating a plan for war. She had the elephants with the military towers on them move, one to the south of the caravan, and the other towards the House of Hoo. Wana sent guard patrols north of the caravan to scout for trouble.

The Japha, Jan sent a messenger telling the Hoo that they were making a big mistake disrespecting their King and Queen of the Northern Houses. That they should reconsider their position and let the Royal Caravan enter the House of Hoo. Before they got a response, the guards from the military tower positioned south of the caravan sent word to Wana that a large army was headed towards the caravan from the south. They were a ways away, but they would be there soon.

Then to make matters worse, the patrols north of the caravan detected an army coming from that direction. Most of them riding on elephants. They immediately reported that to Wana. Wana summoned the other Hellcats, along with the Japha twins, and the Butchers. This was a military emergency, so Wana took the lead.

Ramala and Tara knew how serious the situation was, so they waited to here what Wana would come up with. Wana had a very serious look on her face. She said "We don't have a lot of time, so I'm going to get right to the point. I guess they decided that they weren't going to let us march through the north. We have the Japha coming from the north and a large army coming from the south. There's no telling how many Houses are coming up here from the south. And I can guarantee that the House of Hoo won't stay neutral. Here's what I need to happen. The largest force will be coming from the south. Yin, Dan, and Backir, I need you to take five phants and their guards along with fifteen guards and hold the southern perimeter. This is a tough task even for two warlords and the King from the Hose of Ra. Do whatever you have to, that not one guard makes it past you."

Yin's eyes lit up with excitement and a crazy grin came on his face. Wana turned to the Japha twins and said "Japha, San and Jan, being surrounded, your help is greatly needed." Jan said "Hayee, Wana you know you have our help in any way we can. But since we are the King and Queen of the Northern Houses, we have a suggestion. I, San, and my girls can lead the forces to hold off my family."

Wana thought that that could be dangerous if the Japha twins refused to fight certain members of their own family. They could be over run, and that would be big trouble for the caravan. Jan could see that Wana was hesitant. Jan said "If we face my family. They will have to decide whether to fight me, to get to the Royal Caravan. Whatever they decide, we're not going to let them move south on this position. We'll kill whoever opposes their King and Queen. Besides, if anyone other than me and San start killing Japha. Being this far north with this small a force, I can almost guarantee you would never make it back to the House of Ra. If I can get the Japha under control, we will be able to concentrate on the other threats."

It was a long shot, but Wana figured it might be worth it. At least, it would give them time to come up with more strategies. Wana said "That's a great idea! We can send seven phants to protect your back, along with thirty guards." Wana waited on a response. Jan said "We appreciate all the backup." Wana said "The Butcher girls are going to help me and my cousins fight our way to the House of Hoo, so we can convince them to end this nonsense right away." San asked "How are you going to do that?" Tara smiled at San and said "Desperate times call for extreme measures." San said "I guess that means the Hoo are going to have one hell of a fight on their hands."

Wana looked at Tara, smiled, then looked back at San and said "They started it. We'll do what we have to. To hell with them all!" Ramala looked at Wana and said "Wa! Stay in control! "Wana said "I am in control! I'm just saying!"

It was a quick preparation for departure for everyone. Wana told Ramala that she was going to leave most of the guards to protect Ramala's twins. If things got really bad, the twins would be escorted to the last man back to the House of Hayee. Ramala knew she couldn't let that happen, because that would mean that her and her cousins were dead. She spent very little time with Dan before he left. She walked in on him getting ready, looked Dan in the eyes and said "You're my King. It's time for you to protect our family. I'm counting on you to hold our southern position."

Dan was already just about in serious killing mode. He said "You can count on that." They kissed briefly, then Ramala went to see her twins. When she got there, Yaya was with them, along with some elite guards and the maidens. Wana had already given the guards orders to protect the twins from everyone, including Yaya.

The guards were ordered not to be rough with Yaya, or even stop her from interacting with the twins. They didn't let Yaya know it, but the guards had orders from Wana to kill Yaya if she made one false move towards the young twins. Of course Wana didn't tell Ramala, even though Ramala wouldn't have objected in this situation.

Ramala walked towards Yaya, as her twins grabbed at her legs. She gave Yaya a serious look and said "Very shortly, we are going to be under attack. Things might get rough for a while. You'll have to stay alert and don't panic. Dan and La need to see you calm and in control while I'm gone. Remember, I'm counting on you." Ramala smiled at Yaya, then bent down and said to her twins "Mommy has to leave for a while. Listen to big sister Ya, and do what she tells you. I'll see you later."

Ramala gave both of them a big hug, then stood up

quickly, and told Yaya "I'm going now. Get them." Ramala turned to go just as Yaya grabbed both of the twins and distracted them by wrestling with them. Yaya noticed that the guards were very close to her and the twins. She didn't think it strange that the guards watched her so closely. She knew the situation was serious because everyone was in war mode. Yaya looked briefly at the guards and thought things must really be bad if the guards have to watch as closely as they were.

Everyone got prepared as quickly as possible. Nina and Mia checked Jan's weapons, as well as their own. This was what they were troubled about when Jan decided to run with the Hellcats. Jan getting caught up in warfare. Now wasn't the time to think about that. They didn't want to fight the Japha. They held on to a slim thread of hope that something would be worked out. If not, whoever Jan would be fighting, that's who they would be fighting. Even if that meant fighting the Japha.

Once The Japha twins were ready, they met up with the Hellcats and the Butchers. Jan said "We had better be leaving right away." Ramala said "Right." Then all of the girls hugged each other. All of the men were too serious for that kind of stuff right now. They knew they would have to be at their best for this battle. They just looked around at everyone there, and for a split second, allowed themselves to hope that they would see everyone alive again. They all left with their designated group.

Dan, Yin, and Backir quickly got to the elephant that they were riding on. They hadn't said a word until they got aboard the platform. There wasn't much to talk about. They had to drive back an army with not a lot of help. Now they needed a plan. Backir asked "We need a good plan. Who's got one?"

No one answered right away. These three weren't the best planning type. They were the get it done ones. Someone makes a plan, Then these three got it done. Dan suggested "We spread the phants out, as well as the guards. Us three should fight together from the center of our forces."

Yin and Backir looked at Dan like they weren't completely convinced that that was the best plan. Dan looked at Backir and asked "You got a better plan?" Backir didn't. But still, He offered up his best. He said "We could fight, one of us on one end of the guards, one in the middle, and the other, on the far end." Back looked at Dan, then at Yin. Back said "What do you think?"

Yin looked out at the trees and shrubs ahead of them and

said "If we fight with the guards, who's gonna do clean up if some guards get past the battle line. I like Back's plan, but each one of us should go ahead of the main forces to fight. Let the guards and the phants do clean up." Yin slowly turned and looked at Back, then at Dan. Yin looked at Dan, waiting on a response. Dan knew Yin was testing to see who would back down from his plan. Dan certainly wasn't going to. He said "We can go with that. One of us on one end, one in the middle, and the other, one on the other end. Out ahead of our main forces." Backir said "Then it's settled. That's the plan."

Just then they heard the low pounding of war drums. Yin smiled and said "Now we get to see some real action. I'm going to run through their guards and kill more warlords than either of you two." That caught both Dan's and Backir's attention. They both turned and looked at Yin. Backir said "We'll see about that." Dan just nodded his head up and down. He definitely was up for that challenge. The Butcher men set up the plan with the guards. Then they set out in separate directions. Dan was on one end, Backir was in the middle, Yin was on the other end. All three men started trotting at a steady pace towards the enemy.

This was the first time that Dan was going to face a good number of guards by himself. He wasn't afraid. His Hammer-axes had always served him well. They were strapped to his back . He also had two machetes on his waist. The same as the other two Butchers. All he knew was that he wasn't just going to kill every guard in front of him. He was going to go beyond a massacre. He was going to butcher. He was going to put these men in the Hell of being cut to pieces. He thought it a shame that the other Butchers couldn't witness what was about to happen. Dan wished someone could be here to enjoy the show he was going to put on. He jogged toward the sound of the drum beat until he finally saw what he was facing . He stopped jogging and started walking toward them. It was go time, and he would get to the enemy soon enough.

Backir headed to the front in the middle. He knew that Dan and Yin thought that one of them was going to kill the most warlords. They were going to be in for a rude awakening. He was Backir. It was time for everyone to know who the biggest and the strongest Butcher was. Time for me to step up to the level of top Butcher. Backir finally saw the enemy. He was going to find out what he was made of.

Yin was on the other end. He didn't know how many Warlords Dan was capable of killing. He wasn't that calculating. Yin's plan was to kill whatever guards were in his way, on his way to the warlords. Killing a lot of guards couldn't match killing a bunch of warlords. That's how Yin planned to win the contest. Yin hadn't thought about his nightmare one time since they left the Royal caravan. When he was out in the field, he was in hunting mode. Yin was very good at focusing on killing. He was hunting for Warlords. Then Yin came up on the enemy. He was ready. It was time to start the head collecting.

Dan saw a eight lavishly styled plat formed elephants with men on them. They were just ahead of a sea of warriors. The elephants started towards Dan, while the warriors stood back. Dan had just run into the army that was going to surround the Royal caravan on his side. As the elephants moved closer to Dan. He knew he would be facing warlords right away. The warlords were closing in on Dan. They jumped from the elephants to the ground.

Warlords always looked like they meant business. Now they were close enough for Dan to see their faces, and their weapons. It seemed that the warlords weren't going to try to wear him down with guards this time. They came to take care of this themselves.

Dan knew this was going to be a legendary battle. He wasn't going to be beaten, and he could see in the eyes of the eight Warlords that they thought they couldn't be beaten by one heathen. Dan took in as much information about his enemy as quickly as possible, while he had the chance. He could see that four warlords used Hammer-axes, two had machetes, and two had heavy long poles with spear blades on the ends. The warlords stopped a safe distance from Dan.

All of the Warlords were offended that the House of Ra thought that one Butcher could stop eight warlords. One of the Warlords said "They send one Butcher." Dan stopped were he was. He wasn't here to be questioned. The Warlord asked "Which Butcher are You?"

Dan would answer this question. He said "I'm top Butcher, King of the House of Ra, Dan the Destroyer." Another one of the Warlords said in a slow drawl "We heard that the top Butcher was the Syn, Jara. Doesn't matter Butcher Dan Destroyer. Heathen King to that Hayee, Ramala. We are going to gut you, take your body back and chop off your head in front of the other Butchers. Then we're going to throw your head at your Queen and your degenerate children, before we kill all of them."

Dan stared at the Warlords. He couldn't believe what he just heard. They had to go and make this fight personal. Dan asked "And who are you?" That same Warlord said "We are children of the House of He..." Before the Warlord could continue, Dan interrupted with "That's enough for me to tell your family that I cut you to pieces, before I kill all of them."

The Warlord stared at Dan with hatred in his eyes. Now it was personal on both sides. Another Warlord said "Enough talk. Kill him!" Dan grabbed his Hammer-axes. The Warlords all pulled their weapons and started towards Dan. Dan looked closely at the position of the Warlords. They all were coming together. It was starting to look to Dan that he was going to have to fight all of them at once. They moved in and the four Warlords with the Hammer-axes attacked.

Dan was immediately put on defense. He had to keep an eye on the long pole spearmen, and the machete Warlords, because they had already started getting in to position where if Dan made one mistake, they could make him pay for it with his life. This was nowhere near a fair fight. They had no intentions on giving Dan the slightest chance to live. They had heard about all of the battles that the Butchers had and still were alive. The Butcher's names were known to everyone. To kill one of them would make you a legend.

Dan found that he had to use every defensive skill he had. He even had to pull some new moves out of his ass. The Hammer-axes were right on him. Dan found himself under a constant barrage of swings. He was swinging and twisting his axes as fast he could to block as much as he could, while ducking and dodging the rest.

Every time he thought he had room to make an offensive move, he found that he needed that opportunity to maneuver to a better defensive position to see everything going on around him. Dan decided that defense was his best move for now. The Warlords were impressed that they hadn't killed Dan yet. More than a half hour had passed since the fight started. One thing they were sure of was that Dan couldn't keep going on like this for much longer, not with this kind of pressure on him.

Backir wasn't doing much better. He had six He Warlords giving him pure hell. Backir had managed not to get hit by using good defense and forcing the Warlords to respect the powerful swings from his Hammer-axes. He was already slowly retreating towards the Royal Caravan. He thought for a split second, how stupid Yin's plan was. He couldn't believe he went along with it. Back couldn't think about that. Right now he had to concentrate. He was in a dog fight, and he needed help.

Yin only had four He Warlords to deal with. He wasn't losing, but he wasn't winning either. Yin fought like a madman. The Axes of his Hammer-Axe came at you from every direction that his arm could throw them. Yin's Axe play, you had to respect it. His defense was get out of the way, if he couldn't block it with his Hammer.

Even though there were four Warlords. They had to be careful. They were dealing with a wild animal that didn't want to be put down. The four warlords used Hammer-Axes. They had been putting heat on Yin for almost an hour. It surprised the Warlords that he could withstand the pounding of blocking thirty and forty pound Hammer-Axes. This was a great challenge for them to see how much longer Yin would last under their pressure. They moved in on Yin, trying to surround him. Yin wasn't having that. He attacked the Warlord trying to move behind him on his left side. The other Warlords moved in and started swinging at Yin. Yin blocked and threw his Axes, as far as his arms would allow, before he had to block more swings from Hammers or Axes. Yin was instantly angry with Dan and Backir. They were smarter than him. He couldn't figure out why they would follow a plan that he made up!

Dan Was two seconds from being in the Hell of being cut to pieces. It had been more than an hour and he had already taken a shot from one of the Hammers and half his shirt was ripped to shreds from close calls with the bladed long poles. Dan realized that in the whole time he had been fighting, he had not made one offensive move.

Right now all Dan needed was one chance. Then it came. Dan's feet took off running. Dan hadn't run since he was a young boy. His legs hadn't forgotten how. He took off so fast that it not only surprised him, it also surprised the Warlords. They knew none of them could move that fast. The Warlord with the slow drawl said "Look at how fast Top Butcher Dan Destroyer, heathen King of the House of Ra runs. "The Warlords chuckled a bit at what the man said, and what had just happened. They motioned for their elephants to be brought forward. They were going to ride in comfort until the caught up with the Butchers.

Now Dan was a good ways away from the Warlords. He was pissed that he had to run. He told his legs to stop running. They kept going for a little while longer, just for good measure, before he could stop them. He slowed to a walk, turning to see how big his lead was. He was more than a little embarrassed about the running. He told himself that the only reason he did it was to regroup and get help to protect his family.

Dan was glad that none of the Butchers were here to see that. He made his way towards Backir. Dan's plan was to see how Backir and Yin were doing in their battles. If Dan could help them defeat their opponents. Then he could get some help with the eight He Warlords he faced earlier. Dan wanted to kill them one by one. He'd even take on two or three. Just not eight at a one time. Dan knew one day he would be able to take on eight Warlords at once. One thing was for sure, he wasn't done with them yet!

Dan made it just in time to where Backir was fighting. The Warlords saw Dan coming up fast and two of them turned to meet him. Dan went at them hard. He knew they couldn't waste much time on these Warlords if they wanted to reach Yin before the Warlords he was fighting got the best of him. Also they had to finish these Warlords off before the eight that Dan had faced earlier caught up to them.

Backir was thankful for the help and turned his offense up a notch. This battle went a lot easier for both Butchers. Dan and Backir had just finished off the last Warlord when they saw the eight that Dan had faced approaching. Backir turned towards them, and was about to head towards them when Dan said "Wait! Let's go see if Yin needs our help." Backir turned back to Dan and said "Right!" They both took off, jogging at a fast pace.

Backir wondered how Dan knew he needed help. Backir sad "How did you get here so fast? How many Warlords did you kill before you came to help me?" Dan took a minute, then answered "None." Backir was puzzled for a minute before the answer came to him. He looked at Dan's ripped shirt and said "You were getting your ass kicked before you got out of there, weren't you?" Dan peeked over at Backir and said "Close enough." Backir chuckled a little. Dan gave Back a not so friendly look. Backir said "Calm down! It was a good thing for me you decided to leave when you did. Otherwise you might have got here a little too late."

As Dan and Backir came around a small hill, they saw Yin

running towards them. Backir and Dan knew Yin had fought as hard as he could before he took off. Dan smiled inwardly. He was glad to see that someone else besides himself thought it was a good idea to get some space to regroup. When Yin saw Dan and Backir he stopped running. He gave both of them an angry look before turning and pointing at the four Warlords that were catching up, then saying "Let's get rid of these four Warlords!" Dan and Backir followed Yin to the Warlords.

The Warlords fought fiercely, but the results were the same as the last time. Four more dead He Warlords. Dan said "We have to get the eight Warlords I was fighting, before they make it to the Royal Caravan." Now Yin was puzzled. Yin was about to ask a question when Backir looked at Yin and said "You weren't the only one that had to make a run for it." Dan and Yin both gave Backir an angry look. Backir said "Don't worry! What happens out here, stays out here, right Yin." Yin smiled a little and said "That's right!" Dan took a look around, then said "Let's go!"

The Japha twins moved north as quickly as possible. They didn't have to travel far before they saw the Japha army. They recognized their brother's elephant and several of their cousins right away. They were ahead of the army. Japha, Jett had a very lavishly designed platform on the back of his elephant. Jan looked over at San. He gave her a reassuring look, then looked forward at the approaching army.

The Japha twins were greatly out numbered. The only chance they had was if their family members would refuse to fight them. Once Japha, Jett saw that the small band of guards were headed by his brother and sister, he motioned for some of his guards to join him.

San had the guards stop and then he and Jan, along with Mia and Nina jumped to the ground and moved toward the Japha. Jett saw the twins walking towards him. He jumped from his elephant and walked forward to meet them. His guards followed closely behind him. When the guards got close enough for the twins to see them, they were relieved to see that the guards were made up of most of their cousins. The guards that weren't kin to them, they also recognized. The twins didn't see their other half brothers. Jett stared at the twins.

Jan knew she had to show the Japha that she was the in charge before Jett did. Jan said "My brother and my family came to make sure that their King and Queen would make it safely back home. That is good. What I don't undrerstand is why you all haven't showed us the proper respect."

Jett looked at his brother and sister. He couldn't believe that they thought he came here to protect them. Jan and San both stared at family members that they knew. Then the Japha slowly started getting down on one knee out of respect. Jett didn't get down. He questioned the twins saying "Where's our brothers?" Jan stared at Jett, then said "You dare ask a question without showing respect! I'm going to let it go this time because you are my eldest brother. We'll talk about protocol and the way we expect to be treated later. Right now..."

Jett interrupted with "You think you're going to tell me what to do! Here's what's going to happen. Both of you are going to come back with me. You're going to explain to father what you have been doing all this time and why you haven't completed the mission you were sent on!"

San unloosened the the string holding his ruling cape around his neck. He threw the cape to the ground and said "Enough of these games. If you want to challenge our rule, you'll have to deal with me first." Jett took off his cape. He looked at Jan and said "You're going to come home with us now. Your friends are being destroyed by the He and the Hoo Warlords. If you resist, we'll take you by force. You can fight one at a time, or do you both have to fight together?" San said "I'll be enough for you!"

San started forward, but Jan grabbed his wrist to stop him. San looked at Jan and realized that she had a plan. San waited to see what Jan would do. Jan looked down at the ground, then at her brother Jett. She said with a concerned look on her face. "I don't want us to fight."

Then she looked at her other relatives, the guards and Warlords. Then she said "You would kill us?" She paused for a moment and looked directly at members of her family that she recognized. Then she looked at Jett and said "Dada, Zat, and Tin plotted to kill me. That was a big mistake on their part. They paid for it with their lives. If it weren't for the Butchers and the Hellcats they might have succeeded. Now I see more of my family, whom I love. Led by my own brother."

Jan motioned for San to wait there for her. Then she walked towards Jett. Jett was on guard, watching Jan very closely. When Jan got close to Jett, she talked low so that only he could hear her. Jan said "I know you and the others were in on the plot to kill me and San. We can leave that in the past. Dad doesn't have to know about your involvement. We'll never tell. Right now we have a chance to run the phant trade for the whole north. You can be a big part of it if you choose. If something happens to me and San, the best you can hope for is to run the House of Japha. As Queen of all the northern Houses, and your sister, know that you can do whatever you want to do, as long as it doesn't conflict with what me and San are doing."

Jan paused. She could see that Jett was still apprehensive. Jan slowly put one hand on Jetts shoulder, looked in his eyes and said "You know I have always loved you. I don't know what I have done to make you hate me so much that you want me dead. I just want to go home and be with my family."

Jett could see that his sister was begging him. Still, he wasn't sure whether letting the twins live was a good idea. Jett said in a low voice "I don't want to kill you. Dad wants you brought home alive. The Warlords are here to get rid of those Hellcats and the Butchers once and for all." Jan said "That can't happen. The Butchers are my closest allies and the Hellcats are my sisters. You'll have to kill me to get to them. Then I think you'll find out that they aren't so easy to deal with. They are very smart. Do you think they came up north because they were not smart enough to know that some of the northern Houses would attack them? They have special skills."

Jett said "We know about their screams. We have protection. So do the other Houses. We'll be ready for them." Jan said "Don't be so sure. Don't underestimate them. Besides, right now the Hellcats control all of the trade coming from the south. That's a good thing for us. They will only trade through the House of Japha. Do you know how much power that gives us over the other houses. We could expand north and create the largest House, while keeping the other Houses under our rule. Without the Hellcats the other Houses will not be ruled without another war. Also, if you harm the Hellcats, the House of Hayee will wage war with you."

Jett stared at his sister, then he looked at San. Jan said "Don't worry about San. If I'm not harmed, he'll go along with this." Then Jan motioned, with her hand, for San to join them. San walked over. When he got there, Jan said "You two are going to forget everything that has happened before now. Time to make up. We three will be working closely together, running the House of Japha. "

San looked suspiciously at Jett. Jett looked at his younger brother and said "She makes a lot of since. When did she get so smart?" San let a little smile come on his face and said "Don't act so surprised. She's always been that way."

The Butcher girls were preparing for war. Wana met with them just as they were finishing up. She walked and looked the girls over, then said "I'm going to have the guards move ahead of us and get us as close to the House of Hoo as they can. After that You girls will make sure we get the rest of the way. All three Butcher girls briefly looked at Wana. Then they looked at each other, just before they left with Wana. They knew the score. It was time to put in some work. It was time to kill. That's what they did.

Wana and the Butcher girls met up with Tara and Ramala at the elephants. All of the girls were going to ride on the same platform. Wana wasn't going to take chances. They had to get this right, or, well she didn't let herself think about that. The other possibility wasn't an option. So she concentrated on her plan. Once the girls were on the platform and they were moving towards the House of Hoo, Wana looked at Cat, Ma, and Syn then said "Stay close to my cousins at all times. Protect them at all cost." All three Butcher girls nodded that they would. Tara said "Wa look." Wana turned and saw guards and Warlords of the Hoo, moving closer in the distance. Wana yelled to one of her captains "Speed it up! We want to meet them as far away from the caravan as possible!"

Wana sent a messenger saying that the Hellcats wanted to meet with the elders of the House of Hoo to resolve their defferences. The Hoo sent a messenger back saying that if the Hellcats wanted to resolve this, they should surrender the Butchers and return to the House of Hayee. There was no way that was going to happen. Wana didn't send a messenger with a reply. Instead she moved forward towards the House of Hoo. Now the Hellcats were close enough that they could see The House of Hoo behind the Warlords and many guards that they had with them.

The House of Hoo had a large fortress like wall, made of stone, surrounding it. Guards were on top of the wall looking out over the battle field. Wana looked at Tara and Ramala and said "It's time to get to the ground." The elephant was stopped and ramps were put to the side of the platform. All of the girls walked down the ramp. Once on the ground, the Butcher girls stepped in front of the Hellcats so they could be in a good position to defend them. Wana ordered the guards and the elephants to head back and protect the Royal Caravan. The guards did as they were told. Then Wana said to the Butcher girls "Stay at our sides. That way if we need to blast them, you can quickly move behind us and get low to the ground."

The Hoo Warlords and guards knew about the Hellcats screaming technique. They had special noice blocking pieces for their ears. They knew that the rebels had success blocking the screams with ear pieces, even though they couldn't out fight the Butchers. When they saw the Hellcats move to the ground, they put the pieces in there ears.

The Hellcats and Butchers were now walking towards the Hoo Warlords. The Hellcats were now well ahead of their guards, who were standing with the elephants that they rode in on. There were only six girls.

The Warlords were confindent that they could wipe them out if they let them get close enough. So they were going to let the Hellcats walk right up to them. That way they wouldn't be able to get away so easily. When Wana saw that the Hoo Warlords were going to let them walk right up to them, she told the Butcher girls "That's close enough. We're going to take it from here."

Syn was concerned about how they were going to protect the Hellcats if they got too far ahead of the Butcher girls. Syn said "Are you sure you want to get ahead of us?" Wana said "Yes I am. When you see me and my cousins join hands that will be your sign to get on the ground and cover your ears. Don't get up until we tell you it's alright to do so. Otherwise, you could be permanently damaged. The ear plugs we gave you earlier, put them in your ears now."

Wana and her cousins gave the Butcher girls a reassuring look and a smile. Wana said "Wait here. Remember when you see us join hands, hit the ground and cover your ears." The Hellcats turned and started walking towards the Hoo. The Hoo saw that the Hellcats were approaching, without the Butcher girls. They knew what was coming. They quickly put in the special ear pieces that they had. They weren't going to be caught off guard by these girls. At the least, these three girls would be captured. If the Hellcats resisted to the point that they couldn't be captured, they would be killed.

Chapter 12

What makes the Hellcats scream so effective is the fact that it is a sound vibration. The scream is an extreme vibration that disorientates by vibrating everything it hits. The scream from one of these girls is so violent of a vibration that it shocks the molecules of the entire body by entering the earlobes, then circulating throughout the entire body, vibrating every molecule in the body, and the central nervous system at such a high speed that the affected person can't control motor functions.

The person in effect seems to be frozen when in fact every molecule in their body is vibrating at an extremely high rate of speed from the shock of the scream. Softer object like the human body absorbs the vibration and are affected until the vibration decreases to the point that the person regains control over their motor functions after about ten minutes. That usually take about ten minutes, depending on the person.

The harder the the object is that the vibration hits, the more damage is done to it. An example is the fact that extreme sound can break glass. Plugs covering the earlobes can give protection against one scream in most cases.

The scream from two Hellcats works much like an eathquake. One scream violently vibrates the body one way, while the second scream rips a vibration in the opposite direction. Each one of the Hellcats scream has a different pitch.

Separately, they all are capable of rendering a body completely motionless. When you combine two screams, one scream vibrate the body still, while the second scream violently slams into the central nevous system, and brain with such force that it rips blood vessels apart. Ear plugs can do very little to stop two screams, because with two screams the vibration enters through the skin, as well as the eardrums. Death occurs almost instantly.

Ramala walked straight towards the Hoo with Tara on her left and Wana on her right. They stopped about one hundred feet from the Hoo. Several of the Hoo Warlords jumped from their platforms and stood together in front of their elephants. Now the Hellcats were close enough to the House of Hoo, that they could see the guards on the massive wall that surrounded the Hoo House. One of the Hoo Warlords stepped ahead of the others and said "You should surrender now if you want to avoid a bloodbath." Ramala took both of her cousin's hands.

The Butcher girls saw that and went to the ground and covered their ears, right away. The Hoo Warlords saw the Butcher girls go down so several of them got low, while the others stood their confident that their ear plugs would keep them from harm. All three girls took in air. Ramala squeezed Tara's hand and Tara let out a scream. Then not more than three seconds into Tara's scream, Ramala squeezed Wana's hand and Wana let out a scream. A second after Wana's screamed started, Ramala let out a blast. All three blasts lasted about fifteen seconds.

Sound moves at the speed of seven hundred sixty-one miles per hour. The first scream hit the men and barely disoriented them because of the ear plugs. When the second blast combined with the first, those men fell like rocks a second after the second blast started. Not even the men who got low to the ground were saved from that blast.

When Ramala joined in with her blast, the ground shook from the force of the combined blasts. The stone wall surounding the House of Hoo was hit with the force of a seven hundred sixty-one mile an hour extreme vibration.

When the sound vibration hit the wall, it made the sound of a bomb going off. The wall exploded into pieces, and crashed to the ground. The Butcher girls heard the deafening sound of the blast. They also felt the ground shake and they became very nervous. They wanted to, but refused to look up, because they rememberd that Wana said ' Don't get up until we tell you to '. So they stayed there on the ground. Cat and Ma were terrified. Syn's grandfather had taught her not to be afraid of anything. This was the first time that fear almost took a hold of her.

As soon as the Helcats finished their blast, Ramala pulled her cousins forward. They could hear the Hoo behind the fallen wall in a panic. The Hellcats ran through the dead bodies of the

Hoo warlords and guards until they were right at the crumbled wall. They could see people running around histerically behind the dust coming up from the rubble. The three girls stopped. Ramala looked at Tara, then at Wana. She nodded her head and all three girls took in air again.

This time Ramala squeezed both girls hands at the same time then let go. All three girls let out a blast at the same time. This blast lasted as long as the first one. During that time, every building in the House of Hoo exploded and came crashing to the ground. For the first five second, the noise was so loud from the exploding buildings that it sounded like the continuous boom of thunder from above.

After the sound of falling stones stopped, there was complete silence. The second blast was so powerful that the three Hellcats were disoriented for a few seconds and couldn't move. Once they regained their senses they went back for the Butcher girls.

Ramala and her cousins could see the Butcher girls were lying on the ground terrified, except for Syn. And Syn was very nervous. None of the girls had experienced anything like that before. Ramala said "It's alright now. You can get up." The Butcher girls got up and looked in the direction of the House of Hoo. All they could see was a dust cloud where the Hoo House used to be.

After the Japha Warlords saw Jett having pleasant conversation with the twins, they came over and greeted their cousins. Jan was happy that they were all on the same side again. She thought about the Royal Caravan and a frown came on her face. Jett asked "What's wrong?"

Jan looked at Jett and said with concern in her eyes. "My sisters are being attacked as we speak. They need our help right now. "Jett had made deals with the Hoo and the He to destroy the Hellcats and the Butchers. Now his sister was asking him to help the Hellcats.

Then the elephants caught everyones attention. They were in a panic, causing a comotion. Then Jett and the rest of the Japha heard a ringing vibration in their ears. The intensity of the vibration increased over fifteen second. San and Jan already knew what it was. Jan gave Jett a serious look and said "Get low to the ground now! I'll explain later!"

San and Jan immediately got to the ground. Jett looked at

his brother and sister only for a moment before he knew if they were on the gorund, he probably should be too. He motioned for his men to get down on the ground. Then he got down, looking at Jan for some kind of explaination. Then they heard and felt the vibration again, but only stronger this time. Then they heard what sounded like the boom of thunder several times over. Jett asked Jan "What was that? Was it the Hellcats?" Jan said "Yes it was. I'd say someone found out just how hard it is to deal with the Hellcats. I'm just glad it wasn't you ."

The eight He warlords that Dan faced earlier were headed towards the Royal Caravan when they were met by the three Butchers. The Warlords stopped their elephants and jumped to the ground. The Warlords walked up to the Butchers, and while they were still at a safe distance, the Warlord with the slow drawl said "Look. It's top Butcher, Dan the Destroyer with two friends ready to die or run with him. "All of the Warlords laughed until they saw the Butchers charging at them. They pulled their weapons, then it was all out Warfare. Dan headed straight for the Warlord with the slow drawl.

Dan, Backir, and Yin were in a heated battle with the eight He Warlords when they heard the faint sounds of the first scream and felt the vibration. It was a slight distration to the Warlords that gave the Butchers the advantage in this battle. Three Warlords got sliced up during the first scream. Another three got butchered during the second. The last two didn't last much longer after that.

Yin and Backir were taking a moment to enjoy the victory by gloating. Dan knew if the Hellcats had to blast, danger was near. He said "Let's get back to the Caravan." Dan, Yin, and Backir took one last look at the dead He Warlords before they started jogging towards the Royal Caravan. Both Dan and Yin were glad that none of the He Warlords survived to tell about them running. They both told themselves that they would never run again!

Ramala looked at all three Butcher girls and saw that they were more than a little rattled by the experience, even though they tried to act like they weren't. Ramala said "You can relax a little. We don't have to worry about the Hoo anymore." Syn looked at Ramala and said "You girls stepped it up a notch. That was incredible!"

Tara smiled at Syn and said "Come, we'll show you what we did." Wana looked at both of her cousins and said "We need to get back and check on the caravan." Tara begged "We'll be really quick. Besides our sisters need to see with their own eyes what we did."

Ramala thought that was a good idea. She looked at Wana, letting her know that she agreed with Tara. Wana didn't want to argue, so she said "Alright, let's make it quick!" All of the girls walked quickly towards what use to be the House of Hoo. First they got to the bodies of the Warlords and guards. Cat and Ma looked at each other in astonishment after seeing the bodies lying on the ground with blood coming from their eyes, ears, noses, and mouths.

The Butcher girls remembered that the bodies of Wirlwind Wa's guards didn't look like these bodies did. After they got past the bodies, they could see a low cloud of dust settling over a huge pile of rubble and stones. It was only when they were right at the destroyed gate to the House of Hoo that they could see what had happened.

The House of Hoo covered a large area. That whole area was reduced to rubble. There wasn't one building left standing. The Butcher girls could see body parts covered in dust, imbedded in the rocks that used to be buildings. The girls were staring in amazement at the devastion, when Ramala brought them back to reality by saying "This is what happens when someone tries to do harm to the Hellcats. They get eliminated!" Wana said "Mala, it's time to go!" Ramala looked at the Butcher girls and motined that it was time to go. Each of the Butcher girls took one last look at what used to be the House of Hoo. Then they turned and followed the Hellcats back to the caravan.

The girls trotted at a steady pace towards the caravan. They had to send the elephants back so they wouldn't stampede when they heard the screams. Wana just hoped that the Japha twins and the male Butchers could hold their fronts until they could arrive to help. She also hoped that their voices would be rested enough to get out effective screams.

After two good screams the Hellcats needed to rest their vocal chords, so that they could recuperate enough for them to scream again. Wana knew if Ramala's children were close to being in danger, she would have them blasting screams whether their voices were rested or not. One thing was for sure, if they had to blast a scream or two, they would.

After the Japha twins were relatively sure that there

weren't going to be any more blast, they got off the ground. Jan said "We still need to get to the Royal Caravan." Jett said "Doesn't seem like they need our help to me." Jan said "I'm going to make sure they're alright. If you don't want to help me, my girls and San will go ourselves." Jett said "I didn't say I wouldn't help you. I'll have my guards follow closely behind us. You let them know that we are friends and not foes. I wouldn't want to have to deal with a scream up close." Jan said "Let's go!"

When the Hellcat and the Butcher girls arrived back at the caravan, they could see that besides the guards' patroling, there wasn't anything going on. Ramala went to check on her twins. She peeked in on them for a minute, then she left. She stayed out of their sight because she knew they missed her and would not deal well with a short visit. After seeing that they were alright, Ramala quickly went to meet her cousins.

Wana sent scouts, with guards not far behind them, north to see if the Japha twins needed help. She was about to send scouts south when Dan, Backir, and Yin came running up. The Butcher girls were the first to meet them. Dan saw Wana and questioned "Is everything alright? Where's Ramala?" Tara looked over the Butchers, then said "Calm down. We just got back too. La's checking on your twins."

Ramala was just walking up when she heard Dan's voice. She said "I'm right here." Dan said "The twins?" Ramala said "They're resting. Don't go to them just yet. We still have business to take care of." Wana looked at Dan and said "What are you doing here? What about the southern front?"

Dan said "We took care of the He Warlords. After the screams, the rest of the He retreated to a safe distance. Ther're still out there waiting on us. We have scouts watching their position." Wana said "Good. I sent guards to see if the Japha, Jan needs our help. Depending on the situation, some of us might have to go north to help out." Just then, one of Wana's scouts ran up and begged for permission to speak. He said "The Japha army is on it's way! They'll be here very soon!"

Wana started ordering her guards into position. The Hellcats went to the military elephant with the tower on it. They could see the Japha twins on an elephant with another man. They didn't recognize him as being one of their own guards. The three cousins watched closely as the elephant moved closer, followed by the Japha army. Wana was just about to leave and start giving order, when Tara stopped her. Tara said "Wa look!"

Wana looked out at the elephant. It stopped and the Japha twins, their girls, and the man that was with them, jumped from the elephant and started walking towards the Royal Caravan. Wana looked at Tara. Tara said "Maybe Jan got them to see things our way." Wana wasn't sure about that yet. She said "Still let's be very careful. Let's go and meet them together. If it's a trap, we'll just have to end it with a blast."

Tara nodded in agreement and they left the military elephant. Tara said "La, you stay here. If it's a trap, we'll blast them while you watch for trouble coming from the south." Ramala said "If you two are going, then so am I. We'll have to decide if it's a trap quickly, so we can get back to the caravan and start heading south immediately." Wana paused for a moment, while looking at Ramala. Then she said "Alright then let's go now."

All of the Butchers wanted to go. Wana ordered them to stay with the caravan until they found out what was going on. The three Hellcats started towards the Japha twins. Once they got close enough to see each other the Japha, Jan stopped her two brothers and walked over to the Hellcats only with her girls. When they met, because San didn't come, the Hellcats searched Jan's face to see if she had been forced to come.

Jan could see apprehension in her sisters faces. She said "Are you girls alright?" Ramala said "We are, but what about you? Why didn't San come with you?" Jan looked at all three girls, then back at Ramala before saying "

I didn't want to startle you by bringing my brother Japha, Jett to meet you without first telling you. He has agreed to help me and San in our transition, taking over the House of Japha. Right now, he and his Warlords are here to push back any threat to you and your caravan." Ramala said "He tried to have you killed! Now you trust him?" Jan said "Now he can see that it's in his best interest if we run the House of Japha. He'll do whatever it takes to help."

The Hellcats weren't convinced. Wana said "The only guarantee you have is his word. That's not good enough for me." Jan said "And it shouldn't be. I still meant what I said before. You shouldn't trust him. If anything happens to me or my brother, the last thing I want the House of Japha to hear is that special scream we heard ealier. Who received that?" Tara said "The Hoo. Their House and everyone in it were completely destroyed." Jan said

"What about the southern front?"

Wana said "The Butchers took care of the He Warlords, but their guards are still holding their positions." Jan said "Alright, now we'll see if my brother can be a good general. I'm going to have him convince the He to go home. But first I'm going to introduce you to him." Jan turned and waved her brothers over. The three Hellcats studied Jan's brother closely. Japha, Jett was slightly taller and a little bigger than San. He was just as muscular as San. There was a strong family resenblace to the twins. When Jett and San got to the Hellcats, Jett got down on one knee then got up and said "I am pleased to meet the Hellcats, Queens of the House of Ra."

Wana stared at Jett and said in a not so friendly voice "There is only one Queen of the House of Ra." Jan said "This is my brother Jett. He was just trying to show respect. Jett that's the Hayee, Wana, that's the Hayee, Tara and this is the Queen of the House of Ra. The Hayee, Ramala." Jett went down on one knee again then got up. The Hellcats just stared at Jett. Jett felt uncomfortable and looked to Jan to defuse the situation. Before Jan could say anything, Ramala said "Tell me why you sent your brothers to kill my sister Jania?"

This caught Jett off guard. He said "It was a personal family matter. That's the past. Me and my sister have made up." Jan could see that that wasn't enough for Ramala. Ramala said "It's true that Jan's name is Japha, and my name is Hayee. But still, we are sisters. I care very deeply about Jan. Make no mistake about how very close we are."

While Ramala was talking, Jett looked over at Jan and could see that she was in full agreement with the Hayee, Ramala. Ramala was still talking. She was saying "I was very offended that your borthers attemped to harm my sister. They got dealt with. I'm not very trusting of her brothers when it comes to her safety. You say it was a personal family matter. Well she is my family. And right now, this is very personal. So I'll ask only once more, why plot to have my sister killed?"

Jett realized that he was here with none of his Walords to help him. He heard that the Hellcats screams could paralyze you. All three of them were looking at him with dislike just short of hatred in their eyes. He could see that he wasn't going to get much help from his brother and sister. He had the special ear plugs in his pocket. He wished he had put them in earlier. He knew he couldn't put them in now.

Jett said "There's no answer that I can give you that will satisfy you. Jan has proved how smart she is. She will make a great Queen of the House of Japha. I'm going to make sure that she doesn't run into any opposition at home. She has all of my support now." Ramala said "You support her and make sure nothing happens to her. If one hair on her head is harmed, I'm going to hold you accountable first, then I'll ...."

Tara knew what was coming next. Even though she thought that Ramala was on the right track with most of what she was saying, she didn't want her to go to far. So Tara interrupted with "What my cousin is trying to say is that you'll have the opportunity to protect Jan at all cost. If you can't do that, then you're useless. I sugjest that you visit the House of Hoo on your way home and ask them about our skills. That should be more than enough motivation for you and your Warlords to see how important it is that Jan and San stay alive."

Jett was highly offended. He had just been threatened by this girl. Who did she think she was? But before he could say, or do something that might have made things worse, Jan looked at Ramala and said "My brother can see what's at stake here. He'll do whatever it takes to support me in the House of Japha, and the Hellcats in the House of Ra. Isn't that right Jett?"

Jett held his tounge and said "That's right." Jan continued with "Now that we're done with that business, we have to deal with the theat to the south of us. Jett can take his Warlords and convince the He to end their hostilities."

Wana said "Now hold on here. You want us to stand by, while the Japha army moves to the south of our position as well as the north.That's makes us surrounded by Japha, Jett's army." Wana looked at Ramala then said "I don't agree with that at all." Ramala turned and looked at Jan. Then she looked at Jett, studying his every movement, while talking to Jan. Ramala said "Your brother agreed that he would do whatever it would take to protect you. Because he was part of this whole plan to trap the Royal Caravan, I think he should go and convince the He to go home by himself. That way my cousin won't feel like we are surrounded."

Jan wasn't going to ask Jett to do that. She looked at Jett to answer for himself. Jett thought about it for only a moment, then said "I can do that. I'll take two phants with only my bodyguards and leave right away." Ramala looked at Wana. Wana didn't disagree with that, so Ramala said "That's a start to gaining our trust." Jett wasn't going to mess up this opportunity. It was too early in this game. If he didn't like the way things were going later, he'd plan to make the situation more to his liking.

The Japha, Jett headed around the caravan on his way to meet with the He. The Japha twins and their two girls were going to stay with the Royal Caravan until Japha, Jett returned from his meeting with the He. Then the Royal Caravan would be escorted to the House of Japha.

The Japha twins rode with their brother Jett, until it was time for them to take separate paths. Jan looked at her older brother Jett, and said "It's going to take a lot for the Hellcats to trust you, if ever. So don't mess things up by trying to do something that you think is smart. Stick to the plan. Then everyone wins. In the end, you'll see that what me and my sisters have set up is the smartest plan. Also, I want you to go to the House of Hoo before going to the House of He. That way you will know what the Hellcats are capable of."

Jett said "Do you know what they are capable of?" Jan said "More than you can know." Jett asked "How do you know that you can trust them?" Jan said "I trust them with my life. Which is more than I can trust you with right now?" Jett stared at Jan for a moment, then looked at San and asked him "Do you trust them that much?" San said "I don't have to, but as long as she does, they're good with me." Jan looked out over the plain and then said to Jett "This is where we split up. Met us back at the Royal Caravan when you're done."

The Japha twins and their girls joined the Hellcats and the Butcher girls. They weren't far from the Royal Caravan. Jan saw the Hellcats conversing and joined them. Ramala said "Join us sister." Jan said "Thanks." Ramala gave Jan a concerned look and said "Do you really trust that Japha, Jett?" Jan said "I never said I trusted him, It a matter of knowing him. He'll go along because he knows he has a lot to gain. But still, he's a lot like Chi, smart and always plotting. By the time he decides to get crafty, I'll have the House of Japha runing like I want it."

Ramala warned "You be careful with him. He's already proven that he can't be trusted." Jan said "This is his last chance to prove that he can behave. That's only because he's my older brother. He looked out for me a lot, growing up. That's why I give him this chance. If he messes up this time, it will be his last."

Back at the caravan, Dan was on edge, waiting for the Hellcats to return. Yin and Backir sat back and watched as Dan paced back and forth. Dan was still bothered by the fact that he had to run. It was weighing heavily on him. All the practicing he had done and he still wasn't good enough to take on eight Warlords. He didn't feel like the Destroyer, or the top Butcher, he had called himself in front of the He Warlords. If the Syn Jara could face five priests, surely he could take on eight Warlords. When Dan got back to the House of Ra he was going to rededicate himself to being the Butcher that he knew he was.

Finally, one of the guards came up and told the Butchers that the Hellcats were returning. Dan let himself relax a little. He knew Ramala could almost read his thoughts. When they came up, Dan waited until she came over to him. He played it cool as usual, saying "How did it go out there?"

Ramala stared at Dan for a moment before saying "Everything went as well as we can expect right now. Japha, Jan's brother Jett met with us. He's heading south to convice the He to end this madness and go home." Dan looked puzzled. That sounded to him like they would be surrounded. Ramala saw what Dan was thinking. She said "He went only with ten of his personal bodyguards. Japha, Jan wants to give him a chance, even thoug he tried to have her killed."

Ramala took a quick peek around, then said "If he makes anymore trouble for me, he's dead. Come, let's go see our children. I know they miss us by now. "As they walked to the elephant that the young twins were on, Ramala kept peeking at Dan out of the corner of her eye, She could see that something was bothering him. She knew the only thing that could get to Dan besides her, was if he didn't do as well in a fight as he thought he should, or if he got beat, after that thought she turned her head and looked Dan in the face. Dan said "What?" Ramala said "Nothing." She could at least tell that he hadn't been beat. That was good enough hfor her right now.

Cat, Ma and Syn talked with Backir and Yin about what they saw at the House of Hoo. Now that they were back with the other Butcher, the Butcher girls were calmer. Cat talked with the Butchers, while daydreaming about what it would be like if she could scream like the Hellcats. She wondered if she could learn how to scream like that. She was going to find out when she got back to the House of Ra.

Ma knew that her days of fighting Dan were over. It wouldn't bother her one bit, if she had to fight Ramala, straight up, in a one on one fight. Ma would fight anyone. But after seeing how the Hoo looked after being screamed at. She knew she didn't want to die that way.

The Syn, Jara thought she knew how dangerous the Hellcats were. Now she knew they were near unstoppable. How do you protect yourself from screams like those? That's what Syn wanted to know. Syn knew whoever figured that out would at least have a fighting chance against these girls. Syn knew things could go bad at any time, but with the Hellcats on your side. Let's just say, she knew they had at least a screaming chance.

Tara and Wana didn't spend much time with the Butchers. Once they got back, they met with the guards and ordered them into strategic positions. They told the scouts to let them know the moment that any group of troops moved on their position. No matter how small a group it was. Tara and Wana knew that they were a long way from home. Ramala was slightly distracted with her twins, and Dan. It was up to these two Hellcats to make sure that they all made it safely back to the House of Ra.

Jett didn't have to travel very far before he ran into the He forward guards. Japha, Jett identified himself and requested a meeting with the He elders. Once Jett was identified as who he said he was, he was escorted to meet with the He elders. The whole time he traveled, all he could think about was the destruction that he saw at the House of Hoo. There was nothing left. Not one person had survived. He now knew that even his ear plugs wouldn't have saved him, after seeing the dead bodies with ear plugs still in their ears. Those girls were Hell Cats straight from Hell. If they would do that to some one, there's no telling how far they were willing to go. Jett was glad he listened to his younger sister.

Jett met with the Hoo elders and told them what he saw. He suggested that they should ruturn to the House of He and forget about trying to eilininate the Hellcats. He told them if they didn't think his advise was good, that they should visit the House of Hoo first, before dealing with the Hellcats. Jett told the He elders that he was going to escort the Royal Caravan to the House of Japha. If the He did anything against the House of Ra, he or the Japha weren't going to be a part of it. And he was sure that the Hoo weren't either. One of the He elders asked Japha, Jett "What made you change your mind about eliminating them? Jett said as a matter of fact "Because right now, I don't think that we can."

When Jan and San reached the Royal Caravan, they walked, followed by Nina and Mia, to the covered plat formed elephant that they came on. On the way San put his arm around Jan's neck and pulled her close to him, while they were walking. San said "Good job back there. You handled Jett perfectly."

Jan smile at her brother's compliment. She could feel San's powerful arm resting on her shoulders. He had a good grip on her. Her body was pressed against his as they walked to the elephant. Even though this was the brother and sister touching they had always done. Jan's body was reacting differently. Much like it had done earlier. She tried wrestling away, but San took it as her playing around, and wrestled back. It was too much for Jan. She pulled away from San. San looked at Jan and said "What's wrong?" Jan said "I'm tired. I don't feel like playing." San siad "Alright, all you had to do was say something!" Jan said "I did!"

They both stopped and looked at each other for a moment. They hardly ever snapped at each other. San defused the situation by saying "I must be tired too. I'll let you get some rest and I'll see you later." Jan smiled a little and said "See you later." Nina and Mia acted as if nothing had happened. This happened every once in a while between the twins. The guards put a ramp up to the elephant, then Jan and her girls boarded and took a short nap.

Jett arrived back at the Royal Caravan a couple hours before dark. He told the Hellcats and the twins that the Hellcats shouldn't have any trouble out of the He on their way back to the House of Ra. Jett said he would escort the Royal caravan to the House of Japha. He joined his Warlords and the Japha army moved north towards the House of Japha, with the Royal Caravan right behind them.

Chapter 13

Now the House of Japha was visible from the Caravan. Jan, Nina, and Mia stared at their home, with big smiles on their faces. This was the first time they had been home in almost four years. They were very excited. They could hardly hold back their happiness at finally making it home. The Butcher girls thought that the army that Jett had with him was large, until they saw the rest of the Japha army, as they passed through it on their way to the gates of the House of Japha.

The guards of the Royal Caravan, along with Yin and Backir, stayed outside of the gates to the Japha city. These two Butchers killed Japha family members. Japha, Jett made it perfectly clear to Jan that if the Butchers Yin and Backir entered the gates to the House of Japha, they would never leave there alive. So it was decided that it probably was a good idea that they stayed with the Caravan, until the Hellcats returned.

As soon as the Japha twins entered the House of Japha, their family saw them, and cheered them like they had just won a war for the Japha. The Japha twins were always popular in their family. Now it seemed their popularity had risen to a new level. Everyone in the crowd yelled the twins' names, trying to get their attention. The twins pointed to, and waved in acknowledgement, to as many of their family members as possible. The Hellcats and the Butchers looked at their surroundings. Making sure they remembered how to get back to the main gate.

When the Japha twins walked down the ramp, from the plat form on the elephant's back. Jett was waiting on them. He told the twins and the Hellcats, the building that they would be escorted to. The twins knew that place to be one of the formal meeting halls. Jan told the Hellscats and the Butchers that it was where the Japha greeted their most special guest. The building wasn't far from where they got off the elephants. It was very big, but not one of the largest buildings in this city. They entered the building and saw guards on both sides of a long walk way that led to a throne area. The twins, the Hellcats, and the Butchers walked all the way to the throne area. In the throne area, there were five throne chairs, with older men sitting in them. Behind the five men were a number of huge guards with Hammer-axes in hand, watching every movement in front of them.

One of the men in the chairs was the twin's father, old man Jett, Japha. When Jett two got to the throne, he got down on his knees out of respect. When he did that, everyone else did too, except for the Hellcats. They lowered their heads then raised them, and smiled meekly at the heads of the House of Japha.

Ramala studied all of the old men. They all looked to be at least seventy or better. She looked at all of five of them and tried to see if she could figure out which one was the twin's father before she was told. Ramala didn't have to wait for long to find out. Jan ran up to the throne area. The Man sitting in the middle chair stood up, just as Jan jumped on him wrapping her arms around him, sqeezing tightly. Jan said "Dad! I missed you so much!"

San walked up on the throne and stood there waiting on his turn. Old man Jett pulled Jan's arms from around him, and held her back just enough to get a good look at her. Tears of joy were coming down her face. Old Jett said "It's alright Jania, you're home now."

Old Jett let go of Jan, but she didn't leave the throne area. Jan grabbed her father's hand and stood there with him. Old Jett took another quick look at Jan before turning his attention to San. San came over and gave his father a quick hug. Old Jett said "You look well, for being gone so long. It's good to see you safe and sound." San said "It's good to see you too dad." Then Old Jett turned his attention to the Hellcats and the Butchers. Jan let go of her father's hand and introduced the Hellcats first, then the Butchers.

Old Jett barely paid any attention to the Butchers. They were heathens and far below him in rank. He knew his cousins would be watching them closely. But he and the other elders did take a good look at Syn, Jara when she was introduced. Old Jett studied each of the Hellcats when they were introduced. He paid special attention when Ramala was introduced as the Queen of the

House of Ra. Old Jett said "The House of Japha welcomes the Queen of the House of Ra, the Hayee, Ramala and her Royal Court. I am the Japha, Jett and these men are the elders of the House of Japha." Ramala said "Much respect to you, the elders, and all of the members of the House of Japha."

Then Ramala lowered her head slightly, before raising it back up. Old Jett smiled at Ramala. He said "You are very polished in your speaking to be so young. You're nothing like the reports I heard about you." Ramala said "You can't always believe everything that you hear. But still, there probably is some truth to what you heard."

Old Jett laughed. He said "Well, so far I'm impressed with what I see. I know you had some trouble on your way here. I guess that couldn't be helped. Now you are a guest of the House of Japha. Rest assured that no harm will come to you, or your Court. You have my word on it. Enjoy yourself while you are here." Ramala smiled at Jett and said "Thank you. You are most gracious. May I request one thing of you?" Jett paused for a moment.

Jan looked at Ramala and wondered where she was about to go with this. Jan knew her father wouldn't be bullied, and hoped Ramala wouldn't try that. The other Hellcats were proud of the way Ramala had handled herself so far. Now they were wondering if she was going to say something that might put them all in serious danger.

Old Jett said "Say what's on your mind." Ramala said "I see the love that you have for Jania. It's the love that only a father can have for his daughter. So I say what I say with the utmost respect for you. Attemps were made on Jania and San's lives. I love both of them very much. Me and my cousins along with our Butchers escorted and made sure that our sister Jan made it home safely. I don't know if there still is a threat. All I know is that San and Jan are the only Queen and King of the northern Houses that the House of Ra will recognize. I'm sure you know the agreement that we made to trade to all of the northern Houses, only through San and Jan. Through all of the attemps on the twin's lives, the House of Ra has repelled them all. Now that the twins are home, I expect nothing less."

Ramala paused and walked slowly onto the throne area. The guards behind the throne raised their axes. She stopped. Old Jett waved his hand, and the guards lowered their axes, even though they were still on alert, ready to attack if needed.

Ramala walked up to Jan and reached for her hand. Both girls held hands facing Old Jett and the elders of the House of Japha. Ramala said "I expect the elders of the House of Japha to do whatever it takes to protect my sister. If harm should come to either, or both Jan or San, I'm going to lose all sense of reasoning. First all trade will be cut off to all of the northern Houses. Then I'm going to come here personally and find out what happened to my brother and sister. After that, I'm going to destroy everyone that couldn't protect them."

Young Jett made his way to the throne area and said to Ramala "You think you can come to the House of Japha and threaten us. Who do you think you are?" Ramala ignored young Jett, and said to Old Jett "My words are not a threat to anyone who loves the twins and will protect them at all cost, as I have done . The only ones that should be threatened by my words are those who have ill intentions towards the twins. I'll make no apology when it comes to what I will do if they are harmed. Everyone needs to know that."

Ramala purposely looked at young Jett, when she said the last sentence. Jan stood there in solidarity with Ramala. She didn't let Ramala's hand go, even though she thought Ramala had gone I bit too far.

Old Jett had been staring at Ramala, and Jan the whole time. When she was talking about Jan, he could see that her emotions were rising. It seemed she genuinely cared about his twins. If he had thought that she was trying to sell him a pack of lies, he would have had his guards take her head for talking to him and the elders this way. Old Jett turned, and looked at the other elders. They didn't show that they were offended.

Old Jett turned back to Ramala and said "We can see that you are very passionate in your concern for my twins. Jan and San are special to everyone here. I think I speak for everyone here, when I say that they are safer here than anywhere, including the House of Ra. If harm comes to them while they are in the House of Japha, even though I don't have to promise you anything, I'll say this, if something does happen to them, when you get here, there won't be many people left for you to deal with, because I will have already dealt with them."

Old Jett looked at Jan and said "Do whatever to make sure our guest are well taken care of. When you're done, you and San meet me at my place." Then Old Jett left with the other elders and all of the guards that were on the throne. Jan turned back to Ramala and the Hellcats and said "You heard my father, let's get all of you taken care of."

The Elders of the House of Japha met, in private, right after meeting with the Hellcats. The five elders of the House of Japha were Japha, Jett and his brother Japha, Umbuzec. The other three were Jett's cousins, Japha, Zumecko, Japha, Isecku, and Japha, Jeb-Japolis. They talked about what they had observed of the Hellcats and the Butchers.

Umbuzec said "That Hayee, Ramala and her cousins have to be dealt with. There's no getting around that. If we let them live, there's no telling how long before there're strong enough to challenge us." Isecko said "The Hayee, Ramala is the head of the Hellcats. Kill the head and the rest can't function." Zumecko warned "I watched all three of the Hellcats. The Hayee, Wana watched and observed the position of the guards, us, and everyone else that was in the great hall. She is the top general. This I'm sure of. Then there is the Hayee, Tara. She also watched her surrounding, but most of her focus was on what the Hayee, Ramala was saying. At one point, it looked like she was about to interrupt, but she didn't. I think Tara is the advisor to the other Hellcats. Then there is the Hayee, Ramala, deliberate and cunning. She takes what she wants. What I think we have here is a three headed monster. If you kill one, the other two could still be a big problem."

Isecko said "Then we kill all three." Jeb-Japolis said "These Hellcats can't be taken lightly. Since when have three girls created an army that fought us to a stalemate." Isecko jump in with "If we would have kept fighting, we would have eventually beat them!" Jeb-Japolis said "But at what cost. You have already lost one of your sons. Zumee { Umbuzec } lost two, Jett lost three, and I lost one."

Isecko said "That's all the more reason to kill them all!" Jeb-Japolis stared at Isecko and said "The Hellcats didn't kill them. It was those damn Butchers!" Jeb calmed himself, then said "Remember what young Jett, along with the scouts told us. The House of Hoo was totally destroyed by those three girls. It was reduced to rubble, and they said no one survived. They said it came from a scream. We don't really know how they did it. We don't even know if we could stop it. I'm not willing to take a chance on the House of Japha being destroyed. Even if we did kill these Hellcats, the Hayee would send troops up here to war with us. We have to wonder if the Hayee have other girls that can do this. Let's be smart about this. If Jania has a strong a bond with the Hellcats as it seems. We can take advantage of the situation. As long as we don't harm the Hellcats, and are smart about the way we do it. We can get the Butchers, and eventually the south will take care of the Hellcats."

Jeb looked at Jett to see his response. Jett looked at his brother and his cousins. He said "I'll talk to the twin and see if the Hellcats have any weaknesses. If not, we'll take our time getting rid of the Butchers. We can use the rebellious tribes in the south to help get rid of the Hellcats."

The Japha twins got the Royal court settled in, then they went to their father's place to meet with him. When the twins arrived at Old Jett's place with Nina and Mia, Young Jett was already there. They walked in and sat at a large table in one of Jett's private sitting rooms. Old Jett didn't look too happy with his twins. He started questioning the twins right away. Old Jett asked them "Why didn't you two complete the mission you were sent on in the first place?"

He stared at his both of his twins waiting on an answer. Jan said "Dad, you know that our first priority was to complete our mission. Our caravan was ambushed by Tin, Dada, and Zat's guards. They were trying to eliminate us." Old Jett asked "What made you so sure that that was so?"

Jan said "We were warned by some of their guards. They were going to surround us and finish us off. We had no choice but to have the Butchers help us. The Butchers fought bravely trying to protect us. Once we got to the House of Hayee, my sister Ramala took it upon herself to make sure we got home safely."

Old Jett asked "So you killed your brothers?" Jan said "We had no choice, but to defend ourselves. If we hadn't, we would be dead. That was the only way to make it home." Neither of the Japha twins were going to tell their father Ramala had their brothers killed. That would immediately change every thing for the worse. Old Jett said "Yeah, after you helped her wage war in the south. How could you be a part of that!?"

Jan was slightly shaken by the tone in her father's voice. Unlike Ramala, Jan still had a respectful fear of her father. She composed herself and said "Father, I saw a great opportunity for the House of Japha, so I decided that it was worth it. I didn't expect that you would send armies to attack her. I'm sorry for the Japha that lost their lives fighting her. Dad, these girls have special skills that can't be matched by us. Let them go back to the south unharmed so that we may benefit from trade control of the north. We can expand our House. This is a great opportunity."

Jett said "How do you know they will keep up their loyalty to you?" Jan said "Me and Ramala love each other like blood sisters. We made a pact between us. If some one does harm to one of us, the other will take the heads of everyone responsible." Old Jett said "How do you know she's serious about that?" Jan responded "You see she's serious about it, to come into the House of Japha and threaten everyone here, that I had better be safe. Well, I'm just that serious about nothing happening to her."

Old Jett asked "Do they have any weaknesses?" Jan said "No dad. I love them, so even if I knew something I would never tell." Jett asked "Do you feel that way about the Butchers?" Jan said "I do love the Butchers, but not the same as Ramala. The Butchers are heathens." Old Jett said "Those Heathens are responsible for killing some of your cousins."

Jan quickly said "Not all of them. Only two Butchers were responsible for that. It was the Butchers Yin and Backir." Old Jett asked "Why didn't I see them?" Jan said "No one who kills a Japha is ever welcome in our House. You taught me that. Those two heathens are with Ramala's caravan. The Butchers that you met earlier, I have a lot of love for. I ask you father not to harm them. The other two, they have many enemies. If they are killed, everyone should expect that it was going to happen one day. Just don't let it be known that the House of Japha had anything to do with it."

Jan knew she could never tell her father that Ramala had her brothers killed. There would be no way that Ramala would make it out of the House of Japha, or worse, the House of Japha would be destroyed by the Hellcats. Jan didn't want either of those things to happen.

The Hellcats and the Butchers were treated great while in the House of Japha. Nina and Mia were back home now. They had clothes made for the Butchers, as well as the Hellcats. They showed the Butchers around to the places that they could be shown, at the House of Japha. The Japha were very nice to them. Like the House of Hayee, the Japha let you know where you couldn't go.

The Hellcats only stayed at the House of Japha for less than a week. Ramala requested a private meeting with Old man Jett. The twins and the other elders insisted on being there. Wana and Tara also insisted on being there. They met at one of Japha, Isecku's places. It was a medium sized building with a formal meeting area. Everyone sat a one large table.

After everyone was seated Japha, Jett urged the Hayee, Ramala to speak. Ramala stood up and said "Thanks for granting me this meeting. We have been treated very well, while at the House of Japha. I would like to thank you for that also. All of you probably have heard of how I built the House of Ra. At no time did I ever want to go to war with any of the Seven Houses. It was a supprise to me that I had to fight my own family as well as the Japha. I never want that to happen again. I called this meeting to assure all of you that I and all of the House of Ra want to be strong allies to the House of Japha. What I need to know from all of you is that you are willing to pledge your support to the King and queen of the Northern Houses, right here and now. I would like each of you to make a choice before me now."

Ramala paused and waited on a response. The elders looked at each other. Umbuzec stood up and said "As long as we agree to become allies to the House of Ra. What difference does it make to you who runs the House of Japha?"

Ramala said "It makes all the difference. That was part of the trade agreement that stopped the war." Umbuzec said "So if we don't agree, then you'll start war with us?"

Tara stood up and said "You would go back on you word to support Jania and San as Queen and King of the House of Japha?" Tara remained standing, waiting on an answer. Umbuzec said "I never said that I wouldn't. What I ..."

Tara interrupted with "Pardon me, but it seems like you are trying to get my cousin to say something, before you answer her question. It's not fair to ask questions that have nothing to do with this situation. Do you support San and Jan as the King and Queen of the House of Japha?"

Tara didn't intend for it to be, but it sounded like an ultimatum. Umbuzec wasn't going to answer. Jan stood up and looked at each of the elders while saying "I don't think that my sisters are being unreasonable, asking this Question. Now it has made me curious to know the answer."

Once Jan stood up and started talking, the two Hellcats sat in their seats. Umbuzec sat down after they did. Jan continued with "Tell me right here and now, each one of you. Do you support me and San as the King and Queen of the House of Japha?" Old Jett stared at Jan. Jan didn't flinch. Then San stood up and stared at the elders waiting on and answer. San said "Dad, do you support us as King and Queen of the House of Japha?"

Old Jett stood up slowly and said "What would be our role then?" San said "All of you will advise us. You will still have control over family traditions. Nothing will change that." Old Jett looked at Ramala. Then he looked at his twins. He was proud of the way they handled this meeting. He said "I will support both of you."

Then Old Jett looked over to his brother. Unbuzec stood up, looked at each of the twins, and then said "You have my support." Then one by one, all of the elders stood and gave their support to San and Jan. Then Ramala stood up and said "I too give all of my support to the King and Queen of the House of Japha, Japha, San and Jania."

Tara and Wana stood up and made the same statement. Jan and San ended the meeting. They weren't going to take any chances that the Hellcats and their Elders were going to have another dispute. A big feast was held that night introducing to the whole of the House of Japha, their new King and Queen.

The next morning the Royal Caravan prepared to leave. Jan had tried to spend as much time with the Hellcats and the Butchers as she could while they were in the House of Japha. Jan knew she wouldn't see them for a long time. When they were leaving, she walked out with Ramala.

Just before they were ready to go back to the Royal caravan, Old Jett and the Elders walked up to them. Old Jett looked at Ramala and said "I never thanked you for helping my children make it back home safely. Thank you." Old Jett lowered his head, out of respect then raised it back to eye level with Ramala. Ramala said "Thank you for having such a beautiful, and smart set of twins."

That put a slight smile on old Jett's face. He and the other Elders wished the Hellcats a safe, and speedy trip back to the House of Ra. San said his good-byes as they were leaving. All of the Butcher girls hugged San and Jan. Jan took a look at Dan and then the Butcher girls. Jan said "All of you are welcome to visit anytime you please."

The Butcher girls all had tears running down their faces. Syn, Jara shed tears, even though she told herself she wouldn't. The Butcher girls had strong feelings for Jan. The Hellcats didn't shed any tears. They stayed sharp and looked out for the unexpected. Tara and Wana had grown to like Jan a lot. Ramala loved Jan. Even though she was very sad, leaving Jan behind, Ramala refused to cry. Tears rolled down Jan's face as she watched her sisters leave. She wondered if she would ever see all of them together again.

When the Royal Caravan left the House of Japha, Wana had everyone on high alert. Backir and Yin had already been on alert, waiting on the Butchers and Hellcats to return. But as the Caravan traveled for four days, they didn't meet any resistance what so ever. The forwards scouts didn't see any troops, or guard's patroling, checking on the position of the Royal Caravan. They passed the House of He without stopping. Still they had no problems.

After the first week, Ramala felt comfortable enough to have her twins on an uncovered platform, showing and naming different animals to them. The twins enjoyed this time out on the plains with their mother. Yaya was relaxed now that the danger of war had passed. She noticed that the guards still watched her. Yaya dismissed it as her Queen mother making sure she didn't get into any trouble out here, away from home.

The Royal Caravan didn't stop at any of the Houses on the way home, until they reached the House of Hayee. They stayed there two days while they re-supplied the Caravan and rested the Elephants. The Butchers stayed with the Caravan this time. They didn't want to cause any trouble that might make them have to stay longer than necessary.

The Hellcats and Ramala's twins stayed at the House of Hayee. The twins spent most of the two days with Mashaya. Mashaya enjoyed the twins by spoiling them as much as she could, while they were with her. The Hellcats spent time with their cousins, and other relatives, trying to get them to visit the House of Ra. Once they got them there, they would try to convince them to stay. The House of Ra covered a very large area, and the Hellcats needed more people they could trust, in charge of those areas.

Messengers and scouts brought news of a massacre at the House of Hoo. Roe had a talk with Ramala before she left. He wanted to know if the rumors that were just getting to him from the north were true. Guards told Ramala where Roe was. She didn't need escorts. Ramala knew every inch of Roe's palace. That's where she grew up at. Ramala met Roe at his palace, in one of his private rooms.

Roe was waiting on her when she got there. He stood up from the chair he was sitting on, when Ramala walked over to him. She gave him a big hug, then smiled at Roe, and said "What's so important that we had to meet in private?" Roe's face went from happy to see Ramala, to serious. He asked her "What happened at the House of Hoo?"

Ramala said "As you know, I was escorting my sister Japha, Jania back to her home. Everything was going good, until the House of Hoo refused to let us visit there. Then we found ourselves surrounded by the He army to the South, and the Japha army to the North. We didn't have enough forces to deal with all of them. That's when I decided to make an example of the Hoo. Me, Tara, and Wana marched right up to the House of Hoo. We gave them two triple screams. The first one reduced the main gate to rubble. The second one destroyed all of the buildings and people in the House of Hoo. Not one person survived. You should have seen it! I knew a triple scream was powerful, but I didn't know it could do that!"

Roe sighed, then said "Do you even know what you've done?" Ramala could see that Roe wasn't excited, or proud of her as she thought he would be. She said "I know if we hadn't done that, I wouldn't be here talking to you now. You would be heading North with your armies to take revenge for the deaths of your daughter and your nieces. The He and the Japha backed off after they found out what we did. We didn't have anymore trouble after that. We had no choice."

Roe had a very troubled look on his face. He said "And you think this is the end of it? Ramala, you are making enemies at an alarming rate. It's only a matter of time before they figure out how to get to you. Even if you have the support of those Japha twins, they won't be able to stop the four Houses from making attemps on your life. You can't keep up this kind of behavior. Taking from, and killing anyone who gets in your way. I don't want to see anything happen to you. You're right about one thing.

If they kill my daughter, even though I know you're wrong, I will march my army and take revenge. Don't you see that you may not only end up destroying the House of Ra, but you also might end up destroying the House of Hayee."

Roe paused for a moment to let Ramala know how serious he thought things were. The he said "You have two young children to take care of, and another one on the way. Please tell me that you are not going to try to take over any more territory."

Ramala looked at Roe. She didn't answer for a moment. When she finally did, she said "I could lie to you, to make you feel better, but I won't. I'm not finished yet. If something happens to me. Don't be angry at anyone. Don't put the House of Hayee into danger because of me. This is what I do." Then Ramala gave Roe another hug and a kiss. Then she left. Roe watched her as she left. He had the uneasy feeling that one of these times might be the last time he would see his daughter.

The Butchers were happy to be moving away from the House of Hayee. This was the first time that they were there, and they didn't have to fight for their lives. Well they didn't actually go in the House of Hayee, but it was close enough for them.

Ma rode with Yin, but didn't talk to him much. She could see he was still bothered by, what she thought was Tara ignoring him. Ma smiled to herself. She thought Yin just might calm down a little, once he saw his child. Then she thought about the Hellcats. Ma had already been bested at fighting, by Wana and Ramala. She hadn't fought Tara yet. Before Ma and Cat left the Monastery, Cat was the only person to regularly beat her. Now it seemed, to her, that most every one on her team was better than her. That didn't sit well with Ma. You can't be called a Butcher, if you're always getting your ass kicked! Ma smiled inwardly. They were going back to the House of Ra. She would have time to train. The next time she got into a fight, some one was going to move behind her in the getting your ass kicked category.

Cat was spending most of her time shadowing Wana. Cat knew Wana was the best at what she did. Cat watched Wana as she ordered the troops into certain formations, depending on the situation. Wana was pleased that Cat took interest in security, and would explain to her what she was doing. Cat knew it would be a waste of time to try to learn how to be a conqueror like Ramala. There was only enough room for one Ruler around here. Besides, Cat knew she could kill at will, but she didn't think she could be as ruthless as Ramala. She didn't know anyone as ruthless as Ramala.

Syn, Jara rested most of the way back home. For the most part she enjoyed this trip. It had been very exciting and none of her sisters were killed. She thought about Jan and San. She was pretty sure that they would be alright. She found that she really missed Jan. She thought about her grandfather. Before she met the Butchers, the Japha twins, and the Hellcats, she used to think about her grandfather every day. Even though she still thought about him, from time to time, now she had more family to think about.

Tara was feeling the effects of being with child. On the way back, she was just starting to show. She found herself being easily annoyed and she felt uncomfortable most of the time. She couldn't stand the sight of Yin. That was the main reason she stayed away from Yin now. She wondered what kind of degenerate seed Yin had put in her, to make her dislike everyone so much. Tara had become very sensitive to people touching her and would only put up with it, if it was done by Wana, or Ramala. Even then she could only take so much of them touching her. Tara didn't know why she felt that way, but figured it was because of her condition. Tara thought that if this was what it was like to have a child. Why would anyone want to do this?

Wana rewarded herself with a good time once they reached the House of Hayee. Her cousins were happy to take a shot at trying to fill Wana's sexual needs. Now that they were back on the road again, she was focused and ready for anything. She thought she had done a good job, so far, considering the circumstances. They completed their mission, of proving that the Hellcats couldn't be dealt with. And no one in the Royal court had been killed.

Wana took pride in doing a good job. She always gave herself a reward for doing well. They still weren't home yet. But when they got there, Wana planned on giving herself a real treat. The guards of Ra had it easy on this trip. Wana was going to make them work hard pleasing her, once she got home.

Ramala thought about what her father said. Still he didn't understand that Ramala planned on increasing her territory by moving far into the Southern Jungle. Now that Jan was in control of the Northern Houses, and after the Hellcats showed what they could do. She knew she wouldn't get much trouble from the North.

Now Ramala could focus all of her attention on seeing

why every time that they sent scouts into the Southern Jungle, either they never returned, or they were sent back from a fight that they couldn't give much information on the enemy. Even though that happened three years ago, she hadn't forgotten about it. Ramala had to let it go while preparing for the war. Once she returned home she was going to make plans to move her armies into the Southern Jungle. She also was going to put her twins back on their strict training schedule. Ramala looked over at La, who was sitting quietly looking out over the plains. La had gotten out of hand a couple of times on this trip. Ramala hadn't forgotten about that either!

Even though Dan took revenge on the He Warlords that had him running, it still bothered him greatly. Ramala sensed something had happened in the field, but refused to question Dan about it. She could see that it was a sore spot with him. She knew if she pressed him, it would cause a big fight. Ramala didn't mind a fight at home, but she didn't want one in the field.

Dan went over the battle with the eight Warlords over and over in his mind. He tried to think of what he could have done better to win that battle. He came up with a few things. One of them was simple. He just wasn't good enough. He was going to take his practices to a new level. If he ever faces eight Warlords again, they wouldn't stand a chance in Hell of beating him!

Two days after leaving the House of Japha, Yin had his nightmare again. This time it didn't bother him as much. He thought because he had the dream so many times, it didn't quite have the same affect of him. One thing he knew for sure. When he was in battle, the nights never brought that dream. Yin didn't want to have that dream anymore. He would have to make sure there was always a battle to fight. If there wasn't, he didn't have a problem making one.

Backir was thinking about how soon he would be able to get into some dancers, once they reached Yee province. He knew Chi would have the best dancers waiting on them, back at the Spot. Backir missed the Spot. That place was special to him. After every show, he would have his pick of the dancers. New dancers, old dancers, it didn't matter. Eventually he would get to them all, several times over. Now that was living. Backir wondered if he could get Chi and Han to covince Ramala that they needed him to stay in Yee Province. That's what he wanted. That's what he was going to try to do.

Chapter 14

Scouts from Yee Province spotted the Royal Caravan. They sent word to Han and Chi. Guards were sent to the Caravan to see if they needed any assistance. The Yee guards stayed with the Caravan until it was inside Yee Province. Han and Chi were there to meet the Caravan once it made it to the city. The Hellcats met with Han briefly, to find out where they would be staying. After Han showed them the arrangements he made for them, the Hellcats split up for some down time.

All three girls needed a nap before the evening came. Chi took the Butchers to a new private eatery that the Butchers hadn't been to before. They all sat down, ate, and talked about the last few months. Half way through their meal, the Death Squad came in and joined them. The D-Squad sat at table's right next to the Butchers. It surprised the Butchers to see the D-Squad in the day time. This was the first time that the Butchers and the D-Squad met besides the nights at the spot. The D-Squad had nine members. None of them were related.

The first girl was Dina. Dina was taller than all of the other girls, including the Butcher girls. She wasn't thin, but she wasn't thick. She had some meat on her tall frame. Most of that meat was muscle . Dina was very smart. Even though Dina was smart, she was a very good killer. When the D-Squad had to listen to reason, they usually listened to Dina.

Kiki was about the same height and wieght as the Syn, Jara. Which was medium height, and very muscular, but not thick. Kiki was like Yin. Some how she got killing in her blood, and now she can't stop herself. Kiki also had other skills. Kiki was as crazy in bed, as she was about killing. Kiki had a look in her eyes like Yin. A crazy look, that made her look as closely related to Yin as Ma. Everyone noticed that about them, as soon as they saw Kiki and Yin together.

Like Yin she didn't trust her own judgment. So Kiki stayed quiet and followed orders. Once Kiki started killing, she couldn't calm herself down. Someone had to do it for her. It usually was the other D-Squad members.

Nana was thicker than the other two girls. She was shorter than Dina, and Taller than Kiki. She wasn't fat, but she was a sturdy work horse. She had a solid Hundred fifty-five pounds on her. Men, I'm talking about U.S.D.A. prime Heifer, without the fat! She also had a violent streak like Kiki, but she could turn hers on and off, at will. Most of the time she would do the smart thing, but she could be talked into a massacre, if she was in the right mood.

Then there was Tiger. Tiger was about the same size as Yin. Tiger had good killing skills. He always likes to challenge just about anyone. It didn't help that he had no social skills what so ever. Most of the time he would talk himself into a fight. Sometimes he would just do things that resulted in a fight. Either way, at some point in the day, Tiger would probably get into a fight.

Mangler was next. He was a brute like Backir, only larger. Just like Backir, he wasn't fat. You wouldn't want to find yourself in a wrestling match with him. He was a giant. Besides him being big. The next thing you noticed about him was that he had unusually large hand. Even for a big man. They looked like bear paws. He was a very good killer. They had a reason for calling him Mangler. He liked to inflict serious pain. Most of his opponents end up mangled. After seeing him, it surprised you, when he talked, that he was quite intelligent. He was very vocal, but he measured his words. He wasn't as offensive talking as the other members were.

Dirt was the next Squad member. He was a little smaller than Tiger. He had ripped muscles, and was very strong for his size. He was a good killer. He could fight like hell. But his specialty was torture. Some how he knew just how to inflict severe pain on the human body, with out killing. Mangler was his side-kick. Between him and Mangler, the D-Squad always got information from whoever they tortured.

Went-wrong was another brute on the D-Squad team. He wasn't as big as Mangler. He was about the same size as Backir.They called him Went-wrong because somewhere along the way his mind went wrong. He was a viscious killer. He didn't have much of a personality. If he was told to kill, or thought it was the right thing to do, that's what he did. Besides that he wasn't much trouble. If you started something with him. That's when things went wrong, for you.

Spider was the next Squad member. Spider was quick with his hands. He was the fastest Squad member. In a fight, Spider would be all over an opponent. He also was quick witted, had a quick temper, quickest to kill, quickest to get a woman in bed (but not quick in bed), quickest to kick a woman out of bed (if she had no skills, and refused to be trained at what Spider liked, or if he was done with her), and quickest to get to the food. You get the picture. Like a spider, he was quick.

Then there was One-time. They called him One-time because he had a great memory. If you told him something one time. No matter how complicated it was. He could remember it. If the D-Squad made a plan, he made sure they remembered everything. He would have made a great messenger, if it weren't for his good fighting skills. He wasn't the smartest Squad member, but if you said something, or did something, he could remember it exactly.

The Butchers and the D-Squad members usually didn't say much to each other. The girls would greet each other, and exchange smiles. The girls might have light conversation some times. The men didn't say anything to each other. They didn't know each other that well. Today the girls on both sides were telling of their adventures out in the field.

All of the men were sitting back, relaxing, after a good meal. Cat stood up and stretched her body. The D-Squad men were heathens, just like the Butchers, only not as well mannered. All of them stared at Cat like she was putting on a show, especially for them. Cat had her back to the D-Squad, and couldn't see them staring. The D-Squad girls noticed, but said nothing. Neither did the Butcher girls, but they were focused on the D-Squad men now.

Tiger had a devilish grin on his face. He said "Would you take a look at that." One-time was sitting next to Tiger, and he was just as impressed. He remembered her name. One-time smiled, looked over at Tiger, and said "They call her Cat." Cat heard her name, and turned around. Tiger gave Cat a big smile, then said "I can beat the hell out of a Cat, and she'll like it."

Cat stared at Tiger. Tiger was talking about sex. Cat didn't know that. She thought he was challenging her to a fight. When confronted, the Cat would become very aggressive if she had to. She knew he couldn't be serious, so Cat dismissed Tiger with a smile, and said "You can't handle this Cat."

Now Tiger was sure Cat was flirting with him. He stood up. Dina said "Tiger, don't start." Tiger said "I'm just being friendly." Tiger walked over to Cat. Cat stood her ground and watched Tiger closely. She kept a smile on her face, because she didn't want Tiger to think she thought he was a serious threat. Tiger took that to mean that Cat wanted him to continue flirting with her. He walked slowly over to Cat, as not to alarm her. Cat watched Tiger closely.

Dina Warned "Tiger!" Tiger ignored Dina. She didn't undrestand the play that was going on here. Tiger said "I can handle any Cat." Tiger was close to Cat. Close enough to slowly move his hand and put it on Cat's waist. Cat looked at Tiger's hand, then gave him a stern stare that said she was serious. Tiger let his hand fall down to Cat's butt, and left it there. But only for a second. Cat threw a punch at Tiger's face that she knew he would block with his free hand. A split second later, she threw her other fist as hard as she could into Tiger's ribs. His hand came off her butt immediately. He tried to bring it up to a better fighting position, but Cat blocked it by swinging back the elbow of the arm that connected the blow to the ribs. Tiger was about to swing with his other hand, but Cat threw another punch, this time harder at his face.

Again he had to respct it, and he blocked it. Cat did the same move smashing her fist again into the ribs that she already hit once. This time Tiger grimaced in pain. He backed up quickly to regroup. As he did, he instinctively yelled "You fucking whore!"

In that same second, he attacked Cat. They were swinging and kicking wildly at each other. Everyone on both sides had to back up out of the way so as not to get hit by one of the powerful blows. Cat kept going hard. She wasn't going to be beaten today.

Tiger was furious. This girl had embarrassed him in front of his friends. She was going to pay for that! Everyone on both sides refused to break up the fight. Both sides wanted to see what the other could do. This was the first time they saw each other in action. Cat was finding out that Tiger was no push over. He had regrouped enough to where he was starting to take control of the fight. Cat hadn't been hit yet, but she was starting to run a little.

Cat decided to go for the only advantage she had. She decided it was worth it to exchange blows with Tiger if she could blast him in the ribs again. She knew she had bruised them pretty good earlier. They had to be very sore by now, with all of the twisting and turning that Tiger was doing. Cat was faster than Tiger and landed just before he did. She smahed her fist into his ribs as hard as she could, at the same place where she hit him before. That took almost everything off the punch that Tiger threw. Cat busted up his ribs. Tiger's face tightened in pain as his punch landed with very little force at all.

Cat had the advantage she needed, and she wasn't going to waste it. Before Tiger could regroup, Cat took him apart with a powerful seven piece combination before anyone could stop her. It ended with a kick that landed under Tiger's chin and lifted him off of the ground, flying backwards. He crashed to the floor. Tiger made a couple of gurgling sound, while trying to lift himself up with his arms. He never made it up. Tiger went crashing back to the floor, and died there with his eyes open.

Cat was so pumped up that she stood over Tiger, and let out a scream. Spider was offended at Cat's gloating. He took two steps, jumped in the air, and was on his way towards Cat. Cat heard the two steps, but did not hear another one. She knew serious trouble was behind her. There was no time to turn and look. She tucked and rolled out of the way, just as Spider missed with a powerfully deadly kick where Cat's head used to be. It surely would have killed her if it had landed. When Spider landed, he didn't stop there. Before Cat could get to her feet, Spider was right up on her.

Luckily for Cat, she came up right in the middle of Syn and Backir. Syn blocked Spider and threw a couple of speedy blows that were to fast to be block, and Spider had to respect. He backed up out of the way of Syn's blows, just as a large table was flying through the air, coming at the Butchers, courtesy of the Mangler. Backir smashed the table into pieces with the powerful swing of both his forearms. Mangler came right after the table and started in on Backir. Now it was too late for reasoning. It was a good thing that neither side had weapons, because they went at each other hard as they could.

Wana and the other Hellcats were told by guards that a fight between Tiger and Cat was going on at the near by eatery.

Wana jumped up and raced to the scene, along with Han, Chi, and some elite guards. Wana got there only a few minutes after the table throwing incident. There was only one way this fight was going to be broken up immediately. Wana took in air and let out a powerful scream. It froze everyone in the eatery, while exploding glasses, vases, and other dishes.

The ones that were fighting off balance, fell frozen to the floor. As all of the Butchers and D-Squad member stood, or laid on the ground frozen, Dan realized that Wana's scream was more powerful than Ramala's. At least this one was, compared to the one Ramala gave him back when they were in Anduku's territory. What Dan didn't know was that Ramala took something off of that scream because it was Dan, and they were indoors. Wana looked around the eatery. It was almost totally destroyed. Wana was very angry, and those who were facing her could see it in her face. The ones that couldn't see who blasted them, were glad it was Wana's voice they first heard, instead of Ramala's. Wana yelled "What the Hell happened here!?" No one answered. They were all frozen. Wana yelled again "I can't rest because a bunch of heathens can't control themselves!"

Wana turned and saw Tara and Ramala walking up. Both of these girls' stomachs were just starting to poke through their clothes. Wana beat them to the eatery because they weren't going anywhere in a hurry. They walked there, taking their time. Tara and Ramala looked at the damage and then looked at Wana. Wana said "Can you believe this?" Ramala said "Calm down Wa. We'll find out what happened as soon as they regain movement. We'll wait and see if they have a good reason for this."

Dan and Syn were the first two to regain movement. Everyone else did after that. Syn told the Hellcats everything that happened, just as it happened. She ended it with "That Tiger is dead." Ramala walked towards the combatants. Now the D-Squad and the Butchers were standing there waiting on Ramala to say something. Wana had them line up, all except Dan. He knew he was exempt from whatever punishment Ramala would be dishing out. He stepped over to where the Hellcats were standing.

Ramala looked over at Tiger's lifeless body. She turned back and said "Does anyone have anything to add to the story?" Spider said "She didn't have to kill him. Tiger was just playing around with her." Ramala said "Just playing around! What's this playing around thing? Touching a female killer's ass is what you

call just playing around. Is that the way the Death Squad thinks? Is
that the way the Butchers think? Is that what any of you are here
for! Well, somebody answer me?!"

Ramala wasn't looking for an answer. She just wanted to
make sure everyone was intimidated by her. No one said a word.
Not one of them was willing to risk saying the wrong thing.
Ramala walked up to Mangler, who was the first one in the line
up. He looked at Ramala and quickly received a backhand slap and
the return open hand slap. Mangler quickly debated whether it
would be worth it to kill Ramala right where she stood. He knew
the other Hellcats would blast him with a scream and take his head
after he did that. He would take it for now. Ramala stared at him
looking for the slightest reaction. Even though she was with child,
she still was much quicker than Mangler. She could evade any
move he made. After that, he would be dead. Because he didn't
move, she put up her hand. Mangler took it gently and kissed the
back of it .

. Each of the male D-Squad members received the same
double slap, swallowed their pride and kissed Ramala's hand
afterwards. Backir and Yin only got the back hand slap, but they
still had to kiss Ramala's hand.

Kiki decided that if Ramala slapped her, she was going to
kill Ramala before anyone could stop her. Kiki didn't mind dying.
She knew it was going to happen to her eventually. But for her to
just stand there and let someone slap the hell out of her. Well, that
wasn't going to happen. If one of the other D-Squad members
decided that they weren't going to take it, before Ramala got to
Kiki. Kiki would join them, until they killed everyone, or they
were killed. Kiki looked at the ground, tried to calmed herself and
waited.

Dina was the first girl on either side that Ramala got to.
Ramala didn't slap Dina. She didn't slap any of the girls on either
side. As she got to the females, she lifted their chins so that their
eyes were level with hers. Then she put her hand up. Each girl
took her hand and kissed the back of it. When Ramala got to Kiki
and lifted her chin. Ramala could see that Kiki would rather die
than stand there and be slapped. She stared at Kiki a little longer
than she did the rest of the girls.

Ramala had to stop herself from slapping Kiki, just to
show Kiki that she would. Ramala knew Kiki couldn't deal with
her before her cousins got to Kiki and killed her. Ramala thought

if she wasn't with child, she would beat Kiki in a fair fight, as an example to the others. Instead Ramala smiled at Kiki. She knew she could get this girl to do a lot of killing for her, before she would have to kill her.

Ramala stepped back and looked at the sky. She said "Tiger got just what he deserved. That's in the past now. Let it go. I'm with child now. I am easily agitated, and it brings out my lust for killing . If another one of you touches one of my girls. Whether it is my Death Squad girls, or my Butcher girls, I don't care who it is. I'm going to act like you touched me. Then we'll see just how much that person likes to play."

She paused, and looked at all of them. Then she said "The Butchers and the Death Squad will be working together on some things I have planned. You all had better start getting along a lot better than this. No more fights, unless it's practice. I need to get the most out of my team. Does everyone understand that!?" Everyone on both sides said "Yes Mistress Queen Ramala! "

After the Hellcats left, Han had the two sides separated. This would give them time to calm themselves and think about what Ramala said, without having to look at each other. The D-Squad went with Han, and The Butchers went with Chi. Chi took them to his privte home. The Butchers had been there on their brief stay, before the war. None of the Butchers got hurt in the fight with the Squad, except for Backir. His forearms were cut and bruised.

Once they were at Chi's place, Chi had some maids dress Backir's wounds. Chi looked at Cat and said "You could have roughed Tiger up pretty good. Was it really necessary to kill him?" Cat Said "He got what he deserved." Syn added "Tiger isn't the type to take a beating and leave it at that. I knew that the first time I met him. Cat did the right thing." Chi said "I hope it doesn't cause trouble between you and them." Yin, who fought with dirt said "It already has." Ma said "Yin, don't go looking for trouble. I don't want to have to keep kissing Ramala's hand, and I know you don't like getting slapped."

Everyone including Yin had tried to put that out of their mind. Ma just had to remind them. Yin looked away in anger. He couldn't wait until he could start working on his kill when you get a chance list. And yes, right now, Ramala was on the top of that list. The Syn, Jara said "We'll get along because we have to. If they start a fight with you, finish it. Show them no mercy. These are the kind of killers, if you beat them, you have to kill them. Otherwise, they will get you later." All of the Butchers nodded in agreement with Syn, including Yin.

All of the D-Squad members had a place in Yee province. Han and the D-Squad went to Dina's place. Han had a short meeting with the D-Squad making sure that they knew they couldn't take revenge for Tiger. Otherwise Ramala might have them all killed. After Han left, Kiki stood up, looked at her comrades. She said "Tiger's dead!" Went-Wrong said "Let's take our revenge!" Dirt said "Give me half a day with Cat. She'll wish she had never heard of Tiger!"

One-Time warned "If something happens to Cat, that Hayee, Ramala will have all of our heads. She means business." One-Time looked at Dina to talk some sense into the others. Dina said "Alright, we have to get along with them. So we play it cool. Find out as much as we can about them, without making them suspicious. Kiki, Nana, you two work on the Butcher men. You know, soften them up a bit with some boom booming. (They called sex boom booming) Get them talking.You guys keep your distance from the Butcher girls. They're not into boom booming, yet. But if they want to get friendly, let them. Spider, see what you can do with them, but be careful. Take it slow with these girls. If they think you're trying to play them, things could get ugly real quick." Mangler asked Dina "What are you going to do?" Dina smiled at Mangler and said "What I always do. Watch, and make plans that are good for the Death-Squad."

Later that night, The Butchers headed to the Spot. All of them were a little excited to be going back there. They could relax and watch a good show. The Butcher men wanted to see if there were any new female dancers that they could take advantage of at the end of the night. The Butcher girls just wanted to chill and dance to the drum beats. The Hellcats weren't with them, but Yaya was. This was the first time she didn't have the guards watching her. She was hoping that she could get to the kitchen and talk to her cousins, without the Butchers finding out.

They entered the front of the restaurant as usual, then walked to the back, and into the Spot. Everything looked the same. That was one thing you could count on about this place. It never changed. Most of the same guards, and servants were still there. The Butchers noticed a few new faces. The Butchers sat down. It was still early, so the place was only half full. The D-Squad wasn't in their booth. They always arrived later.

A servant came up to the booth where the Butchers were, and asked if the wanted something to eat or drink. They all wanted drinks . Yaya jumped up and said "I'll get their drinks!" She walked quickly to the kitchen. When Yaya walked through the kitchen door, the first person she saw was Hania. Yaya's eyes lit up with happiness when she saw her cousin. Hania was preparing some food. She had her back turned, and didn't see Yaya at first.

Hania turned and saw Yaya. When she saw Yaya she tried to smile, but winced in pain. Yaya looked over Hania's face. She had been beaten up pretty good. Hania looked at the ground with a defeated look on her face. Yaya walked quickly over to her. Hania looked at Yaya trying to hold back tears. Yaya looked a question without speaking. Who did this to you? Hania's eyes moved to the head servant, then back to Yaya. This was the same man that had beaten Yaya on many occasions.

It took a lot for Yaya to hate someone. She hated this man. Anger rose in her almost instantly. Hania could see it and got nervous. She didn't need Yaya starting trouble, then leaving. That would mean a severe beating after Yaya and the Butchers were gone. The head servant looked over and saw Yaya and Hania. He knew he couldn't say anything to Yaya. The Butcher girls had aready warned him about that. So he said in a stern voice "Hania! That food isn't going to prepare itself! Hurry up! I have guest waiting!" Hania jumped, and started preparing the food again. Yaya was burning up inside with hatred. Outwardly she tried to keep her composure. The head servant could see that Yaya was affected by the way he talked to Hania. He smiled to himself. Yaya looked at him and said "I need a tray to bring drinks to the Butchers." The head servant turned to point to the trays. That's when Yaya pulled out her machete that was on her waist, as quick as she could. Then she plowed it, as hard as she could, as fast as she could, into and through his heart. He was caught off guard. Blood went squirting everywhere. He fell into the trays, sending them crashing to the floor. It made a loud noise. The female servants screamed. The guards that were in the kitchen instantly drew their weapons and surrounded Yaya. Other guards came running into the kitchen to see what had happened. Yaya stood there over the dead body with her machete in her hand.

Everyone in the Spot heard the loud crash of the trays, as well as the screams from the sevants. The Butchers looked at the kitchen entrance, wondering what was going on in there. One of the guards came out of the kitchen and looked at Chi. He motioned for Chi to come. Then the guard looked at Cat and Syn. They immediately knew it had something to do with Yaya and got up with Chi. Ma followed closely behind.

When they walked into the kitchen they saw Yaya surrounded. Blood was all over the floor. Chi looked at Yaya, who was frozen, staring at the body. Chi ordered "Leave her be. Get someone to clean up this mess."

The Butcher girls walked over to Yaya. Syn grabbed Yaya's wrist that the machete was in, and took the machete from her hand. Yaya was still in shock at what she had done. Just as Syn let go of Yaya's wrist, Cat grabbed Yaya and shook her by her shoulders, and said "Snap out of it. Tell me, what happened here." Yaya looked up at Cat and said "I don't know. I just did it. He beat me so many times, I just did it."

In the stress of the moment, Yaya looked over at Hania. Chi and the Butcher girls looked over too. They could see that Hania had been beaten. Hania got nervous, and started to walk away. Chi said "You! Hold it!" Cat said "Chi take it easy." Cat turned back to Yaya and asked "Is she why you did it?"

Yaya looked at Cat, then looked around the room nervously. She didn't want to get Hania in any trouble, so she didn't answer. Chi watched Yaya's reaction as he said "Girl, come here!" Hania walked nervously to Chi with her head down. Chi said "There are a lot of customers that are waiting on food and drink. Make sure there're not disappointed." Then Chi turned and said "Who else can run this kitchen?"

An older lady stepped up. Chi asked "It seems our little Butcher doesn't like it when the girls are beaten. Can you run this place without beating these girls?" The old lady nodded yes. Chi asked Hania her Name. She told him. Chi said "Alright, you can get back to work."

Syn found a towel and wiped the blood from the machete. She turned and gave the machete back to Yaya. Yaya put it away. Cat said in a stern voice "Go back to the booth, and don't get up with out asking." Yaya said "What about the drinks?" Cat said "Your friend can get them for us."

Then all of the Buthcers returned to the booth. When they got there, Yin asked "What was all the fuss about?" Chi said "The Young Butcher just made her first kill." Yin smiled, looked at

Yaya, and said "Nice. How did it feel?" Ma scolded "Yin! Leave her alone!"

Ma stared at Yin for a moment, until she was sure that he would let it go. Then everyone turned, as the D-Squad made their way into the Spot. They walked towards their booth. When they got to the Butchers booth, which was before theirs, they all stopped. Dina and the other D girls were in front of the men. Dina looked at the Butcher girls, then said "That Tiger should have listened to my warnings. He was always looking for trouble. He found it. I hope we can still be friends. It looks like we will be working together. Whether we want to or not."

Dina smiled at the Butcher girls, while the men on both sides watched everything closely, just in case a fight broke out. Then Dina said "I don't think that's a bad thing. I like the Butchers." She turned and walked to the booth, followed by the other members of the Squad.

The Butchers didn't talk about what had just happened. They relaxed and waited on the dancers. It didn't take long for the dancers to come out and get started. Hania brought out drinks for the Butchers. After serving the drinks, she gave a quick look of thanks to Yaya. Yaya wished she could have had time to ask Hania how Mayho and Najay were doing. If she got the chance she would find out herself.

The drums died down and the dancers took a short break. The D girls, who normally dance with the dancers, stayed in the booth this time. They just move back and forth in their seats, to the beat of the drums. Then the drums started up again. The dancers got back on the floor and started their routine. This time the D girls got up and started dancing. They moved onto the Dance floor. They slowly danced their way over to and in front of the Butchers booth. None of the D girls looked in the booth. They just danced there, having a good time.

They weren't there more than a couple of minutes before Syn stood up. Cat and Ma stared at her. She looked at them and smiled. Then she headed onto the dance floor. Cat and Ma followed right behind her. They started dancing next to the D girls. Then all of the girls slowly started making eye contact while dancing. They all started smiling. They were having fun.

As usual, the Butcher men and the Squad men were standing and staring. The men from both sides took a short look at each other. More like a scan for hostile intent. No one seemed to be looking for trouble, so they all went back to staring at the girls. They were figuring out which of the dancers would give them the best time later tonight. That was a lot more interesting than starting a fight.

Dina didn't have to tell the D-girls which Butchers to go for. Just like game recognizes game. The same recognizes the same. That's why Kiki went after Yin and Nana went after Backir.

Kiki had been abused by men at an early age. It taught her one thing. The sooner the man gets satisfied, the sooner he leaves her alone. Kiki wanted to be left alone. So she found out what would get men to the point of satisfaction as quickly as possible. Then she got very good at it. She was a slave to a tribal Warlord who was killed by the D-Squad. What Kiki hadn't learned on her own, was taught to her by this Warlord. As young as she was, she was an expert at pleasing a man. The Squad was going to sell her, along with the other females, until the Squad men found out about Kiki's talents. They kept her for their own personal use.

Dina recognized that Kiki had a violent streak and began to teach her to fight. Kiki quickly took to fighting. She liked fighting. Eventually it kept the Squad men off of her, unless she wanted them. A fight with Kiki could last for days, and would eventually bring the other D-girls in to defend Kiki. So most of the time, it wasn't worth the trouble for the Squad-men to force Kiki to do what they wanted.

Kiki saw the crazy look in Yin's eyes and knew there was something there she wanted to find out about. As Kiki danced, she would stare at Yin until she was sure she had his attention. Then she challenged him with her eyes. Because of the fight earlier, Yin thought she wanted to fight him. He wasn't going to back down from a fight. Even if it meant getting slapped, and having to kiss Ramala's hand. Now Kiki had Yin's attention. He wasn't going to start a fight, but he was going to finish it. She would learn the hard way, you don't challenge Yin.

Nana used a different approach. She danced and show-cased her body for everyone to see. Because she kept a smile on her face, no one could tell when she looked at Backir, that she was trying to entice him. Except for Backir. He knew almost right away. He watched as Nana looked at him a few more times. Each time a little longer than the one before. Now he was sure. He'd been watching the D-girls every since the first time he saw them dance. In his mind, he knew exactly what he would do to each one of them if he got the chance. Nana was thick. He liked that about her. Backir smiled to himself. He knew what he could do. She had better be as sturdy as she looked. And still, she had better bring a friend, or two. If not, it's going to be a long hard night for her!

The energy was heavy in the air tonight at the Spot. Everyone could feel it. Dan looked at all of the dancers. Studying them, trying to see which two or three would be the right combination for tonight. Looking out on the floor, he didn't see how he could go wrong, whoever he chose. In the fight, earlier today, he didn't get to administer punishment to anyone. It was going to be different tonight. Someone's got to be punished! Ramala was with child. So it wasn't going to be her. It might as well be a couple of those girls!

The Butcher girls could also feel the energy in the Spot. Besides the D-girls and the other female dancers dancing with them. Also, there were men dancers. All of the girls could enjoy watching and dancing around these men. These men weren't going to cause any trouble with the Butcher girls or the D-girls. They were going to behave, unless they were told otherwise. But still, the male dancers had very good looking bodies. The girls couldn't help but notice that. The Butcher girls enjoyed looking at the men, but they worked their extra energy out dancing. On the other hand, the D-girls would get worked up with dancing. Later they would pick a male dancer, or two to work off the rest of their extra energy. The other D-girls had a mission. That meant Dina could take her time and choose between the male dancers, and not have to compete for the Dancers with Kiki and Nana.

Chapter 15

It was getting late, and the Butcher girls had seen enough of the Spot to know where things were heading. Dan had two of the dancers, sitting next to him. Backir was talking to some of the dancers, along with Nana. Yin was talking to some of the dancers, when Kiki walked towards him. She stared at him the entire time.

It caught Yin's attention that someone was staring at him. That's when they locked eyes. Yin watched her as she came closer. She didn't scare him, if that's what she thought. Kiki walked right through the girls that were standing next to Yin, and moved very close up on Yin. Kiki never broke eye contact with Yin, while saying "You would pick those girls. You know you could bully them." Kiki bullied Yin with her body, by bumping lightly into him with her hips and breasts, while she was talking. An evil grin came on Yin's face. He said "Forcing me to fight is going to be a big mistake for you."

Kiki bullied Yin again with her body, while saying "I'm not talking about fighting, I'm talking about some boom boom. But I don't care, we can do either." Kiki wasn't smiling. Yin lost focus on the other girls for a second. Yin knew he could beat the hell out of Kiki in bed. If she wanted to fight after that, he could do that too.

Yin looked at the other girls around him. Kiki saw him and said "You won't need them. I'll be enough tonight." This time Kiki's hips and breast pushed a little harder on Yin. Yin thought about how many girls had thought that they would be enough. Only to find out, always bring a friend when boom booming with Yin! He wasn't going to tell Kiki that. She'd find out like the other girls did. The hard way!

The Syn had had enough of this. She walked over to the booth, and looked at Yaya. That meant it was time to go. Yaya was tired and fighting sleep, because of all of the excitement around her. Ma and Cat saw Syn, looked at each other, and knew it was time to go. Ma looked over at Yin, and saw he was busy talking to Kiki. Cat saw Dan and walked over to him, to let him know they were leaving. Cat looked at the two girls with Dan. She knew he would be with them tonight. For some reason, that she wasn't ready to admit to herself, it bothered her. Cat tried to hide her frustration, but Dan could see it. Cat looked at Dan, and said "We're leaving."

Cat pushed her way between the dancers daring them to look at her, and bumped her body into Dan's. Much in the same way that Kiki had done to Yin. But Cat was more forceful with her body. Dan's reaction was grabbing Cat,and holding her there against his body, for a moment. Just as Cat was about to push away, Dan let her go. Cat looked at Dan for a Quick second, then she walked away. Dan thought that would teach her not to push up on him like that, if she didn't want anything.

When Cat turned around, she saw Ma smiling at her, and Syn giving her a stern look. Cat didn't care. She ignored both of them. At first Cat was only slightly attracted to Dan. She wanted to keep him as a close ally that would always have her back in battle. After the first time Cat saw Dan naked, she couldn't get it out of her head. Now, it was more than a slight attraction. The only reason she hadn't let herself be with Dan, was she didn't want to always be second to Ramala.

Emotions were building in Cat. That's the reason that Cat was so aggressive on the trip. It was one of the reasons she killed Tiger, instead of just giving him a stern beating, as a warning to back off. Syn could see that Cat's feelings for Dan were manifesting itself in aggressive behavior. Syn knew the Cat was going to have to deal with her feelings for Dan, or she's going to get totally out of control. Ma was thinking the same thing. That's why Syn had a serious look on her face, and why Ma just smiled. The Butcher girls went back to their sleeping quarters.

This night was an epic battle between two top warriors in their field of superiority. Kiki had a plan in her head of just how to deal with someone as crazy as Yin. She was going to put her plan in motion, right away. Kiki was following Yin to one of his private sleeping quarters. Kiki followed close to Yin and kept pushing up agaist him, bullying him with her firm body. Yin told himself, only a little further to go, then she catches hell. They almost didn't get to Yin's place because of Kiki. Yin was two seconds from dealing with her right on the street.

When they got to the door, Yin opened it. He was going to surprise her with a quick attack. Kiki jammed Yin in the doorway. Yin forced his way inside.

Kiki surprised Yin at how strong she was, by spinning around him and smashing his back into the wall, right inside the door. Just before retreating to a safe distance, right out of Yin's reach, she ripped his shirt while backing up from him. Then Kiki said in her best unimpressed voice "Look at you. They call You Butcher Yin. So far, I'm not impressed."

Yin said "Well me either. You call that rough!" Kiki said "No I don't. Let me get undressed, then I'll show you something." Yin said "The way you've been pushing up on me with that body of yours, why should I wait?"

Then he moved towards Kiki. Kiki was very fast. She out maneuvered Yin. He couldn't catrch her. Yin circled Kiki, while Kiki watched him closely. Kiki said "You should wait because I won't run, once I get undressed. Or you can waste time chasing me." Yin said "Go ahead, I can wait."

Kiki started removing her clothes. Yin watched closely. She did have a great body. He could see Kiki was having trouble with her boots. She looked at Yin and said "Can you help me?" Yin looked at her for a moment, then walked over to help. Kiki said "Grab the boot and pull."

Yin reached down and grabbed the boot with both hands. That's when Kiki slapped Yin right across the face with a good amount of force. Yin grabbed her and slammed her to the floor, on her back, landing on top of her. He held Kiki's wrist, stretching her arms over her head. Yin was two seconds from killing Kiki. Then she started laughing. She said "The look on your face after I slapped you!"

Before she could get another word out, Yin's hands were around her throat. He squeezed and watched as Kiki's eyes rolled up into their sockets. Yin braced himself and waited on Kiki to start swinging with her arms trying to save her life. She didn't though. Kiki regrouped, and her eyes came back. She stared at Yin with no fear in her eyes. She ran her fingernails up and down Yin's arms without scratching him.

Then Kiki started to shake from lack of oxygen. Her face

was calm, not panicked like Yin expected. He wasn't having fun. Yin let Kiki's neck go. Kiki breathed heavily, trying to get as much air back into her lungs as possible. Yin said "Next time I'll kill you."

Yin started to get up, but Kiki wrestled him until they were rolling on the ground. I could say what happened between these two, but I won't. Let's just say they tore up Yin's place going at it. Yin slung, dragged and drubbed Kiki through every room of his place. And I'm not talking about fighting. But it was a serious battle.

Yin had been with a lot of women in his thirty years. He had more than a couple, at the same time on many occasions. But Yin had never been with a woman this physical. Kiki knew just what to do to keep Yin two seconds from killing her the whole night, while Yin did everything to Kiki that he could think of sexually, and physically without killing her. And he was more than a little physical with Kiki. Kiki was good with all that. It was just what she needed.

In Yin's eyes, Kiki was truly a female warrior. She could take it, as well as give it. It took the whole night, and into the next morning to put Kiki down. When he had, Yin staggered into the next room and fell on the floor. Then they both passed out into a comatose sleep.

As usual, when Yin didn't get up on his own, Ma would go looking for him. Cat went along for the fun of it. Chi's guards told the girls where Yin was, and they made there way to his place. When they got there, Ma called out to Yin before she walked in. When Yin didn't answer, Ma and Cat walked in. They couldn't believe what they saw. Chairs were broken. A table was broken. They saw Kiki on the far end of the room laying on the floor next to another table. The whole place was torn up. It looked like someone ambushed these two in the middle of the night!

Ma panicked. She didn't see Yin. Cat saw Ma's reaction and said "Look in the other room. I'll see if she's still alive." Ma ran into the other room. That's where she saw Yin layed out, on the floor naked. Ma looked around. This room looked just as bad as the other one. Ma could see Yin's back rising and falling. He was breeathing. At least he wasn't dead. Then she realized what was going on here.

She Yelled "Yin! Get up!" Yin jerked his head up to see what was going on. Ma looked at Yin and couldn't believe what she was seeing. She erupted into uncontrollable laugher. Besides the scratch marks all over Yin's sides and back. He had a patch of hair missing on the left side of his head.

Yin picked himself up off the ground. He was still groggy. He looked at his hand and saw hair in it. He threw it on the floor. He knew it wasn't his. Then all of a sudden Yin was aware of all the scratches on his body. They were slightly stinging him every time he moved. He noticed his head was hurting. He didn't remember Kiki hitting him with anything, but he couldn't rule it out after last night. Then between laughing Ma said "What happened to your hair!?"

Yin rubbed his head. Something was wrong. He felt a thin patch on the side of his head where he knew hair used to be. He looked down at the hair on the ground. That wasn't his. He put on his pants and headed into the next room. He saw Cat standing there staring in disbelief over kiki. Yin walked up and saw that Kiki was laying on her stomach, with a patch of his hair clinched in her fist. Ma had followed Yin and saw Kiki.

Ma laughed until she had to go down on one knee from the pain in her stomach. Cat started laughing after Ma did. They just couldn't stop. Kiki didn't move. She was out cold.

Yin was so angry about his hair, that he thought about killing Kiki while she slept. He wasn't going to do it now. He turned and went into the next room, trying to make himself as presentable as someone who had a patch of hair missing could. Ma and Cat finally were able to wake up Kiki. She looked up at them, then passed back out. They knew she wasn't going anywhere for a while. Ma looked in on Yin. He was pissed. He said in a stern voice "Don't say anything. I'm coming."

Normally Ma wouldn't take Yin tralking to her like that. But she could see that he was on edge. Just as the three Butchers were walking out of Yin's place, Yin took another look at Kiki. He thought that's one hell of a woman!

Backir took Nana to one of his private houses, along with one of the dancers. Nana knew this would be a tough night, so she brought one of the dancers with her. It didn't make a difference. When backir got a hold of Nana. He stuck with her like a heat seeking missle.

Nana was a strong girl, and took what she had coming. Backir put such a pounding on Nana that her yelling sounded like a cross between an alley cat, a chimp, a turkey gobbling, and an old basset hound.

Sometimes you would here the alley cat, then the chimp, then the turkey gobbling, then the old basset hound bellowing. Sometimes you'd swear you heard all four at once. It was so loud that the dancer, that came with them, stay in the far corner, nervously wathcing the action. She didn't make a sound. She just watched.

Normally, the dancer couldn't wait until it was her turn to get it. Tonight, she just wanted to stay in the corner. Where it was safe. The dancer felt sorry for Nana, but she hope that Backir wouldn't notice her. She got lucky. Backir gave Nana all he had to offer this night.

Chi set Dan up with a place to take the Dancers that he chose for the night. Dan had the dancers making their own symphony of sounds. There was no hiding from Dan. He never lost track of the enemy in battle. He would punish one girl. Then the other, repeatedly. He had learned a valuable lesson from Ramala's aunt, about being teamed up on by women while having sex, and getting worn down. That wasn't going to happen again. At least not tonight!

Dan didn't have the luxury of being able to pass out after he got finished. Ramala had three rules about Dan and other women. He could do whatever he wanted to them, as long as he didn't give them his seed. Her needs came before any other woman's. And he had to be back to her before daybreak. Ramala told Dan "There isn't anything that you can't do, and be back to me before daybreak." Dan knew if he broke those rules, he would catch hell from Ramala. So no matter how much energy Dan expended. He would make sure he got cleaned up, and back to Ramala before daybreak.

Still, that didn't stop Ramala from being discusted with Dan whenever he returned to her, after being with other women. When Dan returned this time, Ramala stared at him as she normally did when he came back from a late night. She would piss herself off, trying to figure out how much fun Dan had without her. Dan knew she was watching him, and ignored her staring, without being rude. Dan knew just what to do. He walked over and laid behind Ramala. He put his arm around her on to her stomach. Ramala shifted a little and said "You had better save some of that for me after I have this child." Dan said" Don't worry. I always save my best for you." Dan couldn't see it, but that brought a smile to Ramala's face. Then Dan thought there's more than enough of this to go around!

The Hellcats could see that if they stayed in Yee Province much longer, things would get out of hand. So they made this a very short visit. They only stayed there two days. The D-Squad would be coming back to the House of Ra to train with the Butchers. After the Hellcats were satified with their training, they would be going on a very important mission. The Hellcats didn't tell either group what the mission was. Both groups knew if it took both them, it had to be very dangerous. They all but figured that it was the Southern Jungle, but with Ramala in control, it could be anything. Ramala even made Chi come along. Han stayed in Yee Province. She knew Chi had been in Yee Province to long unsupervised. There was no telling what he really was up to. The Hellcats didn't trust Chi as far as they could see him. Him going back south would at least keep him honest for a while. If he didn't get himself killed on the mission.

The trip back to the House of Ra was uneventful. There wasn't much room for playing around. Wana had everyone on strict assignments. You had to be where she expected you to be. Both the Butchers and the Squad worked together protecting the Royal Caravan. They all enjoyed a laugh or two at Yin and Kiki's expense. Yin and Kiki didn't say much to each other. They both wanted a rematch to put the other in their place. Neither one of them was convinced that they lost that battle. Although both had to admit to themselves that they enjoyed that night more than any they had before.

Nana thought that whatever doesn't kill you, makes you stronger. Yeah, she got her ass handed to her, and had a lot of fun at the same time. Nana knew that Backir would hand it to her a few more times. She was good with that. While it was happening, she thought it would never end, and she didn't want it to end. Her voice was all but gone for almost two days from yelling. Nana had a slight glitch in her walk. She knew that some day she would deal with Backir a lot better. Then it will be her turn to put the Beast Backir in his place. She knew she wouldn't be able to make Backir sound like an alley cat, a chimp, or a turkey gobbling. At least she hoped she wouldn't. But she planned on having him bellowing like an old basset hound. Just like she did.

Once the Caravan reached the House of Ra, Ramala and Tara decided that it was time to go into seclusion. Ramala put all of her energy into training the twins and training herself. She turned up their training a couple of notches. La and Dan were now spending almost the whole day with Ramala. It cut their play time with Yaya in half. It didn't bother Young Dan. He could get used to almost anything, as long as you kept him fed. On the other hand, even though La did what Ramala made her do. La couldn't understand why she, Dan, and Yaya couldn't spend as much time with out mother watching.

Ramala kept pushing the twins hard with strength training, until about a month before she was to have her child. La noticed that her mother was slowing down. La took full advantage by pushing Ramala. She tested to see what she could get away with. She didn't get to do everything that she wanted, but Ramala allowed her to get away with a few things that she normally wouldn't. That made La put extra effort into trying to wear Ramala down. Once mother got tired, La could do more of what she wanted. Doing what she wanted, if only for a while, was always worth the trouble she got in.

Tara knew Yin and Kiki had a thing going on. That didn't bother her. Tara knew she could put an end to that if she wanted to, one way or another. Tara was glad Yin had someone to take up his extra time. She still didn't know why she didn't want to spend any time with Yin, but she wasn't going to waste time thinking about it.Tara spent most of her time with Ramala. She enjoyed her niece and nephew. Tara watched closely the small battles between Ramala and La. She tried to figure out what she would have done in the same situation, if she had a girl. She did the same with Dan. Tara wanted a boy. She could see that most of the time boys were easier to deal with than girls.

When Wana first got back to the House of Ra, She let herself go wild for the first week. She ran through the toughest of the elite guards. She even put down a few of the brutes just for good measure. Ramala and Tara started to get worried that they would have to interfere with what Wana was doing. But after that first week, Wana toned it down, to what seemed not so bad compared to her first week.

Wana started running the House of Ra as soon as her cousins went into seclusion . That's one of the reasons they brought the Squad along. With two of the Hellcats out of circulation, Wana would need a strong team backing her. She had enough guards. Now she could delegate security responsibilities between the Butchers and the D-Squad as her Warlords. Wana ran the House of Ra like a military camp.

Wana learned two things out in the field. She learned that Ma liked to watched her get some, without getting involved. She also learned that she enjoyed Ma watching her. Those two things brought Ma and Wana closer than either of them had expected. Soon after returning to the House of Ra, usually if you found one of them, you found both.

The Butchers trained hard with the D-Squad. At first Wana supervised the training, to make sure things didn't get to heated. After a couple of weeks, she didn't have to. And a month after the two groups started training together, they became very comfortable with each other. Yin found out that he had more in common with Mangler, Kiki, and Dirt, than he did with any of the Butcher, besides Ma. Those three would teach Yin that there was one thing more satifying than killing. It was torture. Yin proved he could learn a skill other than killing.

Spider took his time trying to find a way to get Cat. He was patient with her. With most girls, he would move a little faster. With Cat he knew he couldn't. He knew she would see past the obvious. So Spider formed a good working relationship with Cat. It took a while, but Cat Slowly started having conversation with Spider. That was a big break, considering how high strung Cat was. Spider knew just like Syn and the others what was going on with Cat. She needed to release the sexual pressure building in her. Spider knew it would only be a matter of time before she let go. He was going to make sure he was in a good with Cat when she was ready.

This was the hardest Chi had practiced in over a year. Back in Yee province, Chi did what he wanted. He stayed in good shape, but training wasn't first on his list of things to do. Now he was going through grueling workouts. He couldn't slack off because of Wana. Wana watched, and evaluated each of her Warlords strengths and weaknesses. She enhanced what they were good at, and worked them hard on their weaknesses. That meant she pushed Chi hard on fighting. He didn't complain. Chi knew that would make Wana work him harder if he did. He couldn't wait until they completed whatever this mission that Ramala had for them. Then he could get back to Yee province, and finish building his own army. He had set things up pretty good before he left.They wouldn't fall apart before he got back. This was Chi's first visit to the House of Ra, and he didn't like it. Chi never really like the Hellcats. He wanted to be as far away from the Hellcats as possible. Chi wiped the sweat from his forehead, and thought 'so this is the House of Ra!'

When Cat returned to the House of Ra, she still was high strung from being out in the field, and from dealing with her sexual frustrations. She would go extra hard in practice and have to be warned by Syn, Jara and Wana. Ramala was in seclusion, but had heard from Wana about Cat. Wana wanted to deal with Cat in her own way, but thought she should talk to Ramala and Tara before she did anything. Ramala told Wana that Cat was dealing with her emotions for Dan. Ramala said she would talk to Dan and see if he would give her what she needed.

Wana said "That will make things worse. She might completely fall for Dan." Ramala smiled, then said "You let me deal with Cat. I knew when I first met her that one day I would have to deal with her. Why do you think I spared with the Butcher girls so much? She will never be able to come close to my fighting skills. Everyone can already see that she has it bad for Dan. They can see that it's affecting her as far as the team is concerned. No one will be able to blame me if she disrespects me and I have to kill her. But that won't happen for a while. By then, I'll be back in shape and unbeatable."

Tara said "'What about the Syn, Jara? She won't like that, I'm sure." Ramala said "In three years time, not even the Syn, Jara will be able to deal with me." Wana said "You're not going to fight the Syn, Jara! If we have to deal with the Syn, Jara I'm not taking any chances. She gets blasted, and we take her head. No arguments. I don't want the unexpected to happen. If I lose one of you, I'm going to lay down a massacre. I won't stop until they kill me!"

Ramala and Tara looked at Wana. They knew she meant what she said. Still, Ramala had it in the back of her mind that she would be able to beat Syn in a fair fight, one day. Ramala said "Alright! We'll do it your way, if we have to." Tara said "Yeah! Don't get so dramatic!" Wana said "I'm not getting dramatic. I'm just saying!"

Later, Ramala talked to Dan. She told Dan that Cat was getting out of control and it was affecting the team. Ramala said "If something isn't done to calm Cat down, she's going to have to be dealt with."

Dan stared at Ramala to see if she was serious. She was, but he could see that she didn't want to have to kill Cat, if she didn't have to. Dan agreed to see what he could do about the situation. He went to the Butcher girl's quarters.

Cat and Syn were sitting, and talking. Ma had gone with Wana, to watch one of her adventures. Dan walked in and greeted the girls. Then he looked at Cat and said "I need to talk to you." Syn, Jara got up and left, without saying a word. Dan watched her as she left. Her body was almost as perfect as Ramala's was before she became with child the second time.

Dan refocused. He turned, and looked at Cat for a moment. Cat was curious and said "What?" Dan said "You know you have been getting out of control, right?" Cat said "I always get hyped up when I'm out in the field. But to say I've been getting out of control, that's ridiculous."

Dan said "Maybe you haven't noticed it, but everyone else has." Cat responded with "I can't help it if I'm becoming a better fighter. I'm tough to deal with now. Like Syn always says, if someone thinks it a good idea to mess with me. I'm gonna prove it's not. Nobody ever says anything when Syn, Jara, or your Mali gets out of control. Now do they?"

Cat smiled at Dan. He had to admit to himself that she was right. Even though he wasn't going to say it. But still, Dan had to get her to calm down, without telling her it was coming from Ramala. Dan smiled at Cat. He said "Well at least give everyone warning when you don't want to be played with." Cat got a puzzled look on her face, and said "Did Mali tell you to come and talk to me?" Dan said "You mean, did she ask me?" Cat said "Ask, tell, whatever works for you." Dan was starting to get fed up with Cat's uncooperativeness. He said "I'm just looking out for you. If you don't trust what I've said is in your best interest, then that's on you."

Cat walked up to Dan, pushed her body up against his, and said "Don't get so serious. I'm just playing with you. I'll calm down if you think I need to." Dan put his arm around Cat and pulled her even closer, knowing that would make her panic. This time Cat didn't pull away. Dan said "There's something else I think you need to do." Cat said "What?" Dan said "Some Boom Boom always calms a girl down." Cat pulled away from Dan. He didn't wrestle with her. Cat said "I suppose you think I should do it with you?"

Dan said "That's always an option, but that's on you. If not me, then find someone. Believe me, it won't make you a weaker fighter. If that was true, Wana would be the worse fighter ever. But she's not!" Everyone knew about Wana by now. Cat laughed, then she moved back close on Dan. She said "I don't know if I'm ready for it or not."

This time Dan didn't put his arm around Cat. He could see that she was starting to get comfortable being close on him like that. He was going to let her get as comfortable as she wanted. Dan said "You're ready, you're just scared. Just like your body was built for fighting, it also can take whatever a man can give. But still, take your time. You just have to be willing to let it happen. Believe me, you'll like it."

Ma walked in and saw Cat close on Dan. When Cat saw Ma, she took a step back. Ma looked at Dan for a second, then looked at Cat. She said "Don't stop because of me. I can come back if you two need some alone time." Ma smiled at Cat. Cat said "You can stay. You might see something you like." Ma looked at Dan and said "I doubt it." Both girls giggled. Dan couldn't see this going anywhere that would suit him. So he said "I got things to do. Cat think about what I said. I'll see you later." Dan walked towards the door. Ma was still in the doorway. Dan and Ma locked eyes. They hadn't had a good fight in a long time. When Dan got to the doorway, he was expecting to get bumped by Ma. Instead, she gently brushed her body against him as he passed. After Dan left, he heard Ma and Cat laughing. That was the first time Ma passed him without giving him a dirty look. And her brushing against him like that. He didn't mind that at all. They both could get it, if that's what they wanted.

Chapter 16

Ramala surprised everyone by having a second set of twins. A girl came first again. Then came a boy. This time the twins looked like a mixture of both Dan and Ramala. The new twins looked more like their older brother and sister, than they did to their parents, even though the first set of twins looked exactly like their parents. Ramala named her daughter Ramashaya, after her grandmother. Dan named his son Don, after his father. The names of two mortal enemies had become brother and sister. Now Ramala and Dan had four children. The Ra, Ramala and the Ra, Dan. Their first set of twins. The Ra, Ramashaya, and the Ra, Don.

All of the Hayee children born in the House of Ra would have the name Ra. So even though Ramala and Tara were Hayee, their children's name would be Ra. That's how it was with all the Houses. That's how the Name changed as relatives from the first House of Japha moved to form the names of the other Houses.

Young Dan was amazed by his younger brother and sister. He watched them and tried to touch them whenever he could. He wanted to pull an arm or a leg to see if it could move like his. Of course, Ramala wouldn't allow him to touch them, with the new twins being so young. La on the other hand was fascinated at first, when she saw the twins. She quickly became jealous when she saw how much attention they were getting from her father. La already had to compete with young Dan and Ramala for Dan's attention. Now there were two more! Was she being replaced? It just wasn't fair! La acted out as much as possible to get the attention she thought she wasn't getting. La had to be watched closely whenever she was around the new twins. That made Ramala get even more stern with La. La couldn't stand the pressure of Ramala, and was back in line after about three weeks. She did what she was told, and had to behave. Even though she didn't like it!

Tara had her child a month after Ramala had the twins. After going through childbirth, Tara swore she would never do that again. She had a son. He looked like the perfect mix between Tara and Yin. Tara named him Ra, Yin. Ramala and Wana didn't like the name Yin, but there was nothing they could do about it. They called the baby, Tara's little man for the first three months, in protest. After that, they called him Yin.

Yin was very proud when he saw his son. Like Dan, the girls wouldn't let him touch the young child. He didn't want to spend too much time with his son anyway. Only because he was to young. Yin couldn't talk to him. The child wouldn't understand. Also, Yin didn't want to start getting soft in the mind, playing with a baby.

Yin tried to think of what he would say to his son. He couldn't. Well, he would have plenty of time to think of something before the boy could understand him. Then he let the nightmare of his death creep into his thoughts. Then he told himself, if something did happen to him, the boy would get good training at the House of Ra.

China and her cousins at the monastery worked hard every day. It had been over two years and the only girl that was learning any fighting techniques, was China. All the Wa girls cooked, cleaned, and hauled everything from rocks and food, to water. China spent about an hour and a half learning fighting each day. She had to keep up with her choirs, or she was told, her training would be cut back. When the evenings permitted, China would teach the girls what she had already learned. Gia, Uma, and Jami, the youngest three, were picking up fighting very fast. They would practice long into the night after China showed them new moves. Mati and Saya were picking up the moves, only not as fast as the youngest three.

The Nuns surprised the Wa girls by bringing all of them into training. At first the Nuns were waiting until the girls were strong enough to take the grueling training that they would have to go through. Now they couldn't wait. The Wa girls didn't know it but the Nuns did it because of the destruction of the House of Hoo. These girls would have to be ready when the time came. The Nuns knew that there was a silent resistance to the Hellcats. Soon the resistance would spill over into rebellion. The Nuns had to get these girls ready. They would have to be good enough to take on the Butchers, and the House of Ra.

At the spiritual temple, The young men from the Wa family were working very hard to be the best fighters they possibly could. Nicko, Hilando, Massiko, and Yawu had become good fighters. They still weren't the caliber of the Butchers, but they could defend themselves very well against the junior priest. The younger Wa men were training very hard, but they were not as good as the older four.

After the top preist of the Spiritual Temple received news about the House of Hoo being destroyed. They went to see the destruction for themselves. When they returned they had a meeting. All of the top priest, except for Ven, decided that they needed to do something to stop the Butchers and the Hellcats before it was to late. Ven warned "If you try something and it fails, this temple will be destroyed." One of the other priest said "If they don't know that the fight is coming from the Temple, they'll have no reason to suspect us. I think that the only way to deal with a Butcher is with another Butcher. If we train ten to fifteen of the orphans to be total butchers, then they can go out and train other rebels to fight. We helped the Syn, Sed train Syn, Jara. I still don't think the other Butchers can deal with her. If we can train these young men to be as good as her. We can at least wipe out the Butchers. That will leave the Hellcats a lot weaker." Ven said "Without the Butchers, the Hellcats are still unbeatable." The priest looked at Ven and said "That's why we get the support of the rebels and the Houses that oppose the Hellcats. The Hellcats are only unbeatable when they are together. We'll just find a way to get them one by one." Ven still didn't agree. He saw big trouble coming if the plan didn't work out perfectly. He was out voted. The priest would train the Wa orphans, along with some of the other orphans. They were going to create their own Butchers.

One of the things that helped La accept the new twins was Ramala letting her help take care of them. Ramala found little things to let La do. This made La feel close to them. She saw that the young twins were helpless. She felt like she had to help and protect them. Ramala also involved Yaya in the care of the new twins. Yaya already had to deal with La and Dan. That helped her a lot in dealing with the new twins.

One day Ramala took Yaya out into one of the gardens around the palace. Ramala dismissed the guards that followed her around. She turned and faced Yaya. Ramala said "You have done well for yourself since being an orphan slave in Yee Province. You have been accepted into the House of Ra as one of our own. I have given you special training, and everyone respect you. Even though I am not your birth mother, I treat you as my daughter. You are big sister to my children. But still, you have not said one word about your family. Tell me what your family name is."

Ramala studied Yaya for a reaction. Yaya didn't say a word. She stared at Ramala then looked away. She looked back at Ramala like she wanted to say something, but didn't. Ramala smiled at Yaya, and slowly took her hand. She said "I have raised you for the last five years. You have turned into a fine young girl. I'm proud of you. I love you. I want us to be able to completely trust each other. Whatever your family name is won't change the way I feel about you. Tell me what your family name is."

Again, Yaya didn't say anything. Her eyes watered up until a tear rolled down her face. Ramala took her hand and wiped the tear from her face. Then Ramala looked out over the garden, still holding Yaya's hand. Ramala said "When I was creating the House of Ra, I gave every tribe a chance to join me. Some of them thought it was a good idea to resist joining the House of Ra. I was force to show them it wasn't. One of those tribes was the Wa. Whirlwind Wa's family." Ramala paused for a second, as Yaya squirmed a little when she heard Ramala say her family name. Ramala continued with "I tried to negotiate with Whirlwind Wa. I gave him several chances to cooperate. He told me I had to be dealt with. I had no choice but to deal with him. One thing I remember is how much the Wa look alike.

When we visited the Spiritual Temple, I saw orphans that looked like Wa. When we were in Yee Province, there were three girls that looked like Wa." Now Ramala could see the tears rolling freely down Yaya's face. Ramala continued with "I even saw girls that looked like Wa at the midrange Mountain Monastery. I didn't single any of them out to be dealt with. I let them live. I have nothing aganst any of them. If they choose to try to do harm to me, or the House of Ra, they will fail. Now tell me, What is your family name?"

Yaya looked up at Ramala. Then she went down on her knees. Ramala ordered "Stand up!" Yaya did as she was told. Ramala said "Always be proud of who you are. Whatever your name is, say it proudly."

Ramala waited while Yaya composed herself. Ramala

looked at Yaya like she was still waiting on an answer. Finally Yaya whispered "Yaya Wa." Ramala said "Alright Wa. You have an important choice to make. You can go and be with your Wa family. The other choice is you can stay here with your Ra family." Yaya said "Can I stay here?" Ramala said "You can stay under these conditions. Never harm any of your Ra family. Always protect your Ra family from harm. And remember that it is I who takes care of you, and will continue to do so. Can you do those things?"

Yaya looked up at Ramala and whispered "Yes." Ramala smiled at Yaya and said "For now, we won't tell anyone that you are Wa. The others might not be as understanding as me. It will be our secret. You have two families now. I don't want you to forget either. I'll make ways for you to see your other family from time to time. Don't let them know I know. Like I said, it our secret. Now go, I'll see you at dinner." Yaya started to leave, then she turned around and wrapped her arms around Ramala, giving her a big hug. Ramala put her hand on the top of Yaya's head. Ramala had Yaya right where she wanted her. Then Yaya took off running. Ramala almost yelled at her, but caught herself. That girl's always running!

Three weeks after Ramala had her second set of twins, she was back in training. She started out slow, just as she did after the first twins were born. Ramala increased her workout as time went on. Most of the time La would be with Ramala during training. Ramala would have La hanging by her ponytail from a low branch of a tree, or a pole hanging from two trees.That was the technique Hayee girls used to keep their necks and hair strong. That's why Hayee girls were known for having strong and long hair. At first Ramala strengthened La's hair by pulling her by her ponytail. Then she started picking her up by it. Now that La's hair and neck were strong enough, Ramala had her hanging by her hair. The first time Dan saw La hanging by her hair, he thought Ramala had lost her mind and was abusing his daughter. It almost started fight between him and Ramala. Ramala quickly explained it was part of La's training. Dan backed off, even though he didn't want to. He wasn't going to stop his little girl from being the best at whatever Ramala was training her.

La also had to hold a small wooden stick in each hand, at her sides, away from her body as she hung by her hair. This was training La's arms to get use to holding Hammer-Axes. Ramala would explain her training moves to La. All of this, while La was hanging from her hair. Then to make sure La was paying attention, Ramala would question her about what she had just explained. That was training La to focus on other things, besides hanging by her hair. Once La got comfortable with something Ramala gave her to do, Ramala added something else. La adapted to all of Ramala's training techniques. Ramala was La's main teacher at this age. She pushed La hard, but only gave La challenges that she could over come. La worked hard to please Ramala. She knew that made mother happy. When mother was happy, she let La do what she wanted. Like I said before, La was learning from one of the best.

Ramala trained Young Dan hard too. But Young Dan got to spend more time with his father, watching his techniques in fighting. Young Dan was forced to stand in place, with a weighted tunic on. He had to keep his arms extended away from his body, at his sides, while holding very light weighted hammers. He had to stand there completely still, while watching his father train. If he moved one inch out of place, Dan got stern with him. Sometimes Young Dan would try to swing the hammers like he saw his father doing. That's the only time that Dan would pretend not to see Young Dan moving. Dan would wrestle with his son. Ramala kept a close eye on Dan's rough play with her son . She didn't want her son injured by Dan's rough play. Rough play didn't bother Young Dan. That gave him and his father a special closeness.

Young Dan could adapt to anything, as long as he stayed well fed. When he got hungry was the only time he got ornery. Ramala kept him fed most of time, unless she was testing him to let him know not to get out of control around her, even if he was hungry.He hadn't passed that test yet.

Soon Ramala was strong and fast enough to train with Dan. They sparred long and hard together. Dan tried to get Ramala to slow down a bit, but she wouldn't. It seemed that she was pushing herself as hard as she could. She was on a mission. When Ramala got like this, Dan had to let her go until she got it out of her system. Otherwise, she would turn all of that extra energy towards him. And not in a good way.

Ramala didn't let La or young Dan watch when her and Dan went hard practicing together. Their practices usually got very intense.That would create a whole other set of problems that she would have to go through with La. La was already hard to deal with, when it came to her father. If she saw Ramala and Dan fighting, even if it was practice. La's mind wouldn't be able to deal with that and Ramala would be forced to take time to deal with La. She didn't have that kind of time. Ramala was working hard to get better than she was before she got with child the second time. She was going to make a push into the Southern Jungle soon. She had to be at her best.

After the Hellcats left the House of Japha, Japha, Jania had an army of guards and servants cleaning up, what used to be the House of Hoo. Once the place had been cleared out, construction started there on the new Province of San-Jania. San-Jania province was being built up as the top province in the House of Japha. That's also where San and Jan had their palaces built. Japha Jan kept herself as busy as possible in the new province. She found that when she kept busy, she didn't think about San as much.

Now that Jan was Queen of the House of Japha, she had a lot of her cousins and uncles trying to court her. It seemed at every dinner, lunch, or family fuction, Jan had to deal with a steady stream of men trying to win her over. Even when she went to San-Jania Province the suitors followed her. Jan didn't mind the attention, as long as the men didn't interfere with her while she was conducting bussiness.

The Hayee, Ramala and the Japha, Jan corresponded with each other through messengers. Ramala kept Jan updated on her pregnancy. Ramala sent word that she had twins and also their names to Jan. She wanted Jan to come and visit, when time permitted. Jan said she would. But right now Jan had to put her new House in order. Jan sent word to Ramala about the building of the new Province of San-Jania. That's as much as she was willing to say, through a messenger. Jan missed all of her girls, but she had a lot of work to do. It took up most of her time right mow.

Instead of dealing with fighters and killers, San was dealing with the politics of ruling the House of Japha. He found that this was much harder. At least with the killers you knew who they were. San was finding out that ruling had a lot of responsibilities. He formed a chain of command to get things done. His father and his brother Young Jett advised and conferred with San, trying to give him as much help as possible. San found that it was hard trying to keep up with the people he made responsible for certain things. He had so many people trying to see him for this or for that. He couldn't remember half the meetings he had to go to. San had people telling him when to go to this meeting. Who to meet on this day, or who he had to meeet with on that day. He thought he was the Ruler, but it was starting to seem to him that he was being ruled. He couldn't keep up with all of the decisions he made. There were to many of them. And the cousins he put in charge of carrying out orders did some of what he wanted, and mostly what they wanted. San realized that he wasn't a good politician. This wasn't the kind of action he liked. He had to find someone else to do this, or he would slowly die in the confusion he called politics.

San went to the new Province and told Jan how he felt. He told her that he couldn't take much more of the meetings and all of the ceremonies that had to do with ruling. Jan didn't like the politics of ruling the House of Japha either. That's why she came to the new Province. She needed to get away from dealing with the way things were done at in the House of Japha. Every one there was set in their ways of doing things. It was a real fight to get things changed. That's the reason Jan formed the new province. She could let the old members do what they were used to doing, while she could set things up here from the start to run like she wanted them to.

Now that San didn't want to stay in the city of Japha and deal with the politics there. The Japha twins had to come up with another plan. San said "You know me and you are nothing but a couple of Warlords disguised as Rulers . What if we let Jett run the city of Japha and report to us what's going on there?" Jan thought for a moment. Then she said "You think we can trust him to tell us everything he's doing?"

San said "You know we can't. But if he can run that city, report to us and get things done that we want, it would be worth it to me. If he can still manage to do things we don't know about, more power to him." Jan said "We can keep him busy doing things we need done in the main city. That would free us up to run trade through San-Jania Province. We will control all of the trade from here." San said "Until we think of something better, that's the plan." Jan agreed. She looked at San and didn't know if it was a good idea having him so close. Then she got an idea. All she had to do was send a message to the Na, Tee to come and visit. Jan was sure that would keep San busy.

Young Jett had no problem taking over the city of Japha. This is what he was made for. He knew all of the traditions that the elders were use to. His father made sure of that. After all, he was the one that was being groomed to run the House of Japha. Young Jett could see that his younger brother and sister were having a hard time dealing with the daily doings of the House of Japha. He knew it would only be a matter of time before they were begging for his help. He never dreamed that they would give him total control of the city. Young Jett was finally getting what was his in the first place. He was going to take full advantage of the situation.

When the Na, Tee received the message that Jan wanted her to come and visit the new Province, she couldn't resist. She packed up some of her things and hit the road right away. Tee made up in her mind that she was going to be with San always, or this would be the last time San would see her. Tee's family had already picked out a couple of Young Na for Tee as her mate.Her parents were in negotiations with the parents of the men that had been chosen. Of course she resisted as much as she could. She told her parents that she would make a decision when she got back from her trip. If San didn't want her, she would settle for one of her cousins.

Japha, Jan didn't tell San that she had sent for the Na, Tee. She needed San to be surprised if her plan to get these two back together would work. Once San came to the new province, he split his time between training, supervising the building of his palace, Jan, and his favorite concubines. He was starting to feel alive again. It would take a war to get him to go back to ruling the city of Japha. Even then, he would rather be on the front lines taking charge in battle.

Japha, Jan kept a close look out for the Na, Tee's caravan. She was going to make sure that she met with Tee before San did. Forward guards told Jan that Tee's caravan was approaching. Jan, Mia, and Nina went to meet the caravan. When Jan and her girls got to the caranvan, they greeted Tee. It surprised Tee that Jan seemed genuinely happy to see her. The Na, Tee searched the faces of Nina and Mia to see what Jan was up to. As usual, Jan's girls never gave any clues. Jan even gave Tee a hug and smiled at her. Even though Tee was surprised and a little suspicious, she played along to see where this was going.

After all of the girls greeted, Jan had a talk with Tee. Jan said "I'm glad you came." Then Jan put a concerned look on her face and said "Once me and San came home, we were greeted as the new King and Queen of the House of Japha. Every Japha girl that didn't have a mate tried to become San's. Of course, I had to interview them all, along with San. We have a lot of good young females in the House of Japha. I thought that San would have no problem finding a suitable mate. But after all of the interviews, I could see that none of these girls would be able to keep San's interest for long. I didn't see the light in his eyes for these girls, like I saw when he looks at you."

Tee could hardly contain the joy from hearing Jan almost admit that she was better than all of the Japha girls. That's what Tee heard. Jan said "He has missed you greatly, even though he'll never admit it. Now he's taking his frustrations out on concubines, wasting himself away." Jan stared off in the distance to add a dramatic touch to what she had said. Of course Jan was lying about San wasting away, but Tee was soaking it all in. It helped a lot that Tee wanted to believe that San would wallow in sorrow at not being able to see her. Tee was thrilled, but she still had her doubts about Jan. Tee said "What about the tradition of only picking mates from your own House?"

Jan turned back to Tee and said "I don't want my brother to have to settle for someone he doesn't truly love. If that means breaking tradition to see him happy. I'm willing to help make it happen. I won't try to influence him one way or the other. That's your job. But if he chooses you, you have my blessing, and I will do everything in my powers to support both of you. If Ramala can go as far as to mate with a Heathen, I guess it won't be as bad if San mates with a distant cousin. At least we have the same blood." Tee smiled at Jan. That was enough for Tee to believe she had a chance.

Jan and her girls escorted Tee to San-Jania. As they entered the main city, Tee could see the city was still being built. Tee as well as everyone in all of the Houses knew that the Hellcats had destroyed this place. You couldn't see any of the destruction now. It just looked like a new city being formed. They passed two large structures that were being worked on. Jan explained that those were her and San's palaces. There were a lot of buildings that were already completed. That's where San and Jan were living for now.

Jan took Tee to see San. He was training, like he did every day at this time. The girls walked into one of the buildings and came out into an open air courtyard where San was sparring with some of his elite guards. Tee froze in her tracks.Tee stared at San and couldn't see anything else for a moment. If there was ever a time for Jan to catch Tee off guard and kill her, this was it. San had on pants, but no shirt. He was dirty and sweat covered his skin. Tee had seen San's body on many occasions, but this was the best shape San had ever been in. If San was wasting away, Tee couldn't see it. Tee wondered if Jan had tricked her. She didn't care about that right now.

Jan stopped and watched Tee's reaction to San. It amused her, as it usually did to see Tee's and San's reaction to each other. San turned and saw Tee standing there looking at him. He took a look at Jan. San knew his sister went behind his back and made this happen. He wiped the sweat from his forehead and stared at Tee. He put up his hand towards the guards to let them know that he was done practicing for now, without taking his eyes off Tee. The guards walked off. Then a smile came on San's face. He started walking towards Tee. As soon as San's feet moved towards Tee, she took off running towards San so fast that it startled Jan and her girls. Nina and Mia's hands quickly reached for their machetes. They stopped themselves a split second later when they realized Tee was running to meet San. When Tee got to San, she jumped into his arms. San caught her and they hugged and kissed each other. Jan looked at her girls with a smile on her face. Her work was done here. She turned and left, with Nina and Mia following her.

San and Tee wouldn't let go of each other. It seemed that they had missed each other more than they both realized. They kept kissing and touching without saying a word. Neither one of them wanted to ruin this moment with words. They stopped and looked at each other for a moment. Then San picked Tee up and threw her over his shoulder. Tee giggled as San carried her off. They spent the rest of the day in San's place catching up on lost time, without words.

That evening Tee and San had dinner with Jan, her girls, and some of the twin's cousins. Jan watched Tee and San with a smile on her face. She could see that these two were very happy now. She looked at her brother and knew this time he would not let Tee go. Jan didn't see how Tee could lose. The only thing that bothered Jan was that as she looked at her brother, she knew in her heart that she still had feelings that a sister shouldn't have for a brother.

Tee smiled the whole time at dinner. She smiled at San. She smiled at Jan. She smiled at everyone. Tee's smile lit up the room and had every one there smiling. It didn't matter to her that Jan had probably gave her something she couldn't get on her own. Tee was going to let that go. She won the prize. The prize was San.

While San ate his dinner, he kept looking at his sister. She was always planning and plotting. Bringing Tee here was the last thing he would have guess Jan was up to. San was very grateful that she did. He wasn't going to send for Tee. He was going to wait until she came to visit. Now that San had Tee, he wasn't going to let her go. He didn't care what his family thought. This was the girl he always wanted from the first time he saw her. When he saw her out in the courtyard earlier in the day, is when he realized that. San told himself that he was going to return the favor, by finding the perfect mate for Jan. She didn't know it, but San planed on making Jan as happy as she had made him.

Over the next five months, San paraded almost every member of the House of Japha that was under forty, in front of Jan. That's when he wasn't busy with Tee. The Na, Tee wasn't going to interfere with San's new obsession. Tee was still grateful to Jan for getting her and San back together.

Now that the other Japha saw Tee with San most of the time, they slowly accepted her as one of them. After four months with San, Tee was carrying his child. Jan went along with San's interview process of potetial suitors in hopes that one of them would appeal to her. Instead, she found that she enjoyed the fact that San was there with her. Jan thought getting San and Tee together would help her. It didn't. Jan could mostly control her thoughts about San, but her body was telling her that it was time that it was put to good use. Jan couldn't figure out whether she had made a mistake in bringing Tee here. Now that Tee was having San's child she would never be able to get rid of Tee.

San was there with Jan while she had zoned out thinking. San asked "Are you alright?" Jan said, without realizing the frustrated tone she used "I don't know if I'll ever be right!" San took Jan's hand and said "Don't worry, we'll find someone special for you." Jan noticed that San didn't take her and pull her close to him. He just took her hand. Now that he had Tee, he wouldn't even hold her close like he used to do. But she wanted San to stop holding her so close. Now Jan didn't know if that was what she really wanted. She was starting to confuse herself. Jan fought jealousy as hard as she could. This was one battle that she couldn't win. Jan fought her emotions, but her eyes filled with water. She knew San saw her eyes before she had a chance to turn away. Jan had to deflect before San figured out what was going on.

Jan put her head on San's shoulder and said "I just don't want to end up alone." San put his arms around his sister and held her close. He Said "I won't let that happen." That was too much for Jan to handle right now. Jan pushed her breast and hips up against San before realizing she had done so. She stayed there like that while keeping her head on his shoulder. This was Jan's body begging for attention from San's body. Now even San was aware that this was not a sisterly hug. Since Jan was upset, San thought Jan was unaware of her body. He didn't want to pull away, seeing that she was so upset over not finding a mate. He didn't want to take the chance that that might upset her more. San would stand there and console his sister.

By the time Jan became aware of what was taking place, she couldn't force herself to move away. She hoped San would push her away. But he didn't. This was what she had been trying to avoid. It was the time when she wouldn't be able to stop herself from doing what she really wanted to. Let her body become totally aware of San's body. San could feel his sister's grown body getting comfortable against his. San knew he had to find his sister a mate before she got desperate and took anything she could get.

Jan finally let go of San when Nina and Mia came into the room. The two girls tried to act like they weren't shocked. San held onto Jan's hand as she moved back. He said "You gonna be alright?" Jan looked into San's eyes for only a couple of seconds, then she looked away. She pulled her hand away from San's hand and walked out of the room. Nina and Mia immediately followed her.

Jan was embarrassed because she had finally let her feeling show. She wasn't going to deal with the situation, right now, anymore than she already had. San was frozen by the look in Jan's eyes. It was the same look of hurt that Tee had in her eyes when San refused to tell her how he felt about her. He stood there for a moment thinking about everything that had happened up to this point. The way Jan treated Tee from the first time they met. If it had been anyone accept for his sister, he would have picked up on it immediately. San was floored by what he saw in Jan's eyes. He didn't know how he would deal with this. No wonder Jan couldn't find a mate. San saw in Jan's eyes, that she was already in love with him.

Nina and Mia followed Jan back to her place. They didn't say a word at first. Then Jan said "I thought I could control it, but now I see I can't." Jan looked at Mia and asked "What's wrong with me!?" Mia said "Nothing. Sometimes things happen that we have no control over. It's not your fault." Nina said "No, it's not you. It's just that you two have spent most of you life together. You have never been separated. It's only natural that you would develop a dependance on him." Jan said "It's not a dependance. It's ...." Mia interrupted with "Maybe some distance will do you some good." Nina said "Yeah! We can go back to the main city of Japha, and San can stay here and supervise the building of San-Jania." Jan's face lightened up a little. Even though she knew her girls would say, or try anything to make her feel better. Jan said "That might work." Nina smiled and said "Maybe with San not around, you might find that you like one of your cousins more than you thought." Jan was willing to try anything. Her and her girls packed their things and left immediately.

Once back in the main city, Jan tried everything to keep her mind off San. She went to every family fuction, every party, and every gathering. None of that kept her mind off San. She even let her girls set up some interviews, or dates with some of her cousins. She let some of her male cousins get close on her to see if she had a good reaction. It was nothing like when San touched her.

San didn't make an attempt to contact Jan once she left. He wanted to give them time apart. He didn't want to make matters worse by contacting Jan. That made thing worse for Jan. She didn't know how San had taken their last encounter. She hoped he hadn't lost respect for her, or even worse hated her. Jan couldn't stop herself from thinking about how it felt when she and San's bodies were pressed against each other. She knew it would be only a matter of time before she headed back to San-Jania Province. If she didn't go there, San would have to come to Japha city for business or something. Jan couldn't face San in front of her father. She was afraid her father would see the truth on her face.

Jan knew she had to put some more distance between her and San. She told her girls that she was going to make a trip to visit Ramala and her new twins. That they were leaving right away. Nina and Mia didn't want to go back to the House of Ra. But they thought it might be the best thing for Jan right now. So they didn't debate it with Jan.

Jan didn't want San to know she was leaving, and they wouldn't be stopping at San-Jania Province. Jan sent a messenger to the House of Ra asking Ramala for permission to visit. Jan didn't wait on an answer. She left a day after she sent the messenger. She knew Ramala would always welcome her visit. Jan also sent a messenger to tell her father where she was going a day after she had left. She never let San know she was leaving. Jan had never run from a problem in her entire life. She always prided herself on always facing her problems head on, and over coming them. She was going to run as far away from this one as she could.

Chapter 17

Ramala's youngest twins were six months old now. They were starting to show a little bit of their personallites. The new twins had a trio of performers that always put on a good show for them. Ramashaya and Don were very comfortable with Yaya, Dan, and Ramala. They looked forward to seeing their brother and sisters every day. La had become very protective of the twins because of Ramala letting her help take care of them. Giving La responsibility made her feel in a way, that the twins were hers too. Sometimes she would stop Dan from getting to wild around them. She couldn't force her hand with Yaya, because Yaya was her big sister. But still La would test Yaya every once in a while. Yaya would contain La in front of Ramala. She would get really physical with La when Ramala wasn't around, if La tested her. La and Yaya got along really well, so there weren't that many fights between them.

One day Ramala was in between practices and had all of her Young ones in the garden with her, while she relaxed. La was sitting on the ground, clawing up dirt with her bare hands, forming mounds with the dirt. Dan was running around kicking and stomping on things, working off some of his seemingly endless amounts of energy. Ramala would let them run around the garden and even tear it up a bit, as long as they didn't get out of her sight, or get completely out of control. The gardeners would take care of any damage they did.

Yaya was there too. She would pick different flowers and show them to Ramashaya, who Yaya called Shay-Shay or Shaya. Ramala watched as Ramashaya smiled and seemed happy with Yaya bringing flowers over for her. Shaya would reach for them, but Yaya knew Ramala didn't want her to give them to Shaya. Ramala could already see a big difference in her two girls.

Ramashaya's attention could be held by showing her pretty things. La wasn't at all interested in the flowers in the garden. She would rather pull them out of the ground. After that, La didn't have much use for flowers.

They were out there for about an hour when a guard came and gave Ramala the message that Jan would be coming for a visit. Ramala got a little excited, but wondered why the Japha twins would be visiting when they were building up their new province. Ramala decided she wouldn't waste time thinking about it. The twins would be here in a few days. She could get any questions she had answered then.

Ramala looked over at Dan just in time to see him tasting something that he found. She yelled "Get that out of your mouth! Get over here right now!" Dan dropped what he had in his hand and slowly walked over to Ramala. When he got to her, she gave him a stern look, but she only lightly scolded him. Ramala was in a good mood now. Then she saw a dirt ring around La's mouth. La wasn't past tasting her own inventions. It was time to leave before her oldest twins changed her good mood. She told Yaya to go and get her younger sister. Then she turned to the younger twins and said "Look at your brother and sister. Sometimes they just don't know how to act."

Ramala smiled at the twins and motioned for the maidens to help her get them. She always talked to the new twins, just like she did the first ones. Ramala looked over and saw Yaya wrestling with La. Sometimes when La wanted to be stubborn, not even Yaya could make her do something she didn't want to. Then Ramala yelled "La! Dan! It's time to go!" When the twins heard the sternness in Ramala's voice, they both ran over to her and nervously hoped that they hadn't taken to long. Ramala let La see that she was not happy about the dirt on her face. She bent down and brushed the dirt from La's mouth. Then she smiled at both of them and said "Let's go."

They followed behind her without making a fuss. Yes, Ramala was in control. The new twins always watched their older brother and sisters. They always saw them jump to attention when they heard their mother's voice. Even the new twins could see that their mother was in control.

After Ramala put the new twins to sleep, she made the older ones take a nap. Then she went to see Tara. Even though Tara only had one child, she was finding that it still was a lot of work. She had just as many maidens as Ramala. They did everything for her, but Tara was used to coming and going as she pleased. Now she had to spend time with her son so he wouldn't get fussy and make her have to spend even more time with him until he calmed down. Yin didn't cry much as long as Tara spent time with him. He had adjusted well to the maidens taking care of him. He wouldn't get out of hand until he missed Tara, was hungry, or needed to be cleaned. Other than that, just like Ramala's boys, Yin wasn't much of a problem for Tara.

Tara was lying down with Yin when Ramala walked in. Tara motioned for Ramala to be quiet. Ramala looked and saw that Yin was sleep. She waved for Tara to come and join her. Tara got up quietly and let the maids know she was leaving. Tara and Ramala walked out of the room. Tara looked at Ramala to tell her what was on her mind. Ramala said "The Japha twins are coming to visit." Tara looked surprised and said "I thought they were busy building their new province." Ramala said "Me too. I wonder if something happened that we didn't anticipate." Tara said "Who knows. I guess we'll find out soon enough."

Ramala looked at Tara. Tara hadn't started getting herself back into shape yet. It was starting to show. Ramala thought Tara needed a little push, so she said "Let's go get some training in." Tara looked less than enthusiastic and said "I don't know. I'm a little tired. I think I need a nap." Ramala said "You already had a nap. If you don't start getting back into shape, it going to get harder to get your mind to make you do it. You've seen those girls that never get back into shape after having a child. You don't want to look like that, do you?" Tara quickly said "No way!" Ramala said "Then come on. We'll go find Wa and we'll have some fun." Tara nodded in agreement and the girls went to go work out. Ramala didn't have to remind Tara about the importance of training and keeping her body in good shape again.

Jan's caravan arrived about a week after Ramala received the message that she was coming. The Ra forward guards escorted Jan's small caravan to a checkpoint just before the main gates. By that time, Wana had been infomed that Jan was about to arrive. Wana went to get a look at the caravan from the high wall that surrounded the main city of Ra.

Wana was surprised at how small the caravan was. There were only five platforms. The largest one was in the middle of the other four. It looked to be only about twenty guards on the elephants that surrounded the main platform. Wana's elite guards stopped the caravan at the checkpoint just before the main gate. Wana saw Jan and her girls on the center Platform. She relaxed a little. Wana signaled for the guards to open the main gate. Wana wondered why the Japha twins would only travel with about twenty guards. Wana told herself that she would bring that up with Jan later. Right now, she found herself hurrying down from the wall, to meet the friend that she hadn't realized she missed so much, until she saw her.

The Hellcats didn't tell the Butchers that the Japha twins were coming. They didn't want the Butcher getting distracted from their training. All of the Butchers had been training very hard. Each of them had their own personal reasons for pushing themselves to their physical limits.

Ma hadn't lost any fights outside the team. But of all of the people she fought within the team, she hadn't beaten any. She told herself that wasn't going to keep happening. She practiced most of the day. If she couldn't find someone to spar with, she practiced alone. But with the D-Squad and the elite guards around, she didn't have to practice alone too often. Ma was determined to win some fights. Even if she had to lose some first.

The D-Squad had a new name for Cat after training with her. They called her Battle Cat. Every training session with Cat was a battle. Soon that name started catching on with everyone, including the Butchers. Cat was quick and she was strong. None of the D-girls could get with Cat. Cat put all three of them in their places soon after they got back at the House of Ra and started training together. Cat gave all three girls the kind of beatings that said we're teammates, but if you get out of line, you get dealt with. The D-girls decided it was too early in this game to get dealt with.

The D-men didn't fool around with Cat either. Cat was wound up tight. She could explode at any time, even though she didn't. They would go at her pretty good in practice, but they let the Tiger thing go. Mainly because they didn't want to get dealt with by Ramala. What bothered Cat was that she couldn't beat Syn. She couldn't beat Ramala, and she had yet to fight Wana or Tara. She wasn't gaining ground on Syn like she thought she would. Cat was pushing Syn hard every time they sparred. Cat thought about Ramala. The next time She tries me, things are going to be different!

The House of Ra was the place Syn, Jara called home. The

Hellcats had houses built for each of the Butchers and the D-Squad members. The Butcher girls usually all stayed together at one of their places every night. Syn knew she had a bullseye on her back. Everyone wanted to beat her fighting. So far, the only one that came close, if you could call it that, was Ramala. Ramala was a year younger than Syn. She had twins and still increased her strength and skill enough to really compete with Syn. That bothered Syn. She wondered if Ramala hadn't had children, how close in skills would they be right now. Syn had to put that out of her mind. She knew Ramala would keep trying her until she beat her. Syn, Jara wasn't about to let that happen. Even though Ramala was almost back in shape and training hard. Syn was already in great fighting shape. Everyday Syn trained very hard for the challenge that not only was coming from Ramala. Syn, Jara was still undefeated. She knew there had to be someone out there with skills just as good as hers. Jara knew she had to keep working hard to stay undefeated. Syn was training for the challenges she didn't know about, but knew were coming.

Dan was dusting off everyone in practice. He was on a mission. He had to have at least four or more of the top elite guards attacking him at once. The only ones he didn't spar with were Backir and Yin. The Hellcats ordered these three not to get into it at practice. The Hellcats didn't want their three top Butchers to kill one another in training. Dan was training for the Day when he would have to face eight Warlords again. He wouldn't be running that time!

Ramala was the only one that sparred with Dan one on one. They went at each other with weapons and without. Ramala got roughed up pretty good by Dan when they fought without weapons. He didn't go all out when he used his Hammer-Axes. Ramala couldn't deal with that kind of heat from Dan. Dan couldn't believe how rough Ramala had gotten in the months after having their second set of twins. She could take a good beating without getting herself hurt. He was very proud of her. Dan knew, because of the beatings he put on Ramala in practice, that she would be very hard to beat, If at all.

When Jan's caravan entered the main gate, Wana was there to meet it. Wana jumped onto the platform that Jan was on and gave her a big hug. Then she looked at Nina and Mia and asked "Where's San?" Nina said "He didn't come. It's just us three." Wana wondered why not, but didn't ask. She noticed that

Jan didn't look her usual self. Wana asked Jan "Is everything alright?" Jan paused, then said "As far as running the House of Japha is concerned, Yes." Wana couldn't help, seeing that something was bothering Jan, asking "And what about everything else?" Jan said "I really missed all of you more than I thought I would." Wana could see that she would have to get back to Jan on this later, so she said "We have missed you too. Let's go see everyone!"

Wana told one of the guards to let everyone know that the House of Ra had guest. There was a certain drum beat to let everyone know guest were arriving. There was a certain drum beat for most every situation. Whether it was danger, guest, or dinner time. You could tell what was going on by the beat of the drums.

It didn't take long for the Butcher girls to find out that Jan had arrived. They raced to the building that Wana had set up for the Japha twins. The D-Girls, who had become close to the Butchers, arrived just after the Butcher girls did. After all of the girls hugged and greeted each other. The first thing they noticed was that San wasn't with Jan. It was so unusual to everyone that the twins weren't together. So every time someone different came to greet Jan, that was the first question she had to answer.

The Butcher girls asked about San, the Butcher men asked about San. By the time it was Ramala's turn to ask about San, Jan was fed up. It seemed to her that not even in the south could she get away from San. So when Ramala asked about San, Jan cut her off before she finished the question. Ramala watched her friend closely and could see that Jan was stressed about something. She let it go for now. Everyone had a good time catching up on things that happened.

Ramala sent everyone on their way and took Jan to see her children. La and Dan remembered Jan and let her pick them up. Jan was amazed at how big they were getting. Then she turned her attention to the new twins. They didn't want anything to do with Jan, even though they saw Ramala and their brother and sister comfortable with Jan. Tara came by with Yin. Of course Tara asked the same question everyone else did. Ramala answered for Jan. That kept Tara from questioning Jan further. After Jan visited the children for a short while, Ramala, Tara, and Jan went to one of the private gardens and sat for a while. They weren't there for five minutes before Wana joined them.

Ramala had guards bring extra chairs over for Nina and

Mia. Ramala said "If it's alright with Jan, can your girls take a seat? I think it's safe around her, right Wana?" Wana said "Safer than anywhere." Jan looked at her girls and nodded that it was alright for them to sit and relax. Nina and Mia would never go completely off guard. That's the way they were trained. After they were seated, Ramala looked back at Jan and said "I'm so glad you made time to come and visit. I want you to know that we can talk about anything. You look very well, but I do see sadness in your eyes. Why didn't San come?" Wana interrupted with "Also, no offense to Nina and Mia, but you traveled all this way with very little protection. That was taking an unnecessary chance that harm could come to you." Wana's voice had a light scold to it, but it also had concern.

Jan looked at both Ramala and Wana. She didn't say anything right away. Tara said "Sister, I don't have to tell you how much we care about you. It is also important to us that you stay safe. When you leave the House of Ra you will have more protection than you need. Anytime you travel you should have maximum protection. San can't run the House of Japha like the both of you can. He needs you to watch his back."

Jan was starting to feel ganged up on. She looked at Tara and said in a frustrated tone "Is there anything else I'm doing wrong?" Tara didn't want to respond to that, so she looked to Ramala for help. Ramala said in a soft voice "Sister, I hope you don't think we are criticizing you. It's just that we're very concerned right now. We should talk about what's bothering you. We don't have to talk about it right now, but whatever it is, it's bothering me too."

Ramala looked at Jan. Jan said "Alright. I'll tell you." Then she paused while she organized her thoughts. Jan stood up and looked at Wana and Tara before looking directly in Ramala's eyes and saying "There is something weighing heavy on my heart. It has to do with San. When me and San were on our way back to the House of Japha, I noticed that it was hard for me to deal with San's brotherly touching.It surprised me when my body started having reactions to San's body that a sister shouldn't have for her brother. I tried to control my body with my mind, and by avoiding San's brotherly affections. San noticed right away and it created friction between us. I thought if I could find some way to keep San busy, I could work this thing out in my head. I sent for the Na, Tee with out San knowing. I knew how much San missed Tee. When she got to San-Jania province my plan worked like a charm. San and Tee became inseparable. Soon after that, Tee became with child. I had more than enough time to sort out my thoughts. They just weren't what I wanted them to be. My mind was starting to side with my body. At that point I couldn't even face my father around San. That's when I knew it was time to leave. I didn't even tell San I was leaving. I just ran as quickly as I could. I can't figure out what's wrong with me!" Ramala stood up immediately and said "There's nothing wrong with you." Ramala walked over and hugged Jan. Jan broke down in Ramala's arms and said "Why is this happening to me? Why can't I put him out of my mind? I don't know what I'm going to do! Why can't I love someone else?"

At that point, Nina and Mia stood up. They weren't going to let Jan get completely out of control. They thought she had said too much already. Then Wana and Tara stood up. Wana looked a warning to both girls that they didn't like but had to respect.

This was a personal moment between Jan and Ramala, and Wana didn't want these two girls to lessen it by interrupting. That only stopped Nina and Mia for a moment. They started towards Jan. As they did, Wana and Tara moved and beat them to Jan. Wana and Tara both put their arms around Jan and hugged her for support.

Ramala said in a very soft voice "We'll figure this thing out together and we'll do what's best for you. We'll do whatever we have to to make sure you're happy." Nina wanted to get Jan out of there, but she had to be careful not to disrespect the Hellcats. Nina said "Please, it's been a long trip and Jan is tired. She needs rest." Jan regained her composure and the Hellcats released her. Ramala took a quick peek at Nina and Mia before loking at Jan and saying "Sister, go get some rest. We don't have to figure this out right now. We'll meet for dinner later. After that we'll have a party and dance. We'll unwind and relax. You'll see, we'll have fun!"

Ramala smiled at Jan. Jan smiled back. She felt better now, realizing how much weight had been lifted off of her shoulders by talking about her secret that she felt was so terrible.

Wana personally escorted Jan and her girls to the building that they would be living in while visiting. After they were gone, Tara and Ramala stared at each other for a moment. They knew they had a delicate situation on their hands. The Japha twins were the key to keeping the northern Houses in check. Without the Japha twins working closely together. They would not be able to keep control of the House of Japha. Without the House of Japha in the Hellcats pocket, they would always have to worry about war coming from the north. Especially after what they did to the House of Hoo.

Ramala had her eyes on expanding her territory into the Southern Jungle. Now she had to be a little more careful in her planning. If she got caught in a war in the south and from the north, the House of Ra would be done. She was almost sure of that. If Jan couldn't get over this thing for her brother, the Hellcats would do what had to be done to make sure Jan was comfortable working closely with San. Even if they had to take matters into their own hands. Now the Hellcats were starting to see the Na, Tee as a problem. That wasn't at all good for the Na, Tee.

San was running the new province with amazing efficiency. He never thought he could do so well without Jan's help. He put what happened between him and Jan out of his mind. At first he was furious with Jan for leaving and not telling him. Even though Jan didn't know it. San sent guards to escort her caravan, without letting her know they were there, as soon as he found out she left. They followed her all the way to the forward guards of the House of Ra before returning. The Na, Tee got nervous that San would go running after his sister because of the way he responded at first. San missed his sister dearly. After a few days San calmed down and got back to the business of building San-Jania. He was starting to understand that Jan's leaving was best for both of them. She was the smartest. She wouldn't have done it if it wasn't best for both of them.

Even though San had put out of his mind what happened between him and Jan. One thing kept creeping into his mind. Before that day he had never been aware of Jan's grown woman body. After she pushed up on him with it, she forced San to realize how her body really felt. The one thing that kept coming back from that day was how Jan's body felt next to his. When that thought crept into his mind, he quickly put it out. San knew how much trouble could come if he started thinking like Jan. San had Tee. She was enough for him. He decided he wouldn't contact Jan. San was going to give Jan as much time as she needed to get over this thing. Even though he missed his sister, he knew it was for the best that they didn't see each other. San knew he had to be strong for Jan.

Ramala's plans for moving into the Southern Jungle were going as scheduled. Her training with Dan and her elite guards had put her back in great shape again. All of her Warlords and Elite guards were in the best fighting shape ever. She rewarded herself by testing her body in bed with Dan. They hadn't been together sexually since before she had the twins. Once they started up again, Ramala found that no matter how much Dan gave it to her, after she recovered, she wanted it even more. They went at it every chance they got until finally, yes, you guessed it. She was with child again. Ramala didn't tell Dan at first. She was just about ready to move into the Southern Jungle. She knew Dan wouldn't go for her fighting in the jungle with four of his children and one on the way. She had to change her plans. She knew she wouldn't be able to go, but she was still going to send everyone else.

Ramala was laying with Dan this night. Once she became with child, her sex drive always decreased dramatically. Dan had been getting rode hard by Ramala at night. Lately she hadn't been so ferocious. He didn't pick up on it right away. He just thought she was like that because of the long lay off. Now that she had got her fill, and knew she could get it anytime, she was starting to slow down. That's what Dan told himself. Ramala snuggled close up on Dan. She looked up at him and didn't say anything. Dan knew Ramala well enough to know something was on her mind. He looked at her and Said "What?" Ramala just looked at Dan trying to find the right words. Dan said "You might as well just say it." Ramala said "You are going to lead the Butchers and the D-Squad, along with my army to take control of the Southern Jungle from the savages."

Dan thought to himself, first she built a kindom in the south by taking land from people she called heathens. Now she was going to take the southern jungle from the people she called savages. Dan wondered how many more degrading names Ramala had for the many more lands that he anticipated she would take over. He knew if anyone could come up with an insulting name, his Queen Ramala could!

Dan said "So you're going to stay here and take care of our children. I can't believe I didn't have to fight you oner that one." Ramala smiled. Dan couldn't stop her from doing anything she wanted to do. She wasn't going to let him know that, unless she needed to. Right now she needed him to be successful, and show everyone that he could be a good leader and the King she knew he could be. This would be his first real test. Ramala was a little concerned. Dan had told her about the encounter with the He Warlords. She knew if that happened again and people found out. Dan would only be a king in name. Ramala wanted him to be a King with big victories behind him.

Ramala said "I'm a little concerned that you might need me out there." Dan said "Since we met, you've always taken the lead. I said I would back you up, just to see where it would lead. Now I finally get to show everyone that I'm not just a King in name. When I return, everyone will have stories about the King of the House of Ra, Top Butcher, Dan the Destroyer."

Ramala had heard Dan use those names to describe himself, after they got home from the last trip. She didn't want him to become over confident. So she said "You haven't beat Syn yet.When you best the rest of the Butchers in a one on one contest, that's when you become Top Butcher.When you carve me out a new territory in the Southern Jungle is when you become Dan the Destroyer."

Dan said "What do you call me now besides shit heathen?" Ramala shifted her body on Dan's and said "In bed, you are all three to me, King of the House of Ra, Top Butcher, Dan the Destroyer. Outside this bedroom, you have to prove it to everyone else." At first Dan was offended. He didn't think Ramala was cofident that he could take the Southern Jungle without her. After he thought about it, he knew she was right. He hadn't proved anything yet. Dan wouldn't let himself call himself those names again, until he proved that was who he really was.

Ramala had planned to challenge and test all of the girls on her team's skills. She was going to do that in a month or two. Now that she was about two months with child, she had to do it now, or it wouldn't get done. She told her cousins what she was going to do the day before she planned on doing it. They would go along, but they were going to watch closely. Ramala hadn't told them she was with child, or they would never go along with her doing something this rough. They knew their cousin could best the other girls easily. What they were going to watch closely was Ramala's match with the Syn, Jara. They weren't concerned with the other girls.

Ramala set it up, and told the girls that it would be happening. Jan spent most of her time with Ramala since returning to the House of Ra. Ramala told Jan. Jan wasn't going to waste her time telling Ramala she didn't think it was a good idea. She knew Ramala was going to do it anyway. Jan decided to sit back and enjoy the show.

Ramala let everyone know the order in which they would face her. Everyone filled the small courtyard where the matches would occur. The Butcher men were seated along side the D-Men. All of the girls that would be fighting were sitting together. The Hellcats, Jan, and her girls, along with Yaya, all sat together. All three Hellcats had on their ruling capes. Wana stood up and said "All of you know why we are here today. Your Queen wants to see what progress you have made in your training."

Wana turned and motioned to Dina. Dina stood up and walked to the middle of the courtyard. Ramala stood up slowly. She pulled the string holding her cape around her neck. The cape dropped to the ground. Ramala could feel Yaya's nervous stare on her. She looked at Yaya and gave her a smile that every thing was alright. Then Ramala walked out into the courtyard where Dina was waiting. On the way, Ramala wrapped her ponytail around her neck and tucked the rest of it in her blouse. When Ramala reached Dina she said "Don't hold back. I need to see how good you are. Besides, holding back will get you hurt. You can start whenever you're ready."

Dina lowered her head out of respect, then went on guard. Ramala smiled and motioned, with her hand, for Dina to start. Dina was taller than Ramala and thought that might give her a slight advantage. Dina attacked. She found out that Ramala was hard to get to and very quick. Ramala countered off of every attack Dina tried. Dina was good but not good enough to compete with Ramala. Ramala touched her up, but not to badly. Then she ended it. She told Dina "I know your smartness is your bigest asset to the team. I still need you to get better at fighting." Then she dismissed Dina. That fight only took ten minutes. Dina was glad it only lasted that long.

Nana was next. Wana sent her out into the courtyard where Ramala was waiting on her. Nana watched the first match and knew Ramala couldn't be taken lightly. Nana was thick and strong. She also was quick, but not like Cat. She could bully an opponent with her size, if it was a woman.

Ramala smiled at Nana and motioned for her to start. Nana attacked. Again Ramala countered off of Nana's attack to the point that Nana was getting hit up pretty good, but didn't get one blow in on Ramala. Ramala stopped that fight after ten minutes. Nana couldn't hit Ramala and had all but given up. She was just waiting on Ramala to say she was done hitting her. Ramala told Nana "If you add some speed to that strength, you'll be very hard to deal with." Nana lowered her head out of respect to Ramala, glad that she ended the fight when she did.

Kiki was next. If Kiki couldn't beat Ramala outright, she just wanted to get one good blow in on Ramala to even the score for having to kiss her hand. As Kiki walked over she looked Ramala in her eyes for a split second. Ramala could read eyes very well and knew what Kiki was thinking. Ramala took her ponytail out of her blouse and unwrapped it from around her neck. It fell down her back past her behind. This was the first time any of the girls would see Ramala fight without her ponytail hidden. When Yin saw Ramala's tail come out it brought back memories of Tara beating the hell out of him with hers. Yin knew Kiki was in big trouble. He smiled at moved forward in his seat. Yin didn't want to miss one second of this fight.

Ramala didn't smile at Kiki like she did the other girls. Kiki had disrespected her by looking Ramala in her eyes and with bad intentions. She just motioned for Kiki to start. Kiki attacked hard. She was fast, but Ramala was managing to stay just out of the reach of Kiki's blows.

Ramala waited until she was sure of Kiki's speed before she moved in and started countering. Ramala moved out of the way of one of Kiki's swings and moved inside. She punished Kiki with a two piece to the body then moved just out of the way of another fast and powerful swing from Kiki. Ramala punished her with three shots to the body this time. Kiki grunted in pain from t he last one. Kiki started swinging again. This time Ramala stayed close to her, avoiding her swings, but not hitting her. Kiki couldn't help but notice Ramala's ponytail dancing around as she avoided Kiki. Kiki was looking for any advantage, so she grabbed Ramala's ponytail and yanked it as hard as she could. Ramala's head didn't move one inch.

Kiki couldn't beat Ramala with two hands, now one of her hands was on Ramala's ponytail. Ramala struck in the same instant that Kiki yanked her ponytail. She took all the wind out of Kiki's body with a powerful, lightning quick eight piece. Kiki let go of Ramala's tail after the forth blow crached into her midsection. After the second four Kiki was a little dazed and breathing very heavy. Ramala didn't give her time to recover. Ramala took a step back from Kiki and started spinning very fast in a circle right in front of Kiki, swinging her head as she spun. With every revolution Ramala's ponytail whipped across Kiki's face. After the hair whip hit Kiki four times in her face, Ramala stepped closer to Kiki and stopped in front of her, letting her tail wrap around Kiki's neck. Then Ramala took a quick step back to tighten the grip of the tail around Kiki's neck.

Kiki tried to reach for Ramala's tail to loosen the grip from around her neck. That's when Ramala showed Kiki that she was better. Ramala blocked every attempt by Kiki to grab her tail. Kiki fought until the lack of oxygen stopped her. Kiki's arms dropped to her sides and her legs begain to wobble. Ramala moved close to Kiki and unwrapped her hair from around Kiki's neck. Kiki gasped for air. All of the strength had been zapped from Kiki's body. She was done. She didn't have anymore will to fight Ramala.

Ramala looked Kiki in her eyes and said "You can be a lot better if you learn to fight without anger. Work harder so you can impress your Queen with what you can do for her." Then Ramala lowered her voice to where only Kiki could hear her. Ramala said "I'm in charge. Challenge me again and I'll kill you before you can think." Kiki lowered her head. She respected Ramala more than she ever had. Not because Ramala spared her life. It was because Ramala was crazier than Kiki and could back it up. That's what impressed Kiki. Kiki walked back to her seat with four welts from Ramala's hair on her face.

The Butcher girls knew they were next. Ma was the first. Ma wasn't thrilled about fighting Ramala, and she really didn't want to deal with that ponytail of hers. But Ma wasn't going to back down from a fight. Ma walked on to the courtyard. Ramala smiled at Ma and then wrapped her tail back around her neck and tucked the rest into her blouse. Ma was a little relieved that she wouldn't have to watch for that tail swinging at her.

Ma got her ten minutes in with Ramala just like Dina and Nana. Only Ramala didn't punish Ma. She danced and avoided Ma. When Ramala was done playing with Ma, she gave her one powerful blow to the midsection, then ended the match. Ramala could see that Ma was upset that she hadn't done better. Ramala said "Don't be so hard on yourself. I know you held back so you wouldn't hurt me. Keep getting better. I know you can." Ma lowered her head and went back to her seat. Ma wished she was good enough to hold back while fighting Ramala.

Cat didn't waste time. She stood up before Ma sat down. That made Syn nervous. Syn knew Ramala saw Cat. After the beating Kiki took, Syn knew it wasn't a good idea to let Ramala see that you're anxious to fight her.

Cat was still wound up tight. Even though she had gotten closer to Spider she still didn't want to trust him with her body. Cat was playing a teasing game with herself and Dan. She wanted to give it to him, but she didn't. She considered giving herself to Spider just to spite Dan. Cat knew it bothered Dan to see her and Spider talking privately. Dan couldn't say anything because of Ramala. Besides, he wouldn't anyway because he knew Cat wanted him to say something.

Cat walked out on to the courtyard very confidently. This was the fight between the Battle Cat, and the Hellcat. Ramala smiled at Cat. She was going to enjoy beating Cat. Cat was good, but Ramala knew Cat couldn't deal with her. Ramala let Dan throw her around wrestling with him, just so no girl would be able to. When Cat got to Ramala, Cat said "Ready." Ramala looked at Cat and motioned for her to start.

Ramala was offended that Cat would ask her if she was ready. What was this heathen thinking? Ramala wondered how Cat didn't know she was ready, when she set this whole thing up! Cat jumped on the only advantage she knew she had. Ramala was angry and thinking about it. Cat attacked while Ramala was still thinking. Cat was very fast and Ramala had to block these blows, instead of avoiding them.

Then Ramala's ego got the better of her. She wanted to prove to herself and Cat that she could avoid Cat with out blocking. That strategy didn't work out to well for Ramala. Cat caught up to her and delivered a shot to Ramala's midsection and barely missed her face with another one. Ramala had had enough of playing with Cat. Ramala turn the fight around right away with a strong three piece combination on Cat. She ducked out of the way of another swing by Cat and punished Cat with a five piece that left Cat sucking air. Then Ramala laid into Cat something fierce with a hellishly fast and powerful seven piece. Cat was stumbling, and almost out on her feet. Syn and Dan were both on their feet ready to stop the fight. Ramala wasn't finished yet. She was going to make an example out of Cat that the others would never forget.

Dan saw something in Ramala's eyes that let him know Cat was dead if he didn't do something immediately. That made him bolt on to the courtyard. Ramala was about to finish off Cat when she felt someone coming up behind her, and pulled her pony tail out of her blouse and spinned her head unwrapping her tail from around her neck. As she was turning to see who was coming fast behind her, she thought it was Syn or Ma, but it was Dan. Ramala slung the tail towards Dan catching his arm just as he was jumping through the air to stop Ramala. Dan wasn't grounded. All of his momentum was going towards Ramala. That made it easy for her to pull her head back with all her might, flipping Dan hard on the ground, on his back. Just before he hit the ground she loosened her ponytail grip on his arm, bringing her tail behind her.

Ramala was furious to see that it was Dan, her King that came to the aid of his heathen friend Cat. Ramala shot a glaring stare at Dan for only a few seconds to let him know how angry she was. Then she turned her back on Dan and Cat. Ramala said "This match is over. The last match will be tomorrow." It took all the control Ramala had not to turn around, attack Dan and then kill Cat. Cat was down on one knee trying to clear the cowebs from the beating Ramala gave her. Tara and Wana saw Ramala's eyes. They knew she was fuming. Ramala quickly walked over to her cousins. One of the guards put Ramala's cape around her neck. She quickly walked off. Wana and Tara stared quickly at Cat and Dan. Then as they turned to walk away, they flung their capes around their bodies out of anger. There was going to be trouble over this incident and the Hellcats were going to cause it!

Chapter 18

After the Hellcats left, Syn and Ma hurried out to see if Cat was alright. She was roughed up and shaken up, but she would survive. Syn said "Dan, go and check on Ramala." Dan looked at Syn like she had lost her mind. He knew Ramala had taken it personal that he came to Cat's aid instead of hers. Even though Ramala didn't need his help, he came to help someone she was fighting. He knew that's how Ramala had taken it. To make matters worse, it was a woman he helps. And worse than that, it was Cat. Dan had gotten off the ground and watched as Ramala stormed off. He figured he couldn't go home tonight, if he wanted to live.

Jan watched everything that went on. She didn't leave with the Hellcats. She wanted to talk to the Butchers and try to help them out of a situation that had spun out of control. She told Ma and Syn to go to their quarters and stay there for the rest of the night. Syn looked at Jan like she had better be right on this, then Syn looked at Ma, and they left. Jan turned and told Cat to go to Ramala's palace and beg for Ramala to take her head or accept an apology from her. Cat looked at Jan in disbelief. Jan said "You played a dangerous game and lost. You have to offer your life as quickly as possible or you and all of your friends will be dead before morning. That I can guarantee."

Cat could see that Jan was serious. Jan continued with "You of all people should know not to challenge Ramala under any circumstances. You did and you lost. Whatever happens to you, you deserve it for putting your friend's lives in danger. Go right now and do what I said!" Cat only looked at Jan for a few more seconds, then she left.

Ramala was walking very fast towards her Palace. Wana and Tara were doing their best to keep up. Tara said "La! Slow down!" Wana said "Mala, tell me what you want done? I'll start taking heads right away, if that's what you want! Whatever needs done, I'll do it!" Ramala said "When we get to the Palace we'll talk." Wana said "I'm just saying!"

The Hellcats didn't say another word until they got to Ramala's palace. They followed Ramala to one of the private meeting rooms. Wana ordered one of the guards to bring food and water. Then all three girls sat down. Wana and Tara looked at Ramala waiting on her to start talking. Ramala just sat there. She was slowly calming herself down. Wana and Tara were very patient with her. Finally Tara said "What do you want done with Cat?" Ramala had a sad and confused look on her face when she said "He came to stop me from doing harm to her. Does he have feelings for her, that he would protect her from me?" Wana's eyes lit up with fire. She said "That's it! They're both dead!" Tara said "Wa calm down! Let La think about what she wants done. Then we'll take care of this." Wana stared at Tara and yelled "I'm just saying!"

Tara turned back to Ramala and said "Tell us what you want." Ramala was about to say something when Yaya came running into the room. Ramala could see that she had out maneuvered the guard outside by the way he ran in staring at Yaya with bad intentions. Ramala looked at the guard and motioned for him to leave. Ramala said "What's so important?"

Yaya didn't say a word. She slowly walked up to Ramala and put her hand on Ramala's hand. Then Yaya looked at Ramala with concern in her eyes. Ramala didn't know if the concern was for herself or Cat. Then Yaya sat down lying next to Ramala pulling Ramala's hand and arm around her. Ramala looked down at Yaya then said "

Don't worry, everything's going to be alright." Tara and Wana watched as they saw Yaya act as if she was Ramala's blood child. Then a guard came in and begged permission to speak. Wana gave permission. The guard said "Mistress Queen you have a visitor." Wana said "Who is it?" The guard said "It's Cat." That was enough for Wana. She stood up quickly with bad intentions written all over her face. Ramala Yelled "Wa!" Wana stopped, turned and looked at Ramala. Ramala shook her head no. Wana put her hands on her hips and waited on Ramala to make the next move.

Ramala asked the guard "Go see what she wants and come

report it to me." The guard said "She already gave me a message. She said she has come to offer an apology for her actions earlier. She said if you will not accept her apology, then she offers her head." A big smile came on Wana's face as she watched and waited on Ramala's reaction. Ramala asked "Where is she now?" The guard said "

She's waiting on the stairs of the palace on her knees, alone." Ramala said "Go back to your post. I'll handle it from here." The guard lowered his head, then left. Tara said "She couldn't have thought of that on her own. A heathen could never think of that! I bet that Japha, Jan put her up to this, thinking you wouldn't take her head. I say you do it!"

Ramala could feel Yaya flinching and nervously squirming when Tara and Wana spoke. Ramala rubbed Yaya's stomach and said "Go check on the twins. I'll be there when I'm done here." Yaya stood up and lowered her head to each of the Hellcats, then took off running. After Yaya disappeared out the doorway, Ramala turned to Tara and said "Can we take the Southern Jungle without the Butchers?"

Tara didn't look as confident as she should have when she said "Sure we can." Ramala looked at Wana and said "I'll be the one who decides if Cat's head get's taken. If I do decide to take it, it won't be until I have complete control of the Southern Jungle." Wana and Tara both smiled. That was enough for them. They knew Ramala well. They knew she would eventually take Cat's head for her arrogance. Of that they were sure of.

Cat went to the stairs of Ramala's palace and was stopped by her guards. She requested to see Ramala and gave the guards a message. Cat was told to wait there on the steps and they would return with a response from Ramala. Cat got on her knees and waited for Ramala. She knew she was wrong for challenging Ramala. She couldn't figure out why she did it. The only thing she could figure was that something had been building in her and she had to get it out. Maybe Dan was right. Maybe she was wound up to tight and needed to release some of that tension through sex. Maybe it was to late for that. Cat didn't feel good about coming here. The only reason she did was to save the lives of her friends. She knew Ma and Syn would have jumped in that fight if Dan hadn't. If Jan hadn't told Cat to beg for forgiveness, Ma and Syn would have stood by Cat, in battle against the Hellcats.

Cat waited and waited but the guard didn't return. She

didn't know whether that was a good sign or a bad one. Cat told herself that she wasn't going to leave until she saw Ramala. If she had to stay there all night, that's what she was going to do.

Syn and Ma went back to Cat's place hoping that she would return soon. Jan and her girls got their after an hour and told the girls what Cat was doing. Ma jumped up and said "We can't let that happen!" Jan said "If you try anything, you'll be killed. All of you." Ma looked at Syn and said "We should just let her kill Cat?"

Syn didn't say anything. She didn't know what to do. One thing Syn did know was that none of them had learned to deal with a scream from a Hellcat. If they got blasted, it wouldn't make a difference how good they could fight, because they wouldn't be able to. If they did do something, they would have to strike the Hellcats before they could scream and kill them. Jan could see Syn thinking and said "Whatever you're thinking, you can't beat them. So don't try."

Jan paused, then said "I'll go and talk to Ramala. Maybe I can change her mind. If not, you two had better let this go." Jan looked at both girls then she went to go talk to Ramala. Jan saw on Ma and Syn's face that if Cat was killed, all bets were off. They would be willing to give their lives to take revenge for their friend. As Jan walked to go see Ramala, she didn't think they would get it.

Jan and her girls caught up with Ramala playing with all of her twins. To Jan, it didn't look like Ramala was in a killing mood. Jan looked at Mia and Nina. They knew she wanted them to wait outside, so they did. Ramala knew what Jan wanted to ask her. Jan came over and played with the all of the twins before she turned her attention to Ramala. Ramala brought up the subject before Jan did. Ramala said "You know I'm not going to kill her this time. But she has to know that I will."

La was listening and said "Who's gonna get killed?" Ramala looked at La and said "Mother is talking. Go play." La could see that Ramala was serious, so she moved a short distance away while watching and listening to her mother without asking questions. Jan said "This is partly your fault."

Ramala looked surprised at what Jan said. Jan continued with "My girls are my team mates. I never challenge them. That keeps bad feelings from developing. Why do you keep challenging your team?" Ramala said "It keeps everyone in line. It reminds them that I'm in charge."

Jan said, as a matter of fact "Everyone knows you are in charge. A person needs to be able to have some pride. You can't take that away. If you do, you'll have rebellion within the House of Ra." Ramala thought about what Jan said. She hadn't thought about it that way. She knew Jan was right. She wasn't going to kill Cat, but she still planned on fighting the Syn, Jara tomorrow.

Ramala let Cat stay out on the steps of the palace for three hours before she went to see her. Cat was determined to wait there to see what her fate was. Ramala came alone. When she got to Cat. Cat said "Please forgive me Mistress Queen! I beg your forgiveness. If not, I offer my head."

Cat pulled her hair up, exposing her neck. She closed her eyes and waited. Ramala said "I am partly to blame for this. Challenging you girls to fights can only lead to bad blood. The only reason I fight you girls is to motivate you to get better. From now on I'll have to trust that you have been practicing hard and are on the top of your game. Stand up and look at me." Cat did as she was told. Ramala said "Don't lie to me. How much of what happened today had to do with your feelings for Dan?"

Cat answered as honestly as she could. She said "Not much, if at all. Dan seems to think that I'm wound up too tight. He thinks sex will help. What do you think?" Ramala said "Sex does relieve stress. But you have to be careful. If you have feelings for the person, you can become very emotional and you'll do irrational things. Some girls like Ma don't need it to keep them balanced. It doesn't affect her. But you, I think it might do you some good. Then again, that might not be the problem. If not, sex could create a whole knew set of problems for you. You have to decide for yourself. You're old enough to make your own decisions. I forgive you. Respect me and never challenge me. If you do that, you'll have no problem from me." Cat said "Thank you my Queen." Then she took Ramala's hand and kissed it. Ramala gave Cat a hug. Then she said "Go and let your friends know that everything is alright."

Cat went back to her place. When she walked in the door, Ma and Syn jumped up and ran to meet her. They all hugged. Syn looked at Cat and said "She just let you go?" Cat said "No, I had to do some serious ass kissing." Ma said "That's all?" Cat looked at Ma and said "That was enough! There's not one inch of Ramala's ass my lips didn't touch. I think I kissed ass she didn't know she had. That's how much ass I kissed!" Syn and Ma laughed. They were so happy to see Cat unharmed, that they were giddy. They would have laughed at almost anything. After a moment Cat started laughing too. They all laughed for a while before they regained their composure.

Dan was staying at Backir's place when the Butcher girls came by. Cat told them what happened. Dan knew if Ramala didn't do anything to Cat, all of the blame was resting on his shoulders. Dan had time to think about what happened. At first, there would have been no way he would go home. Over time, his confidence built up. He convinced himself that he could get out of this by turning the whole thing around, and blaming Ramala. Convincing her it was she that was wrong. It was a bold plan. Not many men would even consider trying this with Ramala. Dan wasn't going to go groveling to Ramala. The only way he figured he could get away with what he had done was with the old trick of deflecting. Dan knew he would have to play this all the way if he wanted Ramala to think he was serious. When he got back to the Palace, Ramala was going to have a lot of explaining to do!

When Dan was walking up the Palace steps the guards alerted Ramala. She was with her twins. Ramala said "Yaya, the maids are going to take you and the twins to Tara's place for the night." Ramala motioned for the maids to take them all. Ramala had already made arrangements with Tara for the children to stay at her place. She planned on having a big fight with Dan tonight. She would settle for nothing less. The maids had gathered everyone and was about to leave when everyone was statled by Dan yelling from down the Hall "Ramala! Get out here right now!" The maids hurried the children out of the room and didn't stop moving until they were on an elephant heading to Tara's place.

After Dan yelled, Ramala felt heat shoot from the top of her head to her feet and back to her head. If Dan was trying to piss Ramala off more than he already had, he succeeded. Ramala tried to calm herself but couldn't. Her heart was beating a thousand beats a minute. Her eyes blinked slowly and studdered as the closed before opening back up. She walked out of the childrens room and down a long hallway that led to her and Dan's sleeping quarters. Ramala knew Dan didn't think she would come to him after he yelled like that. When she got to their sleeping quarters, Ramala looked around the room and took note of everything there she could throw at Dan. Then she heard Dan walking down the hall towards her. Ramala turned and face the doorway. Dan barely got to the door, when Ramala yelled "Who the Hell do you think you are yelling at me you stupid Ass Shit Idiot Moron!?" Before Ramala could start another sentence, Dan quickly said in a stern voice "You owe me an apology right now for what you did today!" Dan was trying to shock Ramala, and he had. She couldn't believe what he said and yelled "WHAT!!?" Dan said "I came over to break up a fight that had clearly gone to far, and you threw me on my back acting out like a crazy ass dingbat!" Ramala stood there shaking in anger, and barely was audible when she said "What did you call me!"

Dan, without realizing the affect that he already caused, said "You heard me. I said crazy ass air headed dingbat! Getting all worked up over nothing and attacking me like that! Have you lost that sick ass mind of yours?"

Ramala stared at Dan not able to answer. She had always taken pride in showing Dan how smart she was. Did he really think of her as an air headed dingbat? Dan had never in his life seen a look of hurt and anger like that he saw on Ramala's face. Her lips trembled as she said "This is what you think of me!?"

Dan had taken all the fight right out of Ramala without knowing it. She was crushed. She stood there staring at Dan with tears welling up in her eyes, waiting for him to say something. Now Dan was confused. This wasn't the way this was supposed to go. Now what was he going to say? He decided that he wouldn't say anything. He put an apologetic look on his face, and walked toward Ramala. When he got within arms reach, she slapped him as hard as she could across his face. Dan flinched in pain, but didn't move after that. He just looked at Ramala. She slapped him again. This time he took her in his arms. She tried to wrestle away at first, but she had no fight left in her. She dropped her arms and cried uncontrollably in Dan's arms. Dan just stood there and held her. He knew he had screwed up big time!

Dan took Ramala over to the sleeping area and laid her down. He lay down next to her, looking up at the ceiling. Dan was just starting to go in and out of consciousness when Ramala got up over him and started ripping off his clothes. Dan didn't say anything because he didn't want to ruin the moment. Ramala looked like she meant serious business and he wanted to get dealt with.

Dan threw everything he had at Ramala, except the kitchen sink. Ramala threw everything she had at Dan, including the kitchen sink. Dan had always been the master in this bedroom. Tonight he couldn't match the emotional fury Ramala was putting out. It was almost day break before she stopped. When Ramala finally got finished with Dan, he had the sheets wedged in between his toes of both his feet. He pulled the sheets from between his toes. Ramala watched him as he did it. He saw her looking at him and was more than a little embarrassed about that.When he was done, he layed back down next to Ramala.

Ramala said in a low voice, with her back turned to Dan "Don't ever leave me." Dan was puzzled by what Ramala said. He didn't remember saying that he was leaving this time. The tone in Ramala's voice also shocked Dan when she said that. She wasn't begging. She had given him an order.

Dan was cautious when he woke up the next morning. He didn't know what to expect. Dan watched Ramala almost dancing around like nothing had happened. She even smiled at him and said "You're not going to sleep all day are you? Let's go have breakfast with our children." Ramala's smile was radiant. She seemed genuinely happy. It looked like all had been forgiven. Dan was going to roll with it.

Ramala and Dan had breakfast with Yaya and their children. Dan watched as Ramala loosened her usually strict grip at breakfast. She smiled and laughed at the twins, who sensed the weakness in their mother and acted out as much as they dared. They didn't go too far into uncharted territory, but it was far enough for being around Ramala. Dan watched as it seemed that nothing could get to Ramala this morning. Dan let his two oldest children climb all over him, while he let his food digest. After that he went to his morning training session.

Ramala met with her cousins, The Butcher girls, and the D-Girls. All of the girls noticed the change in Ramala. She was very pleasant to everyone, including the guards. That never happened. Then Ramala told all of the girls that she was postponing the last match, which was against Syn, Jara until the next day. She knew today it would be very hard to reach the intensity level she would need to compete with Syn.

Cat, Ma, and Syn had only seen Ramala this happy twice since they knew her. Both times were right after she had her twins. They couldn't take their eyes off of her. She was practically glowing. Cat wondered what Dan had done to Ramala last night to bring about this change in her. Cat's body was on high alert every day now, waiting on Cat to let it be dealt with. After seeing Ramala today, Cat wanted Dan to do whatever it was he had done to Ramala, to her.

The other two Hellcats questioned Ramala extensively as to why she was so happy today. Ramala told them that she couldn't explain it. She said "Last night I planned on giving Dan a good piece of my mind, then I was going to give him a fight he would never forget. I was so angry I wanted to kill him. But when he got there, he said something so stupid, that it threw everything out of whack. All of the anger I had was somehow turned against me. I still don't know what happened. But some how we ended up making up. And boy did we make up! After that, I didn't have a drop of anger in my whole body. Strange, isn't it?"

Tara said "Just tell me what he said. I want to feel like that! Maybe I can get Yin to say it to me!" Wana excitedly said "Yeah, tell us what he said!" Ramala smiled at her cousins and thought to herself for a second before saying "Nothing really. What he said wouldn't have affected either of you two. Trust me, it was something that would have only worked on me."

The next Day Ramala was focused on what she wanted to do. Even though Ramala was pleasant to Dan, he could see she was back to her old self. Now Dan had a secret weapon to use on Ramala when she was out of control angry at him. He was going to let things go back to normal. He wasn't going to use it unnecessarily and let her get use to it. Dan was going to use his new weapon when it counted most.

Ramala quickly got her two oldest twins back in line. They thought today was going to be like yesterday. The twins were sadly mistaken. They found out right away that things were back to normal. Ramala ordered everyone around like she had done before yesterday. The Queen Ramala was back!

Ramala set up her match with Syn to start just before noon. The sun was beating down on the courtyard. It was very hot when everyone assembled in the courtyard. After everyone was seated, Wana announced to everyone what they already knew was going to happen. Wana ordered Syn out into the middle of the courtyard. Syn, Jara made her way to the middle of the courtyard, turned and faced the Hellcats.

Just as aways before Ramala fought, she unloosened the

string holding the cape around her neck. It fell to the ground. Ramala looked at Syn waiting on her, and walked out into the courtyard. When Ramala got to Syn, Syn lowered her head out of respect. When she raised it back up, Ramala smiled at her. Ramala said "You can start when you're ready." Both girls charged themselves into fighting mode. Syn started slowly circling Ramala. Ramala started turning with Syn so Syn couldn't get behind her. Then Syn attacked. Syn was instant heat. Ramala had to respect that and tried to stay out of the way. Syn was right on top of Ramala. Ramala was moving and blocking as fast as she could, barely staying out of the way of Jara. Still, right now Syn couldn't pin down Ramala good enough to hit her. So with out pausing, Jara turned the heat up even more on Ramala.

Ramala adjusted her speed to Jara's and managed to start countering off of Syn. It surprised Syn how fast Ramala was. Syn blocked or moved out of the way of all of Ramala's counter moves. The girls went at it hard with Syn mostly on offense and Ramala on defense countering off of Jara's moves.

After fifteen minutes of non stop fighting, everyone in the crowd was on their feet watching the action. The two girls finally paused after thirty minutes of intense fighting. There was a thin cloud of dust low to the ground from the fast and furious foot work from these two girls. Jara knew Ramala hadn't planned on being beat today. Well neither had she! Jara watched Ramala's breatheing to get any sign that Ramala was tiring. Ramala's chest was almost as calm as if she was sitting down. Syn caught Ramala looking at her chest to see her heart beat. There was no way Jara would even be warmed up a half hour in, only fighting one person. She attacked Ramala again putting high heat on her. Syn wasn't going to hold anything back now. If she didn't end this soon, Ramala would start getting more and more confident. That could lead to trouble for Syn.

Ramala was dealing with Syn at Syn's best. Syn couldn't and wasn't holding anything back now. Ramala's defense was tested to the max. Ramala was managing just to stay an inch from being punished by Syn. Syn threw a punch that Ramala ducked under. Then Ramala spun out of the way of the kick that followed that punch. Syn followed that kick with three more that Ramala ducked under, then rolled on the ground out of the way of, trying to create some space between her and Syn. Syn jumped to close that gap in space, and was still right on top of her. Ramala was immediately back on her feet avoiding several more punches thrown by Syn. Ramala was spinning, flipping, and moving out of the way so fast it looked like she was just barely fighting past each move that Syn was throwing at her.

Now they were amost an hour and a half into this fight. Syn hadn't let up on Ramala one bit. Jara knew Ramala couldn't stand up to this pressure all day. Syn was going to keep things at this high level. Although Syn was very impressed with Ramala's level of skill and concentration, she knew Ramala would make a mistake sooner or later.

Even though Ramala was running, Syn was very impressed with her defense. Ramala was patient. She wasn't going to make a mistake trying to be greedy and turn to offense. Ramala was waiting for Syn to slow down. If she did, Ramala was going to attack. Ramala got her chance when Syn slowed down a little to try and bait Ramala to go to offense. If Ramala fell for the bait, Syn was going to counter off of Ramala's move.

Ramala saw the opening she was looking for and connected on a powerful blow to Syn's midsection. The power in Ramala's punch surprised Syn. Syn's body was shocked by the blow. It had a lot of steam on it, being this far into the fight. It looked like Syn was about to take a step back from the force of the blow she took. Ramala started to advance to take advantage of the situation. Syn's step backwards turned into a stiff kick to Ramala's stomach. Syn knew that kick was only strong enough to stop Ramala from advancing. She had already planned her next move that wouldn't miss no matter how fast Ramala moved.

Syn saw Ramala's arms move with amazing speed. Ramala wrapped one of her arms around her stomach where she had been kicked. The other arm moved in front of Ramala's stomach in defense. Ramala's eyes were looking down at her stomach. Syn could see fear and concern in Ramala's eyes. It was a good thing for Ramala that Syn saw all of that in a split second and knew what it meant.

Only a woman with a child in her stomach would leave every other part of her body open for attack, except there. Syn dropped her hands to her sides and yelled in a slightly scolding voice, without thinking "You're fighting while you're with child!?"

Everyone heard what Syn yelled out and now the other Hellcats and Jan, along with her girls were racing to Ramala.

Ramala raised her eyes from her stomach and looked at Syn. Ramala knew Syn was a half second away from delivering a shot to Ramala when she stopped. Ramala turned and put her hand up at Wana and Tara letting them know not to move on Syn. Then Ramala turned back to Syn and said "Not only do you move extremely fast, you think just as fast. Once again you have showed us why you are still undefeated. Thank you for the lesson. This match is over."

Syn stared at Ramala with concern in her eyes. Syn asked "Are you alright?" Ramala said "Yes, I just didn't want to take another shot like that from you." Ramala smiled at Syn. Syn lowered her head out of respect. Tara looked at Syn for a second. She couldn't blame this on Syn, so she turned to Ramala and said "Come on La, let's go!" When Ramala turned around Dan was standing there. He saw what happened and heard what Syn said. Dan was about to question Ramala. She looked at him like he really didn't want to do that right now. By the look in Ramala's eyes, Dan knew he didn't want to question her right now. Ramala said to Dan "I'm alright." Dan said "You look like you need some rest."

Ramala started walking out of the courtyard. She could feel a slight shot of pain in her stomach where she was kicked as she walked away. Ramala was upset with herself. She put her unborn child in danger because she wanted to prove to herself that she could beat Syn, Jara. If she lost this child it would be hard to forgive herself for this.

The Hellcats, Dan, and Jan walked with Ramala back to her quarters in her Palace. When they got there Wana stared at Ramala and scolded "You didn't even tell us! Why would you do such a thing? Putting yourself in harms way like that!" Ramala said "I'm not that far along. Besides, I knew you wouldn't let me fight if you knew I was with child." Wana said "You're right! We wouldn't have! I hope you know you're done fighting for a long while!"

Tara turned to Wana and said "You're not making things better. I'm sure La didn't think something would go wrong. Let's not argue about the past. Let's just deal with now. She needs our support." Wana didn't want to, but she left it alone. Tara turned back to Ramala and said with a hint of excitement in her voice "Even though I think you were wrong, that was the best I ever saw you fight!" Wana snapped "Don't incourage her!" Tara smiled at

Ramala, then looked at Wana and said "I'm just saying!"

Tara and Ramala looked at each other and started laughing. Wana was still serious and said "I'm just saying too!"

Ramala told her cousins "I'm still taking over the Southern Jungle." Tara and Wana looked at Ramala like you're not going anywhere. Ramala said "Of course I'm not going. Dan's going to lead the Butchers and the D-Squad into the Jungle. Any tribe that doesn't want to make a treaty with the House of Ra, will be wiped out. They have to go immediately, because Dan has to be back before I have this child. We'll meet with everyone tomorrow."

The next Day Ramala had her maids get the twins ready. Ramala would take the twins to meetings with her. She would have them stand next to her throne with weighted tunics on. Their arms would be stretched out away from their bodies, with a short club in their hands, pointed towards the sky. Their knees slightly bent.

Ramala demanded nothing less than them standing still in the exact spot and exactly how she told them to stand. Now that the twins were almost four years old, training was starting to get more serious. They were expected to stand their and listen to everything that was said. Ramala would always ask them questions about what was said to see how much they remembered. She as wasn't strict on the remembering part. She knew that would take the twin's time. Still she expected progress.

Today Ramala and her maids got the twins to the meeting hall before everyone started arriving. She had them stand beside her throne, like she usually did. They knew this routine and didn't make a fuss. Wana and Tara arrived and played with the twins until everyone else arrived. Then Ramala made the twins go back into their stance next to her throne. There were four chairs in the throne area. Ramala's and Dan's were on the far right. Tara's and Wana's were on the left. The Butchers and the D-Squad arrived together.

After everyone was seated, Ramala started talking while still sitting down. She said "All of you have had enough time to train yourselves. Now I need you to impress me with your skills." Then she stood up and said "With your King leading you, I expect the Southern Jungle territory to be a part of the House of Ra before I have this child I'm carrying. I want all of the Southern Jungle tribes to have the opportunity to serve me. If a tribe won't agree to be part of the House of Ra, I want them eliminated without hesitation. No playing around. All of you are heroes from the House of Ra. That's what I expect here. It's not going to be easy. They've managed to keep my elite guard out of the Jungle so far. That means they're very tough. We have to teach these savages who's in charge here! ME!" Then Ramala calmed her tone slightly and said "Besides I expect my King to be home before I have this child. Now go, you should be getting to the Jungle." Wana dismissed everyone. Dan stayed and talked to the Hellcats before leaving with Ramala and his twins.

The Southern Jungle was only four hours from the House of Ra. Everyone relaxed on the way there. It would be a long time before they could relax like this again. Dan had the Butchers, The D-Squad, One hundred elite guards, and Two hundred regular guards. They took forty attack elephants. They also had fifteen elephants packed with supplies. The forty attack elephants were there to secure a camp just outside the jungle. They wouldn't be able to take the elephants into the jungle. The trees were so large and it was so many of them so close together that elephants would have a very hard time moving. They were going to have to go into the jungle on foot.

When the caravan was a few miles from the jungle, Dan had them set up a base camp. The place where they set up base camp was on a small plateau, over looking bush land that was just before the jungle. Dan's military cabinet consisted of the Butchers, the D-Squad, Two captains of the elite guards, and four captains of the regular guards. They surveyed the jungle, trying to figure out the best way to move into it.

When they looked at the Southern Jungle from the plateau, all they could see was the vast tops of the canopy of trees that were three and four stories high,stretching as far as the eyes could see. The canopy of tree went over small hills, into valleys, up and over very large hills and small mountains. This was the most jungle that any of them had ever seen before.

The one thing that crossed all of there minds was that they hoped all of that area in the jungle wasn't filled with people. Yin stared out over the jungle and said "If the whole of that jungle is filled with people, it's gonna take a lifetime to kill them all." Ma said "Who says you have to kill them all. After we show them we mean business, they'll cooperate." Yin smiled at Ma and waved his hand, pointing at all of the jungle ahead of them. He said "It's gonna take who knows how long just to cover half of that area. I'm just saying if they don't cooperate right away, there's an awful lot of room to run around in out there." Dan asked for suggestions from the smartest ones in his cabinet for the best ways to invade the jungle. He listened to everyone's thoughts, even Yin's and Went Wrong's before deciding how he would move into the jungle.

Chapter 19

The Southern Jungle was the ancestral lands of the people who where know as the tree dwellers. The tree dwellers started out as a large family or tribe that moved into the jungle about the same time when the House of Japha was still a tribe. The tree deweller found that the jungle had a lot to offer their tribe in the way of food, medicinal earbs, and building materials.

The biggest problem living in the jungle was predators in the jungle. On the ground, it was nearly impoosible to go a night with out an attack on their people. They started out sleeping on the strudy branches of the trees at night to have a better vantage point when the preditors moved in on them. Soon after that, they built platforms up high in the trees to keep the women and children out of harms way. They found out the platform in the trees also gave them better hunting opportunities. It didn't take long before they had platforms in the trees for every living need. They had sleeping areas, hunting areas, lounging areas, then living areas.

The Tribe multiplied and built platforms as they moved out further into the jungle. They had huge villages and tree houses, all up in the trees on platforms that connected. These villages were just as functional in the trees as a village on the ground. You could even travel from village to village without walking on the ground.

But the Tree Dwellers did have to share the trees with some animals and birds. The birds weren't that much of a problem. They lived in the highest parts of the trees. The biggest problem came from the different spicies of monkeys, apes and chimpanzees. They all had territories that the Tree Dwellers had to respect. Some of the troops of monkeys numbered into the hundreds and thousands. If the Tree Dwellers moved into the territory of these animals, they would be attacked by hundreds if not thousands of them.

The Tree Dwellers built there plat formed villages around the largest herds and kept a unesy peace with them. It was nothing for the herds of monkeys to go stampeding through the jungle in the trees. When the monkeys stampeded through the trees, they killed or tore up things in their path. The Tee Dwellers put up baracades to guide the herds of monkeys around their villages when they were stampeding.

The Tree Dwellers even learned how to fight invading armies from up in the trees. Being higher than your enemy gives you an advantage. It was easier for the Tree Dwellers to get to you, than it was for you to get to them. That's why no one had been able to move into the Southern Jungle. The Trees Dwellers had mastered their form of tree fighting.

The Tree Dwellers had a simple lifestyle. Even though some of them lived in differtent villages. They didn't change their first name. First name back in the day was what they call your last name, or family name. Like the Japha is Jan's first and family name. The Hoo's, Hee's, Tat's, Tere's, Na's, Hayee's, and Ra's ancestors are all related, because they migrated from the first House of Japha. All of the populations of the seven Houses added up to about fifty-nine thousand. It was over sixty-nine thousand before the Hellcats wiped out the House of Hoo.

The Tree Dwellers all had the same first name. They lived in an area that covered over fifteen hundred square miles. They had close to one million family members. The Southern Jungle was the land of the Shinmushee family. Their family name was the same as what they called the area that they lived in.

The Shinmushee helped run Ramala's grandmother, Mashaya out of the south many years ago. They watched carefully from the jungle as Ramala took over lands north of their jungle. When Mashaya moved her army into the south, the Shinmushee came out of the jungle to help the tribes push her out of their lands. This time they decided to wait until the invaders came into the jungle. Then they would deal with them. Ramala sent her Butchers and three hundred guards into the land of Shinmushee.

Dan had the camp moved to just outside of the jungle. They sent scouts into the jungle, but they never returned. Only one scout made it into the jungle and made it back to the camp. It was Chusee. He told Dan and the military cabinet that he and the other scouts were attacked from above. Spears rained down on them from the trees.

Also, men repelled from vines and swung through the jungle on these vines taking the heads of the guards. (Ever wonder where the idea of Tarzan swinging through the jungle on vines came from? It was done thousands of years before.) Chusee said he barely made it out alive. Saliva sprayed out of his mouth with almost every word. Even though they stayed out of the reach of Chusee's saliva spray, everyone was disgusted looking at him talk. When he was done Dan promptly dismissed him. Ramala forced Dan to take Chusee with him. She told Dan that Chusee was one of the best scouts the Hayee had ever produced. He never got caught by an enemy. Even though Dan couldn't stand the sight of Chusee, he had to admit Chu was good at scouting.

Chi looked at Dan and said "That's why no one returns from the jungle." Dan said "How do we gain a foot hold into the jungle with out losing most of our men?" Chi said "We have to have protection from the spears and men coming from the trees." Dina said "What if we use platforms from the backs of the phants to sheild us as we go into the jungle." Dan said "That could work. But how do we get them out of the trees?"

Chi said "That depends on how high up they are. If there're not that high, our spearmen can pick them off. If they are too high for the spearmen to pick off, we'll have to go up the trees and get them." Yin asked "How are we going to get into the trees with them throwing spears at us? And when we get in the trees, how do we fight up there?" Everyone was silent. No one had an answer. Then Spider said "I got it!" Everyone looked at him. Spider said "If we start chopping down trees, they'll come to us. One way or another." Chi said "That would force them to fight us on the ground. That's where we have the advantage." Dan said "Alright then, that's the plan. We move into the jungle at day break."

That night some of the guards built shields that could be carried by a long pole in the middle of it. They resembled umbrellas. They made twelve of them to start. Each one could sheild six to eight men.

The next day the Butchers and the D-Squad all headed into the jungle, except for Chi and Dina. They were the two smartest and Dan wanted them to watch the battle from the safety of the caravan. If something didn't look right, these two would spot it and send word to Dan.

As soon as they got under the canopy of trees the sun was

completely blocked out. The light was that of dusk. They could still see well but was aware of the sudden change. It gave everything in the jungle a mysteriously eerie look. Dan, Syn and Backir were under one of the shields, with two guards holding the shield up. Cat, Ma, and Yin were under one together. Mangler, Went-Wrong, and Dirt were together under a sheild. Nana, Kiki and one of Ramala's big brute hatchet men were under one. The other ones were filled with three more brutes and the rest had Elite guards.

They all looked around and peeked from beneath the shields up at the trees. They walked for about five minutes before they could see the first of the platforms up in the trees. Then as they got a little further in, they could see that the platforms were getting larger and a lot of the platforms were connected. That gave Dan an uneasy feeling. This was starting to look like a well organized group of people. Not the savages Ramala tried to make them out to be.

Then all of a sudden spears started hitting the tops of the shields. Dan called for all of the shields to move together as one. That gave them more cover. Then Dan ordered the brutes to start chopping at the base of two of the trees. The bases of the trees were extremely large. It would take a while to cut through these trees. After a few chops on the trees, which made a loud distict noise, the spears stop coming. Dan figured the chopping of the trees got their attention. Their platforms were attached to these trees. They couldn't let them cut the trees down.

The all of a sudden men started repelling from the trees on vine like ropes. There seemed to be hundreds of them. Dan told everyone to wait. He wanted to see if there was a chance for negotiations. From under the shields everyone could see that these were warriors. They all had spears, machetes, and axes. There axes had blades on both sides. Not like a Hammer-Axe with the Hammer on the opposite side of the blade.

When the warriors got to the ground they didn't advance. They stood close to the invading forces, but not close enough to cause fighting to break out. Dan, while still standing under the sheild asked "Who is your leader?" None of the warriors answered. Dan could see some comotion behind the warriors. They were parting for someone, who Dan assumed was their leader. A group of ten men made their way through the crowd of warriors. They walked up and stopped short of the invasion force.

One of the men, which was with the ten took a step forward. He was built like a brute but not as heavy. He had no shirt, as all of the warriors with him, and his muscles were bulging. He appeared to not have a neck, because the muscles from his shoulders went right to his head. He actually looked like a gorilla, but not as big or black. His skin was lighter than any of the Butchers. Probably from the lack of sun. He looked to be somewhere between the age of forty to fifty. He looked at Dan and said "Who are you? Why do you come into our homeland?" Dan took a step forward and said "I am the king of the House of Ra. We come here to give you the chance to show us what you can offer us in the way of goods and services. If you cooperate, we'll make a treaty that will let you keep most if not all of your land. If you don't, we'll do what we want, the hard way. Right now you have a choice, so make it." Dan was confident and full of himself. He was proud of the way he layed down the law.

The man who spoke the first time siad "Do you even know who we are?" Dan had to admit he didn't. So he said "No. Who are you?"

The man said "We are the Shinmushee. These men with me are the warriors of Shinmushee. I am the Butcher of Shinmushee. I cut, I cut well ." All of the Butchers were shocked. They thought that they were the only ones called Butchers. This man actually looked like a Butcher. Looking at him, Dan thought he was the first person to remind him of his father. That wasn't a good thing.

The Man continued with "Are you the ones that call yourselves Butchers?" Backir said "We are the Butchers!" The man cut his eyes at Backir, then looked over all of the invaders before him. He put a grin on his face more evil than Yin ever had, the said "Does any of you even know what a Butcher is?" Backir said "You're looking at us. What do you see?"

The man said "I'm looking at probably a group of first or second rate killers and nothing more. A Butcher kills first rate killers, and everyone less than that. A Butcher also kills Butchers." All of the Butchers were offended as well as the D-Squad. Backir said "Anyone can call themselves a Butcher. Proving it is a different matter."

The Butcher looked at Backir. He said "You talk too much." Before Backir could respond, the man was in the air toward Backir, who was next to Syn and behind Dan. Dan moved to the side to avoid the attack. Syn and Backir pulled their weapons, before the man hit the ground. The man crashed through the wooden sheild and started swinging his Axes before his feet hit the ground. Syn and Backir were right on top of him. Backir with his Hammer-Axes, and Syn with her Baby Axes. They found out that this new Butcher was very fast with his Axes. He was taking Backir head on, while keeping Syn at bay. After the first couple of swings by Syn, the new Butcher adjusted to her speed. She couldn't get close to him without risking serious harm. Dan pulled his Hammer-Axes and joined the fight.

None of the other warriors joined in to help the new Butcher. Then the new Butcher caught Backir retreating from the heat he was putting on him. He took Backir's arm off just above the elbow. Backir would have kept fighting, but Mangler and Went-wrong grabbed him and pulled him just out of the way of another one of the new Butcher's axe swings that surely would have split Backir wide open.

Nana quickly took dirt's shirt and tied it as tight as she could aroud what was left of Backir's arm, making a tourniquet. Backir was furious and had to be carried away by Mangler, Went-wrong, and Dirt.

The battle between the Butchers Dan and Syn, against the Butcher of Sinmushee raged on for over forty minutes before the Shinmushee Butcher retreated next to the nine warriors that stepped up with him. Dan and Syn were too smart to follow him and get trapped by his henchmen. They stopped and stared at the Shinmushee Butcher. The Shinmushee Butcher said "I have proven that I can't be beaten by you. I took that brute's arm because he taunted me. You two, I spared with light cuts."

Dan and Syn didn't realize that while they were fighting, but they both had been slightly cut. They looked at their cuts, then back at the Butcher who had cut them. He smiled at Dan and Syn and said "I cut well. Now go back home before I'm forced to kill all of you." Dan said "Do you negotiate for the Shinmushee?" The Shinmushee Butcher couldn't believe Dan was questioning him still. He said "Why?" Dan said "If a treaty is not made with the House of Ra, we'll be forced to do this the hard way."

The Butchers and the D-Squad hoped that Dan had a better plan than for them to fight the Shinmushee Butcher. They saw what he had done to Backir. They also saw that Dan and Syn couldn't draw blood in a double team against him.

The Shinmushee Butcher looked at his comrades. He looked back at Dan and said "If we fight, you'll lose." Dan said "If we fight you're going to lose a lot of your people. We're not going to lose." The Shinmushee Butcher said "I don't care if I kill all of you or not. I was told to give you a chance to leave is the only reason all of you are not dead now. If you're ready to die let me know. I'll start taking heads now."

Dan wasn't going to leave. He stared at the Shinmushee Butcher. There comes a time in your life when you have to find out what you are made of. Dan knew this Shinmushee Butcher was the best he had faced up to this point. To be the best, you have to beat the best. Dan was only slightly cut across his right fore arm. That was nothing. This day Dan was going to find out if he was a Butcher. Only a Butcher can beat a Butcher.

Dan said "I am the King of the House of Ra, Top Butcher, Dan the Destroyer. I challenge you Shinmushee Butcher to a duel. If I win, you negotiate with me, or take me to someone that can negotiate for the Shinmushee." The Shinmushee Butcher said "There's no way you have a chance by yourself. Your friends can help you. It still won't matter." Dan said "If I win, do you agree to my terms?"

The Shinmushee Butcher said "If you win, I'll take you to see whoever you want in Shinmushee."

Cat said "Dan, don't do it!" The Shinmushee Butcher heard the concern in Cat's voice and said "You should listen to your Queen. She seems worried about you." Dan wasn't going to tell him that Cat wasn't his Queen. That was none of his business. He could think whatever he wanted. Dan said "Don't worry about her. Let me know when you're ready." Now the Shinmushee Butcher was offended. He had been challenged by this man, who was clearly no match for him. He even tried to give him and his people a way out, which he didn't take. Now he was impatiently pushing him to start a fight that he couldn't win. The Shinmushee Butcher was going to give this King of the House of Ra a quick trip to Heaven, or Hell. Whoever would take him, he didn't care.

Both Butchers stepped out in front of each other. They stopped at a safe distance from each other. Dan could see that the Shinmushee Butcher was all business now. One mistake and he would never see his children again.

The Butchers lifted their Axes and went at it. The Shinmushee Butcher was very quick and powerful. He was chopping and slicing at Dan with extreme ferocity. Dan was blocking and countering with his Hammer-Axes as fast as he could. It seemed this Shinmushee Butcher was never out of position. The fight went on for over two hours with neither man willing to give in. Both men were drenched in sweat. Their breeathing was slightly elevated, but there was no sign of tiring from either man. The sun was setting and the jungle was strting to get dark. Torches were lit. The fighting went on for a half hour after dark. Then the Shinmushee warriors stopped the fight. They said the fight would resume at day break.

Both Butchers looked at each other. They knew they had been in a serious fight. Dan had a couple of light cuts, from near misses. The Shinmushee Butcher was uncut. He was just surprised that he hadn't killed Dan yet. He realized that Dan had been holding back when he was fighting with the girl at his side. The Shinmushee Butcher smiled to himself. That won't save the King of Ra in the morning!

The Butchers and the D-Squad headed back to camp for the night. Once they reached the camp, Cat was all over Dan checking him for damage. Dan went to see Backir. The first thing Backir asked was "Is that piece of shit dead!?" Dan said "Not yet. How are you doing?" Backir showed Dan the nub where his arm used to be, and said yelling, in a very frustrated voice "What the Hell kind of question is that!? How does it look like I'm doing!? My arm is missing! This is bullshit! If you don't kill that son of a bitch, I swear I'll do it with one arm!" Dan knew it would take a while before Backir calmed down, so he sat for a while, and let his friend yell and get as much of the pain of losing his arm, out of his mind as he could.

The rest of the night, until Dan went to sleep, Syn advised and counseled Dan on everything she saw of the Shinmushee Butcher's fighting style. Dan let Syn talk. He knew she was concerned, so he let her work through it by talking to him. He listened to her points and took in everything she said, but in the morning he would do whatever it took not to be cut well by the Butcher of Shinmushee.

The next morning the Butchers headed back into the jungle. Backir stayed behind with Dina, and Chi. With one slice from the Shinmushee Butcher, Backir was redused to a military adviser. He probably would have been less than that if he wasn't one of Dan's closest friends.

The Syn, Jara told everyone to stay on high alert, and not get caught up watching Dan's fight too closely. She wanted them to be prepared for an ambush. Syn told all of the girls, if a fight breaks out to watch each other's back. The men would have to fend for themselves. They put up the wooden shields as they entered the jungle. The Warriors, and the Butcher of Shinmushee were there waiting on them.

The fight started about five minutes after they saw the Shinmushee. The action was fast and furious. Sometimes it would slow down for a few minutes, then pick up again. This went on for a little over two hours before the warriors of Shinmushee called for a break. They said the fighting would resume in one hour. Dan wasn't going to argue with that. He would have kept fighting if he had to, but he would take any break he could get. He walked over to the Butchers and the D-Squad. Cat gave Dan water. Dan drank as much as he could before Syn stopped him. She said "You need a light meal. If you fill up on water, you'll run out of energy in the next round." Dan listened and ate some food. After that he rested his mind until it was time to fight again.

The Two Butchers started up again. They fought as hard as they did the first time. They went for just under two hours this time before the Shinmushee warriors called for another break. This break was for an hour also. Dan could see that the longer he lasted, the angrier the Shinmushee Butcher became. Dan knew his opponent was used to being able to impose his will by now. Dan wasn't going to give up. He was going to get out of the way of whatever this Butcher was dishing out. Eventually, he would make a mistake that Dan could take advantage of.

The two Butchers fought one more time this day. This time for only an hour. Then the Butchers were told to be back at day break to start again. When they got back to camp. Dan ate as much as he could. When he was done Cat rubbed the soreness out of his aching muscles. While Dan layed there, he really appreciated Cat's powerful hands on his back and shoulders.

The next five days were the same, except for the third and fourth day when it rained. The two Butchers fought three times a day. On the third and fourth days, Dan could see that his opponent was starting to lose his will to keep fighting. The fifth day Dan put something extra into the fight. He was actually able to go on a sustained offensive run before turning back to his defensive strategy. When the fifth day of fighting was done, the Butcher of

Shinmushee wouldn't look at Dan.

On the sixth day Dan walked out to fight again. The Butcher of Shinmushee said "King of the House of Ra. You have proven that you are a Butcher. I have respect for your fighting skills. We will settle this with a contest between our top three fighters. One on one contest without weapons. The best of three fights wins the contest. If your fighters win, you'll meet with our tribal counsel. Whatever happens there is out of my hands. If you lose, you leave here and never return." Dan said "I agree to those terms." Dan was just saying that. He didn't think the Butchers he was going to pick would lose. If they did lose, he still would have to figure out how he was going to take the Southern Jungle. Dan walked back to his people and told them what was going on. Dan picked Yin, Syn and Went-Wrong. Went-Wrong and Spider were the two best D-Squad fighters. He picked Went-Wrong because he looked insane. Spider didn't look as threatening. Dan hoped Yin and Syn could win their contests. He didn't want it to come down to Went-Wrong having to win.

Dan sent Syn out first. She walked out and stretched herself a little. Like with everyone else, the Shinmushee warriors were surprised that the Butchers sent out a girl. The Butcher of Shinmushee wasn't. You don't send a girl into this contest unless you are sure of her skills. The Shinmushee Butcher decided to send out one of his best warrior. After this fight he would have a one to nothing advantage. He would look at the next opponent Dan sent out and decide who to send then. Syn watched her opponent as he walked out to meet her. He was a good sized man. Bigger than Dan and very muscular. He had an all business look on his face. Syn knew she had to be very careful. They were ordered to get started. They went at it. Syn played at defense and tried to counter off of the warrior. He was very good. His blows were powerful and Syn had to respect them and get out of the way. His defensive skills were just as good. He avoided all of Syn's counter attack moves. He was faster on defense than he was on offense. This made for a difficult and long fight for Syn.

They went at it for over an hour. Dan was getting a little nervous. If Syn got close to getting beat, Dan knew Cat and Ma would jump in the fight. All hell would break loose. He watched the position of the warriors around the Butcher of Shinmushee. How many of them could he kill to gain an advantage before he would have to tangle with the Shinmushee Butcher again. Then

Dan noticed the Shinmushee Butcher was looking at all of Dan's people. It looked like to Dan, that the Shinmushee Butcher was thinking the same thing he was.

Then Syn started to get a counter blow in every few minutes. After a few more minutes she was starting to punish the Shinmushee warrior. She paused and gave him a chance to concede defeat. He didn't. Like most men, the last thing he wanted to do was to be beaten soundly by a woman. He would rather die first. Syn knew this and tried to see if she could change his mind. That's when Syn let loose with a hellishly quick ten piece that sent him to the ground. Syn was surprised that he got up, even though he was shaky. He wouldn't last a minute in this condition. Syn looked at the Butcher of Shinmushee to end it, or she would. The Butcher stopped his warrior from advancing on Syn. He still almost couldn't believe what Syn had done to one of his best warriors, but since he saw it with his own eyes, he had to.

Dan sent Yin out next. Yin was damn near unbeatable one on one. The Shinmushee sent out a warrior that was bigger than Yin, but not the size of a brute. Yin was very confident. He had fought Warlords and was undefeated. Yin looked at the warrior. The warrior looked just as confident as Yin did. That didn't matter to Yin. Yin had a point to prove.

Yin could never be the King of the House of Ra. Dan was given that title by Ramala. And Dan calling himself Dan the Destroyer didn't bother Yin either. Yin thought that name was kind of catchy. It fit Dan well. Yin took being called a Butcher seriously. He was a Butcher and he knew it. What bothered Yin was that Dan called himself Top Butcher. That didn't sit well with Yin. That hadn't been proven yet. Dan hadn't beaten him or Syn. If anything Yin would call Syn, Jara Top Butcher before he called Dan that. Actually, he would only call Syn that if his life depended on it. Still, even then, he could go either way on that depending how he felt that day.

Yin didn't have his usual evil sinister grin on his face. The look was evil, but there was no grin. They were told to start. Yin didn't waste any time. He put on an offensive display that could only be called masterful. He touched the warrior up pretty good for about a half hour. Then Yin finished him off within three minutes of that. The warrior wasn't dead, but he was layed out cold on the ground. Yin didn't go for the kill. He just turned and looked at Dan for a second as he returned to his comrades. Dan had seen that look many times before, but never from Yin. The look was just short of a challenge that said, you can't deal with me. Everyone else that thought they could deal with Dan found out otherwise. Except for Syn. He had to put that out of his mind right now. Dan couldn't afford trouble between him and Yin right now. Dan turned his attention to the Shinmushee.

The Shinmushee Butcher saw what Syn and Yin did to his warriors. He thought that they had played a game of holding their best fighters back. If these two were this good against his warriors, he didn't want to see his warriors fight any of the rest of them. The Shinmushee Butcher said "Come back in the morning. Our tribal counsel will be waiting to meet you." Then he turned and walked away.

Dan and his military cabinet went back to their camp just outside the jungle. Once they got back to camp, Dan called for a meeting. Everyone had food and water, then the meeting started. Dan said "I don't trust that Shinmushee Butcher. In the morning we could be walking into an ambush. If they negotiate that would be good. If not, we need to do some convincing. In the morning, everyone is to be armed to the teeth and ready for all out warfare. That's the plan, unless someone has one better."

Dan looked around the room. Syn, Jara and Cat had become Dan's closest advisors on this mission. They counseled Dan on the day's events every time they got back to camp. When no one said anything, Syn stood up and looked around the room at everyone as she said "If fighting breaks out, stay close. Don't get taken off in a fight away from the main group. Remember, we'll be behind enemy lines, more than likely surrounded. If you go off on your own and get caught by yourself, it may be a while before we can get to you, if at all. Fight in space and hold your ground. If we decide to move in a direction, everyone fights towards that direction. Help make a path. Quick clean kills. No wounding. Finish off everyone in our path. We have to be out of the jungle before nightfall."

Spider quickly asked "Why is that Jara?" Syn said "We're not familiar with this area. They are. They have the advantage at night, while we're in the jungle. We would be fighting until daybreak. Then we would be checking to see how many of us are still alive."

Chi and Dina hadn't been in the jungle yet. They were left at the camp to watch the battle field from there and send help if it was needed. They had to put a picture in their mind of the conditions there, so they could give the best advice they could. The Butchers told them about the platforms in the trees.

Chi said "You said they live on platforms in the trees. What if that's where they want the meeting held? If troubles starts, how do you fight in trees?" There was a moment of silence again. Then Dirt said "I guess we fight the same as always. Kill and don't get killed. Oh, and don't fall out of the trees." The Syn said "We'll do whatever it takes to be successful." Chi said "I'll have messengers at the edge of the jungle. If you need help get word to them. If they see something going on they'll get word back to me. If I don't hear from you by a little more than half the day, I'll assume you'll need help, and I'll send it." Dan said "Also, if you send guards in after us, send for more guards from the House of Ra. "Syn said "Do you think we'll need more guards?" Dan said "I don't know. But if I do need them, I want them here, where they can do me some good."

Chapter 20

The next day everyone checked their weapons before they left for the jungle. All of the girls from the D-squad and the Butcher girls rode on the same plat formed elephant. They did last minute fixing of the hair and clothes, while looking in each other's eyes, reassuring themselves that everyone was ready to do their part to protect each other. They all were ready and were charged up as they got to the jungle. There were no more Butchers and D-Squad. All of these girls were sisters going into battle together.

The men rode on four other elephants. They were use to battle. That's all they could remember ever doing. The Butchers and the D-Squad was one team now. It was time to prove your worth. This was just another day at the office for them.

When they entered the jungle, the Shinmushee Butcher and his warriors were waiting. Syn and the rest of the girls watched the Butcher closely to see if they could get any clues that might help the team. Dan's group was asked to follow the Butcher and his warriors. They followed them a ways into the jungle. The further they went into the jungle, the more Shinmushee warriors joined them. Soon they were surrounded and out numbered at least ten to one. They were led to a tall tree that had a very large trunk. The tree had thick wooden planks wedged into the tree going up it winding around it at measured intervals. They were stairs leading up the tree. Dan's group looked up the tree. They could see the platform above them. It was about three floors off the ground.

Dan's people followed the Shinmushee up and aroud the trees. The wooden planks were very sturdy and held the weight of the larger men very well. They walked up the planks until they came through a large opening under the platform. When they came through the opening they realized that the platform was larger than it looked from the ground. It also was a lot brighter up in the trees than down on the jungle floor.

The wooden platform covered most of the trees area as far as you could see. Looking up from the ground, branches and leaves covered a lot of the platform. Dan's people tested and found that the platform was level and and very sturdy. They could see walk ways that led in all direction. They passed small houses and a few larger wooden buildings. Women and children were walking around taking care of daily business. They would stare at the Butchers out of curiosity, then go back to what they were doing. This was a functioning city.

Dan had an uneasy feeling in the pit of his stomach. This was a very sophisticated society. It was running just as well as any of the Seven Houses. These people weren't savages like Ramala said they were. Dan hoped their military wasn't as advanced as the city was. Something told him it probably was. Now they were escorted by a small army of close to two hundred warriors. They were led to a very large courtyard. The branches had been cut away from over head, and you could see the sky. It was beautiful. Ahead they could see twelve men sitting in chairs, surrounded by close to a hundred warriors.

It was the Shinmushee Trbal Counsel. Now Dan's people were completely surrounded. Dan refused to let himself turn to see what was behind him. He didn't want to look intimidated. He knew Syn and the rest of the Butchers would be watching his back. The Tribal Counsel and their warriors in front of them. The Shinmushee Butcher and a couple hundred warriors behind them.

Including himself, Dan's group was only twelve strong. Dan's people were on high alert, watching everything from the warrior's movements, to the occasional bird and monkey that passed by. The warriors took Dan's group close enough to talk to the Counsel, but not close enough for them to attack the Counsel members before they would be met by Shinmushee warriors.

All of the Counsel members were old men. They watched Dan's group closely as they walked up. When the Butchers stopped before the Tribal counsel, one of the men said, while staying seated "Tell us, why you have come here?" Dan said in a strong confident voice "I am the King of the House of Ra. These are my Top Butchers here with me. I have come here to help you save the lives of many of your people. Make a treaty to become part of the House of Ra. Provide us with goods and services. Give us any help we need while traveling through the land of

Shinmushee. We expect these things and whatever else that will impress the House of Ra with what you can do for us. In return, you will be allowed to keep your land. You will also enjoy the priveldge of being part of the House of Ra."

The old Counsel member who spoke before said "Which of you girls is the Hayee, Ramala?" Dan said "She's not here." The same man said "You go tell your master, Queen Hayee, Ramala or whatever she calls herself, to go back to the House of Hayee and never return. If we're forced to. We'll run her back home like we did her two elder Hayee screamers that tried to terrorize and take over this region many years ago. We've had enough of this nonsense. It's starting to annoy us. You're not welcome here. Leave right now and don't return." Dan said "I don't know what else I can say to convince you that it's in your best interest to cooperate. So I'm done talking for now. It's time to convince you the only other way I know how."

Dan pulled his Hammer-Axes from their harnesses on his back. When the the rest of the Butchers saw that, they knew it was go time. Everyone pulled their weapons as quickly as they could. Dan turned quickly to Syn and said just loud enough for her to hear "We need to capture some of those Counsel members alive." Syn looked at Cat and Ma. That meant follow her lead. The Butchers all charged towards the Counsel members. Volleys of spears were launched at the Butchers as soon as they pulled their weapons. At the same time the Shinmushee warriors raced to meet the Butchers before they got to the Counsel members. Dan, Cat, Syn, Ma and Yin tore into the warriors trying to get to the counsel members. The Butchers blocked the spears just before they were met by the Shinmushee warriors. Mangler, Spider, Went-Wrong, Dirt, One-time, Nana, and Kiki fought at the backs of the others, keeping the Shinmushee Butcher and his warriors busy.

As warriors went down to the Hammer-Axes of Dan's people, more warriors kept coming. The courtyard was filled with as many warriors as could fit in there. The counsel members were watching the action, feeling safe from where they were until Dan and the others started getting a little closer.

The counsel members got up and were leaving when Syn jumped into the air to cut them off. She was greeted with a hail of spears. She blocked them and landed on the other side of the counsel members, surrounded by Shinmushee warriors. Syn had managed to block the exit, but was now fighting ofr her life. Dan and Cat were in the air only a few seconds after Syn landed. They avoided more spears and fought hard at Syn's side. It wasn't long before Yin and Ma made their way towards the counsel members.

The members were trapped. They still had a few warriors between them and the Butchers, but they had no escape route from the courtyard. The Butcher of Shinmushee jumped in the air towards the Counsel members. Dirt, Spider, Went-Wrong, and Mangler were right on his ass. When the Shinmushee Butcher landed, they were right there forcing him to deal with them. It took everything these four had not to get sliced up by the Butcher. Kiki, Nana and One-Time were in a hellish battle with the Shinmushee warriors, trying to keep them too busy to help their Butcher.

Finally, the Butchers were able to capture three of the Counsel members. Syn, Cat, and Ma had their axes to the throats of the three members. Dan and Yin protected the girls from attack. That allowed the other counsel members to get away. The fighting around Dan and the captured Counsel members stopped. Kiki and the others fought their way over to the others. Once there, the warriors didn't attack them. Dan's people took defensive positions around the Butcher girls and the counsel members. Syn motioned for Kiki and Nana to take over for her and Cat. Then Cat and Syn went and stood next to Dan watching every movement.

The situation was desperate to say the least. Dan knew they would have to capture some of the counsel members to have a chance of getting out of there alive. He had succeeded in doing so. He just hoped the ones they had were important enough that the warriors wouldn't sacrifice their lives to kill Dan and his people.

All of the counsel members were held in high regards. Dan lucked out and two of the three he had were the the top men in this region of Shinmushee territory. Even if the warriors were ordered to attack they wouldn't. It was a standoff. The Shinmushee Butcher said "Let them go and we will forget about what has happened here and let you go." Dan said "I gave you a chance to cooperate. Now we do things the hard way. Move back now, or these men are dead! Then we'll start taking more heads!" The warriors moved back and gave Dan's people room. Once Dan was comfortable with the room they were given, he said "One-Time, go meet our messenger."

Then he looked at the Shinmushee Butcher and said "My man here is going to go meet with my messenger and you're going to let him. If he's not back in a shorter period of time than it took for us to get here, we start taking heads starting with these men," The Shinmushee Butcher looked away from Dan. He didn't have to answer, everything was understood. The warriors parted, and One-Time walked off very cautiously.

The Counsel member who Ma had her Axe to his throat, said "You can loosen your grip young lady. I'm not going anywhere." Ma said "Not with your head. That stays right here." The old man said "I'm thirsty." Then he startled Ma when he yelled "Someone bring me water!" Yin turned and looked at the man and said "Who said you could have water!?" The man said "If you're going to kill me over drinking water, I can guarantee this thing you have done is going to turn out bad for you. I'm an old man. Don't stop me from drinking water." Yin looked at Dan for a second, then looked at Ma. He didn't see any opposition to what the man said so he turned back to watching the warriors. At that point it really didn't matter to Yin what the old man did.

The warriors parted after a couple of minutes and a girl who looked to be in her mid twenties walked up with a pitcher of water. She stopped when she got to the Butchers. The old counsel member who yelled for the water said "Over here girl! Bring the water over here!"

The girl looked at the Butchers and slowly started towards the old man. They watched her looking to see if she would make one false move that they would have to take her head for. She was in a very dangerous situation, she knew it and it made her very nervous.The girl walked slowly and deliberately. She wanted everyone to be sure of what she was doing.

When the girl got to the old man and just as she was giving him the pitcher, Syn took the pitcher from the girl. Syn inspected it closely. Then she tasted the water. She gave it to Cat, then Cat gave it to Ma. Both girls drank some of the water. Then they gave it to Dan, who drank some. Syn looked at the girl and said "You heard the old man! He's thirsty! Bring him some water!" The girl ran off to get more water. When she returned, she brought girls with her that also had water. The Butchers made the three council men test all of the water before they drank any of it.

It wasn't long before One-Time returned with fifty elite guards. They were allowed to join Dan. The Elite guards from the House of Ra set up a perimeter in the courtyard around Dan's people and the three Council members. Dan sent a messenger, along with One-Time back to the caravan for Chi to send more guards. Dan knew it would be dark soon and he needed to solidify his foothold in the jungle.

The other council members wanted to meet with Dan. They were ready to talk about a treaty. Dan said he would meet with them in the morning. If things went well over night, he would talk in the morning.

One-Time returned with another fifty guards. The guards had food and water for Dan's people. The three Council members were allowed to get a little more comfortable. They were surrounded and watched very closely. They knew better than to try anything. Dan now had enough gurds to cause real trouble if the Shinmushee didn't cooperrate in the morning.

The Butchers slept lightly over night, while the elite guard listened for the slightest hint that an attack was coming. Morning came and nothing had happened. Dan met with the Shinmushee Tribal Council again. This time the Council wanted to know how the treaty was going to work.

Dan said "Your land, your customs and your way of life is yours to control as part of the House of Ra. What we expect from the Shinmushee is the use of skills that you have, goods that the jungle supplies you with, and the free travel throughout the Land of Shinmushee. Of course there might be something that I have not mentioned. We would talk to the tribal council and expect cooperation after that."

Dan paused for a moment to collect his thoughts. He continued with "I'm sure the Shinmushee have a lot of great warriors that would be willing to give their lives in defense of their land. Again I say this is the land of the Shinmushee. It's just part of the House of Ra. Your brave warriors don't have to die fighting us. You have the power to save the lives of a lot of your people. This isn't the army of the Screaners that you defeated many years ago. This is the House of Ra. Make your decision, so we can go forward, which ever way you choose."

The Council member could see that their captured brothers were being treated well. One of the Tribal members said "You will consult with our Tribal Council before any decisions are made to visit?" Dan said "Any plans the House of Ra have that concerns the Shinmushee will be discussed with the Tribal Council first." Then the member said "A treaty with the House of Ra does not mean that the House of Ra owns Shimushee land, does it?" Dan said "A treaty means that Shinmushee is a part of the House of Ra, but not owned by Ra. If Shinmushee has an enemy or if someone invades Shinmushee, they have to deal with the House of Ra. Also if the House of Ra is attacked, we would expect help from our Shinmushee brothers. This allaince makes both of us stronger." The Shinmushee weren't buying the last sentence Dan said about the alliance making both of them stronger. Th e council knew the House of Ra would use the Shinmushee land as a stepping stone to their next conquests. They would also expect the Shinmushee to help them defeat whoever they waged war against. The Shinmushee needed time to coordinate all of the families in Shinmushee. For now they decided to agree. They made a treaty with the House of Ra. Dan asked if the council members could stay with the royal court a few more days. The council had no objections.

In the next two months, Dan set up some of the elite guard to sit on the Tribal council as representatives of the House of Ra. These Elite guards, or Warlords would be permanently staying in Shinmushee along with their guards. Dan had achieved his goal of giving the House of Ra a strong foothold in the Southern Jungle. Now it was time to get back home. It would be another couple of months before Ramala had their child.

Chapter 21

Ramala was having a tougher time with this pregnancy than the others. She would get pain in her stomach from time to time. It wasn't that bad, and it would go away after a while. It aways made Ramala nervous, because of the kick she took from Syn. She wasn't going to tell anyone unless the pain got worse. It also didn't help matters that the child she was carrying was very active. Some days it seemed this child was doing flips in her stomach. She would have to stop what she was doing until the child stopped flipping around in her stomach. Ramala was slowed down more than with the first two pregnancies. La and Dan took advantage as much as they could.

Ramala had been singing on and off since her grand-aunt taught her the technique of singing. Now she was singing almost every day to her children. They loved the sound of Ramala's voice and would almost be in a trance when she sang to them. Sometimes she would sing with the girls that her grand-aunt sent back to the House of Ra with her. Ramala would test to see if she could make people cry and loose their will to fight. She could bring you to tears, but she didn't know if she could breaks a persons will to fight. She was going to keep practicing until one day she could.

La, Dan, Ramashaya and Don were keeping Ramala very busy. The two oldest twins were training most of the day, with breaks in between. The two youngest were also with Ramala most of the day. The maids did most of the work and took the younger twins away when it was time for naps. Jan and her girls spent most of their time with Ramala. They watched the training that Ramala put her twins through. Jan asked Ramala "Why do you train them like this at such an early age?" Ramala said "I have a lot of enemies out there somewhere. You've seen what all I have done.

My children are going to have to be strong enough to deal with anyone who would try to harm them. You watch and see. My children are all going to be Hammer-Axe champions. They are also going to be experts with all the weapons and without weapons. They're going to be ready for anything when I'm done with them." Jan said "The Hammer-Axe Four with one on the way." Nina said "With her track record of having twins, it might be the Hammer-Axe Six." Ramala smiled then said "Then eight, then ten, then …." Jan interrupted with "We get the picture. You're going to have an army of Hammer-Axe children." Ramala said "That's right!"

San sent a messenger telling Jan that Tee had a boy. San wanted Jan to send word by his messenger when she would be coming home to see them. There was no way Jan was going back right now. She had just got to the point where she could get through most of the day without thinking about San. Some days she didn't think about San at all. She was starting to feel more like her old self. She wasn't going to jeopardize her progress. She wanted to be sure she was over San before she went back home.

Jan sent word with the messenger congratulating San and Tee. She also sent word that she wouldn't be returning for a while. She told San to send word on how things were going with the building of San-Jania Province. When San got Jan's message it annoyed him more than he let Tee know. Jan couldn't hide forever. She needed to get over this thing soon. San missed his sister.

La was now four and a half. She was very smart for her age. She followed directions to the letter when she had to, and did what she wanted when she could. La thought that everything revolved around her. She looked at everything as belonging to her . Ramala was her mommy. Hers. Dan was her daddy. Again hers. The twins were hers, Yaya was her big sister. The Palace was her home. The House of Ra was her home. To La everything was hers in one way or another.

La was also very physical. She liked to get rough, wrestling with Dan and Yaya every chance she could. La loved her big sister Yaya. Yaya would never tell Ramala when La was doing something that Ramala didn't approve of, unless La was did something that might get herself hurt. Even though La was very smart, Yaya was always one step ahead of La. That helped her keep La in line without getting physical with La. La loved the new twins and now that they were crawling and standing up on things, La thought they were open game for her rough play. Ramala saw it once and got physical with La, explaining that the young twins weren't ready for that yet. The next time Ramala saw La getting rough with the younger twins, she really got physical with La. La got in line. The lesson La learned was don't rough up the twins. If you do, don't do it around mother!

Young Dan was getting big at four and a half. Between his father's, his mother's and his big sister Yaya's roughing him up, he was very rough. Dan loved his big sister Yaya. He called her Ya, just like La did. She always roughed Dan up lovingly. Dan was now tough enough to take the physical punishment La would give him on a daily basis. He would get fed up with her from time to time and take an extra beating from her for his troubles. It didn't bother him. He was a boy, and even though he couldn't deal with La, he could take more physical punishment than her any day. Sometimes when he got angry with La, he would wear her out by making her beat him until she was too tired to continue. That's how Dan won a fight against La. For all the fighting they did, they were as close to each other as any twins could be.

Ramashaya wasn't as physical as La. She liked to climb up on things and investigate, while standing. She wouldn't tear things up like her older brother and sister usually did. Ramashaya liked to touch and feel things. She was into the feel and texture of things. If Ramala caught Shaya with something, she would see her rubbing it across her face or arms seeing how it felt. Shaya loved Yaya. Yaya would always bring her pretty things to look at and to touch. Shaya laughed uncontrollably when ever Don did. His laughter always tickled her. She was quiet and sometimes Ramala would lose track of her, watching her other three children. Shaya wasn't as fussy as most girls her age. In fact, she wasn't much trouble at all unless La was pestering her, or if she was hungry, or needed to be changed. She was perfect for Ramala, who was trying to deal with four children while carrying another.

Don was curious about everything. He put everything in his mouth. If he was able to talk, he would be able to tell you just about what everything in the House of Ra tasted like. Ramala worked hard to break Don of that habit. Don would also get into silly moods which would have him laughing at almost anything. That would get Shaya laughing too. These two twins could be very serious one minute and completely silly the next. Don was also very smart. He knew his position in the family at ten monthes. Don loved Yaya. She always made him laugh. Don stayed out of La's way at all cost. He knew she was big trouble. She proved it to him every chance she got. Dan didn't bother Don too much. Dan would push Don down if he was feeling ornery. Other than that, the two brothers got along good.

Yaya was almost twelve years old. She spent most of her day training. She was a very good student and was more than a match for any of the Hayee children her age that trained with her. Ramala trained her as well as the Butcher girls. The days were very hard on Yaya. Whenever she got a break, she spent it with her brothers and sisters. Now she had two younger sisters and two younger brothers. All of Ramala's children loved Yaya. Yaya loved her younger sisters and brothers too. They looked up to Yaya. La looked up to Yaya and watched how she handled everyone, even though La didn't think she was being handled. La would even imitate Yaya. The only other person La imitated was Ramala. That was the biggest compliment La could give you. Yaya missed the Butcher girls. She also missed Dan.

La was starting her training as a screamer. She had a pretty strong scream already. Now it was time for Ramala to take La to the next level. Training for a screamer is like giving a child a drum set in the room next to yours. It gets annoying very fast. Ramala had a huge pit dug in the private courtyard where only her children trained. The pit had steps that went down into it. The pit was about eight feet deep and faced Ramala's palace. That way when the screams bounced off of the walls of the pit. The sound that escaped the pit would travel away from the palace. La loved screaming and she loved the pit. After the pit was built, Ramala wouldn't allow La to scream in the palace. When La got angry, Ramala would take her to the pit and let her scream out her frustrations. It didn't take long for La to become pit trained, sort of like you potty train a child. Ramala and her other children would watch La as she blasted screams until Ramala stopped her. La was always calmest after a good screaming session.

Dan sent word, through messengers, of his progress in the Southern Jungle. He let Ramala know he was coming home the next day. Dan was satisfied that the Warlords he put in charge, had a good relationship with the Shinmushee. They would send regular reports of what was going on in the Southern Jungle.

The Butchers arrived home a couple of hours after noon.

As soon as they got to the Gates of Ra, the drums started beating throughout the House of Ra signaling their return. They were cheered as heroes as they entered the gate. Everyone wanted to get cleaned up so they split up and went to their own prvate homes.

When Dan's elephant got to the loading dock at the main palace, he could see his family there waiting on him. It always surprised him how much bigger his children were when he would return after a mission. The second he stepped off of the ramp, La and Yaya took off towards him. Yaya was faster than La and La knew it. So once Yaya passed La, La stopped and let out a scream that sent Yaya to her knees holding her ears. Then La took off running and yelled "Daddy!" Then she jumped into Dan's arms. She wrapped her arms around Dan's neck and squeezed as tight as she could before letting go, staring into Dan's face with a big smile on hers. Dan said "That's some voice you got there." La said "I can scream louder than that Daddy. Watch this!"

Dan stopped her before she started. He said "You can show me later. What else have you been doing?" That was the wrong question to ask La, if you really didn't want to know. Ramala taught La to remember everything. La started telling Dan everything that happened from the time she got up this morning. Dan was walking towards Ramala with La in his arms, when Dan ran into his leg and yelled "Daddy!"

Yaya got to Dan next and gave him a hug. When Dan got to Ramala, after dragging everyone who had a grip on him, he put down La. She resisted until she saw Ramala give her a serious stare. Dan gave Ramala a sideways hug. Then they kissed . Ramala was big. It was hard to get his arms around her.This was the biggest she had been while carrying a child. Dan bent down and picked up his youngest twins. These two tolerated Dan, but they weren't as happy to see him as his two oldest twins and Yaya were. Dan put them down after a minute or two. La quickly grabbed Dan's hand and started swinging his arm as she was talking. She announced to everyone as if they didn't know. She yelled "Daddy's home!"

La couldn't contain her excitement. She looked up at Dan with a big smile on her face and said "Daddy, I can run fast. Daddy, I'm a big girl now. Daddy, why is your clothes dirty? Daddy, you smell yucky. You need a bath. Where have you been? Daddy, mommy hangs me by my hair from the tree. Sometimes I like it, sometimes I don't. Daddy, look at mommy's stomach, its fat. There's another baby in there."

La and young Dan started laughing. La's voice was light, even though it was loud and her words were clear. La talked Dan all the way into the palace and to his private quarters. Ramala had the maids take the children to their rooms for a nap. Ramala told La "Daddy's going to get cleaned up. Behave like a big girl and don't give mother any trouble. You'll get to see your daddy later." La didn't put up a fuss. Her Father was home and she would get to spend time with him later. La was happy for now.

Dan took a long hot bath, while Ramala sat next to him interrogating him on his trip into the jungle. Dan told her everthing that happened. Ramala asked Dan "How big is the Shinmushee tribe?" Dan said "I'm not sure. It covers a lot of area." Ramala said "Approximately how many warriors do they have?" Dan said "I'm not sure. We saw a couple hundred. They're no match for the Elite guards and the regular guards we left there." Ramala stared at Dan with a disgusted look on her face. Dan said "What?" Ramala said "What is right. You're not sure about the area you say you took. You're not sure about how many warriors they have. What do you really know about these people? How many Shinmushee are there?" Dan said "There are at least a couple of thousand of them."

Dan didn't understand why Ramala was trying to find anything to pick at. He had gained a foothold in the jungle. Dan said "I had to be back here before you had our child, otherwise I would have stayed longer and had all the answers to your questions."

Ramala said "You had close to five months there. That was more than enough time to know what you were dealing with. Once you take an area, you survey that area. You have to know how much land the tribe you took over has. Second and most important, you have to know how large the tribe is. You have to make them bring out all of their members so you can see what you are dealing with. Right now, all you know is what they showed you. They could have another thousand members that you didn't see. Next time be sure."

Even though he knew Ramala was right, Dan was tired of being interrogated. He said "After you have this child I'll go back. I won't return until I know how many Shinmushee there are, and their names, and how many trees there are, and how many leaves are on those trees. Hell, it might take me the rest of my life to find out everything about the jungle." Ramala said "Don't threaten me. There's no where you can hide that I can't find you if I want." Dan said "Who said I would be hiding." Ramala said "You better be hiding if you disappear on me and our children."

Dan didn't want this to go any further. He had to remember that Ramala was with child and her hormones were probably pushing her further into this conversation than she would normally go. Then he remembered, this was Ramala. It didn't matter if she was with child or not. She was capable of taking any conversation too far. Dan got out of the bath without responding to Ramala.

Ramala followed Dan back to their sleeping area. Dan turned and looked at Ramala. He said "Go ahead and get whatever it is off your chest. I'm a little tired from the trip. Say what you have to say so I can get some rest." Ramala looked at Dan for a couple of seconds with disappointment on her face, before saying "Go ahead, get some rest if you're so tired."

Dan stood there looking at Ramala. He said "Just tell me what's bothering you!?" Ramala paused for a moment, then said "Why didn't you tell me you missed me?" Dan said "I didn't hear you say it either." Ramala snapped back "I didn't say it because I wanted to hear you say it first!" Dan said "There you go playing games. You know I missed you. If you missed me, just say it. It doesn't matter who says it first."

Ramala said "It does matter! It matters to me!" They stared at each other for a moment. Ramala was hoping that Dan would just say it. One simple sentence is all she needed to hear, and this would be over. Then Dan turned to go lay down. Ramala picked up a vase that was sitting on the table and launched it at Dan. By the time he knew something was wrong, the vase crashed and exploded on his shoulder and neck, just missing his head.

Dan turned around and looked at Ramala. He said "What the Hell's wrong with you? Are you crazy!?" Ramala was pumped up with anger. She yelled "You're so fucking stupid! You make me sick!" Ramala rarely used profanity to that level. Dan couldn't understand why she was flying off the handle like this. He said "What the Hell is wrong with you!?"

Ramala face was angry. She picked up a small box off the table and threw it at Dan. She said "What's wrong with me!? What's wrong with you!? "Then she picked up the next thing she could get her hands on. Dan stared at her like you better not throw it. Ramala threw it anyway. Dan moved out of the way of the flying object. Ramala yelled "Oh, that's right! You're not smart enough to figure out anything that I don't tell you! You stupid ass ignorant shit for brains heathen!"

Ramala wanted to hurt Dan like he had hurt her when he refused to tell her he missed her. Dan's feelings weren't hurt, but he was offended. He decided because Ramala was with child, he wasn't going to take things as far as he could. But still, Ramala was still picking things up launching them at him. He had to put a stop to that. She was out of control. Dan yelled "Stop it!" He had to duck out of the way of another flying object. Dan moved towards Ramala quickly, hoping to get to her before she found something else to throw at him.

Just before he got to her she bent over and he could see pain in her face. At first he thought she was faking. Then he could see the pain was genuine. Dan put his arms around Ramala and guided her to a chair. She sat dowm and tried to calm herself. Guards and servants were at the door waiting for Ramala to give them orders. Before she could say anything, Dan said "Guards, go back to your posts."

Then he pointed to the servants and said "You two can clean this mess up. The guards hesitated for a moment. When Ramala didn't say anything, they did as they were ordered. Then the servants started cleaning up. Dan got down on one knee in front of Ramala, rubbing her arm with his hand. He said "Are you alright? Do I need to get some help?" Ramala said "No, I'm better now. I just had to calm down." Dan looked at Ramala with an apoligetic look and said "O.K., I'm stupid when it comes to things that I should say. You have to know I missed you. I really missed you Ramala. You know I love you."

Ramala went from looking away from Dan, to looking him in his eyes as he continued to talk. Dan said "I'm probably never going to say the right things all the time. So I appologize in advance. Cut me some slack. Don't get stuck on the little things." Ramala said in almost a whispering voice "Somrtimes the little things mean a lot." Dan said "I'll try to remember that." Ramala smiled and said "No you won't, you just don't want me throwing things at you." Dan smiled and said "You got that right!"

After Tara had little Yin, She didn't pay that much attention to Yin. It didn't bother Yin because Kiki found ways to keep him busy. Yin had Kiki in his system and couldn't get her out. Kiki knew that much. Kiki also knew that Tara came first when it came to Yin. Now that Tara was back in training and Little Yin was getting old enough to play with Ramala's twins, Tara had more time to think about how much she missed being with Yin. Tara wasn't capable of going as far as Kiki would with Yin. Tara liked what Yin did to her, but she would only do so much for Yin. To Tara it was all about her needs.

In Tara's mind, Yin was lucky to be with someone of her position. Even if she did next to nothing for Yin, she thought he should feel privileged for whatever he got. Kiki on the other hand was willing to do whatever it took to get the job done, and then some. Yin loved that extra and then some.

When Yin returned from the Southern Jungle Tara was waiting on him with their son. Yin was happy to see his Tara and his son. He had never seen Tara so happy to see him. Little Yin barely remembered his father and was apprehensive about going to him. Tara let it go. She knew there would be time for these two to get familiar with each other.

Right now Tara needed to get very familiar with Yin and she let him know it. Yin could see it in Tara's eyes. He knew she needed something crazy done to her, and she needed it right away. He was the man for the job. After they hugged and spent a few minutes with their son, Tara had the maids take her son for a walk. Yin smiled at Tara and said "Your place or mine?"

Tara smiled and said "You take your whores to your place, so let's go to mine." Yin said "Today you're going to find out what I do to whores. You're the whore that I need right now. Follow me." Tara smiled at Yin. She was down with all of that. Tara followed Yin to his place. No sooner than they got inside the door, Yin did some things to Tara. He had a lot to get off his chest. So he treated Tara like his personal whore until they both passed out from exhaustion.

Backir was having a very tough time dealing with having his arm taken from him. He was very bitter. He knew he would never be the Butcher he was before. He had some things he had to get off of his chest too. Backir took Nana back to his place. He did everything he could do with one arm to Nana.

Well into the action, he pinned Nana down and tried to balance himself on his nub, forgetting he didn't have a hand. He fell over onto the floor. Nana tried not to let Backir see that she saw him roll off the bed and hit the floor hard. She smiled inwardly at the sight of the big brute hitting the floor. Backir was so angry that after he got up off the floor, he kicked Nana out of his room. She protested for a moment because she wasn't done yet, but She could see that Backir was close to getting violent. So she angrily left the room. Backir sat on the bed and looked at his nub. He smashed it into the wall, and immediately yelled out in pain. He cussed for a few more minutes before calming himself enough to take a nap.

Later that evening, the Hellcats gave a feast honoring the Butchers and the D-Squad. It was a ceremony where again, the top Warlords had to kiss the Hellcats asses. After they were done, Dan got up and addresses his comrades who fought beside him. Dan gave praise to everyone from the regular guards, the Eilte guards, the D-Squad, and the Butchers. He told them that this victory wouldn't have been possible without them. Ramala tried to get Dan's attention so she could give him a stare that told him that he had given them more than enough praise and that they should be praising him. Dan pretended not to notice Ramala getting uncomfortable with what he was saying.

Dan called Backir up to the throne area where he was standing. Then Dan gave a fairy taled account of the bravery that he had witness from Backir since he had known him. He told about the fights that they had that both of them wondered how they would get out of. Dan even told about some of the times when they were fighting just for food. Dan told everyone that Backir was a great hero.

Backir was just entering the age when fighters become legends. Even though his best friend tried to make him seem like a legend, Backir knew he wasn't. Backir looked at his long time friend. Dan didn't have to tell him. Backir had just been retired and Dan was giving him a retirement speech. Even though he knew it was best, when you love what you do, retirement is hard to take when you're in your prime years.

Dan then talked about Yin and how valuable to the team he was. Dan told how Yin performed at top level every time they found themselves in a serious situation. He said Yin's uttter disreguard for human life and his willingness to use that in his battle for the House of Ra made Yin Top Butcher in the House of Ra. Dan said from this day forward, until he was defeated in a fair fight, Yin was Top Butcher of the House of Ra.

Dan walked over to Yin. Yin stood up. Dan held out his hand. Yin looked at Dan. He couldn't believe Dan was giving him this title. No one had ever recognized Yin as anything except a homicidal maniac. Dan had turned that into something for Yin to be proud of. Yin took Dan's hand and shook it. Ma's eyes started welling up with tears. She could see that her brother was proud of his new title. Ma didn't know why Dan did this for Yin, but it got Dan off of her kill when you get a chance list, for now.

After the speech, everyone relaxed and talked. Ramala made it an early night. She figured Dan needed to unwind from his trip. She wasn't going to torture herself watching him find a girl to take care of his needs. She would see him before daybreak.

Dan looked around the room. He was half paying attention to conversation that the Butcher men and the D-Squad men were having. He saw Cat talking to the other girls, and joking around. Cat felt Dan looking at her and turned to catch him doing so. They looked at each other for a moment. Cat smiled at Dan. Syn and Ma saw Cat, but tried not to let her know they had. The look in Cat's eyes was unmistakable. Sometimes a look can say more than a thousnad words. Cat's eyes said all that needed to be said.

The party moved to one of courtyards. Drummers and dancers kept everyone in a festive mood. Cat saw Dan scoping out some of the dancers. She walked over to him. Cat said "Looks like you're planning on a busy night." Dan said "I'm just relaxing. What about you? Doing anything fun tonight?" Cat said "Depends if you want to come back to my place and teach me something new."

Dan was surprised, but didn't let it show. Cat rarely stayed at her place. She usually stayed at Ma's or Syn's place. He said "I can teach you some things if that's what you want." Cat smiled and said "That's what I want. I'm ready to go whenever you are." Dan was surprised again. He said "I'm ready." Cat said "I'll tell Ma and Syn that I'll be staying at my place tonight. Wait for me outside." Dan let everyone know he was leaving. A few minutes after he left, Cat told her girls she was staying at her place. She told them that they should leave her alone tonight. Both girls knew what was going on and didn't protest. Ma said "Have fun." Cat pretended not to hear her.

When Cat got outside Dan was waiting on her. It was quiet and the air was cool. The only light was that of the torches that lit the main walkways. Cat's place was less than five minutes away. Cat and Dan started walking. Cat nervously said "Remember, I'm new at this." Dan said in a reassuring voice

"Don't worry, you'll be alright. Believe me, this will be good for you." Cat said "I hope you're right."

Then they were startled by a scream coming from the main palace. The distance they were from the palace muffled the scream's intensity. Then they heard the scream again. Dan knew who's scream that was. Cat had heard it many times before and knew who it was too. It was La. Cat and Dan stopped walking and looked at each other. Then they heard her scream again. Cat said "That's your little La. I wonder why she's screaming like that?"

Dan was torn between going to check on La, and continuing to Cat's place. Cat could see the indecision on Dan's face. She said "Go check on her. When you're done, I'll be at my place." Dan said "Alright." and headed to the main palace. Cat walked to her place. She was hoping that Dan would have come with her. Cat knew she would always be second to Ramala. Now she wasn't even second in Dan's life. Right now she was at least third.

When Dan got to the palace he went straight to La's room. Ramala was already there with some of the maids. When Dan walked in, Ramala and La turned to see him. La's face lit up and she yelled out "Daddy!" Then she extended her arms reaching for Dan. Dan walked over and picked her up. Dan never had anyone as happy to see him as La. It always surprised him the way La's face lit up at the sight of him. Ramala said "She just had a bad dream." Dan told La "It's alright. You're safe. You can go back to sleep now."

Dan kissed La and put her back down on her bed. Ramala looked at Dan and said "I can take it from here. You don't have to stay." Dan looked at Ramala, then at La. La's eyes were begging Dan not to leave. Ramala was a little less obvious, but Dan could tell by the tone in her voice that she wanted him to stay also. Dan sat on the bed next to Ramala, while La smiled, looking at both of them until she fell asleep.

Dan and Ramala left La's room. Ramala looked at Dan for a moment. She wanted to ask him to come back to their sleeping quarters with her. Instead, she said "I'll see you later." Dan said "Why? Are you going somewhere?" Ramala said "No, but I thought you were."

Dan could see that Ramala really wanted him to come back with her. Most of the time Dan couldn't catch Ramala's subtle hints to save his life. This one he caught. He put his arm around Ramala and said "It's late. I can catch up with everyone some other time."

When they got back to their sleeping quarters and were in bed, Dan was laying behind Ramala with his arm around her big stomach. Ramala whispered "Thanks for coming home with me." Dan said "You don't have to thank me for that." Ramala said "I know. I just wanted to."

Dan was there next to his Queen thinking what it would have been like to be with Cat tonight. He put it out of his mind and went to sleep.

Cat was at her place listening for any sound that would tell her Dan was coming. She was very excited. She paced around and tried to calm herself. Every time she heard something, she got really excited and waited on Dan to walk through the door. When he didn't, she tried to calm herself until he came. After a while, she realized he wouldn't be coming tonight.

Cat was upset with herself for getting so worked up over Dan. At the same time she thought to herself that the next time they had a chance to be together, she wouldn't let him get away so easily.

Chapter 22

The Shinmushee treated the Ra Warlords and their guards that were left behind by Dan, very well. The Warlords watched everything closely for any sign that the Shinmushee were up to something. The Warlords had a system of messengers that could contact the House of Ra and send reinforcements if needed. So far all the Warlords could do was send good reports about the Shinmushee cooperating with them.

The Shinmushee didn't take to kindly to the way they were treated by the War Party from the House of Ra. They definitely didn't like that many of their warriors were killed when the Butchers attacked and captured the Tribal Counsel. The warriors that Dan and his people faced were only a small part of the Shinmushee army. The Shinmushee army had close to two hundred thousand warriors. The problem was that they were spread out over most of the Southern Jungle.

The Shinmushee had underestimated the stregnth of the small invading force. The Shinmushee Tribal Council cooperated with Dan's Warlords in front of their faces, while they sent word for as many warriors to come as could. The Tribal Council met with other Tribal Council from other Shinmushee citties. They all agreed that they would force the House of Ra to flee back north, or they would eliminate them. Dan and his war cabinet left the Southern Jungle before the main army of Shinmushee could be moved into position to deal with them.

The Shinmushee knew that the Warlords had messengers waiting to report back to the House of Ra at the first sign of trouble. The Shinmushee wanted to get rid of the Warlords and their troops that were already in the Jungle. They waited until they carried out the first part of their plan. The first thing the Shinmushee did was flood the jungle north of the House of Ra with warriors. They sent sixty thousand warriors into the jungle outside of Yee Province. They would wait in the jungle until they were given word to attack Yee Province. Han only had three thousand guards in and around Yee Province.

Once those warriors were in place, the Shinmushee place one hundred thousand warriors in the jungle south of the House of Ra. The House of Ra only had a little over four thousand guards protecting it. That included Ramala's Elite guards. Once the warriors were in place, they surrounded Dan's Warlords and killed most of them and their guards. The few that were left had no way of winning or escaping. So they surrendered and were taken prisoner. This was all done in about six and a half weeks after Dan left the Southern Jungle.

One messenger made it out of the jungle. It was Chusee. Chusee hid behind trees, ducked, and spit his way out of the jungle. He was confronted and almost caught on several occasions. When questioned, he answered with a violent spray of saliva that the warriors either got hit with or jumped out of the way to avoid. It was always a surprise to everyone when saliva came spraying towards them unannounced. That was always the split second that Chusee would take off running. He was very fast and elusive. That's why he was the best messenger. He never got caught by the enemy.

When he reached the forward guards he was so excited, he wet them up with the story of what happened in the jungle. If it hadn't been so important, the guards would have killed Chu for spitting on them. Right now it was a matter of life and death for everyone that Chusee reached the House of Ra as soon as possible. After the Shinmushee warriors reported that one of the Ra scouts had escaped. The Shinmushee decided that they couldn't wait any longer. They started moving all of their warriors towards the House of Ra. They were going to finish this as quickly as possible.

At the House of Ra, after the night that Dan and Cat tried to get together. Cat ignored Dan for the next few days. Even though Dan told Cat why he couldn't make it back that night, Cat wanted to be difficult. She even spent more time with Spider than she usually did to get back at Dan. When she finally realized that it wasn't affecting Dan like she thought it would, she asked Dan if they could try again.

They met at Cat's place after Dan had dinner with Ramala and his children. Cat had been waiting like before. If Dan didn't show this time, she made her mind up that she wouldn't try with him again. She would go with Spider. Cat sat there daydreaming and listening to every sound like she had done the last time. Then she heard Dan. Cat got very excited and her heart started racing. She tried to calm herself but couldn't. When Dan walked in, he could see how excited Cat was. Still he told himself that he was going to take it easy on her because it was her first time.

Cat was almost twenty-nine years old and still a virgin. Dan couldn't imagine how someone could keep it to themselves that long. Cat got undressed and even though she hadn't had sex yet, she still had a grown-ass woman's body. That didn't go unnoticed to Dan. He went over to Cat and started slow with her. Cat started slow, but she had a very aggressive nature and it took over. She wanted to take her time, but her body wasn't having it. Her body was making up for lost time. Cat's body was jerking in spasms and ways that it had never done before. Not even Cat could control her body. Cat's body was taking to sex like it took to fighting.

It took Dan by surprise at first. He thought that there was no way this was her first time! The agressiveness of Cat's body made Dan more and more aggressive in his moves. Pretty soon Dan and Cat were in a heated battle. Cat got the best and the worst of the fight that her body picked with Dan.

Eventually Cat couldn't take any more, and begged him to give her a break. Normally she would have had to take what he dished out, but he rememberd that it was Cat's first time. He wanted her to come back for more, so he let her up. Dan and Cat rested for about twenty minutes before Cat pounced back on Dan. They went at it several more times that night.

After the last time, Dan looked over and saw tears running down Cat's face. He asked "What's wrong?" Cat said "Nothing." Dan said "Then why are you crying?" Cat said "I'm not crying. It's just that it felt so good. I never felt anything like that before. It was such a beautiful thing that happened between us. I don't know what I was afraid of all this time." Dan didn't say another word. He wondered what the hell Cat was talking about. It was only sex. Yeah it was good, but he wasn't going there. Now he wished he had never questioned Cat. Whatever she felt was what she felt. Sure they had a good time, but to say it was beautiful. That wasn't in his sexual vocabulary and he wasn't about to put it in it.

After as few minutes of silence, Dan said "Don't let this

go to your head. We had a good time. Now you have to learn how to control your sexual urges." Dan paused for a moment then said "I've been here most of the night. If I don't get back before daybreak, our heads will be trophies for Ramala." Dan could see the way Cat's face looked when he said Ramala's name. This wasn't good. Dan got up and put on his clothes. Cat jumped up, wrapped her arms around him, and held on tight. Dan held her, then released her. He finished getting dressed and left.

As he went back to the main palace he couldn't help but think that what he and Cat did was eventually going to get her killed. If Ramala heard her talk like that, or even if Cat look at Ramala strangely, Ramala would have Cat killed if she didn't do it herself. If Dan had known Cat was going to react like that, he never would have had sex with her. Just to save her life. That's how much Dan cared about Cat. But he didn't love her. He loved Ramala.

Dan returned to to Ramala clean as a newborn baby. He didn't want her to smell any hint of Cat on him. It didn't matter. Ramala knew everything that went on in the House of Ra. She anticipated these two getting together sooner or later. She had guards spying on everywhere both of them were. Ramala was told that Cat and Dan were together before Dan got back home. She even found out about the night they almost got together. Ramala didn't let Dan know she knew about that. She didn't question Dan when he came in. She wanted to see if he would tell her. Of couse he didn't. That bothered Ramala more than what actually happened.

Cat and Dan had sex three weeks before Ramala's water broke. In that time Cat tried to get Dan to set aside some time for them to get together again. Now that Cat got her a taste of some Dan, she wanted a steady diet of him. Dan didn't think that was a good idea right now. If he and Cat started going at it heavy right now, it wouldn't look good for either of t hem. Ramala was close to having the baby and she was having problems. Dan used that as an excuse. Cat went with it. Dan really wanted Cat to get used to not having him whenever she wanted him. He needed to get her used to only getting it from him every once in a while. That way there would be less friction about the matter. Dan's plan was working for now.

In the next six weeks Dan got to know more about both his sets of twins. La was talking perfectly, and could hold a conversation for hours if he let her. She was very smart and tried to figure out everything until it made since to her. That could take a while. Dan learned first hand about La's non stop questioning. Dan had to watch the older twins more than he ever had because of the problems with Ramala's pregnancy. Actually he had never watched them alone before. Dan tried to be patient with La's questioning at first.

La knew how her mother ran the House of Ra. She watched Ramala closely all of her life. Now La was spending time with her father. She questioned him so much because she was trying to understand his routine. To La everyone had a routine. Once she understood that routine she knew how to deal with you. She could learn a person's routine so well that she would even help you stick to your routine.

La also demanded more of Dan's time from him. Ramala wasn't around all the time to calm La down. So La manipulated Dan into taking her with him, when normally Ramala would have her doing something else. That just meant her and young Dan got to watch their father practice more than they ever had. Young Dan had watched his father practice before. Although he liked watching a lot, it wasn't the special treat it was to La. La was fascinated by Dan's Hammer-Axe play. She watched every move he made in amazement and tried to remember everything she saw. This was the only time Dan could get La to stop talking. So what did he do? Every time he had La with him and couldn't get her to shut up, he took her and let her watch him practice for a while. La was a master of manipulation. She learned that from Ramala and Yaya. She caught on to Dan immediately. She didn't talk much after watching him practice. She played his game because she knew she would end up watching him swing his Hammer-Axes. La loved being around her daddy. It was a lot easier to get him to do what she wanted. A lot easier than with her mother.

The young twins were getting more and more comfortable with Dan as the weeks went by. Ramashaya loved the attention she got from Dan. But she wasn't old enough to compete with La for Dan's time. Shaya tried to stay out of La's way when she knew La wanted something.

Shaya was just getting good at walking, but would have to watch her older sister because La would push her down if La felt like it. That's how La let Shaya know that she could do anything she wanted to her when no one was looking. La let both her brothers as well as Shaya know who was boss among the siblings. Dan didn't watch the children as closely as Ramala did, and Shaya learned real fast that La was sneaky and could get away with roughing her up around her father. Shaya was happy with whatever attention she got from her father. It was enough for now.

Don was like young Dan. He loved getting roughed up by his Father. La would rough up Don sometimes, but he wasn't much of a challenge for her. He also didn't challenge La in any way. So she took it easy on Don. Dan would also let young Dan rough Don up a little. Don didn't like that. His brother didn't have the control his father had and would get a little to physical. Don would be at the mercy of his older brother, until his father looked over and thought Don had enough, or if he saw Dan doing something that might really hurt Don.

The last six weeks of Ramala's pregnancy was very hard on her. Besides the pain that she was feeling on a regular basis. She found it very hard to deal with the child in her stomach always moving and seemingly flipping around in her. Ramala would have to stop whatever she was doing when the child became active. All she could do was sit and wait until the child calmed down. In her last two pregnancies blood calmed her children. That didn't help this time. She drank more blood than a hardened alcoholic could do with his drink of choice, but it still didn't calm down this child.

It was so bad that La, Yaya, and Dan felt sorry for their mother and helped her as much as they could. La would rub Ramala's stomach and talk to the child, trying her best to calm the baby down. Sometimes it worked. The child would seem to listen to La and stop moving. La talked to the child always calling it Baby. La would say things like "Calm down Baby, everything is alright." or she would say "Baby, mommy is tired. Stop moving so she can get some rest."

When talking, or rubbing Ramala's stomach didn't work, La would get frustrated. She couldn't understand why the baby was hurting her mother. When Ramala was a few days from having the child, La had had enough. La was becoming more and more stressed over the pain she saw her mother in. She looked at her mother, who was in severe pain from the child inside her. La said in a very frustrated voice "Why won't baby just act right!? Why can't baby leave you alone!?"

Ramala tried to calm La. She said "It's not the baby's fault. It's almost time for the baby to come out. That's why baby is so active. You were the same way."

La thought back to when Ramala was carrying the second twins. She didn't remember her mother having this kind of trouble. La said "Why don't you do what you did when you had Shay-Shay and Don in your stomach? They didn't cause trouble like this." Ramala told La "This baby is a lot different than your younger brother and sister."

Chapter 23

Ramala didn't know it, but Tara and Wana were so concerned about the trouble Ramala was having with this pregnancy that they sent messengers to their grand -Aunt as well as their grandmother. They wanted all the advice they could get. They thought messengers from both their elders would give them some idea how to deal with the difficulty Ramala was having with this pregnancy. They never expected both of them to show up at the same time.

Mishay arrived first, the day before Ramala's water broke. Mashaya arrived the Day after Mishay did. These two sisters hadn't seen each other for decades. It was because when both these women were Young like the Hellcats, they moved into the south with plans of starting their own House. These sisters were screamers too. They just weren't as advanced as the Hellcats. Individually their screams were nothing more than a serious nuisance that could on occasion disorient you. It took both of these sisters screaning at the same time just to freeze people.

They were successful at first when they moved into the south. They would scream and their warriors would take the heads of the people they froze. They had a foothold in the south for a short time before meeting stiff resistance from all of the tribes in the area. Mashaya was merciless in her killing of every tribe that opposed her. Mishay soon got tired of all of the killing. She just didn't think it was worth wiping out every tribe they ran across. Mishay refused to continue freezing people so their guards could kill them. Mishay stopped screaming with her sister. That was the advantage that the tribes needed. After a series of bloody battles, they pushed Mashaya's warriors back north out of the south. Mashaya was so furious that she got into a physical fight with Mishay.

These two girls were very close and had never had a real fight before. After they were separated by the warriors. Mashaya promised that warriors wouldn't be around always and that she would get Mishay for betraying her. Mishay was hurt beyond belief. She couldn't believe Mashaya was angry enough to do her serious harm. That night Mishay left the Hayee camp and walked right into the camps of the tribes that were fighting her and her sister. She was taken prisoner immediately. Mahsaya refused to send warriors out to look for Mishay. After a few more stiff battles, Mashaya returned to the House of Hayee and didn't return to the south until Ramala built the House of Ra.

The tribes that held Mishay decided to let her go after holding her prisoner for a short time. They could see that she was remorseful and tormented by what she had done. They didn't know that what she was tormented by was the betrayal that she felt Mashaya had dealt her by not understanding that she couldn't continue to kill just for the sake of killing. The fact that Mashaya never even sent troops to see what happened to her. Realizing that Mashaya didn't love her anymore. That hurt Mishay more than the killing she had done.

Mashaya always traveled with a large number of guards to protect her. She made a lot of enemies when she was younger. She wasn't going to slip up and get caught by them without a large number of guards with her. When Mashaya traveled, her caravan looked like an invading army. She always had her top Warlords and warriors with her where ever she went outside of the House of Hayee.

Mashaya's guards had to make camp right outside of the main gate of the House of Ra. Wana refused to let them in. Her grandmother was allowed to only bring in her personal servants. Wana escorted Mashaya to the main palace. She told her grandmother that Ramala was having a painful day. When they got to the palace and went to the special room where Ramala was, Mashaya and Mishay were startled by the sight of each other. That's when Wana said "Oh, I sent for grand-Aunt too." These two sisters hadn't seen each other in over fifty years. They stood there staring at each other not knowing what to say. Then Ramala yelled out in pain. They broke their stare and both went over to see how they could help. They would deal with each other later.

The two women worked together with the maids trying to comfort Ramala, and to get her to relax. Then her water broke.

The pain increased for Ramala. This was the worse labor pain she ever experienced. The pain was so great she almost passed out several times and had to be forced back into consciousness by a slap or two from her grandmother. Ramala's grandmother ordered her to stay awake and push the child out. It seemed that the child inside of her didn't want to come out. It was several hours before they finally got the child out. It was a boy. He was plump, and covered with Ramala's blood. Ramala was still bleeding. Ramala barely got a good look at her newborn son before she was hit with a powerful shot of pain. Ramala screamed "DAN AAA H!"

Dan was down the hall and heard Ramala. Then he heard her scream the same thing several times again. He kept hearing Ramala scream "DAN AAA H!" What Dan didn't hear was Ramala telling her grandmother "There's another child in here!" The two older sisters went back to work immediately. The grand-aunt felt around but couldn't get a grip on the remaining child. It took another hour before she finally got a grip on the child and pulled it out. This one was a girl. She was also covered in Ramala's blood. Ramala was dizzy from the pain. She forced herself to look at the child that had caused all this pain. Ramala saw her daughter for a few second before she passed out. The maids took the children to clean off Ramala's blood. Mishay looked at her sister with serious concern in her eyes and said "She won't stop bleeding!"

Mashaya and Mishay did everything they knew to try to stop Ramala from bleeding. Blood was everywhere. Maids kept bringing more towels and sheets, but they all had to be replaced because they were soaked in Ramala's blood. The sweat and the blood from Ramala that was all over Mashaya's face were mixed with Mashaya's tears. She was watching her grand daughter die right before her very eyes. It was the toughest thing she had to do, trying to help stop the blood from flowing from her grand daughter.

Mashaya had seen a lot of people die in her lifetime, but she had never seen this much blood from a relative before. Tara and Wana both watched the whole thing happen. To them it seemed like a dream. Tara and Wana were in shock. They were traumatized to the point that they both had to be removed from the room. Every one of the Butchers, Jan, and Dan knew something had gone terribly wrong when they saw Tara and Wana come out of the room looking dazed and confused, like they had just been through Hell. Still everyone was force to stay out of the room by the two older sisters.

Finally Ramala stopped bleeding. Mashaya and Mishay didn't know if they stopped it, or if Ramala just didn't have anymore blood left. They looked at Ramala's face. All of the color had left her skin. Tears rolled down both women's faces. Mishay grabbed Ramala's wrist and checked for a pulse. She could barely feel one. She checked Ramala's breathing. It was very shallow. Mishay had no hope in her eyes when she looked at Mashaya and said "At least she's still alive."

Mashaya sent for Dan and wouldn't allow anyone else to enter. Dan looked at both Mashaya and Mishay's faces. He saw the blood all over them and the tears coming down their faces. He looked around the room on his way over to Ramala. He saw all of the bloody sheets and towels. It looked like someone had butchered his Queen.

When Dan got to Ramala and saw her face, he froze. He looked at Mashaya. Mashaya said "She's still alive."

A tear rolled down Mashaya's face. She looked away from Dan and said "Say something to her while you have a chance." Dan turned back to Ramala. His throat got thick and his eyes started burning. He felt his head tightening up on him. Dan was filled with a sadness so deep he couldn't even move. Then he said "Ramala! Ramala, wake up!" Then Dan calmed himself and said "I love you Ramala and I always will."

Dan wished he had told her that earlier while she was conscious. Then Dan couldn't hold back his emotions any longer. He didn't want this to be good-bye. He yelled "Wake up Ramala!" Mashaya could see that Dan was about to lose it. So she motioned for the guards to come in and get Dan out of here. It wasn't pretty, but they got Dan out of there.

A short time later, Dan was told that he had yet to name his new children. Dan was distraught over the day's events. Still, he managed to pull himself together enough to name his children. The boy he named Ram. The girl he named her the last thing he heard his Queen Ramala say, Danaaa. Dan looked at the two newborns. Ramala would have been proud. They both were plump. They looked more like the other twins than they looked like Dan and Ramala. He was as proud as he could be under the circumstances.

La knew something was wrong when she was not allowed to see her mother after she had the twins. La and her siblings were allowed to see the new twins. La stared at them both and knew right away that it was the girl that caused her mother all the problems. La looked at the girl. La would deal with Baby later. Right now La needed to see that her mother was alright.

La remembered the last time her mother had twins, that she was allowed to see her mother soon after. La was very smart and even though Dan tried to put on a good face in front of La, she knew he was faking. It seemed every one was acting like everything was alright, but wouldn't take La to see her mother. La turned to the only other person she trusted, Yaya. Yaya found out through the maids, who were spreading rumors that Ramala was on her death bed. Yaya wasn't allowed to see Ramala either. Yaya couldn't tell La what she had heard. Yaya was filled with sadness that she might never see her adopted mother again. La could see Yaya's sadness and panicked. Yaya tried to calm La but couldn't. La kept screaming "Take me to see my mommy now! I wanna see my mommy! Somebody take me ta see my MOMMEEE!" Yaya saw that familiar look on La's face that said she was about to start blasting screams. Then Yaya got an idea. She knew how La had been working Dan with her long conversations. If La could pester Dan enough, maybe he would give in and let both of them see Ramala. Yaya told La the plan. La was going to act on it right away.

Wana and Tara came and got Dan before La and Yaya caught up with him. Chusee had returned with important news form the Southern Jungle. When Chu walked in, they immediately made him face the wall before he started talking. With the mood that every one was in right now, Chu would be dead before he got the message out if he spit on someone.

Chu told The Hellcats and Dan what had happened in the jungle. Dan looked at the wall that Chusee wet up with his saliva. Dan was always disgusted with Chu after receiving a message from him. Dan had to admit to himself that Chu was very good to get them this important message. Dan thanked Chusee, then dismissed him.

Then to make things worse the forward guard sent word that an enormous army of warriors were headed this way from the jungle. The guard said he had never seen this many warriors in his whole life. Now Dan had somewhere to channel his energy. The Shinmushee was going to pay for what happened to Dan's Queen Ramala! Even if they had nothing to do with it!

Epilogue

After Ramala saw her daughter, she lost consciousness. She fell into a deep dream. It was the same dream she always had of herself living well into her old age. The dream was the same as usual, only this time the dream went on longer. Ramala saw herself an older woman sitting in a chair in a courtyard.

A young woman came in and said "La, I'm sure Mistress Queen Ramala is proud of what you have accomplished." Ramala was shocked. The dream had never showed this much! La and Ramala looked so much alike that Ramala thought she was seeing herself later in life. But it was La that she was seeing in her dreams.

All this time Ramala had done everything because she thought she had destiny. She was sure that she was going to live well into her old age no matter what happened. All this time the old woman that she thought was herself, was La.

Ramala felt betrayed by destiny. She would have never done all of the things she did knowing the old lady in her dreams was La. Ramala tried to wake herself up but she couldn't. At first she could hear her grandmother and grand-aunt talking. Their voices had trailed off until she couldn't hear them anymore. Ramala tried again to wake herself. It felt like she was in a dream. If only she could wake herself, everything would be alright.

Panic set in. Ramala didn't want to face what this could really be. She refused to say it to herself. She kept telling herself that this was a dream and she had to wake up. All she had to do was wake herself up!

Then Ramala started dreaming again. She could see six children playing together. She could see her first two sets of twins faces and knew that the last set of twins were the children she just had. Then a voice spoke to Ramala in her dream. The voice said "You have done well. Your children will become known throughout the land. In the order in which they were born,

The Ra, Ramala will be known as La, Cut Faster, The Meza-Cyclone Chop Era, Hammer-Axe One.

The Ra, Dan will be known as Faster Cut, Dan the Destroyer, The Hammer-Axe Champion Chopper Ra, Hammer-Axe Two.

The Ra, Ramashaya will be known as The Angry-Axe-Hammer Ra, Pretty Girl A Chop A, Hammer-Axe Three.

The Ra, Don will be known as Axe-Angry Chop Chopper, The Hammer Went Wrong, Meat Butcher, Hammer-Axe Four.

Then deadly quiet is The Ra, Ram, Low Pressure the Assassin, The Dirty Degenerate-Eco Jin Ram, Artful Dodger, Just Choppin, Stupid Too, Hammer-Axe Five.

And the child that Hell needed a break from is The Ra, Danaaa, High Pressure the Executioner, The Immaculate Degenerate-Dan Jinn Eco, Wrong Place Wrong Time, Stupid, Baby, I Chop I, Hammer-Axe Six!"

Ramala listened to the voice carefully. She didn't know if this was the only information she would ever have about her children. Then the voice said "You have done well. You can rest now." Ramala thought the Hell I can! With names like those, she knew her children would need her guidance. There's no way Dan can deal with these six children by himself!

Ramala tried to wake herself up again. She couldn't. She pleaded within her mind for somebody, anybody to wake her up! Then she started to get even sleepier. She was fighting as hard as she could, but it seemed the more she fought the deeper she drifted off, until finally she was in a very deep sleep. Rest in peace beautiful Queen of the House of Ra Hayee, Ramala.

Together Ramala's children would be known as The Hammer-Axe Six. Separately they were Hell for anyone that came across them. If you ran into all six of them, it was the Wrong Place Wrong Time for you.

They were the most feared family that history didn't have a record of. The massacres they did with Hammer-Axes were beyond belief. They are the reason the Hammer-Axe was out lawed and never used again in Africa.

It was even against the law to metion the names of these six, or their parents after their time on earth. Three sets of twins born from the Hayee (Hellcat), Ramala and the King of the House of Ra, Dan the Destroyer. And yes, all six were Butchers. Killing isn't the only thing they did. But they were one of the greatest killing teams in history.

Join me next time, as I tell the story of :
Hammer-Axe Six!